Red Jacket

D0950256

BOOKS BY PAMELA MORDECAI

Poetry

Journey Poem

de man: a performance poem

Certifiable

The True Blue of Islands

Subversive Sonnets

Fiction

Pink Icing: Stories

For Children

Storypoems: A First Collection

Don't Ever Wake a Snake

Ezra's Goldfish and Other Storypoems

Rohan Goes to Big School

The Costume Party

Red Jacket

a novel

Pamela Mordecai

TAP
BOOKS

Chapter 3 ("The Burning Tree and the Balloon Man") was previously published in *Pink Icing: Stories*. It appears here by permission of Insomniac Press.

Editor: Diane Young
Design: Courtney Horner
Printer: Webcom
Cover Design: Laura Boyle
Cover Image © peeterv/iStockphoto.com

Library and Archives Canada Cataloguing in Publication

Mordecai, Pamela, author
    Red jacket / Pamela Mordecai.

Issued in print and electronic formats.
ISBN 978-1-4597-2940-7

    I. Title.

PS8576.O6287R43 2015   C813'.54   C2014-905056-9
                                         C2014-905057-7

1 2 3 4 5   19 18 17 16 15

We acknowledge the support of the **Canada Council for the Arts** and the **Ontario Arts Council** for our publishing program. We also acknowledge the financial support of the **Government of Canada** through the **Canada Book Fund** and **Livres Canada Books,** and the **Government of Ontario** through the **Ontario Book Publishing Tax Credit** and the **Ontario Media Development Corporation.**

Care has been taken to trace the ownership of copyright material used in this book. The author and the publisher welcome any information enabling them to rectify any references or credits in subsequent editions.
                                                                J. Kirk Howard, President

The publisher is not responsible for websites or their content unless they are owned by the publisher.

VISIT US AT
www.dundurn.com/TAPbooks

TAP Books Ltd.
3 Church Street, Suite 500
Toronto, Ontario, Canada
M5E 1M2

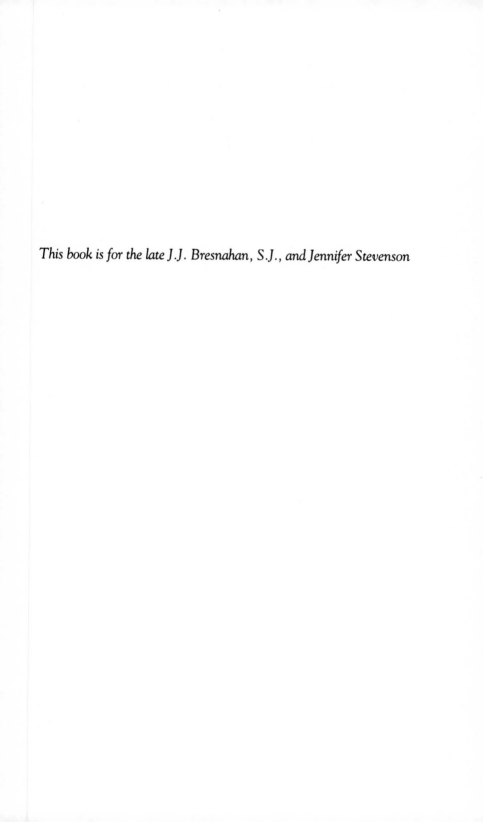

This book is for the late J.J. Bresnahan, S.J., and Jennifer Stevenson

Note

Mabuli does not exist. I have nevertheless tried to be true to the topography, flora and fauna, architecture, climate, and occupations of the republics and peoples of West Africa. I've imagined Mabuli as a small country situated between Mali and Burkina Faso, taking up a bit of each and bordering Côte d'Ivoire in the south. I've tried to be faithful to the conditions in this part of West Africa. If there is any respect in which I have misrepresented anything, I apologize and acknowledge the responsibility as all mine.

One of my readers suggested that my fictive St. Christopher is a thinly veiled Jamaica. I hope not. There are some similarities. I imagine the Spanish as the first colonizers of St. Chris, as they were in Jamaica and Trinidad (though not Tobago), followed by the British. Both colonial powers worked their plantations with enslaved people from Africa, so both populations are of mostly African descent. Geographically Jamaica and St. Chris are different. My St. Chris is smaller than Jamaica and slightly further to the west and north, so just south of the western tip of Cuba. However, both are in the Greater Antilles. St. Chris is not the island of St. Kitts in the Leeward Islands of the Lesser Antilles.

Both Jamaica and my imagined island share education systems constructed on the British model, as well as a strong investment in education, especially early childhood education. Children often learn to read and memorize mathematical tables before they go to school, which is sometimes as early as age three. They are taught to use British conventions when they write. The spellings they use are British; the way they format dates is British. Chrissie Creole is much like Jamaican Creole, although there are some differences in usage. For example, Chrissie Creole does not employ the double negative. Users of both Creoles code switch and code slide in the same way, mixing acrolectal (more English) forms with mesolectal (intermediate) and basilectal (more Creole) forms at will, so that it is often impossible to place speech in any one range of this language continuum: speakers move seamlessly across the language spectrum. Thus "standard forms" of the possessive case, for example, may appear in the same sentence, or string of sentences, as Creole forms.

According to the most progressive practice, words from real or imagined *living* languages other than English are not italicized in this book. Also, words like "coolie" and "negro" are used according to the practice of the time and place and often self-referentially so that their usage is mostly not derogatory.

I have tampered with history in moving the first Blue Jays game from April 7, 1977 to April 7, 1978, but the day of that game was indeed a day of snow and freezing temperatures. I have been true to most other events of climate and human history in North America. For example, the temperature on October 21, 1979, when the heroine phones her birth mother from the John P. Robarts Research Library, was a record high for temperatures on that date in Toronto at the time, one that remained until 2007.

PRELUDE

114 Riverside Drive
United States of America
18 July 1960

Dear baby

This is my firs letter only to say I miss you and speshally feedin you there was so much milk leave in my bres after they take you away doctor give me pills to dry it up. I cry to see it all runin out and I know it so good for you. I am here wit my rite mother Miss Daphne Miss Evadne daughter. Miss Evadne is your great Gran so you have plenty fambili here. my mother Miss Daphne she is reelly your Gran but it hard for me to tink of her so for she look so young. I tink my mother is more Miss Evadne your great gran that mind me all my life up till now.

Hopin you are happy and God bless I will rite soon again.

Your lovin mother
Phyllis

GRACE

1

A Girl Child in Wentley Plantation

Like all children of decent parents in the village, Grace raise in the church. King James Version of the Holy Bible is the first book she ever see, the one book they read every day. Come evening, in their two-room barracks hut, they partake of whatever repast the Lord provide. After that, Ma, Pa, Gramps, and the lot of them listen to the Word, first as read by a grown up, next as reread by one of the children that is sufficiently book-learned to cipher it out. At just past five years of age, Grace can unscramble the longest words, measuring the ancient Hebrew names like shak-shak music on her tongue.

"Then Nebuchadnezzar said, 'Praise be to the God of Shadrach, Meshach, and Abednego who has sent his angel and rescued his servants!' " Grace pause and look around to collect the gentle encouraging nods of Ma, Pa, and Gramps, then she resume. " 'They trusted in him and defied the king's command and were willing to give up their lives rather than serve or worship any god except their own God.' " She lift up her eyes again, shut the Holy Book solemnly, and declare, "Here endeth this evening's reading."

"Amen, Alleluia. Praise the Most High." So say Gramps. "For the Lord defendeth his people and will not see his faithful children to perish into neither pit, nor jail, nor trap set by the unrighteous defenders of Babylon who shall be cast out. Alleluia! Praise his Holy Name."

Long life, white rum, and years of singing in the gospel choir give Gramps voice a deep, sweet sound. Sometimes, if rum recently oil Gramps throat, and he making argument on matters political or spiritual, that voice pour out like waters rushing on the river bottom over a million pebbles and make Grace shiver deep in her deepest insides. Gramps is forever talking about pit and jail and trap. She wonder who ever put Gramps into a pit or a jail, a tall, strong man like him. She never consider a trap, for Gramps is a smart-smart man, and, so far as Grace could see, no trap in all the world clever enough to catch him.

Gramps slap his hands on his knees after this proclamation and ease himself from his chair, and that is the sign that prayers is over and every man jack to bed. Bed is two coir mattresses shove together that Ma take time and extend as more and more children come. She cut down the side and sew on the extra ticking, and then she stuff in more coir and sew it up again. So the two mattresses now filling up most of the little space they calling a bedroom. Lumpy is true, but better than sleeping on the tough wood floor, and the sheets are spanking clean and no bug inside the mattresses to bite for they go out in the yard regular to get fierce beating and fiercer sun.

"All of you children finish homework?" That is Pa, every night.

"Yes, sir," say all but the littlest two who are sleeping already, Sammy on Ma's lap and Princess, sucking her finger, propped up on cushions, head at rest on the table.

"Going to put Simple Bible on that girl finger, make her stop sucking it," Ma say, "or her mouth going to mash."

"No such thing as Simple Bible, Gwen," Gramps say. "How much time I tell you the thing name *sempervivum*? From Latin. Mean the plant always alive, hard to dead."

Ma make a long kiss-teeth and say to Gramps, "Mr. Carpenter, is nough things I got to member in the language I know. So forgive me if my recollection don't stretch to take in a next one."

Gramps shake his head, answer her with a suck-teeth of his own. "I look on the homework. Edgar and Stewie and the girls finish their assignment good enough, but Conrad like he need to settle down with them times tables. He know to do the sum, but he can't get the answer for he don't know the tables, and teacher say, do the sum, but don't look on the tables."

"Don't know how that make sense," Pa observe. "How he can know to do the sum if he don't know the tables? And how he to learn the tables if he don't look on them?"

Pa don't say all that much, but he is kind to them. With his good left hand, he pat each one on the head, from Pansy, the biggest, right down, and say every night, "God bless, sleep tight, and bite back any bedbug that bite you," He don't use the right hand so much, for the top two joints of the first two fingers are gone long ago, chop off by the teeth of a old threshing machine, and the third finger is almost all gone. When each child reach the stage of touching his hand, asking for the lost bits, Pa just shrug.

"Like the Holy Bible say, good thing come from bad, least that's the way it is for all who fear the Lord." He wiggle the stumps, and whoever is sitting on his lap, laugh. "When the machine chop off my finger, boss man look quick for something my brain could do, for he don't want to pay me the severance pay, and that is how I get the work I do today. You mark my words: Is a ill wind indeed that blow no good."

———

25 March 1965

Dear little daughter,
Today you turn five year old so you are a big girl now.
Happy birtday!!! I hope you do something special
today not so much ice cream and cake but maybe go

to the river or the sea or the big waterfalls in Martin's Bay. I remember a little one on the river that run through Grannie Vads place. It drop in a pool deep so my foot never reach bottom in some place. Grandpa Mali try show me how to swim in that pool but I never learn good. I hope you get to know how to swim. I am learning now that I am a big somebody. I think is better you learn when you are little for I don't too love put my head in the cold water I go to YWCA pool with all girls here. I will tell you when I can swim down the pool me one. Your birthday cheer me up for right now the world come like a sad place I don't know what wrong with black people why they always turning on each other. Last month a man name Mr Malcolm X get kill by his own people some saying he was a troublemaker but if we kill everybody that make trouble then half of we who in the world wood be dead. This month some people was marching into a place name Selma with a man name Mr. King and police mash up the march and treat the people like animal beat them up and put them in jail. I glad you growing in a country where everybody look like you. Plenty of our people is here in New York. At my school is eight of us from West indies I am the oldest one so they say I am dear mother. I tell them no is only one child I have and is you.

Your loving mother,
Phyllis

———

"Well, it's never stung me," Gramps say the day Grace ask him about the pretty purple-blue bubble lying on the sand at Richfield. It was the first day she put her eyes on so much water, big shining acres of it that blind her as the truck emerge round a corner from the dark of the forest. "However, I know plenty people who it sting and make well-sick," Gramps continue. He sound serious, like parson at a funeral.

Gramps words taking their time to make meaning in her head, and as he talk, her hand is moving down to touch the shiny mauvish skin.

"Stop, Gracie. Don't touch that!" Gramps say, sharp like flint, and he walk over and scoop her up from the sand and hoist her round his neck, so she is a princess save by a prince who snatch her from danger and settle her high on his horse. Of course, Gramps is the prince and also the horse, and she laugh at that, but not so soft that Gramps don't hear her, never mind the waves bashing the rocks.

"It's not a laughing matter, Gracie."

"Sorry, Gramps." She is a bit annoyed that Gramps stop her from just slightly touching the bladder, which is all she want to do. "Gramps, I wasn't going hurt it," she explain. "Only just pat it a little."

"I want you to learn a lesson, Gracie. Two lessons. First, I would never stand in the way of your having any experience or testing out anything for yourself. Understand?" He is balancing on some crusty rocks, rough white stones that poke into the raging sea as if they daring it to lash them some more. Grace is thinking about his bare feet and wondering if the points in the rocks not hurting them. She know he waiting for an answer because he tilt his head up towards her, so she oblige. "Yes, Gramps."

"That is how you will learn new things, and learning and growing as a person are what you are here for. Correct?"

She nod with plenty ups and downs.

"Second I want you to look good at that bubble. It is called a Portuguese man o' war. It is as deadly as it is pretty, meaning that if you get stung by one of those trailing tails, it could kill you." Which is how the question about the stinging come up, to which Gramps reply that jellyfish never yet sting him.

"You know anybody it kill, Gramps?"

"Well, if you must have an answer, yes, I do, Gracie. It was long ago, and I don't like to recall it."

He look so sad, she never ask him any more about it. Instead she turn her attention again to the sea, green-blue and then darker blue and darker, curving out like a hip until it meet the sky. Sitting up on his shoulders, she feel in charge of sea and sky and wind and all. She like that. With she and Gramps, no bad things would happen. Ever. She close her eyes and behold the bright redness in the dark behind her lids. In a flash she dream a whole, entire dream. She see a big baby fish — not any ordinary baby fish, but a good-size baby manatee like they learn about in school with a cat face and fine whiskers — that is swimming in warm blue water clear as glass beside a big-big mother fish. They are dancing, twirling round and round, sometimes standing on their tails, and sometimes just lying back with their heads above the water. Then in a flash the water is dark and cold, and the little fish is alone, head twisting side to side searching for the big fish who is gone, just so!

She open her eyes. Though the dream is flown away quick as it come, she is glad to find warm air all around her. They stay on the beach until midday, waiting for Lemuel. He is Gramps longtime friend. They pass by his house in the morning when they just reach to Richfield, and his wife say he and his sons gone fishing from before daybreak, not coming back till noontime. So Gracie and Gramps are waiting. Gramps let her play in the water and build things out of sand and stones. The sand is a sort of rusty colour, not like the sand the big trucks haul in to build cement houses for the office workers at Wentley Park. Those houses are a long way down the road from the barracks huts where the Carpenters live. Gramps tell Pa that since he move up in the job, he should tell backra he need a better house. Pa tell Gramps, "Remember, Pops. The higher monkey climb, the more him expose!" The two of them laugh a big laugh. Ma just listen and smile.

Gramps and Gracie see boats come in, watch the fishermen haul in their nets and sort the catch. They choose some to take with them and sell and throw the others back into the sea. It seem to her that many of them are dead and so can't swim away but Gramps explain that other fish will eat them, so they won't go to waste.

Grace gaze at the sea for a long time. Far out on the horizon she make out a ship, and she run to Gramps to point out how it is getting bigger. He start to explain about the roundness of the earth. "I know Gramps. We learn it at school. That's why Columbus never fall off."

"Maybe it would be better if he did fall off."

"But if he never come, we wouldn't be here."

"True. But we were fine where we were. And it was evil to put us in chains and treat us like animals."

Grace has heard Gramps on this subject before. "No sense crying over spilt milk, Gramps."

Whole morning she watch for ships heaving into view from nowhere or slipping away over the edge of the world. Someday she will go too. Someday she will have business to take her to places far from St. Chris.

Midday arrive. Lemuel still don't come back. At half-past twelve Delroy, the man that give them the ride from Wentley Park, come to collect them, and they climb aboard the back of his truck. Gracie have something for everybody: shells, bits of coral, pretty stones, and jewels that are really pieces of deep green, dark blue, and orange glass bottle that the sea smooth over. She have hats for Sammy, Princess, Pansy, and Pa that she make out of coconut leaves, for Gramps show her how. The shells, stones, jewels, and coral are for Stewie and Edgar and Conrad, and there is a conch shell, deep pink inside, for Ma.

Gracie know the Maroons still blow the conch shell, and also the cow horn they call abeng, to send messages, and that long ago, Arawak people used to send messages by blowing the conch shell too. As they leave the beach, she beg Gramps to blow the shell through a hole in the top so it make a sound. Gramps take a deep breath, put the shell to his lips, and blow. The sound is low, thick and steady, not like any horn she know. She want to learn to blow the shell, so all the way home, she puff and puff into it, but all she hear is the *phoo-phoo* of her own breath.

"Gracie," Gramps eventually say, "give it a break and try again later. You will do better. No use puffing and blowing when your lungs are tired."

She put the shell one side like Gramps say.

Early the next morning Gramps leave the barracks house to find her sitting on the big boulder at the back of the yard, hard at work trying to make the shell sound.

"Any better luck?" he ask as he approach, same time searching the sky as he do every morning for signs of the day's weather.

She nod, put the shell to her lips and produce a faint, dithery sound.

"Good for you, Gracie! I am going to crown you Miss Determination! You keep trying, and it soon going be loud enough to call the clans together."

"What's the clans, Gramps? Why we calling it together?" So Gramps sit beside her on the stone and tell her about Scottish clans and African kinship groups, and how families can stretch across the world, and how one time, in the army in England, he meet a man who look so much like him they could be brothers, except the man was fair.

"You know what we discovered, Gracie?"

"That your grandpa was brother to his grandpa?"

"Exactly right, but for a generation. His great-grandpa and my great-grandpa were half-brothers. Can you believe that?"

Gracie grin, nod, and then she ask, "So a bit of you is white then, Gramps?"

"I suppose so, Gracie. In this country, chances are a little bit of almost everybody is white." He look at her for a moment. "Why? Does it matter?"

She shake her head to say no, and right away feel bad because she know it is a lie, a big lie. But if a little bit of Gramps is white, then perhaps she don't need to feel bad about the fact that she don't look so black. Maybe the colour you are is just a matter of luck. Maybe there is lots of black in her that don't manage to find its way out. Maybe, if she ever have a son, he will be a proper black man, dark as Gramps and Pa.

———

25 March 1966

My dear little daughter,
Happy birthday! Today you are six years old! You must be going to school now maybe even big school. I wish I could see you in your uniform with a red ribbon in your hair and your school bag and lunch pan. I am so proud of you. I know you are going to be a good girl and learn as much as you can for sure I am praying for that. I have some news. Your Grandma Daphne my real mother is getting married next month and it is a big thing so she don't have time to think of much more than that. The man has four children and two are small ten and eight years. We don't meet them yet but she say soon. Once she is married she going to live with the whole of them in New Jersey for those children need her. That will leave just me and Granny Evadne. Granny Vads, for is so we call her is mother to Daphne and Granny to me. I am trusting God that we will able to manage. I am eighteen years old now and working at school to make a little money. I help all around sometimes in the kitchen sometimes in the office sometimes to make the new girls feel confortable. Sister Agnes say if I work hard maybe there is a job for me. I will wait on the Lord and see how things turn out.

Lucille Gray who live here with Daphne a long time is still boarding so we make someting from that and Daphne say she will help us. I think her husband have money. They drive a big new car and he have his own house. At least that is what Daphne say.

I have some other news for you. Last time I say I would tell you when I can swim all the way down the swimming pool by myself. Well I can do that now. I remember how I was so scared when I start. Maybe if you can not swim yet one day I can teach you.

Sister say take a interest in what going on in the world so here is the news. Things still don't go so good here in this America. Last year August they have a big palampam in a place name Wats in California. Plenty people die and get injure because police beat up two black fellows bad bad and people get vex and make a riot. I don't know why these police think they can carry on so.
I send you all my love.

Your loving mother,
Phyllis

P.S. There was a big outage here in November last year. Imagine no light anywhere in this big New York City. I have to laugh because they are so boasy saying those things happen only to poor countries. But it happen here for true.

2

The Boys to the Rescue

Gracie feel from she is small-small that she will never be like Pansy, eldest child of all, strong and facety, fearing nothing. Pansy talk her mind, sometimes even to Ma and Pa. Not Gramps though. Gramps can fix her with a look. Mostly, Pansy just go where she like, do what she want, and don't care what follow.

Gracie will never be like that. She is not strong and fearless. She don't fit with the rest of them. She is skinny: "bird bones," they tease her. Her hair is flimsy and red. She have freckles — dots of red-brown colour on her cheeks and nose. Everybody say her nose and lips are "fine," which is to say they are thin like white people own. And her eyes, which are sort of greeny-grey, are the wrongest of all. "Puss Eye," they call her at school.

Ma, Pa, and the others are good and black, with thick heads of hair, and nothing pointy on their face. To Grace everything about them is steadfast and strong: lips and noses and cheeks and chins, strapping shoulders and arms and legs. Ma can carry anything on the cotta on her head: baskets of provisions from market, pails of clothes to wash at the river when the standpipe is dry, planks of board to mend the house or batten it down in storm and hurricane. Pansy can balance a good-size basket on her head too. She have her own cotta, make from part of a old frock that she wind tight on itself to form a rope, then round and round to make a cushion for the basket to rest on.

"Not the only cloth I use now," Pansy announce with a secret smile, when she see Grace one day gazing at the cotta with envy. Grace can make a cotta, but Ma not going to let her put any basket on her head. Grace don't know what Pansy mean about any other cloth, so she just wait till Pansy turn back to her homework, then long out her tongue as far as it will go at her back.

Grace badly need to discover something that will make her feel special, something she is excellent at, something that will make people think good things about her. For a long time she think and think, and she finally make up her mind to learn to read best and fastest, and to practice to recall what she read with the highest powers of remembering. Gramps help her, but he have no idea as he sounding out words with her, how much she is taking in. The first day Ma catch her ciphering out things from *The Clarion*, reading aloud "Five Children Left Alone Killed in Fire," Ma make to grab the paper, and then stop and address Grace with a square, inquiring look. "Grace, you can read that?"

"Yes, Ma."

"Come, read some more," Ma say, turning the pages quick, looking for something a small child can safely read.

That is a long time ago. Now Grace can read anything. She study her tables too, so she can add, subtract, and multiply in her head, no counting on fingers. Mr. Wong say her head is fast as the cash register in his shop. And from the day that she hear Gramps say *sempervivum*, she store the word away in her heart like the mother of Jesus in the Bible story and she take it out and touch her tongue on it now and then. Every time she taste it, she is more sure that something will come of it. She know Gramps will explain about this other language, and he will teach her more words that are strange and juicy on her tongue.

25 March 1967

My dear daughter,

Sister Magdalene say seven is the age of reason.
I think I was reasoning before I was seven but
maybe St. Chris children are smarter than the
ones up here. Smile! I am certain you are very
smart and behave good and work hard. I know
because I pray for it every day. I pray believing
I will get what I am praying for which is how
Jesus say you should pray. I expect you to do great
things when you grow up maybe be the Prime
Minister of our country. There is going to be lots
of Prime Ministers in the Caribbean and I don't
see why you should not be a lady prime minister,
that is if you want.

Granny Vads and me are managing not too
bad and we see Daphne and her husband from
time to time about once a month maybe. One
time I took the train with Granny Vads to the
town of Edison where they live but even though
we take a taxi to the big train station here and
they pick us up over there in their car it was hard
for Granny Vads, so we not going do that any
time soon again. She is feeling stronger now and
the cold don't so much trouble her but she is not
strong like she was in St. Chris.

Granny Vads would send love if she know I was
writing, but is a secret between Mr. Carpenter and
me. God bless and keep you always.

Your mother,
Phyllis

As they grow, and Grace is looking more and more different from Pansy and Stewie and the others, one and two people in the district not bothering to talk behind their hands any more. Don't mind that they are standing right beside her, they throw their remarks into the air like Grace is deaf and can't hear them. The things they say make her feel bad, though she try not to pay them mind, so she is glad for her brothers, Stewie (first boy, tall and stringy), Edgar (third child, thick and solid), and Conrad (after Grace, short and stringy) that help her not to heed these people too much.

Those boys behave like somebody give them happiness sweeties with their cornmeal porridge in the morning, porridge that Grace hate like poison. But the boys sneak and eat her porridge between them, and then they pick whatever fruit is in season from the trees they pass on their way to school — mango, orange, redcoat plum, June plum, pawpaw, starapple — and give to Grace so she don't go to school hungry. Either that, or else they thief out Gramps allotment of brown sugar for his cocoa-tea, for Grace can just see her way to eating the porridge if it have plenty brown sugar in it.

Again and again Ma ask where is the sugar she set out in Gramps cup, first thing.

"No, Ma!" the boys say in chorus. "You don't set out Gramps sugar for his tea yet. We would know. We would see." That time the sugar done melt down into her porridge and she eating it, one small spoonful, then another.

Then come one of those awful, dark days that make Grace believe in hell for true because this is what it must be like when the light and presence of the Lord is withdrawn. From time to time she is mountainously afraid, she don't know why, and with the for-no-reason fearfulness come dark weather days when her head thump like a drum, her stomach want to jump out her mouth, and her skin feel clammy. Today is a day like that, plus today she have a job she hate above all. She is at Mr. Wong's shop. She dash there during a break in the deluges that scouring the sky for more than two weeks now, so bad there is flooding all over St. Chris and four people dead. The sheets of *The Clarion* Ma give her to cover her head soak through in two seconds so she is cold and wet and fidgeting from foot to foot, trying to remember Ma's shopping list, for fear, which is the only thing that can do it, fry up her brain.

She hate the damp, smelly shop full up with people panting their warm breaths above her like a herd of animals in a pen. Ma say she is growing, but she still have to fight for space. She tip on her toe, gripping the coins that sliding through her wet fingers, stretching forward to rap on the counter loud enough so Mr. Wong will hear and notice her, for then he will serve her before the big people, and curse them in his Chinese language if they make any complaint.

That afternoon, Mr. Wong is looking hard at the woman standing beside Grace, his nose trembling like a sniffing mouse, like he know before she open her mouth that she going say something nasty. Grace is trying to make room beside Mrs. Sommersby, careful not to interfere with the woman's plentiful self or step on her fat toes. When Mrs. Sommersby glance down and see Grace beside her, a look like she taste something bad pass across her face, and she start to broadcast her mind, as Gramps would say.

"What-a-way this child colour is red and the rest of the family so black, eh? Just go to show, you can never know how pikni will turn out. And look her fine-fine hair! Her mother must give thanks every morning for this chile's soft hair. No fighting with kink and krinkle. And soft hair is not usual with redibo, for you know those St. Philip red people, their head dry, with hair that sparse and picky-picky!"

Same time as Mr. Wong is glaring from his low height, drawing himself up like he getting ready to do a kung-fu move on Mrs. Sommersby, *braps!* Conrad arrive like a little body bomb.

"Oh, God! Get off me! Get off me, you wicked boy!" Mrs. Sommersby turn into a gigantic bottom as she bend over and grab at her pink stockings. She wear them roll down to the knees and with the roll twist into a knot to make them stay up, but now, sake of the collision with Conrad, they are sliding down her fat legs and meeting up with the contents of his schoolbag: exercise books, string, stubs of crayon, marbles, jacks.

Conrad's red rubber jacks ball bounce right between Mrs. Sommersby's gigantic breasts when she bend over, while his skinny limbs are twining about her fat legs like a wiss vine, tangling everything up in a busy confusion.

Stewie and Edgar enter and start quarrelling with Conrad.

"Cho, Conrad, man. Make you can't look where you going?" Stewie ask.

"Conrad, how much time people tell you to walk and don't run?" Edgar follow up. Two of them put on a song and dance, insisting that Conrad apologize to "Miss-triss Som-merz-bee," meanwhile she complaining about bad boys that love to gaze up under big woman skirt. When she say that, Mr. Wong suck his teeth.

"After no likl boy not so tupid," he mumble, but loud enough for people to hear. "Dat one dry up, drop off de tree, long time." Still, he scrape the woman up and make a show of asking if she is all right.

She sniff, pat down her skirt, roll her stockings up and twist the tops, push her bosom back into place.

After he serve her, Mr. Wong send his son to pull her goods home in his cart.

She leave with a last lick. "Little red jacket! Like we all don't know how the hair so reddy-reddy and soft!"

Mr. Wong make another long suck-teeth and then speak to Grace kind and consoling while he serving her. "Not a nice lady. Not like your Mama, no sir." He frown at the boys as he give them peppermint balls and hurry them home. "Run quick. Rain soon fall! Take care of Miss Gracie!"

Outside Edgar and Stewie help Grace with Ma's groceries, the three of them jumping over orange patches of watery dirt and ditches of dark red mud, dodging the on-and-off, heavily falling rain.

3

The Burning Tree and the Balloon Man

25 March 1968

My dearest little girl,

I wish for you a peaceful and happy eighth birthday
in this world of trial and trouble. I know Ma and Pa
Carpenter and old Mr. Carpenter will do something
special to make it a happy day, and I hope you have
fun with your brothers and sisters and friends.

In some ways it pains me that you are growing
bigger for the older you get, the more you will know
that the world is not the place it should be. All the
same, there are plenty good people. If I could, I
would send some books especially about great men
and women from our part of the world, like Marcus
Garvey and the wonderful nurse, Mary Seacole,
and Sarah Grandby, a great lady from St. Chris
who worked with Mrs. Seacole for a while.

I have a sad story to tell you. I met a woman at a
convenience store on Broadway where I sometimes
go to pick up things I need in a hurry. She was beside

*me doing her shopping. I heard some crying and when
I looked, tears were running down her face. I asked
what was wrong and she said that she just heard that
her one remaining son was killed in the Vietnam War.
He was the third one to die over there. I helped her
finish shopping, and I walked home with her.*

*So never mind I would love to have you with
me, every single day, I am glad you are far from
all this. I pray one day all the children in the world
will grow up in peace. You are lucky that you are
growing in a quiet place. Till we meet, God bless
and take care of you.*

*With all my love,
Your mother,
Phyllis*

———

When the old machine cut off Pa's fingers at the sugar cane
factory, backra look around quick for a next job to give him.
So sake of the missing fingers, Pa get a new work counting the
loads of cane that come to the factory from the small farmers
nearby and also from Wentley Park Estate. Pa let them know
he can write with his sound left hand for he could always use
the two, and they give him the tallyman job that he is better
than qualified for. It never last long, for when they see what
they have in Pa, they move him up again quick enough. Is
liaison with cane cutters and small farmers that Pa response
for now, and that is plenty, plenty people. Nobody don't call
him no liaison officer, for money would have to go along with
that, but Pa know that if they never have him listening to
complaints, discovering small-size trouble before it grow up
and come of age, the whole of Wentley Park Estate would not
be like it is now.

Grace never forget what Pa answer when her turn come to ask about the fingers, for they are not entirely gone, little finger-ends remembering what was once there. "Is not so bad, Grace," Pa say, and he wiggle them and make her smile. "Make me think of my own life, how one day it will dwindle like these two, then vanish once and for all, like this little one here. It's a good lesson."

After prayers the children go off into one room with Ma. Pa and Gramps take to their special corners of the larger space, the "big room" where they eat and pray and do homework at the mahogany dining table, their one good piece of furniture. The big room is where Ma keep her treasured things: the family Bible; a good set of plates (not matching but with no chips); a "Home Sweet Home" oil lamp; a statue of Jesus in lignum vitae wood; and a transistor radio for listening to the news every day and religious programs on Sunday.

In this Wentley Park place Grace come to know from school and church that she must reverence the Most High God, she learn that the wages of sin is death, that pride goeth before a fall, that the mills of God grind slowly but they grind exceeding fine, that God is not mocked, and that she must walk in the fear of the Lord for the fiery pit is the lot of those who disobey him. They tell her too that the Lord is her shepherd and that God love her and will send his angels to bear her up — but not with quite as much conviction as they bring to the terrible sureness of the punishments to be meted out by the Almighty.

Not Gramps, though. Gramps God is different. For one thing, he and Gramps have conversations all the time. Gramps tell her of things that God tell him, not just things that he read in the Bible. Take matters of cultivation, for example. God give Gramps special permission to grow some plants that other people are forbidden to grow. God and Gramps are often scamps together, though if you are God, you couldn't be a scamp. But if you make the laws, you could break them if you want. It sweet Grace to think God change his mind and break his own rules, and it don't at all surprise her that God should give Gramps leave to do things others are not allowed to do. Gramps is special. God is smart so he would know.

There is no prospect of Grace being led astray as she growing up for daily she learn the disastrous consequences of deserting the straight and narrow path. At night, as she lying down beside the bigger ones, for they are all sleeping together in the shrinking room — Pansy and she with heads to one end of the mattress, Stewie and Edgar with heads to the other, Ma with Conrad, Sam, and Princess on the next mattress — Grace listen to a susuing waterfall of information which start tumbling out as soon as Ma is safely snoring: who (whether big-big woman or reckless young girl) thief whose man; who make who pregnant; who lucky to lose baby and who not so lucky; who gone to the other end of the island sake of the belly they carrying; and who nearly dead sake of them try to dash away the belly. Other sins too, but there is no thiefing of stray goat, no destruction of property, no maiming a intruder with machete sake of praedial larceny that can compete with the sins related to baby-making matters.

Truth to tell, no matter what going on, Pansy and the boys are in the middle of it. Ma would say, "If is egg, those pikni into the red!" Unlike Grace, the four of them think they have a God-given right to be anywhere they choose: front bench in Zion Holiness Tabernacle and quick to examine the temple pool if there is a baptism; behind the counter at Mr. Wong shop, so make the old man get well vex sometimes; up under the window of headmistress office at the standpipe where you can drink water or pretend to drink water while you gulp the words that sail out upon the breeze, loud and clear. These are places where you can see and hear every little thing and some big ones too.

It is the said standpipe where Stewie overhear the headmistress explaining to Grace form teacher, "The child Grace is not really the Carpenters' blood kin, you know. Is adopt they adopt her."

The day Grace get that piece of information was a day that she never forget — not for that reason, though. For another reason, having to do with what Gramps call "eternal verities," so that what Stewie say come to her at the time as no big thing. Grace remember it all clear as day, bright as the bolt of lightning.

Behind the barracks hut is a small patch of land where Gramps plant some yam and dasheen; bok choy and cho-cho and callaloo; Scotch bonnet pepper; skellion, onion, and thyme. Ma too, have some flowering plants there that are easy to grow: cosmos and croton, puss-tail, monkey fiddle, and jump-up-and-kiss-me. Every Sunday she cut some of these flowers and put in a jam jar on the dining table.

Gramps love to tend this patch of yard, which he refer to as his "ground," and Grace is his willing helper from ever since. And Grace know that Gramps leave the patch now and then to walk some distance into the forest that start at the boundary of the yard and stretch out to cover the low rise behind and then continue on up to the hills as they get fat and full. Is right there behind the row of barracks huts that the round hummocks begin and spread and grow to form into karst country that bump up and down for acres and acres in the middle of which is the flat place that is Wentley Park plantation. In this forest, Grace know there is another ground, a small clearing where Gramps grow some medicine plants, or so he call them. These are the ones Gramps has permission from God to cultivate. Grace know she can't go into the forest with Gramps when he going to tend that plot, so she always sit and read and patiently wait until Gramps find his way back.

Sometimes he don't come back with anything but his machete and fork, but sometimes he have bits of the plant, which he call "herbs," and those times he would always let her watch as he carefully infuse them (so say Gramps) into a bottle of white rum, and leave them to soak.

This particular day is only Grace and Gramps at home, for Grace is breathing with great difficulty and Ma is afraid she is heading for bronchitis and so she is to stay at home and be quiet and not stray far from her bed. But late in the morning — a morning that seem long as any day and night — she is bored, for she read every piece of old newspaper she can find, so she sneak out and walk up and down the narrow rickety back porch about fifty times. She read all the words she can cipher out in the crossword puzzle that Gramps make sure to do in the day-old paper they get from Mr. Wong, after he drink his cocoa-tea in the morning. The boys always take the paper back, for Mr. Wong use it to wrap up codfish, herring, and pig's tail. Grace learn by looking at the puzzle after Gramps finish and trying to remember any new words and meanings she can make out.

So, bored and daydreaming, she climb off the porch and walk over to the back fence, which is not really a fence but a line of monkey fiddle hoisting their gristly green-and-white stems and pink-red tips from out the dark red earth. As she standing near the boundary of their plot of ground, waiting for Gramps to come back, the sky get dark quick-quick, and thunder start to roll, and lightning flash, and then a trickle of fire catch the small otaheite apple tree that serve to anchor one end of the clothes line and *zzzzt! pitchaw! pow!* Right there as Grace is staring, the tree catch afire and start to blaze.

Grace so frighten she pick up her two foot and take off into the forest after Gramps, never mind she not supposed to follow him. She race down the narrow track, not minding the prickly things that jook her feet nor the long branches that box her in her face. And she so glad when she see Gramps, she running, running up to him, fast as she can go, but she so frighten she can't get any words out of her mouth to tell Gramps about the burning tree, so she only moving her jaw up and down, and hearing no sound from her mouth, and half turning and pointing back to the yard.

And then the strangest thing, for, as soon as he hear her steps, Gramps swing round and shout at her rough-rough, "No, Grace. Not one step further. Go back into the yard. Into the house! Now!"

Grace is wounded. Gramps has called her "Grace." Not "Gracie," but "Grace." Gramps never call her that. Pa sometimes;

Ma sometimes; but never, never Gramps. In her heart she is deeply grieved; in her legs she is paralyzed, for she cannot now move. Instead, she stand up stock still, stuck into the ground like a yam rooted into its hill.

And Gramps have to turn around and shout at her again, not once but twice, before her brain reconnect with her foot, and she spin and race back into the yard quick as a mongoose, making sure to run round to the front of the house, sake of the fire, and into the bedroom and hide her head under the sheet on the nearest mattress and start one big cow-bawling.

But she don't turn and go before she see what is keeping Gramps in the forest: a man lying on the ground. Grace know he is dead for she see dead people before. Never one like this man, though, for the skin on his face, arms, and fingers done lift away from his body and puff up like a balloon. Grace eyes glue on to the man as she see the wind, rising now with the storm coming on, as she see it blow a piece of macca against the man's face, and she watch the thorns pierce his skin and see it pop like a burst balloon. It is in that second that Gramps spin round and shout at Grace the last time, and in that second that she find her two feet and run like her life depend on it. It is in that second, too, that her voice return to her long enough for her to scream "Fire!" at Gramps and point to the backyard.

So when Stewie whisper to Grace late that night that "Eadmistress say is adopt Ma and Pa adopt you," Grace just give a long suck-teeth and declare, "Eadmistress too lie."

Truth to tell, right that moment Grace not thinking about that. Is just the quickest way to deal with Stewie and his minor matters. Her head is full of too much other things: of how Gramps put her on his knee and laugh a soft-soft half-of-a-laugh and tell her he never know she had a voice so big that she could bawl like a bull-cow; of how he commend her for coming to tell him about the fire in the otaheite apple tree, never mind the storm was coming up and she must have been fraid-fraid of the lightning and the fire; of how Gramps explain that he sorry to shout at her, but that he never want her to come near to the dead man.

Grace don't let him get off so light. "But Gramps, I see dead already," she tell him firmly.

"Not like this dead, Gracie. Not like this dead. Don't that's true?"

Grace nod, yes, but she is not yet satisfied. "But how he come to be in your ground, Gramps?"

"I don't know, Gracie. Maybe he came to help himself to some of the medicine plants that I grow there. Maybe he was so sick that he didn't know where he was going."

"Well, that must be a bad sickness."

"Yes. He die from a terrible sickness that eat your flesh away. I see it when I was in the war. That is a long time ago, but they still don't have no cure for it, and they don't know how it spread. That's why I make sure that we all keep far-far till the ambulance come this evening and take the corpse away."

Nobody else see the dead man. Only she and Gramps, and Ma and Pa from a far distance, when they reach home from work, but only the shape of the body for when she, Ma, and Pa go outside, they see that Gramps cover it with a tarpaulin to shelter it from the rain that start lashing down same time she was bawling into the mattress. When all the other children come from school, they stay inside till police come. Is police that call the ambulance and come with it to take the body away.

So Grace don't care when Stewie tell her that headmistress say she is not blood kin to the Carpenters for she feel deep down in her belly that by the events of that very day she is bound even more closely to Gramps, and that, never mind she not able to balance a basket on her head like Pansy and she not using no cloth like her big sister, never mind all that, she is grown up in those minutes, in the time from the lightning hit the tree till she fling herself down on the mattress and start to cry. The dark sky and the fiery branch and the balloon man in the forest are big as any Bible story, and she is brave and stalwart, like Esther and Judith.

4

Grace and Pansy

25 March 1969

My dearest little girl,
Happy birthday! Now you are nine and so I guess
you are thinking about going into high school. I
don't even know if you are in the country or in
Queenstown. I think your Granny Vads perhaps
knows, but she doesn't let anything out, as though
she still hopes that if she doesn't talk about you, I
will forget you. She should know better.

I hope you are at a good school, maybe in
a place like Ramble Village, which is a pretty
town near to Hector's Castle. I remember it
because there was a grove of starapple trees
there, and one time we went on a church picnic,
and Granny Vads let us pick the starapples and
bring them home and that was the first time I
tasted matrimony, which is the sweetest tasting
thing, made out of starapples and oranges and
condensed milk. Granny Vads is not doing so well.

She is up sometimes, but down so often that I worry about it.

There are all kinds of bad things going on right here in USA but I am not going to spoil your birthday with all of that. We have a new president, Mr. Nixon. I don't like him. He looks sneaking. Granny Vads says so too, but we will see what we will see. I have to rush off to work. God bless you for the next whole year.

All my love,
Your mother,
Phyllis

———

From she small, Grace don't like to go into places with plenty people by herself, and as she grow it don't get much better. She never know how to come into or leave a place, any place, no matter where — church, classroom, Mr. Wong shop. When it is her turn to run there to trust things, never mind that Mr. Wong look out for her and treat her specially, she is still full of such fear that she can barely say what Ma send her for. She feel people forever gazing at her, thinking she is funny looking. Try as she try, she can't fix that. Gramps say, "You have to play the hand life deal you." So she keep on studying and learning and hoping that in time, she will know how to play her hand. Lucky for her, she like to learn new things, so even though the work get harder, she don't give up. When she reach Grade Six and go into the class that preparing for the General Entrance Exam, the load of hard work don't frighten her. If she do good in the exam, maybe she can win a scholarship place in high school. A good high school, if she is lucky.

As for Pansy, at age fifteen she is content to be in All-Age school. Ma encourage, Pa frown, and Gramps look like thunderclouds that going to rain down storm, but Pansy taking her own lazy time with her lessons. People just get too tired with Pansy. Conrad, Sam, and Princess still need plenty minding, and Ma is not well every now and then, for babies keep slipping away, and Gramps is getting older, and Pa, too.

From Pansy start hanging round the Ital Cookshop on her way home from school, Grace know nothing good not going to come of it, but what to do? When Grace venture a comment to Gramps about how Pansy always looking for trouble, though she don't say how, Gramps shake his head, declare, "That one own-way from she small. Your dead Granny Elsie is partly to blame. Is she mind Pansy when your Ma was still doing live-in housework, before Stewie and Edgar born. She spoil Pansy rotten. Never say 'no' to that chile."

Grace and Pansy walk home from school together from ever since Grace start going to school. Even when Grace is old enough to know the way, it continue like that. Which sometimes make her resentful.

"Grace, it's not that I don't think you can walk home by yourself now you are bigger," Ma explain. "But I prefer if you and your sister walk together. Pansy can help you if anything happen, if you fall down, or twist your foot, or anything so. You can remind her that she not to take her own sweet time — and you know she is a sweet-time miss — for she have things to do here at home."

The trouble start right as Mortimer arrive. The first time they see him, he is cutting lumber with a big saw on a workbench under a lignum vitae tree near to the boundary of land that used to belong to Miss-Maud-God-Bless-Her-Soul. Mortimer hang his shirt on a bush and is working with only his trousers on, his bare back looking like somebody spit on it, and buff it to a high shine. There are patches of sweat near the waist and on the rear of Mortimer's trousers. They hold on to his body in those places. He have on a belt crocheted in Rasta colours, red, green, and gold. As he slide the saw back and forth, the muscles in his arms and back remind Grace of a picture of sand dunes in her geography book. The colour is different, but the curves and ripples is the same.

The structure he is building is near to the boundary line of the property, with the front of it sitting near the bank side, so their journey take them straight past his workbench.

"Peace and love, and Jah blessing, sistren," he say, nice and polite.

"Afternoon, sir," Grace say.

"You not from round here?" Pansy slow down, smile her best smile.

Mortimer smile back, shake his head, go back to his work.

"So what you building?" Pansy now stop to talk.

"Come, Pansy," Grace say soft-soft, holding onto her hand and tugging her fingers. "We not to stop."

"Then why you don't go on?" Pansy hiss her reply.

"Just a small shop," Mortimer answer, then he solve the problem, for he dip his head respectful-like and turn back to his saw in a way that show he done with conversation.

After that day, Grace notice that Pansy start staying late at school one day a week, sometimes two. She tell Ma she doing extra work so she can maybe pass the Grade Nine exam and get into the senior secondary school in Cross Town. Grace don't think that is true, but she don't say anything, just make sure that when school done, she hurry home if Pansy not coming.

One afternoon when she and Pansy walking home together and passing by the cookshop, which is now finished and painted in red, green, and gold, with a big sign that say "Ital Cookshop," Pansy tell Grace to wait outside the shop, because she need to tell Mortimer something.

"What you could have to tell him?" Grace ask.

"None of your business!"

St. Chris roadside shopkeepers only stay in the shop front when things are busy. The rest of the time, they are in the back tending to their cooking or cleaning or baking or stocktaking or other business, always keeping an ear out for customers. All a customer have to do is rap on the counter or ring a bell, if there is one on the counter. Pansy walk into the front of the small shop like she accustomed, but she don't ring the bell. Instead, she knock on a door in the corner. Grace figure it must lead into the room behind, where Mortimer must be staying, for people live in their shop to keep their goods safe. Mortimer open the door, smile at Pansy, and then look up at Grace as if to give a greeting, but Pansy push him back inside and shut the door.

At the start, Grace can just barely hear the two of them talking. After a time, she hear nothing. Grace stand up, waiting and waiting. She can't picture what it could be that is taking Pansy so long to tell Mortimer, and in her belly-bottom she feel something bad is going to happen. Also she vex that Pansy abandon her, for even if the two of them always fuss, she depend on her big sister. She is thinking maybe she should take out a book and read, for it don't make no sense to just lean against the shop front, doing nothing, and she start to search in her bag, when she hear Pansy shout, "Lord Jesus! Oh God, help me!"

Pansy bawling for help louder and louder, so Grace get frighten. She drop her schoolbag, run quick into the shop, and push on the door to the back room with all her might. After a couple tries, it fly open. Staring at her are one pair of feet with brown socks, one pair of feet with no socks, four legs with no covering and Mortimer's bare bottom rising and falling with a motion that remind her of when he was using the saw.

Grace look, turn right around, march out, pick up her school bag, and start walking home. First she is furious with Pansy, but then she start to laugh. Mortimer have a nice body, but he is short. Pansy is a good-sized girl. Grace remember Gramps say, "Tiny insects pollinate sizeable flowers, Gracie. It's God's way." She not sure this pollination of Pansy's sizeable flower is God's way, but she find it funny all the same.

"So … So you going to tell Ma?" Pansy is panting hard when she catch up with Grace and grab on to her. "You going tell Ma. Right, Miss Goody-Goody?"

Grace stop and study Pansy top to bottom, say nothing, turn, and keep going.

"I ask you a question," Pansy say, rough and gruff, holding on to her again.

"Somebody have to tell Ma," Grace say. "Better is you."

"Make you couldn't just wait outside like I tell you?"

"If is that you was going there to do, why you never just send me home?"

"Is not that I was going there to do."

"So what happen? Is force Mortimer force you?"

"After nobody can force me to do what I don't want to do."

"So you must be force him." Pansy make no response to that.

"So you going tell Ma?" Pansy ask again.

"No need to tell," Grace say. "Your clothes mess up, you smell raw, and you look strange."

"I look bad for true?" Pansy sound worried now.

"Couldn't look worse."

"Well, you go in by the front door and talk to Ma, that is, if she reach home already. Make sure to take up plenty time. Meantime I will go in through the back and make haste and change."

"Pansy, I not helping you hide it from Ma. You is my big sister…"

"Sister?" Pansy give out. "You is most definitely not my sister. After no sister of mine could look like you!"

5

Professor Carpenter

Grace is learning about the reproductive system. She is in General Entrance class, and it seem to her that she is learning like a machine. She can use a potato to make prints. She can use a piece of twine and find out the length of a river or road on a map, never mind how many wiggles they make. She know what things a seed need to grow. She know which food is good to eat and which not so good. She can say her tables up to fifteen times. And she start some algebra and geometry, sake of Gramps. She see him use them sometimes, and he explain them so easy, she take to them like a calf to the udders of the mama cow.

"The alphabet letter is like a question sign then, Gramps!" she declare in great excitement when he show her that in the equation a + 7 = 12, a equals 5.

"Ah, my granddaughter," Gramps make a fist and rap her softly in the head. "You are such a clever ten-year-old. They cut your navel string on smarts!"

"I know about that too, Gramps. The navel string has a name. Umbilicus." She pronounce the u like a o. "Is how a baby breathe and feed from its mother."

"That's very good, Gracie. But you must say uhm-bilicus, not ohm-bilicus. Like hum, but without the aspirate."

Gramps talk like that all the time. She long ago know what a aspirate is.

"Uhm-bilicus," Grace intone.

"Egg-zactly."

"Chicken-zactly!"

"Hen-zactly."

"And the rooster comes along and then there's lots more…"

"Egg-zactlies!"

Two of them collapse into cackles of laughter. Is a joke they make up together.

Grace consider whether she could talk to Gramps about what is bothering her. Most of what she learn in class about the reproductive system is things everybody know long time. They learn in Genesis God say man must multiply and fill the earth, and from they small, Ma and Pa tell them how a man and woman come together to make babies and that this is a good thing, and nice too.

But there is something new. Teacher tell them about genes and say that is how children "get things" from their parents. She need to find out about her genes so she can know where her red skin and freckles and strange red hair and puss eyes come from, or if is true what Stewie hear the headmistress say that day at the standpipe at school, or what Mrs. Sommersby say in Mr. Wong shop, that she is "a jacket," unsanctified fruit of a union between Pa and some red woman. And she need to know what else people get from their mother and father, if there is a gene for learning your times tables, a jokify gene, or a gene for being own-way like Pansy.

———

25 March 1971

My dearest daughter,
Well, by the time you get this you will already be
eleven, and on the way into your twelfth year. In

lots of ways, this is the last year for you to be a little girl, so I hope you make the most of it. Do all the things you really like this year. Play music with your friends using a comb and tissue paper, and a grater from the kitchen and an old pot for a drum and shakas off the poinciana tree. Play Hide and Seek, Hopscotch, Jane and Louisa Will Soon Come Home, Brown Girl in the Ring, and Blue Bird, Blue Bird In and Out the Window. Play all the skipping games: One, Two, Three, Auntie Lulu and Salt, Vinegar, Mustard, Pepper; also Bandy Leg Lily and my favorite, Room for Rent.

I don't know if you have got your period yet. I'm sorry I'm not there to make sure you aren't upset when that happens. It's inconvenient but nothing to be scared of. And this is what makes it possible for you to have babies and you will want to do that in time.

I don't know what you will do to celebrate, but I hope you have a wonderful birthday. Maybe you will go to the Hale bird sanctuary in St. Charles and watch all kinds of birds come to eat and drink. Or maybe you will visit the big cotton tree near Perton with the door in its trunk and the little room inside for the duppies. Up here, everyone goes to a movie and then to McDonalds to eat junk food!

Some good things have happened this past year, thank God, but unfortunately a lot of bad things as well. I remain glad that you are there in St. Chris, though I would love above everything else to have you with me. I pray that you are happy and doing well in school and helping at home, now you are growing up.

I love you so very much. God bless you until next year.

Your mother,
Phyllis

———

Grace win a scholarship in the General Entrance Examination and the whole of Wentley Park Primary into jubilation. Not that it is the first scholarship anybody from that school win, for headmistress is well proud of the results the school get, year after year. But what Grace Carpenter do has never been done before, and headmistress admit she don't expect it to happen again. She get the second highest score on the test in the whole of St. Chris, and furthermore she score highest of all the girls that year. It sweet headmistress so much she give the school a holiday.

It don't usually happen this way, for headmistress normally get the results before the news reach the world through *The Clarion*. On the day of Grace triumph, however, the newspaper with the pass list arrive at Mr. Wong shop at the exact same time as the postmaster in Wentley hand headmistress the envelope with the results. So the news bruck out everywhere same time, and Gramps is wriggling round on his dancing feet when Grace reach home.

"Good afternoon," he greet her. "May I carry your briefcase, Professor?" He twirl his hand in circles before him and then hold it in at his waist, bending forward in a deep bow. Then he stand up and salute. "I hear glad tidings, Prof. I hear you have secured a post that will take you to the big city and away from this humble village. We shall be sad to see you go, but we are elated at the good news."

As she give him her schoolbag, Grace trying to hold in her smile so it is not too big across her face. She know Gramps is talking in that way to cheer her up, for over the waiting time, they more than once have a "Suppose I get a scholarship" conversation. She confess to him that she want to go to secondary school, but she don't want to leave home. There is no alternative, though, because the high schools near Wentley Park are too far for her to travel to each day, and Ma and Pa can't afford the bus fare anyhow. In Queenstown she can stay with Pa's cousin, Miss Carmen, who live close enough to the school so she can walk. And besides, if she get through to her first choice school, St. Chad's, it is a much better school than any of those nearby. So Queenstown it will have to be.

Now the news is here, Grace is happy but also confuse as well as frighten. She not surprise she win a scholarship, for she never think the exam was hard. In fact she not surprise she win a place at St. Chad's. But she wasn't expecting to come so high, and now she don't know how to feel or what to say. So she is scared about plenty things, starting from how to fix her face when she is getting all the praise, and going along to how she will manage all alone in a strange city.

She and Gramps walk up the path between the blooms of cosmos that are yellow, purple, and orange and grow thick and full, even in the dry time, for they drink up Ma's soapy washing water and keep coming back year after year.

"The Professor is pensive," Gramps say. "Has she had a difficult day?"

Grace look up at Gramps and nod, and the smile that was going to break out is overtaken by fat tears that fill her eyes and run down her face, jumping from her chin onto the starched bodice of her uniform.

"I think you've had too much excitement, Miss Gracie. I made some Seville orange drink and there is bully beef and crackers left over from lunch. How would you like some vittles to celebrate?" Gramps don't comment on the tears. They go inside, and he set out lunch while Grace take off her uniform and change into her day clothes. Then they sit at the table.

"Lord, we give you thanks," Gramps is praying, "for this food. Bless it unto our bodies and our bodies to your service. We thank you especially for the great success that Gracie has had news of today. Please help her to be joyful and not afraid, knowing your grace will be sufficient for her. Amen."

"Amen."

"Now eat up, Prof. Ma sends congratulations and Mrs. Sampson, too. Ma say she leaving early."

"Pa coming early too, Gramps?"

"He will come as soon as he can. But you know he is not his own master."

Grace don't understand that, for after all, slavery done long time.

6

Queenstown

Pa's first cousin, Miss Carmen, is older than him, well past sixty, while Pa is forty-nine on his next birthday. She is the straightest, tallest woman Gracie ever see. Her hair is all white, and she wear it in a long plait coil on top of her head like a crown. She wear clothes make out of African cloth in bright colours, blue and purple, green and red. Even when the colours wash out, the patterns are still striking. The large, loose tops go with long skirts and sometimes trousers.

"Miss Carmen," Grace ask one day, "how come you wear those clothes?"

Miss Carmen look down on herself, "These? Why? You like them, Grace?"

"Yes, ma'am. I never see people wear day clothes that look like that."

So Miss Carmen tell Grace how she is a long-time member of the Universal Negro Improvement Association, how she meet the great Marcus Garvey as a little girl and how she go with her mother to the plays and parades in Jamaica that he organize. Miss Carmen born in St. Chris, but she go to Jamaica as a child, and grow up there, returning to St. Chris as a young woman. Gramps long time tell Grace about Marcus Garvey, but Gramps was not so lucky as to meet Mr. Garvey.

"I love these clothes," Miss Carmen say at the end of her story. "They are very comfortable, and they make me feel queenly." She smile. "But," she go on, "I also wear them so people will take notice. I want folks to learn about our heritage, about where our ancestors came from, and I want them to understand the struggles we've faced."

Miss Carmen always talking about heritage: mostly African heritage, but also English heritage, which some Christophians have in their blood, but all have in their head. The English run St. Chris from they capture it in the seventeenth century till the island get Independence nine years ago. "Well expressed in our children's rhyme," Miss Carmen say, "We talk English/we walk English/we run English/can't done English!" Now she is also studying her Asian heritage for she just discover her mother's grandpa was a indentured labourer, come from India to work in the cane fields of St. Chris.

Grace think a lot about that word, "heritage." She wonder if a person's heritage could get into their blood. And Miss Carmen is not even as black as Pa or Gramps or Ma. She is brown, though her hair is kinky. Maybe one day she can talk to Miss Carmen about where her red skin and puss eyes come from.

———

25 March 1972

Dearest daughter,
Well, congratulations my teenager! You are now beginning your thirteenth year! The next thing I'll hear is you are a big married lady! I know you are growing up into a fine person and I pray that you are happy. Today I'm asking God to give you three gifts. I'm asking him to make you glad to be the

person you are. I'm also praying you will always be assured that many people love you: God loves you, everybody in the Carpenter family loves you, Granny Vads and Granny Daphne love you, and I love you. Thirdly, I pray you find the reason for your life. The priest at Mass this morning said that there are two important days of your life, the day you were born and the day you know why.

For myself, I pray one day I'll get to see you and tell you how much I love you. I think you were the reason why I was born, and I long to see My Reason!

I am sorry I have not been so good at the news in my last letters. It's always the same thing over and over, and most of it is bad. The one good thing is that black people seem to be making some progress in getting their rights at last. I don't want to talk too soon, but we are all hoping and praying.

I'm sorry to leave you, but I have to hurry, as I want to post this on my way to work. God bless you, my daughter.

Your mother,
Phyllis

———

Grace is walking home from school, looking at the people around her and thinking that some of these town people look so mix up, she can't pick out any one heritage. She is thinking that life in Queenstown is very mix up too. For one thing, day and night collide, with people always on the street, cursing, laughing, shouting, dancing to sound system music. It so noisy Grace have to sleep with a pillow over her head and descend into a deep underground of sleep from which she wake drugged and headachy, instead of refreshed like in Wentley Park.

Mansfield Avenue is one long stretch of bar and dance hall. There is never room enough, so people dance in covered yards on dry hard-packed earth or on cement that they pour over dirt, so it break up and they have to patch it over and over. The bumpy floors of poor people ballrooms don't stop them, though. As night descend, people start dancing and sometimes, even in the days.

Grace never tired to see the plenty different signs inviting people to come inside and dance. She copy them down and send them to Stewie and Edgar because they are so hilarious. In one part of the avenue, the signs always rhyme. "Cosmo as President Taft, Carl as Chaka Zulu, and Fenton as John Shaft invites you to celebrate The Year of the Water Rat at Steve's Hideaway. A Nite of Passion in the Latest Fashion. Come Even If Your Bones Squeak. We Got the Tonic to Make You Feel Sonic." And "Lord Niney Moon and Lord Tenny Sun with Don the Juan and Sancho the Pancho Call One and All to the Original Mansfield Dance Hall for a Night of Dance Till You Drop at Hal's Honeypot House. Pay the Cover and Be a Lover."

Stewie and Edgar invent their own notices and send back. She hope neither Gramps nor Ma nor Pa see the dance party advertisements they are making up. As far as she is concerned, plenty teenagers in Wentley are parents already, and her brothers' rudeness is funny more than disgusting.

Stewie's English teacher say the class must write poems and send to the St. Chris newspapers. The idea of writing a poem is a big joke to Stewart, but he tell Edgar, who been writing songs and stories and poems since long time ago. So Edgar start to send poems to the paper. He make sure to enclose copies of them in his letters to Grace. No poems don't appear yet, but he is persevering.

Grace is truly glad for the letters from Ma, Pa, Gramps, and her brothers. Even Conrad, who not any fan of putting pen to paper, send a short note now and then. Ma also send a parcel every so often by someone coming in from Wentley:

St. Chris spice cake or Ma special potato pudding as well as pocket money and toiletries that Grace figure are courtesy of Mr. Wong. She will go home when Christmas come. Till then she must live with the noise and confusion of Queenstown and make what she can of her school of first choice and newfound place of torture, the great St. Chad's.

It is such a struggle to focus her mind in the musical commotion taking place on Miss Carmen's street every night that after she board there one month, Grace start staying late at school so she can do some of her homework in the library. By the time she reach third form, Grace is staying at school every day to do homework. Now, in fourth form, she is starting the University of Cambridge's O Level Exam Syllabus and most days it take over four hours to finish her homework.

When November and December come, it is well past dark when she is getting home. As she walk down Mansfield Avenue, it seem to Grace that the dance party craze is getting more widespread. Nowadays the speaker boxes live outside for they take up too much space in premises that want to jam in the biggest number of patrons. The huge black rectangles come like small residences. Grace figure that anyhow a hurricane blow down your house, you could easy move into one of them! Not that Miss Carmen's house is in any danger of blowing down, for it is a sturdy concrete structure, with hurricane straps on the roof and plywood shutters for the windows, just in case. Because she has boarders, older folks especially, Miss Carmen say she cannot take any risk.

Stewie, Edgar, and Conrad still write her faithfully, and Ma, Pa, and Gramps too. *The Clarion* publish two of Edgar's poems, and he is proud as a setting hen. They even pay him a few dollars. She put the clippings of the poems on her wall.

"Mind how you staying on the street till late at night," Stewie caution.

"Careful and don't take any chances in that Queenstown city," Edgar write.

"Please, I beg you, take care of yourself, my Gracie!" Conrad is practising the intricacies of punctuation.

———

25 March 1974

Dearest daughter,

I nearly missed your birthday this year. Granny Evadne took sick in the middle of this month, the fifteenth to be exact and we had to call an ambulance and take her to hospital. It was bronchitis and it gave us a big scare but she came around quick-quick and was back at home in two days. You pay more for hospital care here than for good gold, so it was just as well she was home so soon. I never left her side after that for bronchitis is a serious business in a person of her age. Luckily the nuns gave me leave from work with no problem. Your Grandma Daphne and Lucille who boards here were Trojans. Daphne came and stayed for the first three days after Grannie Vads came out of hospital. Lucille stayed with a friend so Daphne could have her bedroom, but she came to help every day. After that Daphne came on Sundays so I could get a break. I had to mind Granny Vads for three weeks but eventually she was well enough so I could go back to work. Looking after Granny Vads is frustrating, especially making her obey the doctor's instructions. She keeps getting up and dusting and sweeping if I don't look sharp.

I said my usual prayers for you today, begging God to watch over and guide you. I truly wish I were there to celebrate with you, my daughter. Have a wonderful birthday! I have to hustle and finish writing this, for the letter cannot have a

*postmark later than month end. It's cruel, but that's
the arrangement, and I keep my side. Granny Vads
is calling me, so I really have to go. Have a happy
year and study hard.*

*Sending all my love,
Your mother,
Phyllis*

———

There are four other lodgers who live with Grace and Miss Carmen,
for that is how Miss Carmen make her living. Two are sisters, old
ladies with all their family gone abroad. Nobody connected to
them is left in St. Chris, but they refuse to go to the United States,
Canada, or England, where they have sons and daughters.

"We can't stand the coldness and furthermore we not able for
anybody to treat us like we have no nose on our face." So say
Miss Isoline.

"We live here as human being for too long. Better to be poor
and somebody, than rich and no better than a stray dog." So say
Miss Glosmie.

Miss Carmen do everything for Miss Isoline and Miss
Glosmie: cook, clean, wash clothes, get medicine, write letters,
take them to doctor, take them to church, see that every day
they walk around the small yard in the back. Every month their
children send money to take care of them. Miss Carmen manage
their bank business too, pay their tithes at church, put a smalls
in their savings accounts, make their contribution to Burial and
Benevolent Societies.

Grace help Miss Carmen with the old ladies. She iron their
clothes, fetch things from the grocery and the pharmacy, make
them tea and lemonade, walk with them around the yard, read to
them sometimes. Pa and Ma pay something for her bed and board,
but this assistance from Grace is part of the arrangement, and

Grace don't mind, for Miss Carmen is a perfect lady who, never mind Grace's help is her due, always say, "please" and "thank you."

There is space for two other boarders, and in the time Grace been in Queenstown, two young lady students from America come and go. The two boarders who just arrive since September to take their place are connected to Miss Carmen distantly: Mr. Fillmore Buxton is Miss Carmen's dead husband's first cousin once removed. (Grace is not sure how that work, but she will ask Ma.) He look like he is maybe forty or so. Mr. Buxton's wife, Ermina, look plenty older than him. She is on leave from her job as a schoolteacher to get her BA degree, and she is in her second year at the Adventist College in Queenstown. He is supposed to be looking for work. They don't have no children.

Grace don't see Mrs. Buxton often, for in addition to her studying, she give extra lessons to make money. Mr. Buxton is not in the house very much either — Grace presume he is out hunting for a job — except on Sundays when Miss Carmen provide everyone with a dinner fit for a bishop, complete with special beverage and dessert. After Sunday dinner, the Buxtons are accustomed to visit Mrs. Buxton's sister that live outside Queenstown in a settlement called Freedom Heights, almost an hour's bus ride from Mansfield Avenue.

So one Sunday afternoon when Miss Carmen is taking her once-a-week sleep after dinner, and the old ladies are taking their regular afternoon nap, Grace is surprised to hear somebody tap on her door at the time when she usually organize herself for school. That is when she iron her uniform, darn any tear in her middy blouse or her school tunic, clean her shoes, wash and oil her hair. Sometimes, like today, she finish her homework early so she read and maybe have a little lie-down.

When she open the door, it is Mrs. Buxton.

"Miss Grace, I am sorry to disturb you."

"It's okay, Mrs. Buxton. Something wrong?"

"I don't really know. Mr. Buxton leave after dinner, say he was going to the corner to buy cigarettes, you know, from those fellows that sell on the road?"

Grace nod.

"I don't see him since, and if we don't get the next bus to go to my sister, it will be too late, and we can't not go, for she count on us for certain little things ..." She pause, like she not sure how to say exactly what she mean.

Grace nod again, this time to say she understand what Mrs. Buxton is saying delicately. "Certain little things" could mean they take her money or foodstuffs or toiletries. "Certain little things" could also mean she is simple, or not entirely in her right mind, or handicapped in some other way and the once-a-week visit is the only time she get help to clean, cook, or do her hair.

"The ladies downstairs are all asleep, so I am asking you to tell Mr. Buxton when he come back — for he will come looking for me when he don't see me at the bus stop — that I have gone, and he will see me back here by bedtime."

"I'll be certain to tell him, Mrs. Buxton."

"Thank you very much, Miss Grace."

Grace listen as Mrs. Buxton hurry down the stairs and go out. When she hear the door close, she turn back to her book. She is near the end, sucking the juice of the last pages like her favourite mango. After a while her eyes get heavy and close, and she is dreaming the dream of the big mama fish and the baby fish. Together they gently bruise the bright water, leaving behind fine veins of froth in a train of disappearing webs. As the water is turning dark and cold, something wake her — not a noise, more a peculiar sensation in the air, a feeling of stifling, like the room is different and not in a good way. She half open her eyelids to look through the window opposite her bed, but there is nothing unusual outside.

She rubbing the sleep out of her eyes, swinging her legs to the ground, bending down to put on slippers, when she look towards the door and see a man just beyond the end of her bed. She half-think, "He must be come for the message!" In the self same minute, she is frozen with fright, for Mr. Fillmore Buxton is standing between her and the door, stink of sweat and worse stink of liquor, his belt loose, and his hand on his pants front that is poked up in a pyramid. He is a big man, not tall but meaty, and there is no other way out of the room. Oh Jesus! Hard as she try, she can't move hand nor foot. Can't blink. Her mouth can't open to scream.

Fillmore Buxton is pulling the zip down so his trousers are sliding onto his hips, penis poking through the slit of the pants, stiff and swell up like a big cucumber. The falling-down trousers don't hold him back. He take two steps forward, throw her down on the bed, drop himself on top of her. While one hand push down on her chest, the other one is working her skirt up round her waist and dragging down her panty. The stiff penis is ramming her, the insistence of it stifling her breath. She panic, fear in her belly, for if he shove that baseball bat into her parts, she know she will split wide open. Now, hard as ever, it is pushing into the hair between her legs, but it not getting through the thick tangle, and her bursting lungs grab a gulp of air when the thing settle briefly in the V between her legs. The oxygen turn her brain like a crank, and she recall the advice that Ma give her and Pansy since they small. "Pinch. Scratch. Poke. Bite hard, anywhere you can bite!"

Grace can't move knee or elbow or finger, for the thick, heavy man cover her slim body, pinning her to the bed, but one of his cheeks is now and then close by her mouth as he move up and down, trying to get inside her. When next it arrive, she open her mouth and bite, making sure top teeth meet bottom teeth, as Ma instruct. She hear a scream loud enough to jolt a duppy out his grave and the man grab one side of his face, roll off of her and sit up, eyes squeeze tight and face and mouth twist up.

She spit out something soft and fleshy. Warm wetness in her mouth and blood on the side of his face, and she shove him off the bed, run through the door and down the stairs, holding the panty so it don't drop. She can't run like that, though, so at the door, she let it fall, step out of it, and gallop into the street. Barefoot and bawling, she run and run, dodging the oversize speaker boxes, up Mansfield Avenue, past the telephone exchange, past the butcher shop, past the pharmacy, round the corner by Kingdom Hall, up along Meinster Road, past the Anglican Church of St. Bride, not noticing the sharp stones and pieces of glass on the road that cut her foot-bottom. When she come to her senses, she is running to her friend Olive's place. Olive is boarding too and always telling Grace how lucky Grace is to be staying with family.

She bawl so loud and long when she reach Olive that she barely manage to relate what happen. She still sobbing and wiping her nose as she bathe, dress in her friend clothes, lie on the bed under a blanket though it is a hot evening. She gaze up at the ceiling, paying no mind to the queasiness in her stomach, the bad taste in her mouth, the battalion marching through her head in heavy boots, considering for the umpteenth time if it is worth it, all this grief to get a education. Don't life in the way Ma, Pa, and Gramps have lived it, is just as good? But that is daydreaming, for sure. When Miss Tingle, the Latin teacher, start scrawling their weekly test on the blackboard, she always sing out, her back to the class, "*Iacta alea est.* The die is cast, my dears!"

Grace know she can't go home because too many people sacrifice too much for her to be at St. Chad's. The day she and Pa climb on to the bus to Queenstown with her grip was the day the dice land on the table of her life.

She save her lunch money and buy a small knife with a dread blade.

7

Grace Gets Ready

25 March 1976

Dearest daughter,
Happy birthday! There's a small group of us here
who practice playing music together. Today we
started off by playing a "Happy Birthday!" medley
for you in blues, honky-tonk, calypso, and reggae
style. It was great fun.

I realize you must be finishing school this year.
I hope it was a good experience. I'm hoping too
that maybe you are planning to go to college in
September for you are now sixteen, and I know
you are bright as ninepence! It's not likely you can
go without a scholarship, but I'm sure you are smart
and hard-working enough to win one. Last year on
your birthday I started a bank account for you. I
can't save much, but I put something in every week.
I will let you decide what to spend it on. I am still
praying that one day I will see you for I want so
much to be part of your life, not to say money will

*buy me a part after all these years, but I've learned
to be practical. As your Granny Vads says, "Air
pie and breeze patty can't fill anybody belly."*

*By the way, it's not only patty, cocoa bread, and
hard-dough bread you can get here, but all kinds of
Christophian food: avocado pear, plantain, yam,
breadfruit, gungo peas, cocoa, and dasheen. They
have our pumpkin too. It's different from their
pumpkin, though the two of them resemble. Their
pumpkin can only make pie. It can't make soup nor
boil and eat like ours. So never mind all the things
they have, we have a better pumpkin!*

*I will sign off now for I have homework to do.
I'm taking an accounting course. The nuns need a
person to do accounts, for Mr. Lieberman, a Jewish
gentleman who has done that job for a long time, is
retiring to Florida at year's end. He is training me
and so I am trying to soak up the figures.*

God bless you, my daughter.
Your loving mother,
Phyllis

———

Saturday. August nearly finish. Grace lucky enough to get a
part-time job at the Teachers' Credit Union near where Miss
Carmen live in Queenstown, so she work through July and half
of August and just reach back home to Wentley. The two weeks
since just fly past, don't even wave a good greeting!

Dusk coming on and she outside on the rickety steps round
the back of the barracks hut, book on her knee. That is where she
and her friend Edris oftentimes sit reading and talking. Right now
Edris is crying and crying for her Gran, who they bury ten days
ago, who is the only mother that Edris ever know. Mrs. Bird was in

hospital for a long time, and she get bedsores so bad they kill her.

"Parson say is God's will," Edris say, tears dripping. "How that could be and Gran just turn fifty couple years back?"

"Gracie, you reading in that darkness?" Gramps stick his head out the door.

"No, sir."

"So what, then, Miss Granddaughter?"

"Thinking about what parson tell Edris, Gramps. Don't know how God could want anybody to die from bedsores."

"The God I know is not a fan of bedsores."

"Edris say nobody don't contradict parson, for they are faithful believers. So you not faithful then, Gramps?"

"Never confuse church and religion. One is people praising their God, the other is folks running a business — half the time, a monkey business."

He chuckle a gravelly chuckle, and Grace laugh a short laugh. Edris don't laugh, only jump up and say, "Good night, Mr. Carpenter. See you, Gracie," and leave quick-quick, for now, night coming down. Grace get up too and go inside out of the cool night air, but she don't forget the questions of church and faithfulness.

———

Sunday morning, and they sitting around, waiting for Ma and the younger ones. Gramps and Pa go to Methodist Chapel and the big children go with them today. That service is not so long as at Evangel Tabernacle where Ma worship and where this morning she take Princess and Sam. Stewie, Edgar, and Conrad gone to collect the man blossoms of the breadfruit tree for Ma to use and make a special sweet dessert. Meantime they brew coffee from Gramps beans that he grow, pick, dry, and roast himself, and also cocoa-tea for Ma, Grace, Sam, and Princess. No Pansy any more, for is more than a year since she gone her own way with Mortimer. Gramps is the coffee man. Pa is in charge of boiling the balls of country chocolate, flavouring the dark liquid with sticks of cinnamon. There is milk from the Williams cows next door, and brown sugar that Pa bring home, each crystal separate and clear like a tiny honey-yellow diamond.

Today, breakfast is a celebration, for Grace not only pass her O level exams, she come first at St. Chad's and first in all St. Chris. Mark you, she know already that she going to study in foreign, for she take the tests to go to university in America, and she score so high that plenty universities offer her scholarships. It's only a half happy time for her all the same. Edris just scrape through two subjects, and that is after her mother in New York spend plenty money on extra lessons. Edris was counting on good passes in English and Math to get into the school for practical nurses in St. Chris.

"I well vex with God, Gramps. Seem like he arrange whole heap of bad things for Edris, and she don't do him nothing. Is you same one warn me about religion, and I getting to see it as unreliable."

"Gracie, I try to show you the difference between religion as a business and worshipping God in spirit and in truth, like the Bible say. If you are dealing with God in spirit and in truth, sometime you and him going to fuss. Edris and her people mix up with a deity that give orders, count sins, and don't brook argument. I assure you, is not me alone but many I have met who wrestle with their God."

"Don't hear nobody in this house wrestling with God."

"Well, is not polite to fight in public," Gramps retort. "The Lord say you are to retire to your quarters."

Grace smile, sort of. "What I must do about church in foreign, Gramps?"

"I don't say you must join a church, but you should find folks to pray with. Look for a community where you feel at home and not envied when you achieve, where all rejoice at your successes as you rejoice at theirs. And when you pray, let it not be with a caveat that none come off better than you."

Grace feel guilty. She don't need to have more things than

other people, but she like to come first in class, get the highest marks. She wonder if she should confess this to Gramps, for it sound as if he is saying it's a bad thing.

"While we are on that matter, I also wish you to promise me that when you are famous, you will make things possible for others — especially those of your own race." That let her off the hook. She can only be famous if she do better than everybody else.

"What about Edris, Gramps?"

"Be her friend, Gracie."

She hug Gramps tight. Whether she will see him again depend on so many things, she dare not take these last days for granted. More than all, he is the person who stand between her and yielding to the fear of not belonging. Having him beside her in Wentley or a long stone's throw away in Queenstown is one thing. But when they are oceans apart, will Gramps shielding magic still work?

MARK

8

The Chancellor

"They say here that Grace Carpenter is probably the brightest woman to have passed through the gates of the university."

"Who say?"

"Today's *Clarion*, Dr. Blackman." The woman taps the paper. It says here, "On Saturday, 8 November 1998, Grace Carpenter, perhaps the brightest woman to pass through the University of the Antilles, will receive the university's first Distinguished International Service Award — "

"I think that's a bit much. Plus it gives the wrong impression. She was never a student."

He doesn't wish to think about Grace Carpenter. Focuses instead on the aforesaid gates, just discernible through mango trees that flank one side of The Xooana Inn, where he's at the end of a working lunch with Celia Achong, the administrative assistant assigned to him when he visits the University of the Antilles, a.k.a. UA. Not that gazing at the gates mitigates his trouble.

A couple months before this visit, he'd asked Gordon Crawford, the principal, about progress on the renovation of The Xooana.

"Completed last week, on time, under budget," Gordon had said proudly.

Mark thought things in St. Chris were looking up.

"Excellent. Would you book me in for graduation, please? Sorry, not me — us, Mona and me."

"You? The chancellor? At The Xooana?"

"Yes, Gordon — unless you think it's inappropriate?"

"No, of course not. Not at all."

"Thanks very much. We'd prefer to be nearby."

Chancellors have always stayed at The St. Chris Four Seasons. Mark, who is the university's fifth chancellor, is staying at The Xooana to make a point. A training facility for students in the Faculty of Tourism, the hotel also houses the bar, dining, and lounge facilities that constitute the senior common room, and it's where the university puts up its guests. Too late it had occurred to him that, in its wisdom, UA might have decided to accommodate Grace Carpenter at The Xooana as well.

"Does Dr. Carpenter have children? Is she married?" Celia asks.

"I've no idea." He has no up-to-date information about Grace. He doesn't wish to think of her because he's not looking forward to their meeting, whenever it occurs, as it must occur, at some point between today and Saturday when graduation takes place.

At the workshop in Cambridge, she had told him the best way to keep tabs on an institution was to have your ear to the ground — "a cockroach perspective," as she put it. She could be plainspoken. "Get off your bony black ass and tour the place — meetings, offices, confabs, bullshit sessions. Sneak in and listen. All the better if they don't know who you are, and I assure you, love, most of them won't."

She's right, of course. When he visits UA, most people have no clue who he is. Why should they? His face appears only now and then in the papers, and he's not a movie star, recording artist, or sports personality, so it's of interest only to the few who know him.

He'd taken a turn around the bank one morning, shortly after she offered the advice on walkabouts. "Took a long stroll this morning. GREAT idea!" he'd scribbled on a postcard, dropping it into the mailbox himself. He'd wanted to say more, but decided not to. Had the postcard ever reached her?

"I don't think there are many people who'd disagree with *The Clarion*." The sound of Celia Achong's voice bids him back.

"She's a brilliant woman," he allows. "No doubt about it." He wipes away patty crumbs and then inspects the flecks of iron mould in a napkin almost identical to one Grace had given him in Cambridge, snitched from the common room of their hosts. Only senior personnel use this dining room, and truth to tell, he's chosen it in the hope that if she is here, Grace won't venture thither.

Holding his spectacles up against light leapfrogging through tall French windows, he watches it settle on the polished wood of floor and furniture, make shadows for a while, then make new ones as it hops on, hurrying up the day. This morning he'd peeked in near the end of a presentation Grace was making on HIV/AIDS education and seen her leaning on just such a window, face tilted to one side, the same brisk sunlight making a halo round her head, earnest gaze and fervent tone binding her audience. She'd held aloft and wiggled her little finger, as she declared, "When I consider the state of the world, I'm tempted to think there are more brains in this one small digit than in God Almighty's fat head."

He sits still, recalling the ensuing silence. Angel Gabriel passing over.

"Are you okay, sir?" Celia's wide eyes are concerned. She knows he has cataplexy, some kind of sleeping sickness.

"I'm fine, thanks."

Celia looks back at the newspaper. "It says she's at a meeting in Haiti this afternoon and won't be back till Friday evening. I guess it must be exciting to be constantly on the move, seeing the world, meeting people."

He doesn't respond.

"I'm sorry, sir," she keeps on, "but it's a pretty big thing, she being a woman and all?"

He leans his head to one side, half nods, half smiles. She folds the paper and looks at her watch. "Is there's anything you'd like me to do, sir?"

He doesn't tell her she's taken a load off his mind with the news that Grace won't be around until Friday evening. If she is coming back late on Friday, there is little chance of her meeting Mona until Saturday, even if she is staying at The Xooana. With luck, they will be together only briefly then.

"No, Celia. I think everything is under control. And honestly, I'm fine, but I have to run. I've got papers to read before Council. Will you take care of this?" He points with his chin to the remnants of lunch.

She nods.

"Thanks very much. I'll be in Garvey. See you at two."

JIMMY

9

Father John Kelly, S.J.

In August 1974 James Nathaniel Atule enters the Society of Jesus with one other Mabulian novice, Simeon Lubonli, a slender, nervous fellow with a huge appetite that's no threat to his svelte physique. As Simeon dispatches food the first day, he jokes that they will hereafter live according to LHB and LSB — L'Heure des Blancs et Les Saisons des Blancs. Jimmy raises an eyebrow. Colours of time and season, white, black, or otherwise, matter not; nobody thinks he'll be here long.

His smiling countryman throws another buck-naked mango seed into the trash.

Simeon doesn't know how truly he speaks. Nila died in January of the previous year. Cold, or more precisely, snow, White Winter's pretty instrument, killed her. He still craves her, the comfort of her body, the compass of loving her, the promise of making children with her. He misses the family they almost had. Sometimes he thinks God has punished him for committing the gravest sin. He worshipped Nila.

He knows he is self-willed — not selfish, just stubborn. And full of drama, so as a child his sisters called him "star de cinéma."

The only son and next-to-last child, longed for after four girls, the thirteen pounds of him nearly killed his mother, Makda. She was his first love and after her, Mapome, his father's mother. Enchanted in his cradle basket, he poked at their eyes and noses, at their mouths, opening and closing, making noises. Hugged to their warm bodies, he sniffed them. His nose remembers the perfume of the neroli oil with which they anointed themselves each morning, a scent that swelled with the sun and the day's exertions. He also loved his four big sisters, and Angélique, la petite, when she came. Why not? They all fussed round him as if he were a prince, not the least bit jealous of the extravagant attention bestowed on him.

So, long before coming of age, he'd been pleased to exercise his right as the only son to do what he chose and get what he wanted. Then while he was at boarding school in Benke, the demons danced in and Mapome upped and died. The relentless mutiny of adolescence in his body and the tumult of puberty rites jostled him past that, but his future was not to be tranquil. He'd raced through the American University in Cairo, taking three years instead of four, and then joined his father's business as a buyer. He revelled in the travel, using his native French and English and picking up a little Italian and Spanish.

He thrived in his job, and business was booming.

At this juncture, his parents decided that he could support a family and should start one. He'd allowed them to find him a wife, and they set about choosing a suitable mate. His father's grandfather had converted to Catholicism, so the woman must be Catholic. The ceremony would take place in the cathedral in Benke, but the celebrations afterwards would be according to the customs of the Mnkete clan, both families bearing the cost. No expense would be spared. He'd have preferred not to marry just then. He thirsted for the world — the flesh too but the world more — and even a bit, the devil. But it had been decided that this was an auspicious time, and anyway, eventually he'd have to marry, so it might as well be now. He set some conditions. Travelled, educated, and urbane, what he expected of a wife was more than childbearing, child minding, and running his home. She must be lively, articulate, educated, and, he insisted, uncut. Life in the twentieth century was hard enough. Sex should pleasure both parties. They'd chosen, and he'd consented to their choice, so a dowry was agreed upon, the festivities were arranged, and the marriage proceeded: an exchange of vows before the Bishop of Benke and three days of feasting, stick fighting, juggling, gymnastics, singing, music, and dancing. To top it all, a brilliant Italian fireworks display on the evening of the third day. Everyone said there had been nothing like it before; the patriarchs had been more than pleased.

The party concluded, both of them having waved goodbye to their families, he closed the door to their suite and turned to his bride. He didn't know her well. They'd met two weeks before and had spent time together since then, but little of it alone. Still, the more he spent time with her, the more she seemed her own natural, confident self. Now he was taking her in as she relaxed, head back, eyes closed, the white of her gown contrasting with the copper of her face and throat, the henna of her hair, so it quite startled him when she erupted into fits of laughter, no girlish giggles, but skirmishes of robust sound. Nerves, he'd told himself, determinedly indulgent, trying for a tender smile, trusting she would regard it so, for his sisters often called him cruelly inscrutable.

The clamour ceased as abruptly as it had begun. She sat straight up in the armchair where she'd been lounging, set her feet demurely one next to the other on the floor, put a finger to her lips, and inclined her head, as if in deep contemplation. He thought she might be hungry and reluctant to say so.

"Tu as faim?"

She shook her head, voluptuous gold earrings doing a rhumba at her ears. Charming, clever, classy, she'd been educated by nuns in Benke and sent to Switzerland for finishing. When she was in the middle of doing a degree in African History at London University, her father fell ill and she came home to be with him. When he recovered, she'd wanted to resume, but at just that time his father approached hers. Somehow they convinced her he was a prospect she shouldn't let slip.

For something to do he went to the large picture window and pulled back the curtains. It was cool at night, so he opened the louvres beside the window only enough to let in some air. The sun had set some time before. There was no clear view of the dunes, but smouldering against the red sky a sinuous horizon shrugged in their outlines.

"Mon mari," the lushly puckered mouth spoke so softly he had to turn to hear, "Je suis à ton service." At his service? That was sweet, if curious, especially after the hoots of laughter. Not that he minded a wife disposed to do as he wished, though she didn't strike him as the submissive type. Unhooking the gold embroidered fastening of his kiloli, he slipped it off. He was sinking onto the bed, when she leapt up, tearing off her evening jacket, gown, and slip to reveal a flimsy one-piece undergarment secured by tiny buttons down the front. These she undid, swift fluting fingers playing descending scales. Then she plopped onto the bed beside him, stark naked. He gaped.

"Jimmy, cesse de me regarder comme ça! Stop staring and let's get on with it. My family have gone, I'm far from home, none of this is what I planned, and I'm scared to death of being bored. I'm counting on sex hugely."

"Mon Dieu! She's mad!" Panic alighted like a mischievous monkey on his head. That would explain the odd routine of cackling, submissiveness, and then the wild, unseemly disrobing.

She yawned and stretched. He smelled her end-of-day smell as she lifted her arms, saw round firm breasts, nipples plump and alert as the pointy ends on figs. It lit the tree at his belly-bottom. He looked down. She joined his gaze and grinned. "Et bien?"

He was pulling her to him when it landed, no mischievous monkey but a beast that slapped him, shoved him down, toppled him backwards on the bed. He stiffened. His eyes rolled over. His body, hard as board, slammed the mattress.

"Jimmy? Jimmy!" She touched his forehead and recoiled. He sensed her tucking bedclothes round him. He was shaking recklessly, his face contorted, lips peeled back, bared teeth making a ridiculous rhythmic noise. He bit his tongue and tasted blood; felt her finger in his mouth covered by cloth that set his teeth on edge.

"Jimmy … James! Come on!"

Later (he couldn't afterwards say how much) his body relaxed, his face slack, his jaws loose enough so she could pull her finger from his mouth, he twisted in the sheets to wipe sweat from his body and then opened his eyes to see her finger bleeding into white silk. He shifted over to her, peeled the cloth from her finger, and sucked the bite marks. They lay silent for a bit, then she pushed herself up on one elbow to look full into his face. He was still perspiring.

"Jimmy, what was it?"

"What?" He rubbed his head on her shoulder, smearing the moisture on her warm skin. He dared not think about what had just happened. Sex was a saving grace. He prodded her with his penis. "This?"

She sighed. "Ici."

Afterwards he wondered what the nuns had been teaching in Benke. She'd been like a youngster playing games, eager to demonstrate all the things she was good at, now and then slipping in questions tagged with, "But don't tell me, if you don't want to, Jimmy." By insisting he needn't say anything, she dug most of what had happened out of him.

Coming up to daybreak, curled up against him, her back to his front, she asked, "Jimmy, is there more to it than you've told me?"

He risked his morning fart. "Oops," he said. "Sorry."

"Enfin de compte, c'est pas un problème." True, all things considered, it was not a big deal, but he felt he should give her fair warning nonetheless. "It's not always a puff!" he said, grinning his cute grin, looking past her, through the louvres, into a sky sporting the fizzled fireworks of the remaining stars.

Six months later, she was dead.

"Mon ami? Tu vas bien?"

Simeon's voice brings him back to the present. "I'm fine thanks, Simeon. Just a little distracted."

"Tu le veux?" He offers the last mango.

"No thanks. You go ahead."

Simeon dispatches the ninth fruit in short order.

———

Jimmy battles with the sex thing, worrying about it with each damp waking morning. He and Nila were given to extravaganzas of ebullient lovemaking. Now he is like Sisyphus, forever pushing away his lusts only to have them roll back down on top of him. How is he to give himself completely to God or keep a vow of chastity, when the merest memory of her, a glimpse of someone looking like her, makes his body stand to attention and salute?

One dismal morning late in the second year of his novitiate, a short man, white, rotund, ragged at the edges, arrives, "bearing nothing but empty arms" as the Mabuli saying goes. Father John Kelly's arms are hairy, short, and powerful, and plugged into an equally hirsute chest. His cotton shirt, open halfway down and soaked with perspiration, hugs his plump curves. The priest arrives with only a small backpack, for it emerges that the airline has sent his bags not to Ouagadougou but to Guangzhou. He flies into Ouaga because the airport near Benke is closed yet again on account of sandstorms, which occur with frequency because of the drought. No one is prepared to guess when the bags will be found, and the only novice with clothes big enough to fit him has gone home to bury a family member, taking his wardrobe with him.

The novice master approaches the white man. "Father John," he broaches it gingerly, "we have no clothes to fit you. We are sorry. But we …"

"Don't you have one of those wrap things, Erasmus?"

People have trouble keeping a straight face when the pale priest appears that evening in a brilliant green and gold kiloli. Not that he is awkward; it's just the distressing sight of his hairy white legs, networked with blue veins, growing down to splayed feet in a pair of worn sandals. No Mabuli man of any status carries himself like that.

Father John Kelly has come to direct the novices thirty-day retreat. Jimmy has made retreats before, but the Thirty Day Exercises of St. Ignatius are "une toute autre affaire" — another matter entirely. On the next day, Sunday, the day before the exercises are to begin, he and Simeon bounce down the chapel stairs after Mass in the morning. His friend mimes jumping jacks as they hit the ground.

"Ready for the Ignatius workout?"

Jimmy croaks, "A geriatric like me? I'm waiting for an angel to bring me a wheelchair!" Simeon he-haws from down in his thin belly. Head and shoulders sunk in mock submission to their fates, they sniff their way to breakfast.

———

On Monday, Jimmy gets through the "Principle and Foundation," Ignatius's first-day exercise. He figures they let you slide into contemplation's slow eddies before shoving you through the rapids and over the falls, so while he can, he savours paddling about in "reverencing and serving God." It is what he wants, now that there's no Nila. After she died, he was stuck up a stagnant, smelly creek, mired in indifference, so he knows the price of attachment. He longs to be "free from all worldly desires," to have "a wholesome sense of God, himself, and creation" as St. Ignatius recommends. Floating downstream with no wants and no cares will be heaven indeed!

These thoughts are pretty much what he reports to the director on Tuesday, as he reviews his response to the day before. He is relieved to confess to Father Kelly that Nila has been a part of his prayerful consideration. He loved her utterly — indeed he's caught himself weighing her and God side by side, more than once. Isn't that idolatry? Reverencing Nila as much as reverencing God?

Today is day three, the day for grappling with sin. It is going to be a grim business, a trip through the torrents and very likely over fearful cataracts, so Jimmy can't tell what prompts him to bring up the matter of how much they are all diverted by the sight of the priest in his kiloli.

"Father, if I may ask a question before we begin ..."

"You certainly may, Brother."

"Doesn't it bother you?"

"Is there something that ought to be bothering me — remind me of your name, please. I've forgotten."

It irks him that the priest doesn't remember his name. John Kelly is old, but not that old, and there are just a dozen retreatants. Perhaps the foreigner is feigning ignorance to upset his composure, teach him humility, show him he is just one of the bunch and nothing special. He lets himself think this, at the same time that he knows it makes little sense for a strange priest to come halfway across the world to conduct a retreat and begin by dissembling about, of all things, recalling a novice's name. The idea and his irritation nonetheless persist.

"It's Jimmy," he says in his best British. "Jimmy Atule."

"Merci," says the priest. "And I am John." Perhaps realizing there is awkwardness he adds, "John Kelly." Feet and eyes and shoulders shift about in the discomfort. "You were saying something should be bothering me, Brother Atule?"

"No, Father. I was asking whether something was in fact bothering you."

Match language proficiency? Jimmy almost laughs. Does this white American want to compete with him where language is concerned? Well, a competition he'll get for sure! Jimmy thinks of the four languages he speaks, the fact that most Mabulians speak two or three. It is no longer just a matter of the joke with the kiloli.

"Always when a retreat begins I'm bothered, Brother. Right now the Devil, he looks up, sees twelve men, like the apostles, and he knows they're going to take thirty whole days to talk to God, meditate on the life of Jesus, consider their walk with him. The sight motivates him greatly. Faced with such a Satan, I'm very bothered."

Round one to the pale chimpanzee wrapped up like a Mabulian.

––––

Ignatius has a modern wisdom about measuring progress, advising that the retreatant move according to his own pace, not according to any arbitrary regimen of time. Jimmy is advancing pretty much with the days, though, and the third day has loomed, for he knows he has tales to tell. Obsessed as he is with sex and celibacy, he forgets that it is not just *his* sin to be considered; it is the whole story of evil. They are to contemplate the sin of the Rebellious Angels, for which they deserved Hell; Adam and Eve's sin, for which they had long done penance and which ushered in corruption to the race; and finally his own infractions, a miserable many as against the One Mortal Sin that has sent Various Individuals to Hell. Yes, he supposes he deserves Hell well enough. Except he is lured away from the fullest realization of all this sinfulness by his father's steady provision and protection, his mother and Mapome's securing eyes, his sisters' glad affections, and Nila's passion. So many people have cared for him and not counted his errant ways. Surely a loving God won't be scrounging for sin, his or anybody else's?

Jimmy is in John Kelly's office. He looks at his hands, long slim hands, the hands of a musician, Mapome said, or a surgeon, for they put away the film star nonsense once he grew up. By now they know him, and he knows himself, at least a bit: that he is smart, for every report of his teachers confirms it; that he has presence, for people stir when he appears the way a breeze ripples leaves; that he is strong and keen, the way a good horse stows might in his heart and legs. And now the great work of his hands is to be a priestly one. It excites him that he'll hold a circle of bread, and speak words that will make the white bread become, in his black fists, the Body of Christ — a perfect yin and yang.

It brings him to his sinful trouble. "I most of all want to be sure I can keep a vow of celibacy, Father. I'm not so stupid as to think I can fool God about anything, and sex is such an obvious thing. I've loved women. I've enjoyed lovemaking and even now enjoy it in my dreams. How am I going to manage that?"

The priest shifts in his chair. Ha! He is uncomfortable! Jimmy had determined long before that white people can't figure out sex, largely because they resist seeing the plain-as-day reason for it, which is to procreate. No Mabulian has that trouble. Nila and he made no attempt to prevent her getting pregnant, so he lost not just a wife but a child as well. That increases his guilt and makes the bereavement harder to bear, and, in some contorted way, aggravates his libido.

A priest who squirms at sexual matters? He'll hardly be much use. That Jimmy takes pleasure in the thought is itself sinful, as sinful as the fact that he keeps thinking of the priest as a chimpanzee. But why not? Surely Africans suffer precisely that characterization at the hands of whites? Still, this one is no chimp: a bit of a gorilla maybe, but not a chimp. He doesn't have the chimp's playfulness, its kindergarten penchant for mischief.

The priest breaks into his thoughts on matters simian. "You love women?"

"I confess I do, Father."

"What do you suppose the correct priestly alternative to that might be?"

Saints preserve his temper! The man is perfectly cognizant of what he is talking about. He's no intention of pussyfooting around, not during the few times when he can talk in thirty days of silence.

"Father, I don't think I can be a good priest if I keep on wanting women, desiring them as sexual partners. "

The white man's eyes are fixed on the wall behind Jimmy's head where the paint is peeling, as it is elsewhere in the room and in many buildings in the seminary. That, too, makes Jimmy angry, at whom he isn't sure.

"Let's talk about it when we meet this evening. Meantime, why don't you consider whether Joseph desired Mary? Chat with him. See what he says."

That one takes Jimmy by surprise, but he doesn't let it show. He rises, saying, "Very well, Father. Till this evening, then."

"Have a good day and on your way over, do ask Brother Simeon to come in." Simeon's name the priest remembers.

Three big baobab trees, according to tradition the Father, Son, and Holy Ghost, stand on the line that marks the eastern boundary of the seminary garden. There is a small chapel inside the trunk of the Holy Ghost, where they can go to meditate if they wish, but it isn't Jimmy's favourite place, perhaps because of a story Mapome once told of ancestral spirits living in baobab trees. The big trees have retained their grandeur never mind the drought that for too long has parched the Sahel. Beyond the fence, néré trees mount occasional guard over valiant fields of millet.

Mabuli has been lucky. Tributaries of the River Bani, next door in Mali, traverse Mabuli's long, thin caterpillar shape, hugging the western border of Burkina Faso. Once the rains cease and it is clear there will be no further celestial blessings for a good long while, the Oti, the association of all Mabuli's holy men — imams, shamans, priests, and marabouts — begin to preach the husbandry of water. People hoard it in containers sunk in basins of sand and stored in dark places. If they travel with it, they hide the water gourds in larger vessels of sand or seeds. The drought tests them, but the country weathers it. By God's grace and by dint of many prayers, the Mabenke, largest stream feeding the Bani, runs low, but never dry.

As he approaches Simeon, a graceful figure, his long, thin body bending forward, a reed in a gentle wind, he reminds himself to pray for those who have died in the drought and to keep praying for rain. "Your turn, Simeon."

"Il est très étrange, très blanc?" his friend frets.

"He's white, but not so strange. In fact, he's okay. He's fine." Jimmy feels free to say this. Simeon will hardly be talking to the priest about wet dreams — though as he watches the other man quicken his steps across the stone path that leads to the main house, he thinks, what does he know, after all? The rest are younger men, one or two still in their teens.

He stays in the chapel through lunch, emerging when the midday meal is over to go to the refectory for a drink. Alone, and glad of it, he helps himself to water from a fridge that belches as he pulls open the door, something else to grate on his nerves. A grey smudge in the distance catches his attention on the way back, and he muses hopefully that rain clouds might be gathering. He prays for rain once more, as he slips back into the cool dark of the Angelus chapel and lifts his eyes to the Manokouma windows.

Three stained glass windows show Mary in kilolis of different colours. One of the two small windows shows her, a little girl at riverside among the rocks, jubilant in red and green, brandishing njamra, fat river prawn endemic to the Mabenke; in the other, she is clad in her undergarment, her dead son folded into a blood-encrusted grey kiloli. In the main window behind the altar, the artist has conjured a teenager with burnished skin in a kiloli of cerulean and indigo, mouth half-open in astonishment, eyes matching the gaze of an incandescent angel with a halo of crinkly hair. Nearby a Mabuli Joseph stands at his workbench, hammer in hand, perplexed.

Jimmy sits watching as the pools of light from the large window chase the darkness from here to there. At school he disputed with his mates about whether or not Mary remained a virgin.

"Gospel says Jesus had brothers and sisters," his friend, Tjuma, maintained. "They weren't all the sons of God, so either Joseph had more than one wife or Mary bore him children." That is not so much the present point. At home and at school, he has heard about Joseph's roles: protector during Mary's pregnancy on the trek to Bethlehem, and the flight into Egypt, and foster father to Jesus. But no one spoke of Joseph as a normal male with a man's desires. It is such an obvious, human question. Did Joseph want Mary? And if so, did the wanting obligingly evaporate once he started having angelic visitors who hustled him off to foreign lands so as to dodge tyrannical baby-killers?

At sunset he makes his way past neat lines of beans in the kitchen garden to the retreat director's office. He imagines himself tranquil by then, soothed by meditative prayer, but as he stoops to sit in John Kelly's room, what calm the radiant windows brought him flees like a mbuni rat, leaving him nervous and bereft of control, much as he felt when wet water gourds slithered from his hands as a small boy.

"Did you hear from Joseph, then?" John Kelly asks.

"We spoke, Father, but he didn't answer my question directly."

"Why not?"

Given his anxiety, Jimmy is surprised to hear himself say, "He felt that we do not know each other well enough for me to put a query like that to him."

The priest's laughter sets up a quarrel with the kiloli, which quivers bawdily across his belly. "Perhaps he's suggesting you not make too much of the whole business."

"That may be."

"Or perhaps he said something you prefer not to tell me. That's fine too."

Jimmy does things with his face that he hopes suggest amiable assent. During the day he examined his conscience again, worried over a lack of charity, perhaps even hostility towards the priest. But he absolves himself. He is the younger man, the man in training, and more than that, the party offended by history. Mabuli is his place, Africa his continent. It is an ancient land, birthplace of man and civilization. Strangers of all colours are welcome, but he is sure God does not wish him to behave with any of them like a subservient nincompoop.

And the priest is right. He did gather something from Joseph. It has to do with loving a woman as a woman, for he is sure the saint loved Mary so. He isn't sure how that can be since it puts Joseph in competition with God, but then she was Joseph's before Gabriel came calling.

"Aren't you going a far journey in ten words?" John Kelly resumes.

"What ten words, Father?"

"Let's see. 'I keep on wanting women, desiring them as sexual partners.' "

"I don't know about a journey, but I mean the words."

"I've no doubt. Tell me, will you stop wanting food and water, air and sleep when you take vows?"

"I'll keep on wanting women, but I shouldn't worry? Is that it, Father?" It is rude. He is sorry at how it comes out, but he doesn't take it back.

"Worry's the Devil's weapon, Brother."

Very insightful, Jimmy thinks, but holds his tongue.

"Shall we go a bit further on your ten-word journey?"

"I'm sorry. I'm not following you, Father."

"What's needed is for us to follow your words, precisely. You went from wanting women, to desiring them as sexual partners, I think?"

"They're the same thing, aren't they? I've always thought them the same."

"What do you mean when you speak of wanting a woman?"

"I'm not sure what you want me to say." Jimmy is immediately furious with himself, but he moves for swift redress. "Are you asking me for a description of my emotional state or a definition of the word 'want?' "

"The dictionary is for definitions. It's how you feel that I'm interested in."

"It's a physical thing, isn't it, a burden in the flesh, a need to be inside a woman." Again Jimmy watches John Kelly's face to see if the plain talk upsets him, but the ruddy features betray only attention. "I was married to a woman whom I worshipped. I know wanting isn't a penis looking for a cozy place to burrow into."

"So what is wanting, Brother?"

"Wanting is how a baby is till it has its mother's nipple in its mouth." Again, he is startled at the sureness of his speech. "It's as the psalmist says. 'My soul thirsts for you. My flesh faints for you as in a dry and weary land where there is no water.' "

"And what of desire?" the old priest asks.

"That's a plainer thing. You desire a meal, a good Arabian horse, or a robe of the best silk. Desire has an object."

"And you grasp it, this object?"

"You do, or you intend to. Perhaps that's why Jesus says you've sinned if you desire your neighbour's wife in your heart. Maybe it's reprehensible because you are treating her as a thing."

"That may very well be. Is there no object at the end of wanting, then?"

"Your wanting reposes in a person. That's its nature. But you do not seek the person as an object, no."

Silence, then, "You've said that wanting a woman comes with the maleness of you; desiring a woman is an act of your will. Wanting blooms, like a yawn, whereas desire plots, as a wild beast hunts prey. It's bloody-minded like an ass, bent on its

Red Jacket 89

own way. If you let it run off, it won't be easy to pull up, lead it to drink, eat, do ordinary things to sustain its life."

"That's very subtle, isn't it, Father John?" The confusion of images amuses Jimmy, but he likes their simplicity.

"Subtle? Aye, maybe, but there you have it." The priest looks content. Jimmy wonders what he does with his lusts. The word suits him: he is a lusty man. His face glows in the half dark, and not with heat. "That's the whole thing, Brother, in a nutshell. Grace is subtle. God is subtle, sensitive, following us into light and dark, tones and hues, little yearnings and grand obsessions. Too often we won't let him be God, for even our sins are in his charge. He knows them in and out — he even makes good of them. For sure he's not an Almighty Machine with two counters, one to number sinners, the other to tally saints."

"But God does count, Father John. What of those Old Testament stories, the angel looking for a hundred men so God would spare the city, then ten, then one? What of the parable of the talents, what was done with the five and the two and the one? I'd say there is much numbering in the Bible."

"It's not a book for lazy brains, nor people who have no imagination. Suppose I tell you of a soccer match where the score was nil-all, another where the score was three-nil, and another where the score was ten-nil. What do those scores mean to you?"

"I'd hope the side getting nil all the time isn't the one I'm supporting."

"Nah, that was my side," says the priest. He takes a rag from his pocket and wipes his brow, a rash of drops on it despite the coolness of the night. "Do the scores tell you nothing else, then?"

"They say that in one game, your team was as good or as bad as mine. In another mine beat yours fair and square. And the last time mine trounced yours."

"Good. And if you thought about them a bit longer, they would tell you more, lead you to wonder about the side getting nil all the time, and the one getting better and better scores. In the Gospel of Matthew, Jesus says his father has numbered all the hairs on your head, but that has nothing to do with counting."

"Nor hairs," Jimmy acknowledges.

The sun has almost set; the puff of cloud Jimmy saw earlier has long since blown away. Instead, the day has shrivelled like an overripe mango. Through the window, he can hear the cries of nightjars and owls and glimpse, beyond the three baobabs, an intermittent wind plaiting and replaiting the fields of grain.

Jimmy looks at his watch. "Our time's almost done, Father, but I don't know if we've solved the problem of me and my desires."

"We need to discern whether you have a problem. Desire, you know, is among the easier ones. Pride now, or envy, they are real challenges."

Jimmy gets up to go. Whatever the reason, his loins no longer appear such a dreadful threat to his vocation. On his way out, as he discreetly adjusts the offending instruments, he turns to the priest and inquires, "Father John, you know they're laughing — we're laughing — at you in your kiloli. Don't you mind?"

"Should I?" His grin is impish. There is chimp in him after all. "Please ask Brother Simeon to come in."

Bible in hand, Simeon spins around and asks, "My time?" when he hears Jimmy's step. Jimmy nods. Simeon bounds forward, nimble as a gazelle.

10

Baggage

At the halfway point in the exercises, the day they break their regimen of silence, John Kelly's belongings arrive. The novices straggle in from hunting njamra in a stubborn stream on the south side of the property to find his baggage at the bottom of the front stairs. Probably brought from Benke with the rest of the week's provisions, mail, newspapers, magazines, and packaged and tinned food supplies, it's been discarded as nonchalantly as a school bag shed by a child on its way out to play.

The harvest of shrimp is disappointing — a pity, since they eat as much from the property as they are able. The shrimp are fat but hard to find, their dark shells melding into the gloom of rock and river bottom. The outing has still been fruitful. Frustrated by the njamra search, Mike and Gabe Assalé, brothers from Cameroon, went exploring on a track that runs through bourgou grass and patches of gallery forest, and came across two black crowned cranes. They spotted the elegant curling necks and gold headpieces in a grove of acacia trees. Warned to be circumspect, since the birds might well be guarding nests, the others snuck up to join the two brothers and gazed in awe. Red-cheeked, their black berets sporting golden plumes, the birds sat composed as judges in their singular headgear, dark robes, and white wing sleeves.

There is something poignant in the novices returning from the majestic birds — "deux oiseaux majestueux!" as Gabe described them — to greet the priest's sorry baggage, which comprises a single, very large, tightly packed suitcase with a long tear. The valise is tied together with thick string. No one imagines it started out in this state, but John Kelly makes no complaint. He unties the string and opens the case, exposing its contents: plain white T-shirts, light-coloured trousers, shorts, underwear, handkerchiefs, socks, a few toiletries, a pair of black leather shoes. The bulk is mostly books folded into his clothes. He has one priest's outfit, a suit in black wool.

The black costume unsettles Jimmy, who is detailed to help the man discover the state of his belongings and arrange for his clothes to be washed, if need be. In an odd way, when he pictures the priest in the suit, he is reminded of the cranes. He sees the priest all in black, cheeks red, untidy thatch of mostly orange hair standing on end like the cranes' golden cockscombs — a sad parody.

"But you will be hot in this, won't you, Father? From the rest you packed, you clearly bore the heat in mind."

"The nuncio might ask me to dine or the bishop."

"You're joking, Father?"

"No, I'm not. Father Azikiwe warned that either man might pay us a visit, and then I would need to seem imposing, serpentine, albeit I am harmless as a dove. You get my drift?" His smile is complicit.

Jimmy has no idea whither he is drifting.

"For sure it's near twelve, but we can have most of these laundered today, and you'll have them for tomorrow, or perhaps later this afternoon, if you wish, Father."

"But I've done so well in my kiloli," John Kelly displays his upper body proudly. His face, shoulders and arms begin by peeling, but he and the sun have come to terms. "I knew I'd get a tan," he boasts. "The Irish are from Africa, you know. They came by boat to the fair green isle three thousand years ago."

"I've never heard that."

"My sainted Mum maintained it. Said it explains why both sets of people are loud, quarrelsome, superstitious, drink like fish, fight like fury, and have dark skins, curly hair, and lots of children."

This seems to Jimmy at best bizarre and at worst insulting. He gives the priest an appraising look, but holds his peace.

"Naw, don't puzzle, Brother. She was a mad woman, to be sure. We're all children of Eve, you know, fruit of the same womb, the one bleeding placenta. They'll find out soon enough. We Irish aren't so bad. If Africans have to resemble any white folks, we're their best bet."

Jimmy lets this pass as well. "I'll take the clothes to the laundry, Father. And I'll show the suitcase to Philip. Perhaps he can figure out how to mend it."

"It's hardly worth bothering about, though I'd thank you for arranging for the clothes to see some soap. I'll put a bunch of these books in the library and the rest in the chapel. I want you to have them right off. Perhaps Father Erasmus could tell the others that they're here?"

As they start in different directions, a flock of starlings takes off from under some date palms near the cobblestone path, as if pelted by six or seven shrill wails from across the courtyard. Jimmy and the priest halt and look in the direction from which the sounds came, but they stop as abruptly as they begin and there is no sign of movement or any indication of what has caused them. Indeed, nothing any longer stirs or sounds. Bird calls, insect cheeps, animal noises have ceased.

Erasmus Azikiwe does not reveal what caused the midday screams, although he can't hide the fact that something bad has transpired. That evening the novices watch as staff leave the premises, baskets and bundles in hand, crowding about Elise and

Lili, twins, young women in their early twenties who are part of the kitchen crew. The others surge round them, a huddle of dark figures, taking turns talking to them, putting an arm around their shoulders, squeezing their hands.

They hear the dreadful news during vespers, when Father Kelly asks them to pray for the twins' father. He was attacked the day before in their village, his skull concussed by a ferocious blow. He is a marabout, famous as a healer, and his sanctuary room has been ransacked, his medicines stolen, many of his ritual objects broken. The attack on the twins' father is all the talk at supper, for the tiny women are favourites with everyone. Also, as everyone knows, random assaults often presage larger conflicts: a man here, a man there, then twos, then tens, then pretty soon, a war. And who ever knows the plotters?

By the next morning, things are back to normal. Though the twins are still absent, the other staff have returned. Breakfast appears at seven, and lunch and dinner at the appointed times, and the novices find snacks and juice in the refectory if they need refreshment during the day.

Over the last day and a half, Jimmy has been uneasy, his mind disturbed by a series of small, unnatural events. Coming back from the laundry where he deposited Father Kelly's clothes, he notices the dogs, a ragamuffin crew who had been growling at the priest up until then, wildly wagging their tails, leaping up to greet him and rubbing themselves against his legs. He sees mongoose-like mbuni, rodents who scrupulously avoid human contact, halting their lightning dashes across the yard to approach the priest's feet. He notices presents of seeds and cones, select mbuni morsels, piled up near the retreat director's door. Mabuli sand puppies, dedicated underground dwellers, peek from dirt hills that thrust up to form a quaint honour guard under his window.

Surely, on the way to and from the director's office, his brother novices must have observed the mbuni piling up their votary offerings, the sand puppies watching from their mounds?

Jimmy doesn't know about anyone else, but he needs to make sense of it. Has hysteria induced by the attack on the marabout rattled them all into imagining bizarre versions of the ordinary? Has the hunger for food and everyday conversation prompted mass hallucination? Or perhaps, and this is the interpretation he most favours, the animals sense the imminence of some type of geophysical phenomenon like an earthquake or a giant rainstorm or sandstorm, and this explains their behaviour. He decides to speak to Father Kelly about it. The man has come a long way: he deserves the satisfaction of earning his keep.

There is mostly, though not always a homily at vespers. That night, the retreat director speaks about verses 28 to 31 from the Gospel of Mark, chapter 12, which was the reading at morning Mass. "Jesus says to love our neighbour as ourselves. We keep forgetting that last part. He exemplified that proper self-love, daring to be who he was, the Messiah, son of God, and getting killed for it. Whenever we are rejected, we need to remember that and to remember too that he rises again and his resurrected self renews the sacred self of each of us, making each of us more lovable. Think of it as lungs, hearts, kidneys, corneas, revived, new cells, new organs transplanted from the risen Jesus into us."

Jimmy sits in the chapel, closes his eyes, and tries to meditate on the reflection, but the matter of his initial response to the director keeps intruding. What does he not love in himself that has led him to be hostile to the foreigner? Eventually he gives in and recites the *Confiteor* to ask forgiveness for his initial suspicion of the man, his arrogance at their first meeting, his glee at the sight of the white man in his kiloli, his scorn of the priest's worn sandals and unkempt feet. He thinks of John Kelly's easy good nature, his ready ear, of the fact that their hilarity at the sight of him in a kiloli seems not to bother him. He is ashamed.

After half an hour, he walks back to his room, the night clear so it seems he can count the points of light in the great stars, the dry air a sculptor's rasp scraping dust and detritus from his lungs.

He lies in bed and thinks of Jesus and organ transplants and Africa. Adam and Eve are set down in the Garden of Eden in East Africa. The first heart to find its way from one human body to another does so in South Africa. Jesus lived up the coast in Palestine, so, in a way, in Africa as well. He is transfixed by a vision in which Africa's vastness throbs at the end of God's outstretched finger.

And then, Oh holy ancestors, assist us! Blue Mother of Sorrows, pray for us! At the tip of God's finger he beholds a field of maggots feasting on tawny bodies, corpses tumbled down hills of sand, rotting on roadsides, putrefying in ditches, piled in middens that seethe and hum. He can hear the larvae squirming in an ecstasy of eating, the brush of a plague of tiny wings, the munching of a swarm of mouths. A bloody filter tracks across sand dunes and rocky desert, as gory bodies, baked in the sun, turn every hue of brown and black. The mouldering flesh stinks so high that it invades his senses. He can taste it. Dried blood encrusts his fingers, intrudes under his nails. Chorales of gnawing insects sing in his ears, as God folds his finger, and pulls his hand away.

Shivering, clutching his belly, he hunches over, ready for the fit, stomach muscles taut, bladder squeezed tight, chin tucked into collarbone. He curses the fates for hurling this at him now, when he is just kneading his life into some kind of shape.

The seizure never comes. Foresight but no fit! After minutes of shivering, arms still hugging his middle, breath in long draughts, he feels a trepidation so great he knows he must tell somebody. He drags on his shoes, grabs a shirt, and never mind he's had his consultations for the day, runs to the director's office, praying he will still be there. Mbuni are dozing near his door, eyes closed, pointed heads at rest between their front paws. In the scrub, tree frogs puff their tiny cheeks, trilling *ko-kee* noises. Night birds hoot and howl.

Jimmy raps and hears a sleepy, "Come in."

"Sorry to disturb you, Father John."

"Are you still up then, Brother Atule?"

"As you see, Father."

What he's doing is unprecedented, Jimmy knows, but he's leaving it up to the director. The priest can send him back, if he wishes.

"Have a seat and say what's on your mind."

"Thank you." Jimmy sits. "I'd better just confess it. Bless me, Father, for I have sinned. I'm a soothsayer. I see the future: I divine, foretell, whatever the hell it is."

"It is hell, is it?"

"It is."

"Why don't you tell me about it?"

"You believe me, Father?"

"Shouldn't I?"

"Yes. But first, I must assure you that I've never dabbled in the occult, nor my family. We've always had good teaching on that in Mabuli and not just from you Christians." He smiles briefly at that; the priest smiles too. "We Mabulians know the difference between asking the intercession of the saints, and of our holy ancestors, who are watchful for us, and trafficking with evil spirits."

"Understood. Tell me what happened, or happens, if it still does."

"It does, Father. It just did … That's why I'm here."

"So tell me."

He might as well begin at the beginning.

"I was twelve." The sound of his voice in the silence helps. Proper self-love, Jimmy thinks wryly. "They'd closed school for a month because of an outbreak of mumps. One morning I went tramping through the forest with Tjuma, my best friend. We were looking for mushrooms, the hallucinogenic kind, and we were lucky. We found a whole lot. We made a fire, and brewed up a drink. He had half the tin, and I had the rest, then we sat waiting, all excited."

"And?"

"Nothing. The fungi were perfectly safe. We trudged home, terribly disappointed. I had lunch, and went outside to nap on a bench in the yard. I slept — how long I don't know. And then it happened." He stops.

"Go on," the priest encourages.

"I opened my eyes. Or so I thought. But I couldn't move. Not my hands. Not my feet. Not anything. Couldn't breathe. Not even wiggle a finger. My heart shut down in my chest. My whole body, cold and stiff, lay rattling on the bench the way corpses bounce in the undertaker's cart when it rattles over the unpaved village roads."

"Sounds like fun. How long did it go on?"

"I don't know. A long time."

"And afterwards?"

"I had a … a prescience, I guess you could call it."

"Of what, Brother Jimmy?"

"I knew Mapome, my father's mother, was going to die."

"Had your grandmother been ill?"

"She was perfectly healthy, and not especially old, not by our standards anyway."

"Did she die?"

"The next day."

"You told no one about this?"

"How could I? I was terrified of what they would do if they found I could dream a person to death."

"And there have been other times?"

"Yes."

"Do you want to talk about them?"

"I don't know, Father."

"Call me John, or J.J., if you prefer."

"I don't know, J.J."

"So, what happened just now?"

"I was following up on your reflection, thinking of how Africa had been the birthplace of man, how the first heart transplant happened here, how Palestine, Jesus's homeland, is next door. I saw God's finger outstretched to touch the

Red Jacket   **99**

continent the way it stretches out to Adam in the Sistine Chapel. And then ... Oh, Jesus!"

"We needn't talk about it now. Perhaps in the morning."

"But what must I do? Twice I've foreseen frightful things happening to a single person, a person I loved deeply and wished no harm, and they've come true. This was hundreds of people — a desert people, children, the elderly — driven from their homes, terrorized, murdered. And the seizure never came."

"Some form of illness may yet come, especially if it was as bad as you say. But let's leave it till tomorrow, Jimmy. Sufficient unto the day."

"But the fit, it's like a warranty. I knew Mapome would die. I was sure the other time too, without a doubt."

"Your wife?"

Jimmy nods. J.J. pats his knee, as one would calm a child, and then they sit quietly together as night sucks in the day's leftover smells: jollof rice and fried chicken, reminders of supper next door, rotten-sweet mangoes on the ground, billy goats in heat, ripening animal excrement.

"We used the desert fathers' *Lectio Divina* in this retreat, Jimmy, their way of employing the scriptures to talk to God. Maybe we should be more modern."

"More modern how?"

"Maybe the mystics can help us discern the uses of this gift of yours."

"Gift?"

"Would you rather it were a curse?"

II

Father John Goes for a Walk

Father John opines that the Old Testament is full of prescience, and the gospels too. There are many instances of Jesus's knowing beforehand, up to and including his warning that one of his friends is going to betray him. So why assume that intuitions, visions, and premonitions must be from Satan? The director promises that he and Father Erasmus will discuss Jimmy's visions and decide how to proceed. Meantime, he should make his own inquiries of the Deity, who, having bestowed the talent, can be asked what should be done with it.

Jimmy spends the next day in bed with chills and a fever so high he is delirious. Simeon searches him out after he misses Mass, breakfast, and his morning consultation with Father John. After that, the novice master comes to see him, and later Simeon again, with a broth that the cooks promise will make him "new as a just-born babe." J.J. comes twice as well, but Jimmy is dead to the world both times, for, because of the broth, or his illness, or both, he sleeps all day and far into the next night.

As Father Erasmus tells it afterwards, late in the evening he reminds Father John that they are to meet with the vicar general at seven-thirty the next morning. Though the Very Reverend Nat Nkosi is only making a quick stop en route to Bamako, he'll not be pleased to see the retreat director looking like a Peace Corps volunteer.

"I'll wear my coffle if you wear yours," Erasmus says he quipped to John, at which they clinked their beer mugs, emptied them, and shambled off to bed.

Next morning Jimmy gets up feeling better and anxious to see J.J., in part to reassure himself that their late-night conversation actually took place. By the time he reaches the refectory, the priest has left on his early morning walk to look for "birdies." There is a book about Mabuli birds in the library that he's spent a few minutes thumbing through every evening. On the day when they broke silence, he'd favoured the novices with reports of his finds, proud of the coucals, thrushes, fire finches, and kingfishers he'd sighted. He'd startled Jimmy with a superior imitation of the laughing-doves' soft chuckle.

"Me mum again," he smiled, a little sad. "She could imitate bird and beast."

Father John sets off for his stroll just after daybreak, clad in his black suit. For a long time afterwards Jimmy blames the vicar general, sure that if J.J. looked more Peace Corps and less priest, things would have gone differently.

The staff find him just off a path in the forest, beheaded and eviscerated.

Three days later the vicar general returns to celebrate a Mass of Thanksgiving for the life of Father John Kelly, S.J., with clergy from the nearest parishes and the Jesuit Superior who comes from Benke. All twelve novices take part in the ceremony. It falls to Jimmy to do the first reading from Revelations.

"And I saw a new heaven and a new earth; for the first heaven and first earth were passed away." Simeon takes over when Jimmy can't go on. He cries quietly as his friend finishes the passage. His tears pool in his scars, and then overflow the tiny reservoirs. They send the American priest home the day after that. With his family's approval, the seminarians drape his coffin with his kiloli.

The horror isn't that the murdered man is white or a foreigner. It is that he is a guest and a priest, two conditions that tradition says are violated only at great peril. A guest is welcomed and offered hospitality in Mabuli, while a priest is accorded the esteem proper to one who mediates between the divine and human beings. So it is hard to believe that a Mabulian did it. John Kelly's murder seems ordained to make trouble, attract worldwide attention. It is Africa according to foreign TV.

J.J. was a wise, funny priest. Jimmy mourns his death, but he grieves more over what he knows will follow, for there is something else he senses. It shakes him, body, mind, and spirit: he sees the hand of death that took John seizing all of Africa, then reaching across oceans, tearing apart the world.

The Oti convene at an ancient amphitheatre near Kenbara shortly after John Kelly's murder. Of many stone circles in Mabuli, the Kenbara Stone Circle is the most famous, its stelae taller than the tallest man, its keystone "crying" sporadically, its tale one of three great legends in the sung history of the Mabuli Chronicles. Soon after the attack on Elise and Lili's father, it is rumoured that stones in the circle near their village start to walk. The walking is reputed to spread to other stone circles, and finally to Kenbara, but there is no real evidence until November when an article appears in an issue of the *Mabuli Messenger*. It is a feature about the Oti convention.

> *Mabuli Messenger (English Edition)*
> November 5, 1976
> Kenbara Keystone Cries as the Oti Consider
> State of the Nation
> By Ahmad Kahl
>
> This morning the Oti, Mabuli's priestly federation, and the tribal chiefs from the four major ethnic

groups will convene at 10:00 a.m. for a "State of the Nation" meeting, the first in living memory. The meeting takes place at the open amphitheatre near Kenbara, site of the largest of the Mabuli stone circles and the only one traditionally regarded as having chameleon or colour-changing stones.

At sunset last night the newsroom of the *Mabuli Messenger* was inundated with calls and visits from numerous persons reporting that the keystone of the Kenbara Stone Circle had commenced weeping. More startling, several insisted the stones had begun to change colour. The intermittent weeping of the keystone, though unexplained, is widely documented and has for many years been the subject of study by local, African, and foreign anthropologists, geologists, hydrologists, and other scientists. The changing of colour in the keystone as well as other stones is recounted in the Mabuli Chronicles and in many songs and recitations, but there is no written record of such an event.

This reporter visited the site and noted a puddle of water about an inch deep in the concave depression atop the keystone, the receptacle for supplicatory and sacrificial offerings. The keystone also seemed to have a bluish cast to its normally slate-gray hue. However, it would be an exaggeration to say that the keystone had changed colour since it is possible that the unusual presence of water or uncharacteristic optical effects may have produced a persuasive *trompe l'oeil*.

Indisputably, between this reporter's first visit at sunset, and the second, early this morning, the entire circle had moved, approximately eight inches, in a clockwise direction, as these before and after photographs show.

Although the organizers have given no official reason for this meeting of the Oti, there have in recent months been unconfirmed reports that imams, diviners, dervishes, marabouts, contemplatives, and priests attached to animist, Sufi, Muslim, Christian, and other communities were urging chiefs and elders to come together for a colloquium, indicating that they themselves planned to meet. Increasing violence, including the recent gruesome murder of visiting priest Father John Jeremiah Kelly, SJ, is no doubt part of their motivation.

It would be surprising therefore if the breakdown of law and order were not high on the meeting's agenda. In the circumstances, the behaviour of the chameleon stone and the ambling of the Kenbara Circle will also very likely receive attention.

A subsequent issue reports that the Kenbara Keystone, having wept to overflowing despite the dryness of the time, turns a deep blue on the morning of the meeting, and cries all through the conference, ceasing only when the Oti depart.

There is a resolution at the end of the meeting, expressed in the form of an old chant, also published in a final report in the *Messenger*. Jimmy frames both articles with a picture of Simeon, J.J., and himself. The collage goes everywhere with him after that.

The shed blood of a kinsman defiles the clan.
The shed blood of a guest defiles the nation.
If the lion eats his paw, he lames himself.
The lamed lion cannot hunt.
The lamed lion cannot fight.
The lioness is set upon.
The cubs are devoured.
Let the ones with eyes see.
Let the ones with ears hear.
Let the hard-hearted understand.

Jimmy will forever remember every minute of this time. The trinity of deaths — Mapome, Nila, and J.J. — paste the line of his life together so that it becomes like the never-ending surface of a Moebius strip. Thereafter, events meet, join, and let go of each other like waves of the ocean, separate, all of a piece.

MARK

12

Femina Ludens or The Chancellor's Wife

"Mona?"

"Who else it could be, my dear? Nobody else call at eleven-thirty at night."

"Well, maybe some fellow who discover that the sexiest woman in Washington is alone, so he climb up to her window with hope in both hands …"

"Mark, I've heard a willy called many things, but never hope."

"A willy? Who said anything about a willy? I said, hope in his hands. It's a metaphor. If he try climbing up to your window with his willy in his hands, he would drop and break his neck!"

"Oh! A metaphor. Well, my husband, it have not a soul here, real or imaginary, with either hope or their willy in their hands. "

"Don't dismiss hope. You know how many men walking round with only hope in their pants?" Chuckles, listens in vain for Mona's answering laugh.

"I not even bothering with the fact that you say I sound like a fellow! I see you must have slept, since you firing on all cylinders."

"Did I wake you, Mona love? I'm sorry."

"I never say that."

So what's wrong? Ah well! Just press on. "I meant to call as I got in."

"So you only now reach to the hotel, Mark. What time it is? Don't it's about half-past eleven?"

"Yes. According to my watch, anyway. I reached here at about six-thirty, to be greeted by a pile of papers for council tomorrow. Thought I'd start on them straight off — you know me — took a break and went downstairs to wet my whistle. I guess jet lag hit me when I got back. I lay down to take five and next thing I know, it's middle night."

"Poor you," her tone belies the comment.

"So how are things, Mona?"

"Things? Things are fine. Fine as usual." She's provoking him again.

"You don't sound fine, my darling."

"You never asked about me. You asked about things."

He can't recall where he'd read it, some smart ass saying that since man was changing from *homo sapiens* to *homo ludens*, we'd all have to go back to school to learn to play games. All except Mona, that is. He tries to dredge up Mr. Singh's Latin class, recall the word for woman. Ah. *Femina. Femina ludens.*

It's easy to forgive her, though.

"Mark?"

"Sorry, love. Distracted. Thinking about you. Look, seriously, are you okay? You sound like you have flu."

"Since you now get round to me, yes, Mark, I have a sniffle."

"So you're in bed?"

"Nope. Lover-boy having gone, I'm disposing of the evidence." Ah! She's making a little joke, at least. Since Adam's death, he works hard to make her laugh. She'd miscarried three times and when she finally had Adam, it was like Jesus came, except he died like Jesus, only sooner, at six months.

"Mona, you're aggravating, you know."

"Me, Mark? Aggravating? But is you send the man in through the window!"

Ah! Good! Now she's taking him on. He has counted every jolly exchange between them since Adam's death, which devastated her — him too, but her worse. She had no job to distract her, nothing to occupy her in the days and weeks that followed.

He stops himself. Better pay attention to the conversation.

"What's the Washington weather like, my love?"

"Weather, Mark? You mean temperature and rain and so? It was below freezing this morning. Thirty maybe."

"So cold? But is only the first week in November! And it wasn't anything near that when I left! No wonder you're sick. You know your mother says rapid changes of temperature cause flu."

"I never say I have flu, Mark. I say a sniffle: headache, drippy nose, sore throat, general bad feeling. Your commonplace fall-and-winter ailment."

Testy, like she's pretty much been since Adam's funeral. He'd sent her on a Caribbean cruise with her sister Nora in an attempt to cheer her up. Nora said she'd stared at the sea, cried, barely spoke, hardly ate.

"That don't sound commonplace to me. Anyway, cold or flu, just park yourself in bed."

"Yes, boss. You know me. Your 'patient mule.' "

Who was that? Some poet-type? After the cruise, he'd come home each day to find her, not just in bits and pieces, more like puréed over some poetry book or other. So he'd again dipped into his pocket for a back-to-India trip. He'd been glad to see her trying on saris, jumping to raga as she packed.

"Don't come with your Trini picong. The first time I had a bite to eat in your house, your Ma spent hours telling me about your delicate constitution."

"No way, Chancellor. My mother listened politely to you talking about yourself and your prospects, even though you were black and she hoped I'd wed a wealthy son of India. Plus, she laid on a lavish spread."

"Whatever. Just don't take your health and taunt me."

"Taunt you? Mark, how am I taunting you?"

"I worry when you not a hundred percent, Mona. You enjoy making me feel helpless and without recourse, not so?"

"Husband, whatever things you lack, recourse isn't one of them. But is like you forget I'm flying down day after tomorrow?"

"Sufficient unto the day, or in this case, the day after. Just promise me you will get some rest. And don't yank my chain because I'm too far away to do anything more than beg you to be sensible."

"Yank your chain? Not me, though if I did, it wouldn't be amiss — a mistress, more like." A chuckle he's not pleased to hear.

"Mona, I not making any fun with you."

"By the by, have you met the lady of the moment yet?" The line prickles.

"You mean Dr. Carpenter? No."

"She's there, though, isn't she?"

When she'd come back from India, she seemed like her old self, and things had gone well for a bit. Recently, though, they seemed rocky once more. In many ways, the instability had been there from the start. Perhaps it was a coolie thing and part of her attraction, as his brother had once suggested. Maybe that was true. Whether it was or not, she'd gone off completely after Adam's death. He'd been a perfect baby, happy, well behaved. Then one morning she had lifted his cold body from the crib.

"SIDS?" she'd raged. "Some cretin pick a word rhyming with kids for a disease that kill children?" She smashed every breakable thing, ripped up her clothes, howled like a lunatic. The hardest part was that he couldn't touch her. If he put out his hand, she flinched. If he tried to kiss her, she turned away. He wondered if she was trying to mash up the marriage as well.

GRACE

13

Grace Settles In

Edris's grandaunt would die if she ever know that Grace's roommate, Stephanie Scott, is a Roman Catholic that wear medals and hang a rosary on her bed. Enough to contaminate the air that good Christians breathe! The day after term begin, the said Heathen Idolater hand Grace a letter, saying, "Went for mail. Mail guy must have dropped this. I rescued it. Turns out it's yours."

Grace so glad she nearly grab the letter out of Stephanie's hand. It is from Gramps, first to write Grace, which is not surprising, for Grace know Ma is bustling to fix up school uniforms, shoes, and books for Conrad, Sam, and Princess, and Pa is hustling to find money for those things as well as put aside some for Stewie, in case he get through to Pursea's, a Methodist college in St. Charles parish that still operate the pupil-teacher system. If Stewie do well on the entrance test and give three references, don't mind he never been to secondary school, they will take him to train in industrial arts. Gramps is tutoring Edgar who finish at the All-Age school, but is trying to do four subjects in the Cambridge exams. He still sending his poems and stories to the newspapers.

Grace only glance at Gramps letter. She going to read it carefully when she get back to the dorm. At present she looking for the admissions office so she can speak to somebody about whether she fulfill all the entry requirements. Just now one of the other overseas students say something that make her think she better check. She rummage in her pocket for the letter, so she can touch it again for reassurance, but then she decide she can't wait whole day, so she cross at Bloor and Spadina, go in the bank, find a armchair, and open the letter.

> *Hut No 15*
> *Wentley Park*
> *St. Christopher, W.I.*
> *5 September 1976*

My dear Gracie,
I have been looking forward to writing this letter since the day Ma Carpenter found you reading the newspaper! I am glad to be putting my pen to paper in the first of what I hope will be many letters to pass between us. Before I go on to the "reasoning," as Mortimer would call it, some practical things. I hope you are settling in without too much trouble, for I know things are very different there. The cold especially can come swiftly and without warning, so it is best to be prepared. A good bit of advice that my Irish sixth cousin gave me in the war is, "Keep your head and your feet warm!" That is half the battle won against a formidable enemy. Money spent on wool socks and warm headgear is well spent. Also, if you haven't bought them yet, invest in a good pair of boots. When winter comes, you will be glad you did. In fact, on the whole, buy one good thing rather than two cheap ones. It works out less expensive in the long run.

Nor is it only the weather that you will find a challenge. It is also the draining away of colour, the death of everything around you, the absence of the sun. You will need to fight that in many ways. Here are my suggestions. Put a plant in your room or your dormitory — wherever you are living. Remember my story about stealing the piece of syngonium from Kew Gardens? Those few leaves kept me going through the gloomy winter months. I paid no mind to all those limey fellows laughing at me. When the bombs rained and the racist insults flew, I'd remember it and resolve that I too would thrive.

Next, put cheerful things on the walls of your room. Cut them from old calendars or magazines or those glossy advertisements that proliferate in the North. And buy clothes in cheery colours too, so that you brighten up the landscape. A red sweater or coat can do wonders for your spirits. And give yourself a treat, no matter how small, from time to time.

Now for our usual discourse.

We have a habit here to speak of what education has done and can do for poor people in a small ex-colonial country. I want to say at the start that you must struggle, now that you are out in the wider world, not to think of yourself in that way. God gave us all brains, black and white, brown and yellow. What you are part of, and what you are yourself contributing to, is something much bigger than a bootstrap operation to benefit yourself. Everybody at the university to which you are going is after the same thing. We all need to know, and knowing improves us all, or at least it should. It is

*our common pursuit, and we all benefit. You are
learning with lots of other people and you have your
part to do. I know that you will do it well.*

*Here now is the challenge. Promise me please
that you will not take on every skirmish that comes
your way. There will be battles aplenty. Pick the
ones you join. You are a black person in white
people's country and you are there on sufferance.
They will not be afraid of telling you so. LEARN
TO SWALLOW YOUR SPIT. You know you can
believe me for we have talked about this before, all
those times when I told you stories about being in
the RAF. That was a World War. People's lives and
freedom were at stake. But the colour of a person's
skin was what people saw and reacted to. Don't
let them shove that view of the world down your
throat any more than you allow them to turn you
into somebody bawling the whole time about how
you have been slighted because of your colour. That
is no way to live. It is also letting others box you
into perceiving the world in the way they define
it — and a narrow, poisonous view at that. Your
colour is not your culture nor what makes you who
you are. If it were, any tar-brushed white foreigner
could be a Christophian. It is certainly part, and an
important part, history being what it has been, of
a sometimes splendid, sometimes vile set of events
that have contrived to make you into yourself. But
it isn't by any means the whole of you. You are a
brilliant country girl from Wentley Park Plantation
in Westland Parish in the island of St. Christopher.
Do your do and say your say and know that nobody
deserves to be sipping at the fount of knowledge any
more, nor any less, than you.*

As for news here, things are pretty much as usual. The Queenstown goings-on do not presently affect us in Wentley Park, but I wonder how much longer that will be the case. The problem with these overseas-educated politician fellows is that they eat up the overseas culture and way of seeing things. Don't let that happen to you. Remember the contribution I just spoke about? One part of it involves putting forward the way of thinking and the points of view that you bring with you, those you have because you come from this place and are who you are.

Mr. Wong asked me to enclose the ten-dollar bill. He knows your mother wouldn't take it, but he and I are worldly men so he entrusted it to me.

I close by reminding you again to pick your battles with care: it's sometimes prudent to lose a battle so you might win a war. I am so proud of you, Gracie. All of us are proud. We are praying that you will have great success.

God bless.
Gramps

Gramps missive hurt her heart, but it comfort her too, so she resume her mission feeling better. Inside the administrative building she find her way quick, join a line, and soon reach the front. She land up facing a woman who is maybe fifty and whiter than anybody she ever see. The woman's hair is dark and soft, with plenty gray in it, especially near her small ears. Also, it is crinkly. According to Gramps, in Lisbon during the War, he see plenty women with hair like that, women so sure they were white that they always cross the street to get out of his way. Gramps always laugh and say, "Ah, the Moors! Those Blackamoors!"

Grace say, "Good morning," and smile a little. Ask if there are still admission requirements she need to fulfill. The grey eyes in the face before her light on hers and fly off like they touch a hot surface. Must be really hot, for in the rest of the conversation, the eyes don't make four with hers again. Now, they travel to a pile of papers on the counter, but don't look up, while a hoity-toity voice ask, "What did you say your surname was?"

Grace is on the verge of saying, "Carpenter, ma'am" but instead she just say, "Carpenter."

"You know of course that you must take a language proficiency test?" The woman is face to face with Grace again, her raised brows lifting the rest of a mean face, her eyes staring down at her narrow, quivering nose. Grace know the meaning of all these signs. It's not merely to let her know that she's not welcome; it's to let her know she's hardly there. In a second she is standing again at the counter of Mr. Wong's shop, clenching her teeth, struggling to force out Ma's short shopping list in the loudest voice she can manage. She do the same thing now like she do those times: take a deep breath, swallow, open her mouth, and force herself to speak. But she swear yet again that one day God going tell her why he breathe life into her, give her a good brain, then leave her with such a small conviction that she deserve a space on earth.

"What language is the test in?" Grace ask her. "I speak two — three, if you count my Creole." She sort of stretching things with the three-language bit, but she do have a little Spanish, never mind it's not fluent.

"Your what?" The question explode softly from the woman's mouth in the way you shoot out a coolie plum seed that you finish eating.

"St. Chris Creole, my native tongue," Grace answer. Grace not sure if the woman hear her, for the eyes now staring past her to the rest of the line, then moving across the room to check a old-fashioned clock on the wall opposite, then rolling up to the high ceiling, then sliding down the marble columns. They are looking everywhere but at her.

"I'd like to know the time for the test, and if there are forms, I'd like them too, please." There is a eloquent absence of response, as the woman turn back to some shelves behind her, select some papers, turn around, and hand them to Grace, same time saying, "Next." She is still withholding her gaze. Grace take the papers, consider, decide she will say, "Thank you very much." As she turn to leave, the woman is amiably asking the next person, "May I help you?"

Outside the four o'clock sun is wading through thick clouds, icy gusts whipping bits of old paper along Bloor Street, everybody passing every other body as if they are alone on the planet. She feel a drum starting to beat in her head, no doubt sake of the rude woman. But Gramps say to pick her battles, and he wouldn't rate the woman as a minor skirmish. Plus Ma would say, the rudeness is probably a sign of worries. Which don't make the experience any more pleasant when you just arrive in a strange place.

She decide to think of the nice people she know, like her roommate, Steph, she with the jade plant on her desk. "My mother says even a murderer cannot kill this plant. I tell her not to kid herself. We have a ten-dollar bet that it will die by Christmas."

So her roomie is a gambler too. That don't surprise her. Everybody know Catholics with their bingo and raffles. Lord have mercy! The Worshipper of Graven Images and Wearer of Evil Amulets is now also a what — Punter? Wagerer? Nor is that the end of it. Steph's iniquity extend in other directions as well, for she promise to take Grace to Allan Gardens to snitch a piece of public plant for Grace to grow in a private pot in their room — on Gramps's instruction and by his example.

Grace think of the boys thiefing Gramps sugar and fibbing to Ma, bad things that they did because they love her.

14

A Blinding Headache

Through the glass windows at Coffee Coin, Grace is gazing idly outside, waiting for Maisie's tall, slender figure to stride into view. Though it is only fall, Grace is already a roundness of tights, jeans, and sweaters, an outfit completed by a balloon of a wool hat and smaller balloons of warm mittens, for the cold reach so far into her body, it feel like her pee is frozen into ice. In its approach, winter is no betrayer: it fixing to keep every promise it make to Grace the day she buck up the rude woman in Admissions, a day that seem five years, instead of five weeks, ago.

Grace know Maisie from St. Chad's, her snobby high-school-of-choice in Queenstown, where the girls used to call her — Maisie, that is — "choucune," which they take to mean "yellow girl." Grace was dubbed "redibo," the day she arrive. The light-skin girls at St. Chad's had a rhyme to chant, adjusting it to suit whoever they were torturing. Maisie's version go: "She's a high yellow gal/with hair that straighten well/hair that straighten well/so it's very hard to tell."

As for Grace, if in Wentley Park her red skin, "fine" features, and soft, red hair are the envy of some, at St. Chad's she is at the bottom of the colour/class curve for, first, skin that is light in Wentley Park is dark at St. Chad's, and soft hair there is tough and kinky in this uppity neck of Queenstown.

And she is clearly poor as a scrawny puss.

Maisie not the bookish type and since her family is well off, no way she and Grace were going to be friend and company at St. Chad's, even if they were the same age. In fact, Maisie is a big girl in sixth form when Grace arrive so there is all of seven years between them. Maisie know Grace, though, for everybody in the school know her. Grace arrive with the highest marks in the General Entrance Exam of any student who ever attend the school.

Right now, apart from Maisie and her roommate, Grace know not one other soul in all the length and breadth of Toronto. She meet plenty people, mark you, but it's just plenty hello and goodbye. She don't take it amiss and she hold on to Gramps advice: "Don't shun people, Gracie, when you reach to foreign. There is none of us that cannot profit from a friend. Give a helping hand whenever you can, and if somebody put one out to you, don't box it away."

So here she is awaiting Maisie.

Their first meeting was a buck-up in a expensive supermarket on Bloor that Grace usually avoid, but which she patronize that day because of a urgent need for sanitary napkins as well as on account of the fact that it have a clean bathroom. Grace see Maisie first and say a timid, "Hi!" Maisie see Grace, pull her to one side, and move through her recent history like bran through bowels. Cramming to keep up with her informant, Grace learn that shortly after Maisie graduate from St. Chad's, her family pack up and come to Canada, she find a job in a bank, marry a Canadian widower with a eight-year-old daughter, and settle down to be wife and mother.

When Grace ask what make her family leave, Maisie look solemn. "My father was a civil servant. Remember how they kill Mr. Ogle on his way to work?"

Grace nod. Mr. Ogle was a honest man, so they put him in charge of government contracts in the Ministry of Construction. He institute a fair system of awarding them and get paid with a bullet.

"Next day Father go to the Canadian High Commission and apply for papers." Maisie's sculpted eyebrows take off like soaring birds. "He say he learn to read from he is three, so he can see the writing on the wall, and it not worth being Permanent Secretary when a bullet from a ten-dollar gun can land you up as permanently secreted in God's earth as any dead dog." The crudeness of the dead dog bit take Grace by surprise. "We reach here one year later, which is four years gone."

So Grace now waiting, taking in the scene, and taking her time over a cup of Coffee Coin mint tea. She never expect Maisie to acknowledge her in the supermarket, so when her schoolmate phone her, she is properly astonished. True, they exchange numbers at the store, but if she was to hear from all the people she give her number to, she would be a speedy car on the social highway.

Maisie finally arrive, full of apologies. She not alone. "Meet a friend," she say. "Lindsay Bell, this is my schoolmate, also from St. Chris, Grace Carpenter."

Lindsay say, "Hi, Grace."

"Gracie, I hate to do this for it's the worst manners!" Maisie say, all smiles. "I have to run and leave you. School call to say Sylvia look like she getting chicken pox, so I must pick her up. I bounce into Lindsay outside, and he say he know your brother, Edgar. I say, 'Come, meet her!' So see him here!"

Lindsay is tall, black, and sturdy like Gramps. His somewhat slant eyes put Grace in mind of Miss Carmen, but the whole shape of him recall Gramps. He nod his head in greeting and look unsure of what to do next.

"I don't come here often, but I hear their coffee is good," Grace find herself saying, "and this mint tea is not like the one at home, but it will do."

"I've time for a coffee," Lindsay say. "Can I get you another tea?"

"No, thanks. I'm fine."

Maisie look relieved. "Great! You two get to know each other. I hurrying. Call you later, Gracie." She jangle off, model-on-the-runway, keys twirling.

"So how come you know Edgar?" Grace ask Lindsay, who now facing her across the table, warming his hands in the steam rising from his cup of coffee.

"Haven't known him long," he say. "I know his poetry. It's good. I'm a journalism major at Carleton, and I did my co-op at *The Clarion*. I spoke to Edgar on the phone once when he called about a poem of his being published without his name, and I met him once when he came to get a cheque. Nice guy."

"All my brothers and sisters are." Even Pansy! She's glad she thinks it freely. "So what you doing in Toronto?"

"On an investigative assignment."

"Sound mysterious. I guess you can't say what it is?"

"Not yet. What if I send you the story when it comes out — if it does?"

"Okay."

"I'll need your address."

Grace amaze herself again by tearing a piece of paper from her notebook and scribbling the address on it.

"What about you, Grace? Maisie says you are at U of T?"

"Doing education, supposedly. Still don't know what I really want to do."

"You just come, then?"

"Green as grass, Lindsay." Two of them laugh.

They chat, or mostly he chat, answering her. How come he's at Carleton? Best place for journalism. How come he did his co-op at a paper in St. Chris? His father's idea and connections, him being the St. Chris parent, his mother being from Trinidad. His dad thought Lindsay could do more challenging things at a small paper, plus have the St. Chris home experience. Had it turned out that way? Yes.

Looking outside, Grace can see it's darker. The sky is getting lower; she can taste it. Something swimming in the mint tea in her belly take a dive, creating a raw, acid, disgusting splash in her throat and a peculiar taste in her mouth that mean headache-soon-come. But while this is not her first headache, it's the first time she's doing what millions do every day. She will bear it.

When Lindsay finish his coffee, he say he can't linger, but he hope to see her again, and he renew his promise to send the story. At the corner of St. George and Bloor, they say goodbye. Lindsay head into the subway, and Grace stand up in the same spot where he leave her. Maybe Lindsay really want to see her again. Maybe he will send the story. And he know Edgar! That make her feel warm and near home. She rub her nauseous stomach, but it don't help. As she is calling up the energy to head for her job in the library, a cold breeze clap her in her face like a fast ball crash a wicket. The icy blow relieve the oncoming headache a bit, all the same, so she will see the good side.

She putting foot in front of slow foot, thinking. Who she fooling? Lindsay will not write her. Lindsay have a life. Moreover, what is she doing in this strange place where everything freeze up, even the people, and she don't know neither puss nor dog?

Saturday morning, the headache is mounting a determined attack, keeping Grace in bed all day, lights flickering round the edge of her vision. By evening, it call up reinforcements, and they establish a beachhead in her neck-back. Come Sunday, yielding none of the captured terrain, it start to bombard her stomach. She take two Anacin, close the curtains, get under the covers. The Anacin don't work its usual magic, though; the attack now extend to her eyesight, which is punctuated by black blotches. She decide she imagining them to start with, but by noon she's seeing only half what's in front of her.

"Come," Steph tell her. "We're going to check emerge at General." General is Toronto General Hospital, attached to the university, where medical students cut their teeth. Emerge is the emergency ward, full when they arrive, never mind Sunday is normally a slack day. Steph shepherd her, icepack on her head, through the system, and after half an hour, she is talking to a nurse.

"Name?"

"Grace Carpenter."

"Problem?"

"I can't see."

"You're blind?"

"She's lost vision in half her ..." Steph start to put in her two pence.

"I didn't ask you."

"I was just trying to help ..."

"You must be deaf. I repeat. I am not addressing you, so kindly shut your mouth." The nurse turn to Grace. "Are you going to answer my question?"

Grace, terrified at what is happening to her eyesight, irritated at the whirl of people kowtowing to other people, the lowliest being tawny orderlies, cleaners, movers of trash, the highest being pink Canadians decorated with stethoscope necklaces and clipboard hand-gear, is past fury when she hear the woman address Stephanie like that.

"You ask me," she tell the nurse, "and you better take your face out of my face, like how I have a very queasy stomach." She give a long kiss-teeth, continue in her most correct English, but with a broad Christophian inflection. "I have had a rass cloth headache for two days, and now half of my vision is impaired. Do I make myself clear?" Grace, already shocked by the language emerging from her mouth, is astounded by the menace in her voice.

A short, dark old man wielding a mop look up when she "rass cloth", wink, a sly droop of one eyelid, enjoy a barely audible cackle, and resume scrutinizing the black-and-white checkerboard tiles like he planning his next chess move. The nurse glance at him, look back at Grace, do a soft suck-teeth of her own. She proceed to take Grace's blood pressure, pulse, peer into eyes, and ears. Then she latch a plastic cuff on Grace's wrist, point to some chairs, and instruct, "Wait over there."

"Why, thank you so much for your kind attention," Grace give out, as she stand up, take Steph's proffered hand, and move to the contingent of chairs.

"You okay?" Steph whisper.

Grace nod, then ask, "Washroom?" as she stop in the middle of sitting down, hand over her mouth.

"Right over there, sweet daughter." A soft Christophian voice.

"You need to go?" Steph ask Grace, as she nod thanks to the man.

Grace shake her head. "Just need to know where, in case."

"Don't worry. I going fix you up." It's the chess master with the mop again, speaking into the floor, and then moving swiftly, crab-like, disappearing around a corner.

Grace sit. Steph offer her the bottle of warm Coke she been sipping all day. Suddenly, another dark man is with them. He is the spitting image of the first, except he is younger, taller, green clad, stethoscope around his neck, clipboard in hand. He say to them, "Please follow me."

He is Manny, son of Aloysius-the-Mop-Man's cousin, and a nurse practitioner.

"I'm sorry Caroline was rude," he say. "Her son was murdered last year, by one of ours. Yesterday was the first anniversary of his death."

Grace shrug. She think of all the black people in the world with murdered children putting on their best face in a million service jobs. If every grief had a rude mouth, is only rude mouth that the world would be hearing.

During half an hour's consultation with Manny, she discover that she has had migraine headaches since she was a child. Relief is at hand, though, for there are pills, and she can also learn to relax her way out of them.

On her way out, pills in her pocket, Grace look for Aloysius to thank him.

"Got to look after a countrywoman," he say with a twinkle, rocking on the mop.

"I can't thank you enough."

"Tell you what," Aloysius say, sweet mischief in his eye, "come visit my church some time. Just down the road on Baldwin." He push his hand in his pocket and pull out a couple of tracts, which he give her. "Bring your pretty friend too."

Next day, Grace still can't see straight. She stay in the dorm at Steph's insistence, castigating herself the whole time for not complaining about the nurse. Then she recall Gramps advice. "Gracie, don't be too hard on yourself, and don't expect too much of the folks you meet." So far, people are not so bad. Some are disdainful, but many are kind. She admire Aloysius and Manny, subverting the deferential dance at the hospital, helping to cure not only sickness of the body, but sickness of the way the world conceive of and construct itself.

Maybe she shouldn't study teaching. Maybe medicine would be better. But she don't think she is doctor material, unless it is Gramps kind of doctoring, a basic set of ministrations that include pulling teeth, snapping palates to cure tinnitus, and brewing home remedies from banned substances.

15

Grace Finds a Church

Rufus, the student advisor, is a handsome Bajan who like to grab passersby at the waist, spin them around, and guide them down the corridor in one-two-three steps of a crazy dance. When Grace decide to abandon teaching and do economics instead, she consider switching universities, so she ask Rufus advice. He ask her if she have any cute brothers. She is learning the ways of this pagan place, so she hold up her right hand, and raise four fingers, one at a time. Rufus smile broader at each raised digit.

"And I have two sisters, Rufus, but a question can't answer a question."

"Girl, is much of a muchness where a first degree is concerned. What you put in is what you get out, though it might look different after." He giggles. His Bajan accent does strange things with vowels and the letter "r."

Grace don't bother take on the slackness, for it's nothing new. Wentley Park is not backward in that. Having got the advice she is looking for, she decide to stick with the evil she know. She will stay at U of T, but change her major.

It leave her as the one black person in every course.

"You write so well, Grace."

"Thank you, Professor Letchman."

"Where did you learn such excellent English?"

"At my mother's knee, sir."

And she tired of people being surprised at how she come to be so bright. Sometimes she want to say she is surprised at how they come to be so dumb.

One afternoon at mid-term, when she reach the dorm nearly dead after three tests, back to back, she find a letter from Ma.

6 October 1976

Dear Gracie,

Is Ma here saying sorry it take me so long to write. I know Gramps write and send you news not to say that is a xcuse but you know how things go. We are all okay thank God Pa go to doctor for he wasn't seeming so right and doctor say he have pressure and give him pills. Stewie and Edgar and Conrad growin so fast it hard to keep them in clothes and shoes but your Grampa always find xtra dollars say it come from his agrcultural money. I give God thanks for him everyday he holding up but like the years starting to take their toll. The little ones doing fine Pansy and Mortimer going along good so far praise God. She managing with the children I can't believe is two already and they come so close the baby is two weeks now and look like Mortimer cant done. Him and she growing some things round the back he put a bigger bell in the shop front so they sure to hear customers. I not paying no mind to the politics is in God hands but I do fear with the voilence not thinkin it will harm me or mine but God don't like those things. Only the Maker have any right to take life and he

*is a Jealous God. Everybody send greetings and
prayers. God bless.*

Ma

Grace know is a effort for Ma to put those words down, the
same mother at whose knee she claim to have learned English.
Gramps is the one with the tutoring knee, of course, but
what difference that make? The question about her language
competence is a comment, not a question. But how is she going
to make these people understand that their one-note English
is nothing like the keyboard of language that every St. Chris
child in primary school can play? The school part is important.
You are lucky if you get a cane in your hand-middle and not on
your backside if anything but her Majesty's English come out of
your mouth inside the school! Once through the gate, though,
Chrissie Creole can reclaim its place. That time the language
rock-and-roll can begin, crissing and crossing from English
English, to Creole Creole, and hitting all notes in between.

The blue air letter in her hands wrinkle in a tickle of breeze.
The finger is sharp, a coolness that say "colder to come." She
ignore it. All she pondering is the difference between here and
there, how disinclined she is to bother with educating herself
away from sights, sounds, smells, and tastes that she inhale with
every lungful of air since she born. Some days she feel like it is,
in Gramps terms, a battle she join since she step off the plane.
Yes, it "ought" to be "stepped," she know it is "stepped," but she
choosing to say "step." Too bad!

She miss home so much, she put down a shameless bawling.
When it decline into sniffs and damp intakes of breath, she
consider the Wentley solution to problems: praying or reading
the Word. Here they say religion is a panacea for the lazy and
stupid. She don't care. She only want it to work. Trouble is, in
five years of going to the Church of England at St. Chad's, God

become distant, cold and, well, Anglican. Even if he exhale fire, God is lively in Wentley. She hunt up Aloysius's tracts and decide to visit his church to check out whether God down there is jumping, or if he have a stiff upper lip.

"The Beloved" church on the tracts is, in fact, "The Evangel Church of the Father, Beloved Lord Jesus, and High Holy Spirit." That sweet her no end. There and here can be the same, after all. It sweet her too that Reverend Douglas, the pastor, is a woman. And plenty people from the Caribbean come there, so the congregation resemble the one in Wentley. So "Beloved" is the place Grace start going to worship. She give them her address and phone number, and they tell her of their many ministries: music ministry; temple ministry; ministries to children, the poor, sick, prisoners, students, the disabled, and the emotionally ill. They ask her if she would care to join a ministry, but she say, like how she just come, she will wait and see.

She attend a couple Sunday services. One or two Bible studies and social events. But she soon miss one Sunday service, then another, then three. The third time she miss service, somebody phone to ask how she is, whether she need anything. They are so kind, Grace feel guilty when she find herself staying away, but like spite, life get busier, work increase, and every week she promise herself to go, and then she break the promise. But, she tell herself, toiling at the books is her duty, for Gramps charge her with making a contribution. Now Sunday worship is at the Church of Robarts Library with evening prayers at the Chapel of the Laundry.

Next thing you know, autumn come and gone. Any time now is cold and snow. True, Gramps arm her with counsel about how to survive winter, but she never experience nothing like this. Thank God her one, two friends come to her rescue: Maisie, in a coat purple as a ripe otaheite apple, taking her for treks in the snow, crunching alongside in flashy boots, cowing down winter with her classy clothes; Steph, cheeks red with cold, dragging her out to make snow angels, buy roast chestnuts, search the sky for northern lights; Lindsay, arriving one weekend with grater cake and gizzada, insisting that they go to a documentary on St. Chris.

The clamour of Christmas in the last days before it arrive is the loud noise of how much she ache for home. Maisie and family are visiting her parents in Miami. Lindsay is in Ottawa being a waiter, trolling decent tips in the season of goodwill. Steph ask her from early on to spend the holidays with her family in Warsaw, a village near Peterborough, but she don't want to impose. Besides, don't mind it was long ago, she still bearing the scar from the last place she stay that wasn't home.

Christmas Eve, trying to study in the library, she can't stop thinking about the smell of pudding boiling in kerosene pans, Jonkonnu jumping down dirt tracks with their drum and penny-whistle music, the Devil and his long fork still sending a shiver through her. She can hear clear-clear the sounds of carol service, first the one at school, and then the watch-night service at church, for which people are at that very hour bathing and shaving, putting on their best. Tears hop-skip-jump down her face. She wipe them away quick, gather up her bangarang, scurry like a squirrel back to the dorm, throw her books down on the ground, fling herself onto the bed, and let out a bellow that wake up a gently snoring Steph, who she never even notice on the bed next door. Her roommate stir, open her eyes and say, "Pick up your toothbrush and come. My mother says we're not eating Christmas dinner without you."

That night find her at midnight Mass in Our Lady of the Assumption Church in Peterborough, the one black lamb. When she look out and see snow to the nth power, she wonder again why she choose to be a alien in this forbidding place.

Come January, cold white matter issue from above, dropping non-stop and blotting out every shape and contour. Grace run to the mailbox so many times a day that Steph ask her if they are serving food there. Grace tell her yes, for in truth letters from

Gramps, Ma, and Pa are good, filling starch, as satisfying as yam, rice-and-peas, dumpling, or roast breadfruit. Also solid protein — cascadura, curry goat, oxtail, and tripe and beans. As for the boys, from she was boarding with Miss Carmen, letters from them provide her with rainbow-coloured vittles — vegetables in light and dark green, orange, and beet red, and fruits in all the colours under the sun.

She worry a little about the news from home. Stewie write now and then from Pursea's, but his few lines are hard to take. "Book and me don't agree, Gracie," he write. "My brain and my hand have the best connection a man can want but the book learning confuse me bad." Grace know that industrial arts require some studying. She say a prayer for Stewie.

Edgar's first letter for the New Year give her a terrible pain in her belly-bottom. Edris nearly die from a botch-up abortion. They disfellowship her at her grandaunt's church, whereupon that lady pack her off to a cousin in Queenstown. Then news come to say that Edris run away, nobody know where. When Grace first reach Toronto, she make sure to send Edris a postcard, then a letter, then another postcard, but she hear not a word back. Grace answer Edgar quick sticks, begging for information about Edris — reliable, hearsay, anything.

At least Conrad's letters are still cheerful. He write about poems they are learning the tunes for at school: "Blow, blow, thou winter wind" and "The north wind doth blow/and we shall have snow/and what shall poor Robin do then?" He is all of eleven, but it's still his small-boy voice that she hear asking: "You see poor Robin yet, Gracie?"

Near the end of January there is a tease of warmth, a titillating melt, and plenty slush and dirty water. Grace don't let her defenses down, though. She gird up for February and March, for they warn her not to be hoodwinked by this vamping. And she faithfully patronize the letterbox. Edgar's missives keep arriving once a week, long as ever, well into the New Year. She can tell something is up with this brother who love language, though. He was always into a book while Stewie and his friends were fooling with a ball. Now his words drop, clunk-clunk, heavy, like he perpetually losing his footing as he struggle up out of a deep, dark hole. In March he write to say he going to town to stay with Miss Carmen and try to get a job at *Kris-eye*, a rag surviving on girlie pics and gossip, for he anxious to get a foot, any foot, in the journalism door.

The letters from home are not merely food but also the company of those closest to her all her life long. But where are Gramps offerings? Nowadays he not writing so often. She miss his advice, a staple ever since she know herself.

As for Lindsay, he don't phone since Christmas, and she know she not seeing him before summer. She keep close watch for his letters, short, but always with extras, a clipping from *The Clarion*, a report from a Canadian paper about some Caribbean personality, and sometimes a poem by Edgar who he hear from occasionally. It strike Grace as funny, this other, roundabout connection, via Lindsay, to her brother and her island. She is proud of Edgar for keeping in touch with Lindsay, maintaining a contact abroad in the journalism field.

One of Edgar's poems is titled "Anancy Me." She paste it on her wall.

Anancy Me

Once Brer Anancy was divine.
In the great kingdom of Akan Ashanti
Spider Man was the Creator God.
Unwitting he crossed the wide divide
the long Atlantic water stowed away
in some dark swaying limbo
harnessed and bought like all of us
and brought across to raise sweet cane.

Now tricky webber he spins story
threads playing the fool — wise fool —
his former Majesty crawling about
on eight fine legs the only bug with eight
no decent kind of ant or bee
but Some Thing Else — arachnid,
two legs more and one less body part.
Distorted. Strange. Like me.

She don't entirely get it, but Steph will help her figure it out, or maybe Lindsay, for he write to say he will be in Toronto during the last week in May and the first two in June. Lindsay is bright, down to earth, funny. It don't seem to matter that his father is a lawyer and his mother a teacher. She like him, but she try not to look forward too much to his arrival all the same.

So she and Steph press on, through March and April, Grace abusing the weather, Steph thumping the books. For Grace, the books are plenty work, but not a major challenge. She keep at them, reading and reading, doing assignments and extras, remembering Pa who was briefly a fisherman when times was so bad he couldn't get a job: "Check the currents; study the stars; set course. Then steady as she goes." Her roomie always wavering, can't hold to a straight path.

On the first of June, Grace write home.

Annesley Hall,
95 Queen's Park Crescent,
Toronto, Ontario,
Canada, M5S 2C7
1 June 1976

Dear Gramps and Ma and Pa,
I promise a better letter soon, but I am writing on this
last Sunday of the semester to give an accounting to
you and all the Wentley folks. I've not only passed

*all my courses, I've done as well as I could have in
all of them. The fact that I survived the weather and
the strangeness of the place and still managed to do
my lessons properly is as much a credit to you and
my few friends here as it is to me. So this comes to
say big thanks for all the support, encouragement,
and prayers. I count myself very lucky.*

God bless.
Grace

Summer. Poor Grace, looking forward to a movie, a trip
to the Toronto Islands, a walk on Queens Quay with Lindsay.
When he come, it is for three days during which they talk, briefly,
on the phone. He is full of news and excitement. On the last
day of the semester he hear he is selected to go on an exchange
to the School of Journalism at the University of Queensland in
Australia, an attachment that is to begin in the summer term.
He is therefore rushing to arrange paperwork, store his stuff, be
in touch with powers-that-be in Ottawa and Brisbane, and make
six months' worth of arrangements in two weeks.

Grace can't understand his eagerness to go. Everybody know
Australians don't like black people. They treat their aboriginal
people bad, so they not likely to be won over by his dusky charm,
though, she assure him, he have, and to spare. He just keep
chattering on about "U of Q's top-class journalism program,"
about how it's the opportunity of a lifetime, and how lucky he is
to be selected. So she undertake to keep him au fait with things
in Toronto's up above, in return for news of down under. But she
crank down the level of her investment in Lindsay Bell. She can
always put more money in, if the prospects improve.

Steph, who is in the city taking a couple summer courses,
is concerned that the whole summer long, all Grace is doing
is working in the library and studying, so come the beginning

of August, she propose that they go to some Caribana events, or at least go to watch the festival parade. For sure it must be a good place to meet some other Caribbean people, maybe even a couple interesting guys. Grace don't know anything much about Caribana, although she hear people talking about it. When she do some research in the library, she confess to some alarm. The costumes are not like anything she ever see before. Ma would say the women's outfits are brazen. Pa would say vulgar. Grace can't say she approve of them. Plus dangerous things seem to happen. People fight and get hurt, even killed. And some students at U of T still agree with the opinion of the Black Students Union that boycott the festival in 1971. According to them, is time black people learn that they must struggle, not dance, if they going to survive. Grace know about the struggling part, for sure. She tell Steph, maybe next year.

Then just so, early one afternoon near the end of November in the looming harsh at the start of her second winter, Grace discover someone to consume all her attention. She meet him when she is in Toronto General Hospital to visit Steph, who, having suffered a serious concussion, fractured three ribs, and broken one hand and one foot while skiing on a gentle slope near Kitchener, has just come out of the operating theatre and, as Grace discover upon attempting to do so, may not yet be visited. Cold air stream through Grace's teeth in a long steups when she first hear of Steph's misadventure. Not supposed to happen! Steph is a excellent skier.

Back downstairs in the lobby for a cup of tea, she find herself beside a nurse chatting to a child in a wheelchair. The child not making no answer. Two large eyes sunk in a high forehead, carved cheekbones, flared nose, and full mouth. It's a intelligent face, but the eyes seem far away, unfocused, as if the child is hypnotized. His arms and legs are skin on bone. His belly is distended; his hair is red, thin, and brittle. His skin is red. On his battered sweater is a tag saying, "Colin Jones." He is holding a thick-skinned silver balloon of a sort Grace hate. He hold it tight, but he not looking at it.

They are all close to the rotating door, so he is likely on his way to Sick Kids Hospital across the road. She know what is wrong with this child. She know that never mind he look like he is eight, more likely he is ten, maybe older. She know it is kwashiorkor that draw down his body, suck the muscles, stiffen and red up the hair, and thin it out: kwashiorkor, a Ghanaian word for malnutrition. The child is starving.

Grace feel guilty, but when she go back up, she is glad when the nurse in post-op say she can't yet see Steph, who is still under the effect of the anaesthetic. She decide to go back downstairs and if necessary cross the street to The Hospital for Sick Children to find Colin Jones. In the lobby of Toronto General she check for him near the door, but she see no sign of him. She cross to Sick Kids and ask at the information desk. They are helpful and direct her to the floor where he is, at least for the time being.

When she get to the floor and approach the nurses' station, she don't see anybody, but she spot the child with no trouble, sake of silver balloon. She setting off for his bed, but something make her glance back, and she see a nurse at the station, a dark-haired, young woman who look, maybe Asian, maybe Spanish. Probably Filipina, Grace decide. She go back to the nurses' station and ask the nurse about Colin's condition and if she can visit him. The nurse smile and say, "Of course." Grace never expect the ready agreement, but by the time she reach Colin's bed, she figure out that since she and Colin are both black — or, more correctly, red — the nurse take her for family.

Halting at the balloon stoplight, she say, "Hi, Colin."

His eyes move, but he don't answer her. She come closer to the side of the bed, avoiding the pole on which an IV bag is suspended, and she repeat her greeting. He take a long time, but eventually he focus his big eyes, and she see the slightest smile, so she sit down on the straight-back chair, side of his bed. She think she best talk about herself like she relating a story. She tell him her name, where she live, where she come from, what she studying. She describe Wentley Park and Pansy, Stewie, Edgar, Colin, Sammy, Princess, Gramps, Ma, and Pa. Now and then, she pause, leaving a space for him. But he is silent.

After a few minutes, she feel eyes on her again, like a crawly insect on her neck-back. She glance at the staff station and see the Filipina nurse talking to another, older woman, stout, grey-hair, a pair of glasses at the end of a string riding on a bosom like the prow of a old-time sailing ship.

"Excuse me." The older nurse is beside her, pleasant but not smiling.

"Yes?"

"I wondered whether you were related to Colin. I don't mean to be rude, but he has no family we know of."

"I'm not family," Grace say. "I asked for him by name, but I'd just noticed his tag when he was waiting over at Toronto General. I was visiting someone there."

"In that case, it's good of you to spend time with him." The nurse turn up her mouth-corners and incline her head politely, then pad away to rejoin the younger one.

Grace decide to read to Colin from one of the books on his bedside table. She read a short Winnie-the-Pooh story, which he seem to enjoy, so she read a longer tale, "The Whale and the Pilot Fish," from the *Just So Stories*. When dark descend and streetlights come on, she realize Colin is fast asleep. She put down the book, take up her backpack, walk up to the nurse's station, and ask about visiting hours.

"For Colin?" The older nurse inquire. "At any time. Normally it would be at regular times, but having someone would be good for him. He's not in immediate danger, but he's pretty sick. Not," she add hastily, "with anything infectious. He just hasn't eaten good food for a long time."

"I know." Grace is dry. "He's starving. It's called kwashiorkor."

Unmoved by her acerbity, the nurse continue. "He was glad you were there. He's often almost comatose, but sometimes he's quite aware."

Grace nod. "Can I ask how he came to be here?" She have no idea why she asking, nor why she just spend two hours by the child's bedside.

"We found him downstairs. He had a scrap of paper pinned on with his name. Neither Children's Services nor the police have located any family, but it's early days."

"So it will be alright if I come back?"

"It would be good if you did."

Grace look back at Colin. She can feel the prick of the needle at the end of the IV catheter in his thin forearm. She figure the drip is most likely to rehydrate him. He is sleeping soundly, so she say good night to the nurses, and head for the lift.

Back at the dorm, she is overjoyed to find a letter from Pa that seem to take a unusually long time to reach.

8 November 1977

Dear Gracie,

I hope you are keeping well, for I know it is getting cold where you are. Please make sure you stay warm. Ma say Mrs. Sampson was telling her about some stores where you can buy secondhand clothes. She say that Salvation Army run some, and there are some named Goodwill. That is a nice name. She say you can get good clothes cheap, things like sweaters, coats, hats and scarfs. Also they sell bags and suitcases, glasses and mugs and cutlery, if you should need any of those, as well as books to read for entertainment and plenty other things. You should try to find one of those stores. Money saved is money earned as Gramps always say.

*Here we are going along. There was some
ruction in Queenstown with the Chris People's
Party Union last week, and police intervene and
shoot one person. Lucky it was not fatal. Their
people come down to Wentley Park a while back,
but since the Island People's Union was also down
here not long ago, they have to take a poll. I don't
trust them, neither one nor the other. Not to say
that a union wouldn't be a good thing, but we need
one that will fight for a better deal for us, not any
thiefing Anancy organization.*

*This is a early Christmas letter for we want to
make certain it arrive in good time. Enclosed is a
card where all of us have a word for you. Your Ma
made a Christmas pudding, and Mrs. Sampson
promise that a friend of hers who is going up to
New York for Christmas will mail it to you from
there. We hope it will bring you some cheer. Please
write or phone Ma at Mrs. Salmon and let us know
the number where you are going to be over the
Christmas season. We will phone from Mr. Wong.
All of us send lots of love and plenty blessings.*

Your Pa

The following day, after she visit with Steph, who is being
her rowdy self, talking about cross country skiing, never mind
she wrap up in casts, Grace go up to Colin's ward with three
proper balloons, red, yellow, and green, that she purchase from a
Rasta fellow standing outside the hospital. She hurry in, pleased
with her purchases, sure that Colin going to be brighter-eyed,
more responsive. When she find his bed, closer now to the
nurses' station, he is dead to the world, his ruddy body curled
up like a play-dead caterpillar. Today there is another bag on

the IV pole. Grace figure maybe they are feeding him or giving him extra nutrients.

She tie the balloons to the bed-head, disappointed that he not awake to see them. The silver balloon is still there, but she note with satisfaction that it is creased all over, air steadily seeping out. She sit down. If and when Colin wake up, she going do same as yesterday: talk, read, and sometimes just be quiet. After about fifteen minutes, he stir, open his eyes, and when she say hello, he smile as if he know her.

"So how you do today?"

No answer.

"Tired?" The slightest nod.

"Want me to read?" Another nod, distinct this time. So, never mind she read it yesterday, she read "The Whale and the Pilot Fish," her favourite, again. As she come near the end, she hear him say softly, at exactly the right place, "By means of a grating, I've cut off your ating." She look up from the book. Except for a slight tremor, the sort of swift quiver babies and puppies make in their sleep, he is lost to the world.

———

When she is home and in bed, Grace rootle around under the blanket till she find a good spot and then read a letter from Gramps that she been saving all day.

22 November 1977

Dear Gracie,
This is a surprise letter, for I know your Pa sent you our card and greetings a while ago. I've just come back from choir practice for the Christmas service. They persuaded me to come on board, for the older men are few these days and the young men are lost to our ranks. They flock either to the evangelical churches or the rum bars. I daresay they could

do worse! I enjoy it, never mind my voice wavers often, and it prompted me to wonder if you have found some folks to sing with. It is a satisfying way to bond with people, to be in company with them without having to be their friends, unless of course you wish to be. "Birds of a feather don't need to flock together" your great-grandfather, the Moses after whom your Pa is named, used to say. In this case they are songbirds, so they need only gather to make music, which is reward enough.

Though it is not your first Christmas in "foreign," I am very concerned about you at this time when it is hard to be away from family. I want you to know it is not only on your side. Christmas is different because you are not here, not just sake of the touch you give to the sorrel and the pudding that you make so well, but because your wit and good cheer and your thoughtful reading of the Word are absent.

You know I have been a faithful believer all my life, not necessarily in the ways that the parsons specify, but rather according as I discerned from the Word and figured out from my own fusses with the Lord. I started the struggle with God when as a young man, I found myself fighting a war with men who would spit on me when we all went on home leave, but who counted on me, as I had to count on them, when we were lying stinking in trenches, deaf from the noise of artillery, wrapped about one another so close that it came to the point where you could identify your fellow soldiers by the smell of their farts. We have wrestled, God and I, since that long ago time. There are a great many things I still rail at him for, but over the years it's probably the fight itself that has convinced me He is there.

I need to remind you that you will likely feel the need to quarrel with Him now, in your circumstances. Go ahead and quarrel. That is what fathers are for, and the better the father, the freer you can be about your true feelings. The cold and gray of winter are not good for the spirit, and when they are married to the unpleasantness of people, the absence of family, and of the warmth and beauty of this place, the birthday of Jesus might seem like a bad joke. So complain, but at the same time, do your part so Satan won't have the satisfaction of thiefing the Baby's birthday! One way to make sure that he doesn't do that is to find those less fortunate and help them to have a good Christmas. No matter how small your contribution, those who receive it will be cheered and you will gain many times what you give.

Sorry for the preachment, but old folks get that way as they prepare to meet their Maker. We all send much love and pray Christmas blessings on you.

Gramps

Gramps would be pleased to know about Colin. Not that she set out to do any act of charity, for she count herself more than comforted by the child. She will write Gramps about it in her Christmas letter, also Lindsay, who finally send a koala bear postcard saying he is settled in.

So while Steph looking forward to her release from restraints and busy with plans to drive home to Warsaw, Grace visiting Colin every day, squeezing time from her studies, reading to him, taking him little gifts. He is not better. There are more tubes stuck in him now, and once, for a few days, she never see him at all for he was in the ICU, and since she not family, they wouldn't let her in. Now she is praying hard, so frantic that she is making a novena, with Steph's guidance. So much for Edris's fundamentalist aunt! She don't know why she feel this burden to make him well, or at any rate do what she can to help him.

"We'd love you to spend Christmas with us," Steph is asking Grace to Warsaw for her second Christmas in the cold. "Don't know why you insist on being here alone when the world is sitting round the fire, partying with family and friends."

"Steph, I tell you already, till last year at your house, having never been a girl guide, a cowboy, or a cannibal, I never yet spend time sitting round a fire."

"Very funny! Okay. I can't see why you'd rather stay alone here than be somewhere with people, having some fun."

"It's generous of you to ask me, but I can't. I have plenty studying to do."

"Blah, blah, blah. I know perfectly well why you're not coming. You're staying to visit Colin."

"I'm not staying to visit him. Not saying I won't, but I have plenty to keep me busy here."

"You is a big woman, my dear." Steph is learning Chrissie Creole. "Suit yourself. But if you decide you rather sit by the fireplace and watch drifting snow, just jump on the bus to Peterborough, and call me when you reach."

Two days before Christmas, a jolly Grace in a Santa cap arrive to visit Colin with a bundle of storybooks from the library and a bunch of red balloons with reindeer on them. She find a empty bed. The buxom old nurse tell her Colin died early that morning. She don't reply to the nurse's news, just stand for a minute, then say, "Thanks for letting me know. Bye now. Happy Christmas!"

She take the elevator down, release the balloons as she step into the cold, pass by the library, slip the books into the return slot, walk over to the dorm, throw some stuff in a bag, and head for the subway.

She have to steady her voice to talk to Steph, when she call her from the bus station in Toronto. What with Colin's dying, never mind the novena, the visits, the muttered prayers, it is clear that the Almighty Father is again toying with her. No way is she busing it to Peterborough only to find that plans in the Scott household have changed and they are gone to Tenerife to spend the holiday season in the sun!

"Hi Steph? It's me, Grace. If it's okay, I'm coming down today — in fact, now, on the twelve-thirty bus. Can you please pick me up?"

Snow-white sheets obliterating every contour leave her wrapped up in her thoughts. What was it with her and this child? In truth he and she resemble, and in truth she long to have kin that favour her, so maybe it was that? Is not because she want a child, but maybe she was thinking it was time to have a man in her life, and as every woman know, the two things is one.

But none of that is important. Colin was here, didn't have enough to eat, and died. She not sure what else she could have done, but it hadn't been enough.

16

Grace Joins a Battle

Grace never figure out what make her write to the white people's newspaper! Maybe it was Gramps advice to say her say. Maybe she never close the door on Colin tight enough. Maybe she was just blind vex. No matter what, it come like a bad joke that she get herself tied up in affairs right up Lindsay's street when he was way to the devil on the other side of the world. Lucky she have Steph, or not a doubt that Ma and Pa would be flying to Toronto to rescue her from the psych ward.

> *2 January 1978*
>
> *The Editor,*
> *The Globe and Mail*
> *Dear Sir,*
> *I write concerning an event that took place two days before Christmas: a ten-year-old boy died of kwashiorkor in Toronto General Hospital. Kwashiokor is a starvation disease. I am appalled that in a country so wealthy, a city so fine, a*

state-run health system that is celebrated as one
of the best in the world, anyone, let alone a child,
should die for lack of food. Or did he die because
he was black? It would be interesting to see the
statistics on malnutrition in this city and province,
broken down by race.

Yours sincerely,
Grace Carpenter

Next day the newspaper publish a response from a man name Mr. A. King — ha-ha! "Is this the voice of an ungrateful immigrant bleating about healthcare in a country with the best system for delivering it in the world?" Whereupon he proceed to complain about "delinquent immigrant parents" and say is on account of them that the child die.

4 January 1978

The Editor,
The Globe and Mail
Dear Sir,
Your reader, Mr. A. King, is mistaken in thinking I
am an immigrant. I am a student at the University
of Toronto, and I have every intention of returning
to my country once I have completed my studies.

I was raised to live up to my responsibilities
in any community of which I find myself a part,
however briefly. At this moment, Toronto is
that community. What I find enlightening, and
frightening, is that there is not a word addressing
the issue I raised — one of social welfare — in Mr.
King's response. The community of which I speak
is after all, his. I will leave it in due course, while
he perforce will stay.

I would have expected him to be more concerned.

Yours sincerely,
Grace Carpenter

Mr. King come back with the advice that she "shouldn't worry her head about the health and welfare of this community," since it was "fine before she came and would remain so after she had gone." He also remind her that Canada was in the First and not the Third World. At that point, she elect to let the matter drop, for the back-and-forth not achieving anything.

Wishful thinking! Polite disagreement blossom into a big kas-kas. The fuss in the *Globe and Mail* hop nimbly over to a magazine called *City Weekly*, and another called *Current*, where a writer name Mary Hellman take it up in her column. People now writing letters and columnists taking sides, but by this time, Grace staying out of it. The flare-up in *Current* was early in February, and she despair when the sparks from that fire ignite the student papers in March.

At that point, the Foreign Students Association get in on the act. Unhappy with the lightly veiled racism underlying some of the commentary, they arrange a discussion on April 7. Grace never want to have anything to do with it, for she have plenty work, but they press her, and she finally agree to participate. Flyers trumpet that the forum will encourage a "frank and free exchange."

So at seven o'clock in the lounge at Hardy House, Grace, Malcolm Hinds, presenter of "This City Now," a program on the campus radio station, CIUT, and Mary Hellman from *Current* are scheduled to be on a panel. After that, there will be comments and questions from the floor. Grace share her misgivings with the chairman, a Nigerian medical student named Kwame Edo. She tell him she not up-to-date on the relevant figures concerning incidence of death among youth in the city, whether by sickness or otherwise, and other statistics and information relevant to the discussion. Also, she suspect that her mouth going lock up with fright, plus she not able to compromise her scholarship. He assure her it will go well.

Grace present herself in the student lounge at 6:45 p.m. to find that Steph is already there, gently flirting with Kwame and a next man, still in his winter coat, who must be Malcolm Hinds. She see one, two other people in the room, but the attendance is sparse. Kwame wave her over, looking at his watch as she walking across.

"We've made a big blunder, and also hit some bad luck," Kwame get right to it. "We've just been discussing what to do about it."

"What kind of blunder?" Grace ask.

"As you see, there aren't many of us gathered here."

"I can see that. Yes."

"Also, we've had a phone call from the columnist at the *Current*," Kwame is irritated, "to say she'll be late. We're wondering if we should reschedule."

"Okay. That's the 'also.' What about the big blunder?"

"Tonight's the very first Toronto Blue Jays game. Ever." He shrug. "We forgot. I don't think anyone else is going to show up. Plenty people are either at the game or watching it on TV. Several of the Trotskyites were here earlier, but when a fellow came in to report that police were working over some students in front of Robarts, and they heard that there was violence, they scooted off."

"There's something else." Malcolm Hinds, flecks of snow still decorating hair and coat, sniffle into a handkerchief. "Some senior ladies who run the William Wordsworth Society have been promoting a free event, with Donald Sutherland reading Wordsworth's poetry, for today. It's on at Hart House, donuts and coffee afterwards."

"Donald Sutherland? How could they manage that?" Kwame ask.

"U of T graduate. It's his birthday. He's two hundred and eight," contributed by Steph, helpful, smiling at Kwame.

"Sutherland?" Kwame, incredulous.

Steph gurgle, "No, silly. Wordsworth!"

Hinds, restless, ready to leave, snort into the hanky again. "I'm going there after this. There's a rumour one of the ladies had an affair with Sutherland. She was here as a mature student. I'm interviewing her."

He shake Kwame's hand, nod goodbye to the others.

"I'll be in touch about a reschedule. Thanks, man."

"No trouble. You have my number."

The Toronto Blue Jays won, the city was euphoric, the old ladies produced a fine actor named Donald Sutherland, but not the movie star. Grace wrote Lindsay about the whole affair. He never answered. The event was never rescheduled.

In the end, good come from bad, as Pa maintain. When she add Colin's death to a discussion about hungry-belly children preempted by a ball game and multiply the sum by the controversy her letters cause, the result equal a revision of what she intend to study. It was like, by means of the letters, she reach out to touch a set of circumstances larger than herself, a web of contemptible attitudes and behaviours that recall Manny, Aloysius, and the kowtowing dance in Toronto General on the day she find out migraines been tormenting her since she was a child. She going ally herself with her Christophian countrymen at the hospital, join the struggle, and "do her do" as best she can.

———

At the end of August, Lindsay come back, looking tall and suave. She could see he was dressing instead of just putting clothes on, and he have the tiniest bit of a Australian accent. He greet her as if he write her a letter every day, proclaim how rigorous the program was, how he scurry around with assignments all year long, how every letter from her make him glad.

He say he staying in Toronto till fall and he hope to see lots of her. He is very charming, and so Grace forgive him. Once he come, Steph tease her, say she look gorgeous and glowing. True, whether sake of Lindsay, summer, or both, she feel good: no migraines, no sick stomach, no splotchy vision. But she always feel better once it get warm, even when the temperature rise a little in winter. Anytime that happen, she is bouncy, cruising smooth. Studying is easy — she understand with no effort. Lindsay persuade her to go with him to watch the Caribana festival parade. She enjoy the music, but not the dancing and the daring costumes. Lindsay tease her and tell her she is a prude.

Many a time afterwards, as she contemplate the mad course she plot that summer, she wonder if the up-and-down cycle of good-then-bad feeling is because she is really crazy. After all, madness run in the blood, and she, poor she, don't know whose blood is in her! The crazy course she set concern a lovey-dovey affair.

Lovey-dovey is all around, hand holding, bum squeezing, deep-throat kissing in the library stacks, on the street corner, at every kind of event. Pa had a way to hum a calypso tune, "Love, Love Alone," about how the ex-King of England love Miss Simpson so much he give up his throne for her.

She don't know about that kind of love, don't have no example of it in her life. Pa love Ma for sure, but nothing like that. And Pansy was just force ripe and ready for big-woman business. Grace know about sex, of course, like every country pikni. Sudden as a midday rainstorm, she is back on the mattress in Wentley, listening to the susuing nightly news, as delivered by Pansy, Stewie, and Edgar, after Ma fall asleep, all ears upright, alarmed by the multitudinous dangers awaiting those who risk the highways and byways of illicit sexual activity.

Ma tell her before she leave that never mind she is a big brains, she is a woman too, so she better be thoughtful about any attachment she form and she better make sure not to rush into anything. "Don't make any sweet-mouth man coax you to open your legs before you good and ready!" Lindsay arrive back in Toronto when she make up her mind she is ready — for what, she never really know. She know the mechanics, of course, and courtesy of Beastly Buxton, a swell-up penis come near enough to her parts. But as she make her plan that July, the memory of what she flee from at Miss Carmen's should have prompt her to consider "good" as well as "ready."

True, she like Lindsay; he like her; they are easy with each other. He is sort of shy; she like that about him. And true, he probably need encouraging, but she confident she can do that. And she is not any immature adolescent, seducing him like Pansy seduce Mortimer. She is a big woman, old enough to do what everybody else is doing, Lindsay no doubt included. But also true that Lindsay never send her any romantic signals, and equally true she never really have any romantic feelings about him.

It turn out worse than her wildest imagining. She never throw herself at him for it never get that far. All the same, she end up feeling trashy. And poor Lindsay! Embarrassed to confess he never like her "in that way." She couldn't stop bawling, she feel so shame. She vex with Steph for going home for the weekend. She vex with Lindsay for coming to Toronto. She vex with everything and everybody. She so mash up that next day, Sunday, she find her way to Beloved, first time in months. She jump and clap in the service like a jack-in-the-box, glad when they fuss round her, vowing regular attendance after that.

One week later she get a letter from Lindsay to say that in truth he love a Carpenter, but not she — her brother, Edgar, the sad poet. It never take her long to get into the ring with her favorite boxing partner. *Buff!* Why, if he is God Almighty, he never whisper caution into her ear? *Buff!* Why he so bad mind when she never do him anything? *Buff!* How come he hate her so, hate her since she was little? *Buff!* Why he don't want her to fit anywhere? Not into the Carpenter family, not properly. Certainly not into the snooty high school in Queenstown. Not in this cold, foreign place where they count her as a alien. *Buff! Buff! Buff!* Not even in a normal man-woman relationship!

Buff! She throw blows so fast, the Deity don't get a chance to land a return punch.

Then she remember Edgar and Lindsay. Lindsay insist they are a couple, from as long ago as when he was in St. Chris. Couple or not, her brother is in big trouble. Sodomy is illegal in St. Chris. Homosexuals have to hide, all except the rich and powerful. But she can't think of anything to do to help. Edgar have to tell the others, if he choose. Then, if he smart, he will escape, maybe here to Toronto, where they mostly live and let live in those matters.

She take more tablets than she should, go to bed, and stay there for three days, pillow on her head, drinking warm Coke, eating plain crackers, cursing a God who keep picking on her and who now take set on her poor brother. A pebbly voice remind her she is going to a fine university, free of charge; she have forebears and siblings that love her; a down-to-earth roommate she get along with; a church community that always glad to see her; and the very best marks.

So what?

MARK

17

The Chancellor Considers

The chancellor's suite at the University of the Antilles is a stunning combination of state-of-the-art and down-home. It boasts TV viewing on a gigantic screen, music on a Bose system, a kitchen to make a gourmet chef's mouth water. At the same time, the rooms celebrate the island, from bamboo floors through furniture of blue mahoe to intuitive paintings by Pamungo and Ngosao. If the North thinks it knows posh, St. Chris is where it must come to be set straight.

Eyes closed, Mark is relaxing in a leather recliner, a surprise gift from Mona. It had been waiting there when the principal showed him the suite on his first visit as chancellor.

Celia sticks her head in just as Mark settles back in the large leather chair.

"Can I make you a cuppa to start the day, sir?"

"No, Celia. I'm fine, thanks."

"I'm off, then. I've still a few things to do." She turns to go and then swings round to ask, "Have you spoken with Dr. Carpenter?"

"Actually, no, not yet. Why do you ask?"

"I just wondered." She smiles again and he thinks he detects something. For a split second he has a vision of the St. Chris trash weekly, *Kris-eye,* with front page headlines that shriek, "Honoured Guest Back to Rub Chancellor's Belly?"

Mind made up to set the outlandish imaginings aside, he goes into the kitchen, turns on the kettle, and finds that he's still wondering about the look on Celia's face. He's being paranoid. It's been years, and besides, they were discreet. Except of course for the farewell at Logan Airport, for which he now curses Grace. But it's absurd. Nobody who knew them had been anywhere nearby.

Now Celia is gone, he does want a cup of tea. Feeling lazy, he sprinkles tea leaves straight into a china teapot — Mona insists tea only tastes right in china. He pours the tea when it's brewed, sips, sets the cup aside, tips the recliner back, and closes his eyes. Time to work out what the chaps are up to, what the agendas are.

He wishes he knew more about the brain, about the relationship between intellect, intuition, and imagination. He'd been surprised at his invitation to the seminar, a three-day meeting in Cambridge sponsored by World Resources Institute, for his research and writing had been confined to what was needed in his job and therefore had constituted mostly reports for the bank in the previous few years. Six working groups, and yet somehow Grace and he had ended up on the same one. They slogged on, three women and one man, late into the last night, and then Agnes, a South African, and Fatima, from Delhi, begged off. Though both were staying in the hotel, they had spouses put up in nearby bed-and-breakfasts whom they were anxious to join. There'd been nothing for Grace and him to do, as the unencumbered ones, but volunteer to tidy up the report for the plenary next day.

They fell asleep on the divan in Fatima's room where they'd all been working. At just after three they woke together, roused by a noisy heating vent, for though the days were unseasonably warm, the nights got pretty cool. A hiccup at the start, then it ran smooth and sweet as molasses.

"There's just one thing, Mark. I take it you're not married? Because if you are, we can't do this."

"I am married, Grace, but we haven't lived together as man and wife for almost three years." It was true, word for word. Mona and he hadn't made love for about that long. He and Grace ended up having great sex for the next couple of hours, after which they'd napped. He'd stirred first, content, and so cursed, as Mona said often, to be reflective.

"There are two people inside of you," he declared, rolling over to face her.

"Two people in me?" Grace raised an eyebrow. "No way. One's plenty."

"Not just you, or me. Two people in all of us," he insisted.

"Sorry. I'm not following you. It must be the recent, exhausting activity."

"One must examine one's life," he persisted, "to gain perspective."

"Some folks have a cigarette after sex. Some have a shower. Some have sex again. You philosophize?"

"That's because I always wanted to be a teacher." He'd wanted to be other things too, but that one popped out, so he didn't take it back.

"Okay. Shoot. If you can." She smiled at his penis.

"There's the ideal person, the one you'd like to be, and the real person, the one you are."

"That's the actual person. According to Steph."

"Who is Steph?"

"My roommate at U of T, who saved me in foreign. She did English."

"Okay. Two people, one ideal, one actual."

"So who bedded me?"

"Since it was indubitably idyllic, I would have to say my ideal self."

"Cor-*nee!* I've been had by a vintage, sweet-mouth, St. Chris saga boy."

"That's heartless!"

"As for me, I'm happy to say that was the actual me. See?" She leaned over and licked his ears, nipples, navel. They'd gone at it again till the bells rang six.

"I've never done this before," she'd announced as they picked through the clothes on the floor. It stopped him. She was no virgin.

"Are you on the pill?"

"Why would I be?"

"Suppose you have a baby, Grace?"

"Suppose you do?"

The last day went superbly: good reports, the concluding statement not too ambitious, the final reception affording thanks, toasts, no speeches. They'd spent the last couple of hours old-talking by the river before going to the airport. She was going to London, then Geneva, and then some place in Africa.

He couldn't believe his luck: a halfway decent meeting; unexpected and excellent sex; a clean leave-taking, the woman off to be occupied with her life.

"If I get pregnant," she said over her shoulder as she got in line at the gate, "I'll name the baby for Ma or Pa. Just tell me if you want to know."

A couple nearby looked up. He flushed, black as he was. She saw his discomfort, smiled, and went through the gate.

JIMMY

18

Ordination

On Thursday, 15 September 1988, the feast day of Notre Dame des Douleurs, patron saint of Mabuli, Bishop Ndule of the diocese of Benke will ordain Michael Nathan Nabene, Simeon Peter Lubonli, and James Nathaniel Atule.

Crowds of tourists, believing and unbelieving, flood Benke for the national feast day. They come mostly to gape at the great church and to be part of the Procession of Renewal of La Cathédrale de Notre-Dame-des-Douleurs, as Mapome, when she was alive, always called it. When the church was built in 1806, the Mbula, a clan related to the Fulani who live in the North, near the desert, created the decoration for the cathedral in a style similar to that of the Gourounsi. Mbula artists had renewed it every year since.

The ritual preparations for this annual maintenance process involve treks to forest and kouris to find a special tree bark and a fine, loess-type dirt, which yield dyes that contribute two colours to the decorations: a deep indigo and a brilliant cerulean blue. Both, it is said, are not to be seen anywhere else on earth. There are costumes, music, dancing. At first, anyone could join the search and festivities. Now it costs ten US dollars or the equivalent in buleles.

If visitors wonder at the choice of the Sorrowful Mother of God as the country's patron saint, it has never been a difficulty for Mabulians, who agree that the story of the Dame Bleue des Douleurs, one of three great fables from the Mabuli Chronicles, foreshadowed her selection.

Mapome began telling Jimmy the story of the Blue Lady of Dolours before he could talk. When he was old enough, they had acted it out together: she played the grandmother and he played the children's parts.

"Heheme!"

"Haheme!"

"Long ago, in a terrible hot time, a grandma was leading some sick and thirsty children up a dry kouri, through wasted country, past skeletons of dead animals, in search of food and water. Tired and despairing, she huddled with the children under a dolmen used by sheep and goats, for the sun was fierce."

"What's a dolmen?"

"A kind of stone table, Jimmy, a house meant for those who have left us."

"You mean a grave on the top of the ground?"

"Yes, you could say that. May I go on?"

He nodded.

"The infants were hungry. Their mouths were dry and their clothes ragged and dirty. They missed their parents, so they cried and wouldn't stop though their big sisters kept blowing in their faces."

"Why did their sisters do that?"

"So the little ones would stop crying."

"You used to do it to me?"

Mapome nodded.

"Did I stop?"

"Sometimes. Sometimes you cried louder."

He said no more, and she continued the story.

"The babies scratched at rashes and blisters that had grown on their arms and legs and chests in the heat, and they howled till their bodies went limp."

At this point, Jimmy threw his heart into the howling.

"Suddenly, it was quiet."

"Heheme!"

"Haheme!"

"It is well, my grandson, that you are listening, for this is the marvelous part." She rolled her eyes heavenward to stress the wonder of it and resumed. "Weeping softly, a woman in a blue kiloli appeared from nowhere. She slipped the children's hands, one into another, and began leading them."

Jimmy and Mapome's journey began right then. It looped through the mango orchard in his grandparents' front yard, round through beds of tomatoes, yam-hills, and clumps of eddoes beside the house, and down to the slope behind.

"The grandmother watched as the tearful woman led the children into the tinder of afternoon. The children wept quietly, like the Blue Lady. Tears washed down their faces, arms and legs, slowly merging to form a stream at their feet."

Jimmy was good at howling, but better at quiet weeping. His features crumpled into a tragic, sniffing, lip-quivering assemblage that broke Mapome's heart every time, but she never interrupted the tale.

"After a while, the Weeping One directed the children's bare feet onto the damp earth. Soon they were stepping strong beside a steady trickle. They bent, cupping their hands to sip the clear water. Near the bank were reeds and plants, white lotus lilies and blue water hyacinths. Small fish swam among the waving stalks. And then like magic, they were splashing in a river, looking for njamra among the rocks, bringing them to the grandmother to cook on a bramble fire."

Mapome sank to the ground beside a shallow creek that ran for much of the year. By now Jimmy had discarded his mask of misery. Gleeful, he raced up and down gathering leaves and dry grass for the make-believe fire.

"At the end of the day, they looked for the Blue Lady but she was nowhere to be found. That night, they slept under new gallery forest, bellies full of fat shrimp. Twigs clicked softly, and leaves twitched as trees rose beside the river. Tree frogs squeaked in the branches, cicadas cried, and bullfrogs grunted. Night birds trilled. The ripening moon, rimmed with haze, shed a blue light."

Curled up on the grass, he and Mapome often fell asleep.

———

On the last Sunday before his ordination — now every day is some kind of "last" day — Jimmy wakes, looks through his window into a sky blue as the sapphire in Nila's engagement ring, and feels his chest squeeze in on itself. What the hell does he think he is doing? What is he doing? He is young, not bad-looking, loves women, and thrives on sex. And he is becoming a priest?

He pulls himself together, goes through his misgivings again, and again dismisses them as being of little consequence.

"There is something of very large consequence. You're just not facing it."

He knows what the voice — his conscience, isn't it? — is referring to. Compared to that thing "of very large consequence," an occasionally energetic prick and lusts he can kill with a lime were small sappi. What if he is a seer, some kind of evil mage? After all, he has seen two people to their deaths. There is a world of evil — demons and devils — no doubt about that. It isn't just the stuff of shrill books and Hollywood movies. Suppose he has unwittingly been caught up in that world? And if he has priestly powers, will they not make him more appealing to malevolent forces? How can he go through with it?

Thanks to the bizarre incidents of his life, he doesn't lack the courage to tell his superior that ordination will be a mistake. He doesn't know the new man, Leviticus Kitendi, well, but by all accounts he is a good sort.

His mother raps on his door. "Are you hungry, mon fils?"

He isn't hungry, merely exhausted, though the day is only five minutes old. "Un moment, Maman."

"Good. I'll wait for you. We have peanut porridge today."

It doesn't usually take him long to get downstairs for peanut porridge, but today it requires a huge effort of will to make his limbs obey the smallest order. His mother's dark eyes ferret out trouble, even before he pulls out his stool and sits down. "What's wrong?" She shakes the *Mabuli Messenger* at him. "You are big news, you three. All over the front page."

Jimmy shrugs. "I can't go ahead with it, Maman. I'm going to Father Kitendi as soon as I've eaten to tell him so."

"I think you're having wedding jitters."

"I've already had those."

"You think they're like mumps, that you only have once?"

"Maman, don't joke. This is not something I can proceed with. Now that I know, I have to put a stop to it."

"Has this just occurred to you, or has it been troubling you all along?"

"I won't say it hasn't occurred to me before, but I wouldn't say it has been bothering me all along."

"It overwhelmed you this morning, then?"

"Buried me like the worst sandstorm."

She folds the paper, swift, and exact. "I too was scared on my wedding day. My mother gave me a test. She said, 'Think of three things that you would much rather be doing today.'"

"And?"

"I couldn't. So she said, 'Think of one thing you'd much rather be doing.'"

"And?"

"I couldn't. So I married your father."

Jimmy swallows the last of his porridge, stands, and kisses her. "I won't be long."

"Are you going to walk?"

He nods, pats her shoulder goodbye, goes out on to the back verandah, runs down the stairs, and pauses at the bottom. The sun, set upon by feisty grey clouds, isn't giving in. It elbows its way to a thin splinter in the murk, breaking through in an apostrophe of pure light that falls on his father's most recent undertaking, a grove of red sorrel. Funny, he thinks of it by its St. Chris name, sorrel, rather than bissap, the name they give it in West Africa. Bissape is a popular drink in Mabuli. Sappi is a beer brewed from the flowers of the plant.

His father Andri thinks the plant might be commercially viable. The evening before, he'd stood on the steps at sunset swinging a bag of dried blossoms back and forth on its string as if it were a censer. "We Mabulians mostly use it for bissape and sappi, but other people use it for syrup, jam, chutney, even a sort of liquor. White people use it for food colouring. The seeds make good chicken feed, and yield cooking oil. And you can eat the leaves like spinach or add them to soup."

"If it's such a versatile plant, Papa, why aren't we using it for all these purposes or growing it for export?"

"Exactly what I say, my son. One reason is we're not scientific farmers. We're leaving crops to the vagaries of rainfall, which is inefficient. Rain is hardly dependable in these parts. If you're serious about growing a crop, you have to work out good irrigation practices. Angélique has some friends at the college who've taken it on as a project. If this little effort here works out, I'll fund a proper experiment." Andri pursed his lips till they touched his nose, then slid apart in a smile of benign self-satisfaction.

Jimmy picks his way down the path through the bissap bushes. He stopped to put on one of the pairs of water boots that live at the kitchen door, because the ground is still muddy from unusually heavy rains in August. Mabuli was lucky. Floods have devastated several districts in Burkina Faso, some right on the border, but Mabuli has suffered comparatively little damage. Instead, trees are flagrantly green, pastures stout, mini dams brimful.

Vexation shoves him through the back gate into a lane potholed with shiny brown pools and embraced by acacias. He slops through the puddles. What a waste of the Jesuits' resources! Maybe he can still hang around with them, teach, or work in one of their social action centres. Sadly, Maman's test won't serve. Marriage is a commitment to one person. Being a priest is, to use Mapome's metaphor, a camel with another kind of hump. He'll tell Kitendi the whole story, prophesying, womanizing, and all. The superior knows about Nila, but she's not been the only woman in his life.

In the superior's study, Jimmy inspects Leviticus Kitendi. He is an awkward man, given to looking absent, inattentive. It is Kitendi who told him four Christophians were coming for the ordination: the Watsons, Father Aston Cole, S.J., and Sister Rita Rose. In September 1979, his first time in St. Chris, the Watsons put Jimmy up because the island had a "visitation," as Harry Watson put it, from weather associated with Hurricane Frederic, and the badly damaged Jesuit house was being repaired. Marva was Harry's wife. The priest, Aston Cole, taught him Rhetoric and Caribbean Literature during his teaching stint on the island while Rita Rose, a Dominican nun, was a nursing sister in the Catholic hospital where he was helping the arthritic chaplain to get around.

Preparing to recite his woes, Jimmy isn't sure Kitendi will be helpful, but he proceeds anyway. "Father, I have to make a confession."

"Another one, Jimmy? If it will make you feel better, sure, let's do it. Shall we go to the Lady Chapel?"

"Not that kind of confession, Father. I have to tell you why I can't go through with my ordination."

"The Lady Chapel will still do, if that's okay with you. And please, call me Levi. We are labourers in the same vineyard, remember?"

So he confesses. He tells the older man how he became friends with Marva and Harry, that Harry taught him how to cook St. Chris food and Marva gave him his first lessons in St. Chris Creole. "She made it clear she'd have been happy to give me other lessons too, and I was tempted. She was a former Miss St. Chris and in her forties at the time, but you'd have needed her age paper to know. She was stunning."

"Ah, women from the Caribbean certainly are," Levi muses.

"We got past that, thank God, and she was invaluable in cluing me into local customs and into the behaviour I could expect from 'yout' in St. Chris. They were very influenced by American TV and movies, she said, and most important, I shouldn't lose my temper, because that was their aim and purpose. Plus, she said, it would be no big deal that I was from Africa, but if I cooked up a good tale about my clan markings, it might hold them for a bit. I did, and it did."

"Sounds like quite a woman, and Harry must be a very special man. But she's not why you can't be ordained, Jimmy, is she?"

"No!" a not-so-small demon says. "That was Rita Rose."

Not true, but Jimmy is stalling so he tackles her next. "Have you met Sister Rita Rose who's coming, Levi?"

Leviticus shakes his head.

"For sure she is no Marva Watson, and she was certainly issuing me no invitations. She merely worked havoc on me — completely upsetting my equilibrium. She was like Nila, not so much in looks but in disposition, a pressure cooker, oodles of seething psychic energy. I fell desperately in love, and was going crazy with worry. The regional superior at the time wasn't in St. Chris right then, what with the hurricane and all. Lucky for me, Aston Cole was teaching me Rhetoric, and a sort of survey course in Caribbean Literature."

"I know Aston," Leviticus interrupts. "A good man!"

"He should have been superior, I tell you.

"Avoid the politics, Jimmy! There's zero to be had from them."

"I'll do my best, Levi, but sometimes there's no sidestepping them. Anyway, one day we were reading *Another Life*, by that St. Lucian poet ..."

Smiling with self-satisfaction, Leviticus pronounces, "Walcott. Derek Walcott. It begins with that wonderful image of the waves as pages of a book that's been left open by a reader who's somehow got caught up in a life somewhere else."

"Right! Him! I was complaining that I couldn't get a handle on the damn poem, and then I read his description of a woman who's a nurse. She's hanging onto her books and walking with some other nurses. They're all laughing, and he says, and this exactly caught the way I felt, that his hand is 'trembling' to say her name. I read them, and there I was looking at Rita Rose with the student nurses behind her! I just fell apart and the whole story came out!"

"What did Aston have to say?" Levi's look is tenderly amused.

"He didn't beat around the bush. He asked me if I loved her, to which I said yes, and then he asked me if I found her sexy, which shocked me for sure."

Levi laughs. "For sure I'm most eager to hear the end of the story!"

"He said if I wanted her to go off with me to Shangri-La, I should ask her."

"Well, I know you both didn't make it, but did you ask her?"

"No."

"So don't keep an old man in suspense! What happened?"

"Aston helped me figure out I had the wrong g. The problem was not with girls, but with God, who kept assailing me with extraordinary women with whom I wasn't being allowed to enjoy anything, let alone a life."

"You did marry Nila," Leviticus interposes mildly. "And you seem to have been diverted by Marva and Rita Rose, even though you never 'lay them flat' or tickled their 'feminine gender' as our Latin rhyme says."

"Aston said God wanted me for a permanent partner, so of course She did her best to wreck my relationships with other women."

"Aston clearly hasn't changed a bit. We were both novices at Weston College. He insisted on a female God, or aspect to God, even then."

"To tell the truth, Levi, I wish he were here now. Maybe he could help me again. You see, I still haven't told you my terrible secret."

"I know, Jimmy. Why don't we deal with it?"

When Jimmy ends his tale, Levi is silent for several minutes. Then he asks, "Do you love God, Jimmy?"

Jimmy beams. "Indeed, I do love Her."

Kitendi assesses him through grimy glasses, steps forward, and places his hands on Jimmy's shoulders, surprising him by being taller than he seems. "I can't speak for anyone else, but I do this one day at a time. I realized early on it was the only way I could do it. Did I want to be a priest? Yes. Was I sure I'd be able to be a good Jesuit till I died? No. So I decided to take it one day at a time. I'm still doing that."

"But mustn't a priest have a core of holiness to count on?"

"We all have a core of holiness, and we do count on it, but if you're wise, not too much. You count on God's grace."

"But what about the clairvoyance?"

"This is Africa, Jimmy, a place where the spiritual world is alive and well. I have known clairvoyants, good people whose gifts on occasion saved bodies and souls. It's a burden, yes, but it's not, in itself, an evil thing."

In the end, nobody from St. Chris comes, for Gilbert, bad-John of all hurricanes, grinds its way through the Caribbean in the second week of September, and relegates planes to the tarmac at the Queenstown Airport for four days. By the time air traffic is taking off again, it is too late.

19

Mapome's Game

Two weeks after his ordination, Jimmy presides at the funeral of the husband of his eldest sister, Alleme. Munti died of AIDS-related pneumonia. The doctor is certain: the white fur in his mouth and throat says so. No one speaks about it at the time of his death or in the days after, but they all have the look Mapome referred to, chirruping her wry laugh, as the "chimp-chump" look.

A week after the funeral, at her father's and Jimmy's insistence, and at Andri Atule's expense, Alleme flies to a clinic in Paris with her daughters, one who is four and the other not quite two, to be tested for HIV. Jimmy meets them at the airport when they come back, and drives them home. He helps Alleme give the children supper, and put them to bed. Makda Atule cooked, and sent food to the house so there is something to eat when they arrive, but Alleme isn't hungry. So he stays with her, asks questions about Paris and about how she feels, having heard the results. She says she is glad the older child is okay. She and the younger one have medicine. They'll have to go back to Paris soon.

His other questions elicit mostly one-word answers, so they just sit. The radio is on, turned down, a local music station, and they keep company, not talking, for perhaps an hour, watching the fireflies doing a jitterbug outside in the mango trees, observing the sky darken, and listening to the rain tap out its first notes, then grow into a drum recital drowning out all other sound.

Raising her voice, Alleme finally speaks into blackness, for neither has turned on a light, and the house, an old one set in from the street, is far from its neighbours.

"The irony is, Jimmy, that I feel at fault. I should have been a better mother, kept house better, cooked, washed, and cleaned better. Fucked better." Alleme is a poet, unafraid of words. "Then he wouldn't have gone to whores!"

"That makes no sense, Alleme."

"Then you tell me what makes sense. He just wanted a whore every now and then, the way you feel you'd like a nice mango?"

"That's probably closer to it."

He leaves her at about nine o'clock, having coaxed from her a promise that she will not stay up all night. He undertakes to call when he reaches the priests' house, but he is glad there is no answer when he does, and after a few rings he hangs up.

What the personable, aristocratic, educated man married to his sister might want from prostitutes defies Jimmy's understanding. He thinks this lack of imagination must be a serious failing on his part. How is it that a clairvoyant whose dreams can assume epic dimensions has such difficulty in figuring out why Munti would, as some American movie star put it, dally with hamburger when he can dine on steak at home?

He isn't quoting verbatim, just delivering the movie star's dictum.

D for delivering. D for dictum.

D for dally. D for dine.

D for disease.

D for done. D for dead. D for "done dead," like they say in St. Chris.

He is playing Mapome's dictionary game. Or rather, it is playing him.

Mapome loved words, language, stories. She taught him his first rhymes, taught him to read, to pore over the dictionary, and see it as a game board, storybook, history book, sacred text. She showed him as a ten-year-old how to play the game, which had many purposes: to teach him vocabulary, word derivations, memory gems, to impart values, and to tune his ear to sounds.

"You don't go looking for words. Just follow them as they come. The letter that chooses you first is the leader. If you find yourself straining for a word, it's time to stop."

Desire. Danger. Death. He's done some disputing with the Deity about desire and death.

Debility. Disablement.

Doubt.

Debate. About divine decrees, destiny, pre-destiny. About determination, whether he'll have dead sisters, whether their descendants will die.

Dearth of doctors. Dominicans. Devotion.

Dolour. Dame des Douleurs.

In whose domain, he's done the deed, become a designate of the devotees of Melchisedech.

Designate? Devotees? He is reaching for words. Time to stop.

He eases up out of the armchair. These last days he is fatter. There was a lot of eating during and after the ordination celebrations and at Munti's wake. He pats his stomach, recalling Bagbelly in St. Chris, a fat teenager who befriended, and fiercely defended him, and then the Watsons, Aston, Rita Rose. She would be the perfect person to talk to right that minute. Since Munti died, he's been doing research in every kind of library in Benke and by now has pretty much exhausted what there is on HIV/AIDS. Rita Rose is in obstetrics and gynecology as well as pediatrics, and he is seeing a lot in his reading about the problem of mother-to-child transmission of the disease. For sure she's up on that.

He slips a bookmark into the book he's been reading. He needs to find Levi. The priest has just returned from Bamako.

Maybe he is still in the chapel, for he often reads there until quite late at night. He has to ask him about Alleme, if he'll have time for a chat with her. He is no doctor but a jackass would know she is depressed, although she is refusing to see a psychiatrist.

"I'm not taking drugs so I can deal with life, Jimmy. That's crazy."

Also, having had another change of heart and direction, he has to explore it with the superior. He is to leave for Georgetown University, soon, to do postgraduate work in education. He isn't sure he wants to do that any longer.

The next morning, Jimmy goes to see Alleme just after breakfast. She says she will talk to a sensible person, if he can find one. She has a parish priest, of course, a very dry, very old, very deaf man from Bamako who has been their pastor since they've been in Benke. What would result from a session between him and Alleme, Jimmy doesn't wish to consider. The idea has some virtue because when he suggests it, she laughs out loud. He is glad when she agrees to see Levi, who is a trained spiritual director. There aren't that many of them around and they are good listeners. He was also a journalist in his layman days. Alleme and the superior will have things in common.

"There's something else, little brother."

"What is that, Alleme?"

"What about the others?"

"What others?"

"What about Ansile and Aisha? What about Angélique? Shouldn't they be tested?"

He has indeed thought that his other sisters and their spouses should be tested. He's not sure about approaching Angélique, but Alleme reminds him that sexual contact isn't the only way to contract AIDS and that Angélique is a woman of the world.

"Besides, Jimmy, she may be sexually active. Do you want her to be at risk because we are too delicate to raise the matter?"

"Of course not, Alleme. Don't be foolish."

"I don't think I'm the foolish one here. I will talk to the others if you want. Their chances are better if they find out early. And ideally both spouses should be tested. I know I'm pretty far-gone, but I'd feel better if this at least served some purpose. And the children, they should have the tests as well."

When Jimmy speaks to his father, he is not surprised that Andri has been busy, investigating the behaviours of his other sons-in-law, and getting in touch with a friend who knows a woman at the World Health Organization. When the elder Atule contacts her, she strongly recommends that they all be tested as Alleme recommends.

"Though I am unsure of how this matter should best be handled," his father says, "I propose to speak plainly. I won't hide my anger."

"Alleme says she'll speak to her sisters. She makes the point that sexual transmission isn't the only way the disease spreads, so no one need be offended."

"Yes, yes. The woman in Geneva said that also."

So it is arranged. Alleme speaks to them the next Sunday after Mass, as Makda Atule serves orange juice, bissape, and coffee laced with her own palm wine liqueur to fortify fearful spirits. Ansile and Angélique are concerned about costs, but agree it should be done. Aisha sulks at the impugning of her virtue, a quarrel to which Alleme puts paid. "Has my virtue has been compromised? I'm ill, my dear, not evil."

In the end, it is decided that the screening should be done as soon as possible. For now, Andri Atule will cover the expenses. He doesn't speak at length, but it is clear he is on the warpath, and that the matter is not by any means done with.

Calamity befalls swiftly. Both the husbands test positive. Ansile's test is negative, but Aisha is HIV-positive, and when the children are tested, her one-year-old daughter also has the disease. Angélique is fine.

Andri Atule alters like the desert reconfigured by a violent sandstorm. Jimmy tries to persuade him of their good fortune in having everyone tested early, being able to send them for treatment, having the resources to pay for expensive drugs. The elder Atule is beyond consolation. His sons-in-law are from powerful families, but it is his children who have been violated, his grandchildren despoiled. Often he cries out as if in physical pain. He summons the parents of his sons-in-law. There are lawyers and accountants. Negotiations are conducted and binding agreements made. Monies are paid into medical funds, trusts set up for wives and children. Elders guarantee the behaviour of their sons — much too little, far too late.

Jimmy has no trouble persuading Leviticus Kitendi that Georgetown should be postponed. He can honestly say it is not only what has happened in his family that weighs on him, but the plight of his country, of Mabulians. When Levi asks what he feels immediately called to do, he says he wishes to do something about HIV/AIDS.

"What do you think that might be, Jimmy?"

"Can I take that one step at a time, for a while, anyway?"

Jimmy's research into how the disease spreads takes him to shanty-bars in Benke where he sips sappi and watches women service men in the cabs of trucks, hopping up to check them in turn, like customs inspectors or border police. Truckers from the west via Bamako, the east via Kano and Niamey heading north through the desert to the Mediterranean and those making the journey back mostly pause to rest overnight in Gao, but they come to Benke often enough. So it isn't just to Gao that the disease, dubbed "the Skinny" in Mabuli, comes with the truckers. No doubt it also comes with tourists or traders, but truckers are obvious culprits, always coming and going, promiscuous on the road. Sex traders collect it from them, and pass it on to Mabuli farmers, tradesmen, itinerant workers who "suck a sweetie" while they are away from their wives. And to his distinguished brothers-in-law!

When all things are equal, water from the Mabenke's few tributaries allows farmers like the Atules once were to plough and be assured of reaping, but for much of the seventies the drought that parched the Sahel brought farming to a halt. Benke swelled as refugees from stricken holdings came to the city to find jobs, ply trades they knew, or learn new ones, or, in desperation, fall into the oldest trade. So maybe the drought is to blame for HIV?

"Blame the sun, the moon, the Milky Way!" Mapome often said. "But there's no millet to be had from that!" She is right. One needs to assign a useful blame. It comes down to how you apply the word: as censure, or as verdict, diagnostic, with a view to improving things. Sometimes it is hard to figure which is which. Something else keeps bothering him: why didn't he have the slightest inkling about Munti's death or the disaster that was to overtake his sisters and their children? Or is it that his gift is indeed a curse and his having no warning of this scourge on the Atules is a kind of inverted payback? Shouldn't he have foreseen what was going to befall his family?

Ansile and he are having a cup of tea on the verandah of the family house. They are both visiting. When the Atules moved north, Alleme and Aisha were already married and set up in their own households, but Ansile and Angélique still lived at home. Now, only Angélique, who made bold to be born after Jimmy, still lives with their parents.

"What am I to do, Jimmy?" Ansile asks. "How can I have sex with Raphael? It's suicide!"

"I can see it might be a problem, Ansile."

"It's no time for irony, Jimmy. Should I divorce him?"

"I don't know. Perhaps."

"That's not helpful, esteemed little brother!"

"Do you want to divorce Raphael?"

"I don't know what I want, except that I don't want to get AIDS."

"Well, you do know something you want."

"He says he's never been with anyone else."

"Do you believe him?"

"I don't know what to believe, so I tell myself to deal with the facts. And he is HIV-positive. So what are my options? There's no way this marriage is going to proceed in a state of celibacy, so the only solution to us staying married is his using a condom."

"That seems logical enough."

"But the Church says we can't."

"The Church isn't married to a man who is HIV-positive. Besides which, you have a conscience. In the end, it's your conscience that you answer to."

"You mean that?"

"I do. It's ethically sound, as far as I know."

"Well, that's reassuring."

"You could talk to Father Kitendi."

"And run the risk of his trotting out the church's line? I think I'll just hang on to the leeway you've given me, and obey my conscience, thank you."

"Why don't you pray about it?"

"What's that going to do?"

"You won't know till you do it, will you?"

Jimmy is glad that Ansile goes home feeling better. For days he thinks about her dilemma, and the advice he has given her. His work clearly has to be twofold: to assist with stopping the spread of HIV/AIDS and to minister to those with the disease and their loved ones. Perhaps Rita Rose will come, and help. They need scores of her. The supply of nurses in Mabuli is each day more depleted. They keep falling ill, but nobody knows what ails them. The Skinny is like rumour: say nothing, and it doesn't exist.

MARK

20

Doublespeak

En route to the council meeting on Thursday morning, the first letter Mark wrote Grace comes to mind, word for word. He knows the text perfectly because he'd drafted and redrafted it until he was satisfied.

> *Dear Grace,*
> *It was a pleasure to see you after so long and to work with you on a matter that, though not on the agenda, proved an important one for our consideration.*
> *I must admit that I'm not aware of all the parameters surrounding the issue in question, and so precisely what we are faced with. Nevertheless, we made such excellent progress at our first meeting, despite time constraints, that I'm optimistic about what we might accomplish with steady and consistent application. Thus, I'm suggesting that we meet soon again, or at least find a way to discuss concerns that I'm sure are paramount in both our minds.*

I'd be glad if you could call me as soon as you can. You could be anywhere between Venice and Vladivostok, so over to you!

All good wishes,
Mark Blackman

The second letter was shorter; he's pretty sure of its wording too. He'd been annoyed at not having heard from her, and in two minds about writing. He tells himself now that he was equally careful, never mind his irritation.

Dear Grace,
I am concerned at not having had a reply to my recent letter. I hope it's the burden of work that has delayed your response and not ill health.

This comes simply to reiterate my earlier sentiments. As I said previously, I feel that the project we worked on together is important and has a great deal of potential, never mind the considerable challenges it presents. I would like to pursue it and to meet with you soon, to that end.

If you feel the same way (and I must assume, given the enthusiasm you displayed, that you do), I'd be glad to hear from you as soon as possible, so that we can make appropriate plans.

All good wishes,
Mark Blackman

People busily on the move greet him as they pass. He nods, noblesse oblige, holding course for the council room.

Grace hadn't replied to the second letter either. Why had he written at all? Why not phone? The cloak and dagger appeal of coded messages? The sweet angst of anticipating a response? Fear of rejection, better delivered on paper he could crush and throw away? Whatever, it hadn't occurred to him to call. He'd left his home number with his personal assistant, though, so if she called, she could get him.

GRACE

21

Back to St. Chris

Ma at the door of the barracks hut, her hair just now starting to grey, but her stance solid as ever, bosom thrust out, shoulders thrown back, legs straight and firm as the sides of Hogman Gorge. She watches as the Half-a-Million, a fast, new bus named for its price, sets her daughter down, and Grace collects her backpack and starts walking up the path. The cosmos, purple, yellow, and mauve, wave welcome right and left, their green eyelash leaves making a low forest of shade to cool her dusty feet.

Up the wooden steps, backpack just inside the door, and then Grace gives her mother a long, tight-tight hug. It feels strange for now her head is not as usual on Ma's shoulder, but they are nearly jaw-by-jaw. Either she has grown taller since she went to foreign, or Ma is growing down, the way old people do. But Ma is not old. Gramps is old, but not Ma, neither Pa.

When finally they come apart, Grace asks, "How you stay, Ma? And Pa? Gramps? Sam and Princess? And the boys?"

"Everybody fine, Grace. Well as can be expected. The young ones is at school and your Pa at work. Gramps taking some shut-eye just now, but he soon wake. Doctor put him in bed for a week, say he have a touch of pneumonia."

Gracie hugs her mother again, smelling carbolic soap, sweat, and the faint odour of seasoning, thyme and pimento.

"You must be dead beat. Sun hot already, and the year just start!" Ma smiles, lifts up Grace's backpack and takes it inside. "Come sit down and drink a glass of lemonade and eat something. I have the escoveitched fish that you like, hard-dough bread and pickles from the last batch Gramps make."

Grace sits at the table. Ma disappears for one minute, comes back with a basin of water, a spotless white washrag, and some sweet soap. Grace nods thanks, washes her hands, and then takes Ma's hand and holds it against her cheek. She smiles as Ma retrieves the hand, puts ice from a Styrofoam container on the table into a tall glass that she takes from a small curio cabinet, and pours out lemonade. Grace bows her head and blesses the food, mostly a concession to Ma, Pa, and Gramps, but also because here in Wentley, God is already nearer. She takes a long suck on the lemonade and starts with her fingers on the fish and hard-dough bread.

Ma talks as she watches Grace eat, filling her in on all the news "Pansy expecting again. This one make four, and she lose one. That girl don't even allow a good year between making those babies. I tell her, 'Pansy, if you take the pikni off the breast so soon, you going to start a next one in no time.' But you know Pansy. Say she don't want no baby to drag down her breast. I don't know how she work that out, for each new baby is another breast-feeding and more dragging down!"

"So they doing okay? The children? She? Mortimer?"

Ma shrugs, eyebrows and shoulders lifting up one time. "Give him his due, Grace, he treat her with respect, and he is a good provider. And he don't oblige her to wear locks nor cover herself from neck to foot. The ital food, yes, he insist on that, but that not such a bad thing. We pretty much eating ital."

Grace examines this room where she has perhaps spent most of her waking life. On a bookshelf are books she has sent home, second-hand books on health, nutrition, house repairs. They are from her exile, a way to keep connected.

Ma sees her look, says, "Thank you for sending the books! Gramps read the medical articles, recommend them to your Pa. And you know your father. When he see it write down, it persuade him. So we not eating so much of the stew peas and salt beef and pig tail no more."

"I'm glad, Ma," Grace says. "Is Gramps make the shelf? And the cabinet? I never know he was a woodworker."

"Stewie! Bring them in here Christmas last, proud as any peacock! He doing good at Pursea's."

Grace is glad. Stewie struggles so hard. "You don't finish about Mortimer and Pansy and the children, Ma."

"Oh, Mortimer love those children bad, Grace. The man would give hand and foot for them. And he look well pleased every time Pansy belly start swell."

"So what bout Gramps, Ma? Where he is?" She is wondering where Gramps could be sleeping. Ma points to the door leading to the back porch.

"Go on and see if him wake, my darling."

Grace pushes the back door open, preparing her eyes for the bright afternoon light, waiting to see the low banks of monkey fiddle and jump-up-and-kiss-me, the skeleton of the burnt tree supporting one end of the clothes line, and the pole bearing the other end upon which, by Stewie's account, he has hung a wire ring so Conrad can dunk balls. Gramps will be asleep in the old wicker-bottom rocking chair that was still rocking Princess when she left.

Stepping through the door and down, for the porch is at a lower level, she finds she's not standing on rickety boards but on a firm floor. Nor is there any green glare from the sun on its journey home. Instead, soft light coming through a curtained window shows Grace a long, thin room created from enclosing the back gallery. Under the window Gramps is lying on a high old-style metal double bed. Grace is overjoyed to see him propped up on pillows, asleep in his singlet, breaths of air gently billowing his chest and fluting his broad nostrils.

Clearly plenty things have changed in the time she has been away. So Gramps bed, which had always been in storage under the house, its metal cool even in the hottest time, is now rehabilitated and brought inside. Tucked into the far corner of the porch, it is pretty much taking up the width of the room. Someone, maybe Stewie of the just-acquired joinery skills, has made a table the same height as the bed, thin, so it fits into the narrow space between the bed and the outside wall. On this table are Gramps Bible, spectacles, a newspaper, a pen, and a parcel wrapped in brown paper and tied with string. As she stands watching him, Gramps snorts, an exhalation that pushes him into wakefulness. He opens his eyes, looks at Grace, taps the bed with his heel and pulls up his knees to make space for her.

"Come, Gracie. Take a kotch. Tell me how the colonizing of the white folks coming along. Everybody up there eating patty and singing 'Slide Mongoose'?"

"Don't know bout the singing, but everybody eating patty, for sure."

"Good. I know you would fix up them Toronto folks."

When Ma calls her "darling," Grace knows she's home, but it is Gramps calling her "Gracie" and confident that she "fix up the Toronto folks" that persuades her at least momently that she has a place in the world. Gramps could give lessons to Papa God.

22

A Parcel

Last thing before bed, Grace skims a letter that's just come from Maisie.

> *Larkins' Home*
> *14 March 1979*

Dear Grace,

Sorry to be hounding you all the way across the ocean, but when I tell my story you will know why. Sylvia is pregnant, and I don't know what to do. Is not any big deal that she is pregnant. Woman getting pregnant ever since, but when I think of that girl with a baby, I tremble. She can't take care of herself much less a small, helpless human being. Remember I told you the last time we talk that I had a feeling she was up to something? Well, about three months ago, one week after she turn fifteen, she find a little basement room and a pyah-pyah job and say she done with school and not coming back home either. I try to pass by where she live, but half the time she not in her basement hovel. Of course once morning sickness start, she quick-quick find herself back into this house. Now she only sleep and watch TV. If I push her, she give me a hand, but sometimes I have to ask when last she bathe. I tell her she need to go and see a doctor, but she refuse to go to our family doctor. As for who the father is, if I bring up the subject she fly into a rage. I hope she don't have any baby that yellow and wiry-head like she, for her mother was a very black woman, not light skinned like me. Sometimes I think all this is because they used to taunt her at school, call the poor child "yellow turd." And nobody do a thing till I come on the scene. I find myself to that school one time, and it don't happen again. By God's grace her father don't know yet that she making baby for luckily he been working in Calgary since just after she leave here. That time he say he tired to fuss with her and if she want to go out on her own so be it. I myself think she must have some mental sickness. If you have a phone anywhere near, Grace, I beg you to call me and I will call you right back. Not to say I expect you to tell me what to do, but I always feel better after I talk to you. I am sorry to be weighting you down like this for I know you gone to see your sick Grandpa, but who else am I to talk to? Church people up here is for when things going good and you paying your tithe and not causing any disturbance. I going now to try coax her to go to the hairdresser and buy some clothes that can at least fit her. I hope your Grandpa is improving. He always sound like such a decent man when you speak of him. PLEASE call if you can. Enjoy the sunshine and home cooking. Your good friend,

Maisie

The letter is there Monday, the day Grace reaches home, waiting for her. Today, Tuesday, Ma goes off early to work at Mrs. Sampson's as usual, and Pa leaves at the same time on his way to his tiny office at Wentley Park. By half past seven, Princess, Sam, and Conrad have set off for school, Conrad, who is all of eighteen, bossing the other two though they are not very much younger, annoying them by asking whether they have their homework and their lunch pans, shepherding them out the door in a state of mild rebellion.

Ma makes breakfast for all of them before she leaves. Gramps isn't awake when time comes for her to set out, so she asks Grace to give Gramps his breakfast. Shortly after eight, Grace hears him getting up and moving around. When the door leading to the stairs into the backyard gives a squeal, she knows he is going to the outhouse and will be back before long. She spoons the porridge into bowls and takes down mugs to pour cocoa-tea from the same thermos that has been there since she was small-small.

Gramps climbs the stairs, goes back into the narrow porch-room and lingers there for a while, and then he comes through to the big room where they eat, do homework, and relax. Since she's gone abroad, the three youngest sleep in this room, and Ma and Pa have the one bedroom to themselves. Ma says Edgar and Stewie, when they are home, sleep on a mattress they roll out at the foot of Gramps bed.

When he comes to the table, Gramps rests the brown paper package Grace noticed beside his bed at his place and sits. He smiles at Grace, his face and eyes bright like he's just knocked back a couple glasses of white rum or pimento dram, but she knows it is because of how rejoiced he is to see her. They sit across from each other and join hands as Gramps says grace. After that, they start on the porridge. But there is something ominous that has not escaped her notice. In the prayer, Gramps has called her "Grace."

"Grace," Gramps says when he finish eating, "I have a hard task, and I think I best get right to it."

"What kind of hard task, Gramps?" She looks up from her contemplation of the last honey crystals on the side of her bowl. Gramps licks away the remnants of cornmeal, his tongue making a tour of purple-dark lips, collecting tiny yellow blobs from the hairs in his moustache.

"I want you to bear with me, Grace," he says. "I have a long story to relate, and you are at the centre of it. It behooves me to tell it because I alone know all the ins-and-outs. I must tell it now as I don't know when next I'll see you."

Grace feels the cornmeal rising in her throat.

"I have in this parcel, exactly nineteen letters. They are precious things, full of love and concern for you." He pauses, tenderness overtaking his countenance. "Have you any idea who might have written them?"

She doesn't understand Gramps. Of course she has no idea! True, if the letters are wonderful, then she has nothing to fear. But down in her-belly bottom, she knows something is not right. She shakes her head to answer Gramps.

Gramps is merciful. He doesn't take long, and he holds her hand, and he looks straight in her eyes, and does his best to soothe her with his voice, as he tells her an unbelievable story.

"The truth is you are very lucky, Grace. You have not one, but two mothers: Ma Carpenter, who raised you like you came from her own womb, and your birth mother, the one out of whose belly you did come. Her name is Phyllis Patterson. She wrote these letters to you, the first one shortly after you came to this house, and one on each of your birthdays after that. I am glad, and, in truth, relieved, to give them to you. They have been a heavy burden all these years." Gramps looks out past Ma's cosmos to the road beyond. "Indeed, this long time I've wondered," his voice is close to a whisper, "again and again, especially when that blue air mail letter arrive every year, if we had any right to take you from her, give her no news of you, not even tell her your name."

She takes the parcel Gramps passes to her. She doesn't say anything, and they sit there at the table looking at each other. It is she who first looks away to consider the bundle in her hands.

"It don't make sense, Gramps. Young girls in St. Chris make babies all the time, send the babies to other people to raise, or give them up for adoption. That is routine matters, as you would say. Why this big secrecy with me?"

"Your father take advantage of your mama when she was only a child herself, not even thirteen yet. It was not any boyfriend-girlfriend business. She had just barely start her menses. He never care for her, never had no thought for the seed he put in her belly. We wanted to give her a chance to have a life."

"So what about my father, Gramps? Where he is? He live in St. Chris?"

Gramps face turns into stone, and the gleam in his eyes vanishes, like you dash water on a fire. "Less said about that one, the better."

"What you mean, Gramps?"

"He was a wicked fellow, Grace, barely a human being."

———

Grace is sitting on the big tree stump in the yard, looking at the package wrapped in brown paper and tied with coarse string in one hand and her friend's perfumed letter in the other. She hasn't opened the brown paper package. She is struggling with what Gramps has just told her, so no way can she afford to think about Maisie and Sylvia yet.

"In every way apart from the bond of flesh, you are truly Ma and Pa's child, Gracie, for you joined this family as a baby and they raised you as their very own." These are Gramps last words.

She closes her eyes, crosses her arms in front of her, envelope in one hand, package in the other, hugging herself.

Not that she is cold, for this brisk Wentley air that shakes you, wakes you, but doesn't slice through you, is one of the things she misses. The yard is still cool, for she can imagine the sun taking its time nibbling the wet grass as it saunters up the other side of the low hill behind the forest where Gramps grows his medicine plants. When it breaks the ridge, that time it starts to gallop. Before you turn round twice, it's three o'clock and the day done race away, gone.

What challenges her now is how to grasp that these things concern her, Grace Carpenter. She must own them, for, as Gramps says, they are her life. But Gramps tale sounds to her like a St. Chris version of *The Young and the Restless*. Does anyone deserve a life made up by a third-rate screenwriter? Does she? Do Ma and Pa know all that Gramps has just told her? Why hasn't she asked Gramps if they know? On top of everything, she is vexed. How come nobody gave her the slightest inkling she was coming home to be loaded down with this? And it is only a couple weeks away from her birthday. What a birthday present!

23

First and Last

Last year's letter from Phyllis Patterson is the first one Grace reads. She doesn't really read it, just skims, but she's a good skimmer.

25 March 1978

My dearest daughter,

Today you are eighteen years old. That means you are grown up, an adult under the law. You can vote, and you can take your place in society. I am so proud of you. I don't know what you look like, or whether you are still at home in St. Chris or out in the world making your own way. But it doesn't matter, because there are some things I do know, for I have prayed for them all my life. I know you are a good person. That means you care about other people, starting at home and then going out into the community where you give service. No matter how you contribute, I am certain you do. I also know you have worked and studied hard, and so you have had good success in all your efforts. I know that whatever path in life you choose, you will achieve your goals and be a shining example to others of your race. I know you love God, whether or not you are a churchgoer, for not all those who go to church love Him and many serve Him who never darken a church door. I smile at the word darken, as if all the faithful have coloured skins.

And I know that because of all these things, you are happy with the face you see in the mirror each morning.

There is a last thing that I have asked God for all through these years. When they took you away from me and refused to even let me give you a name, I know your Grandma Evadne and Mr. Carpenter thought they were acting for the best. Their concession was that I could write these letters, and even then there were stipulations: write on your birthday (which I haven't always done, but how were they to know?), and post by month's end. I think they were convinced that I would stop, once I forgot you. But Mr. Carpenter said he would give you my letters. I am holding him to his promise. You have been a part of my life all these years and kept me going through many difficult days. I'm sure your adopted parents love you, but I want you to know that I have loved you too.

I pray for you with all my heart today. I pray that you continue in good health, loving God, and being a credit to your family and community. My heart is full, so I will end now just as I began. Have a happy birthday, my grown-up daughter. God bless you today and all your life long.

Your mother,
Phyllis

The next letter, from the same address, is dated 26 March 1977. She doesn't think she can read through the whole bundle. It occurs to her that it's near the end of March. Her birth mother must be about to write this year's letter. She doesn't want another letter. Maybe there is a way for Gramps to tell this person she needn't write anymore.

It's cool still, though the sun is gaining on mist and cloud. Next door she hears the squeak of the Williams gate, opening and closing to let Miss Constance in. Miss Constance goes to Mass every morning, and she just has time to go and come back before her invalid parents wake.

Grace is not sure she likes how this new mother sounds: she's too full of praying and God, especially for somebody that grew up in a big, foreign city like New York. Then she recognizes the silliness of that. Caribbean people go all over the globe and carry their God, whether Jesus, Jah, Allah, Krishna, or whoever, with them. But it's hard enough to find out that you have a mother you never knew about: she is not able to cope with any saint. She'd rather a mother who, like Gramps, is a rogue who knows God is one too.

All this trouble sake of one little hole in a woman's body! "Woman Hole." She had forgotten Woman Hole, a place near Tavern Town where, never mind the dangerous curve, people stop on the road to pitch their garbage down the hillside. There's no actual hole, and nobody can see where the filth lands up. Which tells her how people conceive of a woman's vagina: a hidden-away place where you off-load stinking, rotten things. It's good agricultural soil all the same, for plants are forever rooting there. Weeds take root in the refuse heap; dump pikni catch in vagina dungle.

That decides her on what to tell Maisie. There's no reason why Sylvia can't have the baby. She seems to want it, and it has grandparents who will love it, no matter what. Sylvia is lucky. The baby will give her something to care about, her parents aren't poor, and at fifteen she is over the age of consent. It's a horse of a very different colour from the one Phyllis had been obliged to ride. Maybe that explains her pious-sounding birth mother. Maybe religion is like Tiger Balm, and when you have pain and trouble, you just rub it all over your aching self to get relief.

27 March 1979

Dear Maisie,

First, I have to say a Big Sorry. I know you said I was to call, and I had every intention of calling, but every day turns into the next without my going with Pa to Wentley Park, or with Ma to Mrs. Sampson. I think I am reluctant to leave Gramps for however short a period. I may well be back in Toronto before you get this, but I'm writing anyhow.

The good news is that Gramps is better than I expected, for when they brought me home I thought he would be on dying, which he is not. It's only two and a half years since I left but those years have made a big difference. He looks tired and a lot older. It seems to be his heart, the organ itself or the blood vessels, for I don't think it is yet sorted out. My problem is that I have never thought of Gramps as old — after all, he's only seventy-seven and plenty people here live until they are eighty and ninety, and some even make it to a hundred.

A lot else has happened and even if I wanted to tell you about it, I wouldn't know where to start for I am still trying to put it into some kind of order in my own head.

Anyway, this was to be about your problems, not mine.

Don't pressure Sylvia. She's pregnant, the baby-father is not around, and she's probably depressed as well as overwhelmed. Just go-long with her, and try to get her to cheer up and take an interest — doesn't matter in what. The baby could be a very good thing for her. That is how you have to look at it and get her to think about it. If the two of you are on the same side when her father gets back, things are bound to go better.

No abortion though. Plenty things are going through my head now that lead me to give you that advice. We will talk more. Meantime, just put on the best face you can manage for Sylvia's sake, and the baby's, for you don't want to mark it with a sad spirit!

I will call when I come. Take good care of yourself, and Sylvia and the baby.

Grace

MARK

24

No Rest for the Wicked

The chancellor's suite in the administrative building is named Garvey, after the Jamaican national hero who spent two months in St. Chris before going to Panama to commence his American adventures. A painting of the great man hangs in the vestibule along with portraits of UA's first two chancellors.

It's early Thursday afternoon, and Mark is lying in his recliner, awake. Foiling his efforts at an afternoon nap before council starts are memories of his first and last conversations with Grace at UA. At the time he had been both Head of Department and Dean. Though she was only a part-time member of the faculty, come to do research for her doctoral thesis, she'd made a splash by publishing a paper entitled "A Model for Real Time (RT), Real Circumstance (RC), Tailor-Made Interventions (TMI) in Communities Affected by Vector-Transmitted Diseases." It had got attention as far afield as the World Bank. Because she'd arrived with funding and wasn't just any old grad student, he'd duly stopped by to check on how she'd settled in.

"Hi, Miss Carpenter. Are you very busy?"

"Always busy, Dr. Blackman, but do come in and have a seat."

"Mark, please. We're informal here. I won't stay long, as I know you must be busy." Idiot. She'd just said that!

"I could do with a break. And you may as well be comfortable, even if it's only for a minute."

"Thanks," he said, sitting. "I thought I'd see how you were doing, check if there's anything I can help with. You know, stubborn issues, intractable people. We've been known to have those."

She smiled, but didn't say anything, so he rambled on about workload, office hours, and library access. He was running out of topics when she spoke.

"Mark, you really want to know what I find hard to deal with?"

"Absolutely."

"Everybody here is forever talking about plantation: plantation economy, plantation society, plantation attitudes, plantation this, plantation that. I tired to hear it and I just come. And this place is the biggest plantation!"

He was surprised at the plantation label. That was an old quarrel made by rabble-rousing students. She had a reputation as a fine scholar, with the objectivity that implied, and she hadn't struck him as the activist type.

"You see me?" she went on. "I grow on a plantation, and I find it hard to see people who're supposedly educated, intelligent, travelled, behaving like gorillas, jealous about territory, real backra massa style."

Aha! All politics is local! She'd clashed with some departmental high-up!

"Would it help," he spoke in a way meant to convince her, "if we talked about what's bothering you? We won't be able to fix it entirely, or right away, but it might be useful to have a chat?"

She seemed to consider it and then said, "I'm sorry. I'm new here, Mark. I shouldn't have spoken so quickly. I should give UA a chance."

After that she'd seemed happy, productive in her work, liked by the students, respected by her colleagues. Then one day she'd resigned; not had an altercation with anyone; not been found wanting in any way. Just upped and gave notice.

He'd been off on sabbatical for the year, and her letter had arrived during his leave period, effective at the end of the Michaelmas Term, so pretty much the calendar year's end. The acting dean mentioned it while bringing him up to speed on their way from the airport. He went to see her the next day.

"Hi, Mark. Welcome back. Did your sabbatical go well?"

"Very well, thanks. Better than things seem to have gone for you here."

She shrugged, said nothing.

"I understand you've resigned. Is there no persuading you to stay?"

"You know why I'm leaving, don't you, Mark?"

Through the window he saw rain, drops plump as ripe St. Chris cherries. September was a rainy month. A lake covered the quadrangle, which was enclosed by cement buildings housing the Social Sciences Faculty. Someone had convinced officialdom to leave them unpainted.

"Suppose you tell me again."

"You remember that incident just after I came? A charge of sexual harassment that a post-grad student brought against Dr. Hazelton?"

"Very clearly. The student's name was Vie MacMillan."

"Right. You wouldn't forget her. She was very bright."

Hazelton was memorable too: a fine teacher and remarkable scholar.

"When they set up her committee, I was asked, not to be on it, but to hold a watching brief, because she was working on a model similar in some respects to the one I propose in my paper. I said yes, and I've taken an interest and offered her any help I could."

The rain increased. It sounded like they were talking inside a waterfall.

"Please go on." He had to raise his voice.

"She told me he showed her his — glowing, by the way — report on her dissertation. However, he threatened to tear it up unless she withdrew the sexual harassment charge retroactively."

"But why is he one of her examiners? It's *ultra vires*. And he can't have threatened her. That's unimaginable."

"She says he did, and why would she make it up?"

"I agree. I don't see her doing that. So has she lodged a complaint about this latest incident?"

"No, she hasn't."

"Well, what has she done? Nothing?"

"Withdrawn the harassment charge. She said she had it sufficiently tough the first time around, and if she tried to make another accusation, it would be her word against his, and who would believe her. Last time she at least had some proof. Besides, she said, his report is enthusiastic."

"Did you do anything?"

"I went to her supervisor, Colin Hall, who happens to have been a friend of Hazelton's — still is, I think. Dr. Hall dismissed it as outrageous and accused me of having a personal grudge against Dr. Hazelton. Said he was very pleased Vie had eventually come to her senses and set the record straight."

"So you went to the Chair of the Committee for Postgraduate Affairs?"

"I did. He said Vie would have to lodge a formal complaint."

"And what did Miss MacMillan say?"

"She says she's 'going along with the fiction.' She's hoping they will set a date for her defence early in the New Year. Two reports are already in, including the external's. Hazelton's is the third. She has an attachment at UCLA starting in the fall that turns on her completing the degree, and that's what's important. If UA is happy with sexual predators on the faculty, so be it."

"And that's why you decided to resign?"

"It was the straw that broke the camel's back. Made me think of all the many things that oughtn't to go on that we allow to go on anyhow."

"And you won't change your mind?"

"Remember? I grew up on a plantation and that experience was enough."

"Bad as that?"

"Plenty worse. I'm getting out of this place before I turn into a house nigger, especially like how I'm red already."

"I'm very sorry that's what you've decided."

"White backra massa, brown backra massa, black backra massa! Same breed of dog."

He checks his watch. God Almighty! He best get at least twenty of the bespoke forty winks. The damn meeting is in a half hour.

GRACE

25

Gramps Travels

Dear Gracie,

Sorry I never get to say much when I phone on the first from Mrs Sampson house to tell you the news that Gramps take in bad, but you know I dont like to take advantage. Gramps never last long once he reach hospital and he pass on the 7 August. We sorry but is only Thursday just gone your Pa find out his office never send you the telegram they promise to send and Mr. Wong say he try your number whole day Friday and yesterday but nobody answer. we going keep on trying but is so long now I make up my mind to put pen to paper for maybe something wrong up your way with the phone. We bury Gramps today Sunday afternoon it was a good turnout. Pa handle all the church arrangements. No mind it was Methodist chapel Rev. Leslie the Anglican parson from Hector Castle that teach your father from early school days insist he will do the honours. he and Gramps was in primary school together and he was one of those that was groomsman when Gramps and Miss Elsie get married he retired now but he refuse for anybody else to do the service. Wentley Park people turn out well out of respect for your father. We bury Gramps right there in the churchyard the boys hold up good to make their grandfather proud but Princess and Sammy never stop cry when I see Pansy and Mortimer and the children it come to me that taking in Gramps is four generation of Carpenter people in the church. The boys look so much like big somebody that I frighten. Not going on more for I crying right here as I write Gramps living here with us and helping us in every way this long long time so is like a piece of my own body that is gone.

Some more lines to follow soon everybody send love God bless.

Ma

30 August 1979

Dear Ma and Pa,

Thanks, Ma, for your letter. The phone in the dorm has been giving trouble this last little while sake of construction outside that mess up the connections. We complain but it hasn't done much good up to now. I'm sorry Gramps is gone, but I'm not devastated. When I think of him and "water come a my yeye" like the song says, I swear I can feel him behind me, hand on my shoulder, saying, "Death is the end of life, Gracie. That's how it is, and I can't say that I'm not grateful, for the world is a mighty trying place."

Then I hear him chuckle, and I laugh too, and I see him putting infusions into white rum, and I smell them, and I smell him, his jackass rope, the coffee that he brew for us on Sunday morning, and the wet earth when he come to the door with mud on his shoes from his cultivation. I'm not saying it don't hurt plenty to know that I won't see him again, but it's as if I can call to him, as if he hasn't gone far.

Steph says I can ask the priest to say a Mass for him, and that seem like a good idea. I don't go to Beloved so much these days, for it come easier to follow Steph to Thomas Aquinas, which is the university church, and the Catholics have those things organized. Edris's grandaunt and Ma's parson at Evangel would be alarmed if they knew that I even light a candle now and then. I know you won't be upset, Ma, for you always had your own ideas about those things. I like to think of that flame flickering when I'm no longer there, keeping my prayer going.

I hope you and Pa are keeping well, especially after the stress of Gramps funeral. Please take care of yourselves. Hope Edgar, Stewie, Conrad, Sam, and Princess are doing okay too, and Pansy and Mortimer and their babies. Also please say hi to Mr. Wong for me, and to the Williamses. I'm rushing as usual but promise to write soon again.

Much love,
Grace

She loves Gramps, but she's still furious with him. Brooding through her library job and an extra stats course during the summer, she sometimes wondered why he never gave her Phyllis's letters earlier, sometimes why he gave them to her at all. She is not to blame for any of this mess. Why should she have to fix it? But it is clearly up to her, for it seems like this other mother has no clue where she is or what she's doing. So what ought she to do? Phone her and say, "Hello. This is your abandoned daughter, Grace"? Humph, as the comics say. And why has the word "abandoned" come into her mind? She never felt that way growing up — different, yes, but not neglected. It surprises her at first, but after a while she perceives how accurate it is. Dumped — by Phyllis, Daphne, Evadne, Gramps. And of course, Papa God.

26

Grace Meets Phyllis

Annesley Hall,
95 Queen's Park Crescent,
Toronto, Ontario,
Canada, M5S 2C7
8 September 1979

Dear Phyllis,

I don't trust myself to phone yet, though that was the first thing that occurred to me. I hope you understand. It's taken me long enough to get around to putting pen to paper. I also hope you don't mind my calling you "Phyllis." I fretted for a while about what would be the right thing and then gave up. I don't mean any disrespect when I use your first name. My roommate calls her parents by their first names, and she respects and gets on well with them. I couldn't write "Mother" or "Ma." It's Ma Carpenter who's been that all my life.

Gramps, bless his memory, said he would let you know that he'd given me the letters, and that you needn't write anymore, because we could now be in touch and talk, person to person. He never mentioned his writing in response to any of those letters, nor any other communication with you. He did say he and Miss Evadne kept in touch, but I guess it wouldn't have suited their purposes to mention me to you. I don't suppose you have any idea of what I look like either, so I've included a photo of the skinny, freckled, red girl who is your daughter. That way you will know what to expect, if ever we meet.

I think it's better to talk by letter first, for I am still unsettled by all these things, not to mention Gramps's passing. It's been a lot for me to take in at one time.

Right now I am beginning my final year at the University of Toronto, having spent much of the summer in the same library job I've had for a couple of years now. I am working towards a degree in economics with some sociology and a bit of psych on the side. So far, I'm doing pretty well. I don't have much of a social life, and though I found a church that I like, haven't been going regularly. I tell you this up front because it is plain that you are religious. I live in the dorm and have a white Canadian roommate named Stephanie Scott with whom I get along very well. She is a Catholic and I sometimes go to church with her, so at least my most immediate influence is a good one.

I am curious about your day-to-day life. Where exactly do you live? I don't know much about New York, so your address doesn't tell me anything. I read about a convent in your letters and assume that you still work there. What is your job now?

Why didn't you leave the convent as soon as your schooling was over? Surely you must have been dying to get away from that atmosphere and those memories? What about my grandmother, Daphne? And my great-grandmother, Miss Evadne?

I look forward to hearing from you. Please take care.

Sincerely,
Grace Carpenter

She can do no better. She thinks about whether to add the "Carpenter," for Phyllis is her blood mother, after all, and in a way it is not kind to add her surname, but she decides she's going to do it. She's going to stand firm in her displeasure. If anyone is to blame for her abandonment, it is Gramps, he and Miss Evadne. She can bet he was the one giving Miss Evadne advice, concocting her life like one of his infusions. Her birth mother is least to blame, and everybody had the best intentions, she's quite sure. But, sake of them, there is now, and has always been, all these crosses in her life.

She can't dwell on it. She has work to do.

23 September 1979

My dear Grace,
I was so happy to get your letter. I could hardly believe what it was that I held in my hands! I've been trying to behave in a composed fashion ever since, but without much success. I long to talk to you and to meet you! However, I respect your position. We can write letters for as long as you wish. Still, I'd be glad if you would let me know when you decide that it would be all right for me to call you.

Forgive me. I should have started by saying how sorry I was to hear about old Mr. Carpenter's passing. Please accept our sympathies and prayers. We know you will all miss him very much.

As for what to call me, I am perfectly happy with Phyllis. I am old-fashioned in a lot of ways, but it would be silly of me to expect you to relate to me as your mother — not at this point, anyway. By the way, I think you have a wonderful name. I hope you like it. I have never been especially happy with mine. They say it means leafy or green bough. I don't know how leafy I am, and if I am a bough, I grow more dry and brittle every day.

Congratulations on your success at school. Those are not areas about which I know much, though I enjoy reading popular articles on economics and even a little layman's psychology. These days we all need to understand how the world works, as well as what makes people tick. What kind of career do you plan? Of course, it's early days yet, so you may not have decided. Thank God you have a roommate whom you like! When that is not the case, it can be horrible.

As for your questions: I live in an apartment in a charming old building at the corner of Riverside Drive and 114th Street in Manhattan. Riverside Drive runs along the west side of Manhattan Island, close to the Hudson River. It is the apartment that we lived in with your Grandma Daphne, and that your great-grandma and I have continued to live in since Daphne married and went to live with her husband and his family in New Jersey. I haven't told her that I've heard from you yet. I thought it might be wise to wait a little. She's a young woman,

*just fifty-two, very smart and determined. She and
her husband have set up a beauty business and are
doing very well.*

*I still work at the convent. The nuns were
good to me from the beginning, and they operate
a miraculous institution. They are mostly bright,
talented women who love life and enjoy giving
service, and they have an excellent program. I
have no desire to leave. I have a good job: I am
responsible for managing the kindergarten and child-
care centre. I've always loved the babies, and that
is where I did practical training when I first came.*

*Last but not least, thank you for the photo. I am
indeed glad to know what you look like! I won't go
on any longer, and you mustn't feel obliged to reply
at length. I'll be happy just to hear back from you.*

*With love,
Phyllis*

Having read the letter, she plunges into the dark of the covers.
No mind the pills she'd taken, her head feels like an anvil in
a busy smithy. True, Phyllis hasn't acquitted herself badly in
the letter, but her resentment still sputters, refusing to be put
out. Whatever fear, confusion, and isolation she's ever felt, she
now puts down to what they'd done, the lot of them. While
everybody else is living life, she's been scrutinizing herself,
assessing, deciding she wasn't good enough, and then setting
herself some giant task to prove she was not only good enough,
but better than everybody else. More than once she decides
that the migraines are a way to punish herself, inflict pain as a
reminder of her sentence to perfection.

She'd been out earlier to see Carlos, Sylvia's baby, a wonder
child, to hear Maisie tell it. They are relocating to Calgary at

month end and not planning to be back for three years, by which time she'll have moved on, where she has no idea. In all likelihood, she'll never see them again.

———

It's October twenty-first, a Sunday, and twenty-four degrees Celsius outside, some kind of record, according to the news. Rugs of leaves in love-bush colours curl over themselves. From a payphone near a window upstairs in Robarts Library, Grace looks at people scooting about on bicycles and on foot, in shorts and T-shirts. Lord! It's not that hot! Still, better a bright, warm day to do what she is about to do. After hours of debating about whether, when and how soon to call her birth mother, she has decided the phone conversation is inevitable and so better done sooner than later.

"May I speak to Phyllis, please?"

"This is she. To whom am I speaking?"

"It's Grace. Grace Carpenter."

"Grace? Grace! Can you hold one minute, please?"

"Yes, of course."

A few seconds' silence during which Grace recalls Phyllis's letter in response to hers, a kind of proper, stiff writing, nothing as simple and forthright as the letters she'd written to her as a teenager.

"Sorry, just closing the door. Are you all right? Is everything okay?"

"I'm fine. Everything's fine, thanks. I was just calling to touch base ... finally ... I'm ... I'm sure you must have heard that Gramps, old Mr. Carpenter, passed away last month?" It's the first thing that comes to mind, and a stupid thing, for of course Phyllis knows. She'd sent condolences in her letter.

"We do know. Someone sent a telegram to Granny Vads, a man named Mr. Hector. But thanks for making sure. How are you?"

"Like I said, things are fine. Not easy, but that's nothing new. I'm sure you know how it is."

"How is the weather, Grace? It doesn't seem too cold yet."

"It's colder here than in New York." Small talk, white people talk. Safe.

"Since you wrote, I glance at the Toronto weather too."

"I'm now accustomed to it, more or less. I don't really think I'm ever going to like it. Gramps says ..." Grace stops, remembering there's no more Gramps. "Gramps gave me advice about staying warm, from when he was in the war. I have good boots and I make sure to wear something on my head."

And, she recalls absurdly, a stolen green plant in my room.

"Do, take his advice, dear. I still hate all the clothes, but every time I cheat, I regret it. Garlic and white rum and honey take me through every winter."

Grace takes comfort from the mention of the white rum. She wonders what Phyllis would say if she knew that, though white rum may be hard to find, there's plenty of ganja in her dorm. She thinks, *Why not?* "Garlic is easy to find, but white rum would be a different thing. There are other herbs I could put my hand on easy, though."

"That mayn't be worth the risk!" A chuckle. "Of course, your Granny Evadne still swears by Mr. Carpenter's infusions."

"I was there. I saw him make them, and give them to people and treat himself with them. I can tell you for sure that they work."

"I still think you'd better not try any remedies of that kind. Not till you finish and get the white people's piece of paper."

The two of them laugh.

"You know what you're doing for Christmas, Grace?"

"Well ... not yet."

"No pressure. Just asking. You could come here if you want. Granny Vads and I can offer a rollaway bed and of course some good St. Chris food."

The cooking tempts her, but Grace thinks, Don't spoil things by rushing them. So far, so good! "Thank you, but I don't know yet. I might have to stay here and study. The last couple Christmases I spent at my roommate's house, and I can go there again if I want. I usually don't decide till the last minute."

"No pressure at all, Grace."

"I have to go now. I have a class."

"Thanks for calling. Call again whenever you like, and reverse the charges next time. Okay?"

"Okay." Grace appreciates her offer. She doesn't have a lot of spending money. "Thanks a lot. Bye."

———

It's just as well things happen the way they happen. Since the first phone call, she and Phyllis talk on the phone a couple times and write letters now and then. So when Phyllis calls the Scotts on Christmas Day to wish her Happy Christmas and say that she just now found out she has to come to Toronto for a meeting right after Christmas and is wondering if she could spend the evening of the twenty-seventh with her, Grace isn't sure what to do. She feels she shouldn't say no, especially as it is Christmastime, the season of goodwill and all that. However, according to plans, they are supposed to stay in Warsaw till the thirtieth, then go back to Toronto to meet Gilberto, Steph's boyfriend, who is coming back from LA so the two of them can go out on New Year's Eve.

After three Christmases, Grace and the Scotts are good friends. She spends a few days there during the year too. They are down-to-earth people. If you factor out house, car, and middle-class comforts — ha-ha — they are not so different from her family. Gramps would say they have class; Ma and Pa, brought-up-cy. She feels kin with Andrew Scott, Bruce, and Susie, maybe sake of their red hair, freckles, and red skin. Not that her red and their red is the same, but still. Mr. Scott puts her in mind of Pa, not saying much but always there, so you feel he will fix anything that needs fixing.

Phyllis says Grace must consider and let her know. When Grace tells Steph why she may have to go back to Toronto on the twenty-seventh, Steph spins out of the room and rattles downstairs. "Alicia, can Grace's mother stay with us? She's coming to Toronto on the twenty-seventh and wants to see Grace."

"Heavens! Is she coming from St. Chris into this cold?"

"No, Ma. Not that mother; her New York mother. She's coming to Toronto for a meeting after Christmas."

"If you two sleep in the study, she can have your room."

"That's what I was thinking."

"And if she takes the three o'clock bus, she can be here by five."

"Cousin Albert, Alicia! She can get a ride with him."

So Phyllis is coming to the Scotts, where they will meet each other for the first time. In a way, she's glad that somebody else decides. She is still put out by this whole two-mother business.

———

Three days after Christmas, at a quarter to six, Albert's BMW stops in front of the square brick farmhouse. He hops out, scoots round to the passenger side, and opens the door. A tall, slim woman steps out, wearing a long, fur-trimmed black suede coat, leather boots, and gloves. Over her shoulder is a commodious bag made of tie-dyed African cloth, its purples, blacks, greens, and reds a little faded. Her head sports a low Afro of feathery reddish hair. She smiles thanks at Albert, looks around, observes Grace, and makes straight for her. Grace sees puss eyes, red skin, a face freckled on cheeks and nose. A "fine" nose.

Phyllis doesn't give her a hug, for which she is grateful. She'd decided it would be hypocritical to run into the arms of a person she's never seen before. Instead her mother takes both her hands, leans back, looks at her face for a long while, then says, "May I kiss you?" Grace nods and awkwardly offers a cheek.

Alicia Scott slides up, introduces herself, Andrew, Steph, Bruce, and Susie, tells Bruce to take Phyllis's suitcase upstairs, ushers her inside, takes her things, sits her down by the fireplace, offers everyone drinks, and asks about the ride down.

"As usual, I drove too fast, Alicia," a grin splits Albert's face.

"Phyllis, I'm sorry if he flew at his usual speed. Albert, please apologize."

"No need. I like going fast," Phyllis smiles at her chauffeur.

"You look exactly like her!" Stephanie shrieks when she and Grace go into the kitchen to fix snacks.

"No, sir!"

"Don't be daft. It's like she spat you out."

Well, it may be she's spat out where looks are concerned, but Grace is sure the similarity ends there. Thank God Phyllis doesn't seek her out or try to be chummy. She talks quietly. Her laughter is genuine, but restrained, her clothes nice but Grace sees neat patches on purse and scarf. Though she doesn't seem to say much, by next day they know she plays the flute well, drums and piano a bit, likes classical music, has a vinyl collection of classics in ska, reggae, calypso, and Chrissie tambu, likes long walks, sews, embroiders, and knits, in addition to her work running the children's centre at the convent.

Grace doesn't know if she likes her or not.

When Alicia Scott says, "You must be very proud of Grace," Phyllis responds, "I am." When Andrew says, "She's a great credit to you," Phyllis replies, "Sadly, I had little to do with it." When Steph declares, "You two are like peas in a pod! Grace can't have inherited much from her dad!" Phyllis studies her hands.

27

Letters and More Letters

4 January 1980

My dear Grace,

I won't try to tell you what it was like to see you. Only to say that God is good, and his grace truly amazing! I am so proud of you! Mr. and Mrs. Carpenter and Gramps were clearly God-ordained. I knew, never mind how much I missed you all those years, that they had a home and family, brothers and sisters to give you, none of which I had. I have given God thanks for them, every day, and those thanks I now repeat many times over.

Of course, I realized when I came back how foolish I'd been! I'd brought my camera, for I'd faithfully promised Daphne and Granny Vads pictures. I couldn't believe that I'd left without taking a single one! Perhaps you'd be good enough to ask Stephanie if she would let me have copies of the ones we took on the steps? I would be very grateful.

I am back at work, stealing a little time to write. It's always a challenge starting a new year. Some of our mothers are lucky enough to have somewhere to go with their babies at Christmas — to their relatives, or to families who volunteer to share Christmas, or to the homes of the fathers of their babies, one or two, that is. We work hard with the fathers if they are around. We try here, make a big effort, but there is no hiding that this is an institution.

I must go. Have a good semester and please write when you can.

With much love,
Phyllis

P.S. Granny Vads and I would welcome a visit during March break, if you'd like, and I will underwrite the bus fare. She's not so well, and it would cheer her up greatly to see you.

4 February 1980

Dear Phyllis,
I am sorry it has taken me so long to reply to your letter, which got here quickly. I think it only took two days. My excuse as always is work and more work. I am truly grateful I'm not one of your young mothers! Starting the year is hard enough with me alone. If I had a baby, I don't know what I would do!

I was pleased to finally meet you too. Of course, I didn't spend years and years imagining what you looked like, since I didn't know you were there at all. But I have wondered one or two things since Gramps gave me your letters. I've wondered if I resembled you, and sounded like you, and what other things we might have in common. Stephanie says I look like you "spat me out," so I guess that's one query satisfied. I've decided we do have one thing in common. You must have been very determined to keep writing those letters, and Gramps was always saying he was going to crown me Miss Determination. The first time I remember him saying it is when I was trying to teach myself how to blow a conch shell. I must have been five or six!

My life in Wentley Park seems so far away now, like another life, never mind I left not very long ago.

Thanks a lot for the invitation to visit you in New York and the offer to pay my bus fare. I can't afford to go away for reading week. I have so much studying to do at that time, and after that I must keep my head in the books until finals. I promise to keep in touch, though. Please say hello for me to Grandma Daphne and Granny Vads. Perhaps I can finally meet them in the summer.

Must go. Till next time,
Grace

12 April 1980

Dear Gracie,
Nothing I would love more than to see you walk up and get that cerfiticate but we cant make it for money tight and we have to try to use it the best way. We save what we can ever since you leave, but is that money bring you home so you could see Gramps before he pass and since that time things continue tough same way. Mark you I am thankful we are in the rural and not town where people fighting the whole time for sugar, rice, and flour

what a pass things come to when country people better off than town people. God have a way to run his jokes sometimes never mind that this is no time for joking but when you is God you could make joke as you wish and we are lucky that he laugh and distract himself for if he look hard down here he get so vex that this time he swallow the whole island for it plenty more sinful than the wicked Port Royal city in Jamaica that he so long ago send earthquake to swallow up under the sea. You never say if you get the letter Princess write to say thanks for the book of poems by the Red Indian young people. She read them out loud for us the ones she like. She and Edgar like pomes and the two of them make up some together when he come to visit us.

All of we send love sorry to take you away from your studies to read this please write when able Mister Wong ask for you every time I go to shop he say to tell you to walk good and take care

God bless,
Ma

27 April 1980

Dear Ma, and Pa,

I well understand why nobody can come to graduation. I will miss you and Pa. Don't worry, though. I know you will be thinking of me and the Scotts promise to take plenty photos. I will make sure to send.

Phyllis thinks she can come, so I will have family present. She and I get along pretty well though it is still strange for me. Ma is the mother I grow with, the mother I know and love with all my heart. Also

Phyllis is so close to my age. Since her Christmas visit, we talk on the phone and write, so we are getting to know each other better. She says if I want, I can come back to New York with her after graduation and stay there for a while before I begin my studies at University of Michigan. That way, I can meet Daphne and Granny Evadne. Only thing is Granny Evadne is suffering badly with rheumatoid arthritis. If Phyllis has her hands full, I won't burden her further, so I'm still considering. Of course, if I go, I will help all I can.

Phyllis says I must know I am smart for I've done so well at U of T and so many universities have offered me fellowships for graduate work. I think I'm fortunate. If I know to work hard, it's because you, Pa, and Gramps have given me such good example, so I am saying a big THANK YOU and I promise to keep trying.

How are Pansy and Mortimer and the children? And Edgar? Is he still at Miss Carmen's? And Stewie, Conrad and Princess? I pray Pa continues strong and the two of you are keeping your pressure under control. Salt beef and pig tail not worth dying for!

I send love and hello for all, esp. Mr. Wong and the Williamses.

Grace

28

A Graduation Fuss

"I can't take this, Phyllis. I wouldn't feel right."

"Why not?"

"A thousand dollars is a lot of money."

"It's yours, Grace."

"Not if I don't take it."

"It's yours whether or not you take it. It's been in a bank account with your name on it for years."

"There's plenty things you could use it for."

"That's true. But you've read my letters; you know when I opened that account. I put in a few dollars a week, whatever I could. There's still money in it. I'll keep putting in what I can, for as long as I can."

"I don't need it. I've managed. I can still manage."

"It has nothing to do with whether you can manage or not. How could it? I didn't know where you were, what you were doing, anything. I just put the money in, probably more for my sake than yours."

"Please don't get upset. It's the end of a long day, a day that's supposed to be a happy day …"

"Can't you see it as part of the celebration, my contribution?"

" … and it is late and everybody is tired. And is somebody else's house."

"Grace, I fully appreciate that this isn't my home or yours. I wouldn't think of causing any kind of upset. But I've looked forward to this for years, thought about a moment like this every time I got a pay cheque."

"Look, I'm really glad you could come, that somebody from my country, of my race, and my family was here to see me graduate. That's plenty. You don't need to do any more. You certainly don't need to give me money."

"I need you to have it for the same reason I needed to deposit those few dollars week after week."

"Okay, fine. I accept. Thanks. Argument now over."

"Is that how you talk to your mother?"

"You are not my mother."

"I am your mother, like it or not."

"Blood is not everything."

"Blood is plenty. Didn't you say just now that having family around you today made a big difference?"

"That's not the same thing."

"Same thing or not, you can take my word about the blood business. Some African cultures have a concept of spiritual blood, something that's passed down through generations and contains the memory, history, and wisdom of the tribe."

"Nobody use the word 'tribe' anymore."

"What kind of work you say you studying to do?"

"Development planning, something of that order."

"Perhaps you should think some more about it. Those jobs need empathy, imagination. But we can speak about that another time. Good night."

Grace was fixing up a cut-eye but she stopped herself, said a muted "Night," put the cheque on the hall table and went to join Steph in the study.

———

That afternoon after the convocation ceremony they'd opened a bottle of champagne outside the hall, toasted Grace and Steph, and then headed back to Warsaw for the real celebrations. She and Phyllis were dozy and didn't say much on the drive down with Albert. When they got to the farmhouse, they cooked a St. Chris dinner: codfish balls with hot sauce, pumpkin soup, roast pork, rice and peas, roast plantain, boiled breadfruit, and a salad of avocado pear and greens. Andrew made coconut ice cream for dessert.

It had been a happy day till Phyllis produced the cheque!

The whole incident confuses her, not least because of her vehement reaction. She can't understand why Phyllis would give her money: a card, yes, or a present, but money? And her response was so bizarre! Phyllis hadn't done anything to her, after all. But she is exhausted and sleeps like a bear, despite the kerfuffle. The summer sun wakes her early. Grace dresses, pulling on a sweater, for in Warsaw it's still cool in the mornings, and runs downstairs just in time to see Phyllis, one arm bandaged wrist to elbow, getting into Albert's BMW. She pelts out onto the porch, halting beside Alicia who is waving goodbye. She lifts a hand to wave, but the car has gone.

Alicia turns inside to the business of the day just as Stephanie tumbles out onto the steps and begins dragging Grace down into the yard.

"What's wrong with you, Steph? Where you hauling me to?"

They are on a path leading downhill into a grove of young birches, funny, spindly white creatures with tiers of notched knees on shifting, slender legs.

"You had a fight with your mother last night?" Steph is whispering.

"What?" Grace is dazed in the morning's blue chill. "Why are you whispering?"

"Me aksin you if you fight with your Mumma las night? And don't bother tell me is not mi business, like how her hand bandage up and all!"

"You think we had a fight, and I hurt my mother's hand? Are you nuts? If nothing else, I'm too well brought up to fight in someone else's house!"

"Me just love how you talk posh when you vex!"

"I do not love *your* fumbling attempts at Creole."

"You get up really mean this morning. The bed was so uncomfortable?"

"I apologize, Steph. Yes, we had a fuss, my Mum and me. And your Creole is excellent."

"You hear yourself, Grace?"

"What? What did I say?"

"You call Phyllis 'Mum'!"

"If you say so. But how did she hurt her hand? It looked bad!"

"If you promise to stop being nasty." Steph affects hurt.

"Okay. No more nasty."

"Three o'clock this morning, there's a crash in the kitchen and a little scream. My mother, who sleeps like a puss, runs down the stairs to find Phyllis standing in a steaming puddle of cocoa, crying, one hand under the tap."

"Lord have mercy! Just because I didn't want to take the cheque?"

"She never say anything about a cheque, but she spill her guts to Alicia."

"Phyllis spilled her guts?"

"You talk as if Phyllis is some kind of ice queen. She's in bad shape. That's why she dropped the cocoa and burned herself. The burn wasn't too serious, though."

"Well, praise God for that. But I can't see Phyllis falling apart, especially if it wasn't about the cheque."

"Like Mumma, like pikni. You're a pretty tough cookie, yourself. People always spill to my mother. I have to be careful around her, or she'll have me confessing every last thing. Anyway, seems your Granny Vads is so ill that looking after her has become a big trial. Her sickness makes her mean, and Phyllis is having a tough time. Plus, something she said led Alicia to believe you two had a disagreement yesterday."

"But Phyllis never said a word to me about Granny Vads."

"Apparently, your grandma who is looking after your great-grandma while Phyllis is away — Grandma Daphne, right? — is willing to stay longer, but Daphne's husband is raising a ruckus about her leaving his children."

"Hang on a minute." The only way Steph can know this is if Alicia repeated it to her. That doesn't seem like Alicia. "Your mother told you this?"

"Did I say that ..."

"How else could you know?"

"My mother's not the only person that sleeps like a puss."

"You listened?"

"Thought you might like to be up to date."

Christ! A mother she doesn't need causing trouble the second time they meet by proffering an extravagant and uncalled-for gift of money she certainly can use herself. So she's to feel bad about her mean response, and about her parent disrupting the household, keeping people awake, injuring herself — and God Almighty knows what else?

It isn't fair. Papa God is on her back again, like Old Higue.

29

A Letter of Apology

Scotts' Farmhouse
Warsaw
2 June 1980

Dear Phyllis,
Thanks, belatedly, for your card and for the cheque.
I'm so very ashamed. If I were you, I'd not have
had anything to say to a bad-minded child whom
I'd kept faith with for twenty years, tried to get to
know when the time came, and presented with a
gift I'd been planning for ages, whose response was
as callous as mine.

Steph keeps harping on how much I look like you.
I love the Carpenters dearly. They're the only family
I've ever known, but one had only to look at them,
good strong black folks, and look at fine-featured,
puss-eye, wispy-hair, red me, to know I wasn't a
Carpenter by blood. And here you were, obviously
my kin, and someone who cared about me. I can't
think of one other soul who would have kept writing

letters for eighteen years to a person she'd known for
two months and hadn't seen even a photograph of.
It's a sour child, I fear. And who am I to blame for
the acid that repeats into my soul, spoiling the taste
of everything? Not Gramps, the best grandfather
anyone could hope for, nor Ma and Pa, who are
perfect parents, nor Edgar, Stewie, and Conrad,
nor Sam and Princess — not even Pansy, who's
been horrid sometimes, but who I know loves me.

I can't bleat about white racism either. It's not
like there wasn't any in St. Chris. I went to St.
Chad's after all — as good a preparation for living
in the North as any. And I've made good friends
here: Steph, the Scotts, Maisie, who popped up out
of nowhere. God I can blame, maybe. I can't go on.
It seems as usual to be all about me. I know you
burned your hand because you were upset. I hope it's
better now and that you'll call. I won't bother you by
phoning first, what with all you must be dealing with,
sake of Granny Vads illness. I hope she's improving.
Please take care. Look forward to talking soon.

Grace

Steph feels like getting out of the house so they drive to
Lakefield to post the letter.

30

Death and Disappearance

The staging area is stuffed with boxes and parcels, everything labelled "Ann Arbor." Steph says she will mail them. God bless Steph!

The fuss with Phyllis still has her knotted up. Did insolence arrive from nowhere and just take charge of her mouth? Or was it a spontaneous blossoming of deep resentment at abandonment as a baby? In a way she feels like a hypocrite for telling Phyllis that if she's sour, she has only herself to blame. Given the circumstances, which respectable psychology book would buy that? Didn't Gramps have a part, Miss Evadne, all the bad-minded Wentley people? Not to mention the professional tormentors at St. Chad and vile Fillmore Buxton!

She looks up from addressing another box, sees her BA "cerfiticate" in pride of place on the chipped mantelpiece, and permits herself to feel proud, just for a moment. Over the weeks, she's done plenty considering, finally deciding there's nothing wrong with being satisfied that she's done a good job of studying her books. She's also decided it's okay to enjoy telling people who ask that she's going to Rackham, a great grad school, on a fellowship. She's mostly silent on the many other offers, though.

Now and then a rude little demon with a Christophian voice encourages bad behaviour. "Why you never just tell Phyllis where to take the cheque and stuff it? If you was vex with her, why you never say, 'You leave me as a baby. Don't come now with your big-money present and your "Please may I be your mummy?" Far too little, lady, and much too late!' That would at least be honest."

Steph says she is a pretty tough cookie. Since when? Had her brothers and baby sister loved a tough cookie all this time? Gramps? Pa? Ma? So she fooled them, all but Pansy? Above all, she fooled herself?

She finds a letter from New York that night in her mailbox. It's forwarded from Warsaw, only thing is the return address is not the apartment at Riverside.

> *Religious Sisters of the Heart of Jesus*
> *Our Lady of Good Hope Convent*
> *New York, NY 45678*
> *9 June 1980*

Dear Grace,

Thanks for your letter, which came quite quickly. Please forgive this brief response, but you'll understand shortly. I won't pretend I wasn't distressed at your reaction when I gave you the cheque, but we're still getting to know each other, and there will be misunderstandings. Apologizing must have been hard, and I appreciate the effort. So we'll just put it behind us. I'm writing from work. I didn't have a chance to fill you in properly, but Granny Vads has been quite ill and took a turn for the worse the day after I came back. I'm glad she waited till then because Daphne had a hard enough time while I was away. Yesterday, she was so bad I had to call 911. They took her to St. Clare's, where she is now. I'm staying here at the convent, since it's close by. Say a prayer for her please. I don't think she has long for this world. I'm sorry you didn't have a chance to meet, but heaven waits. I know you weren't going back to your old apartment, and we were all so topsy-turvy when I left that I didn't have a chance to get the address in Toronto where you are now. I'm hoping this will reach you at the Scotts before you leave. If not, I know Alicia or Stephanie will forward it.

With love,
Phyllis

On 15 June, Grace scribbles a reply to say she's leaving early the next morning, Monday, and that she will stay in the dorms at the University of Michigan to start with, but she will call Phyllis as soon as she knows her permanent address and phone number. She contemplates it, but decides she's not going to sign "Your daughter."

Next day, the plane does the boogie from the time it climbs up over Toronto until the moment it lands in Detroit. It's rainy in Michigan in June, so she makes sure she has pills — migraine headaches don't love rain. When the aircraft slides into Detroit Metropolitan Airport on a beam of brilliant sunlight and she sees green and more green below, she loves the place.

On Tuesday morning as she threads her way from Couzens Hall across East Huron to the office at Rackham, she walks past groups of students talking, laughing, romping, flinging Frisbees in Felch Park. She is struck by their energy, a kind of effervescence that she doesn't recall at U of T. While she is getting things straight in the office, acquainting herself with the social contours, as Gramps had a way to say, a young woman waves a letter at her from across the room. "I think this is for you. Grace Patterson, don't it?" Grace smiles at the "don't it?" A countrywoman! Try as it may, American overlay can't hide St. Chris underpinning.

Odd. The letter is from a Sister Mary Agnes at the convent where Phyllis works. She pockets it, as she now almost always does, for later perusal. Sitting on her bed in the dorm after lunch, she reads.

> *Religious Sisters of the Heart of Jesus*
> *Our Lady of Good Hope Convent*
> *New York, NY 45678*
> *21 June 1980*

Dear Grace,

Please accept our congratulations on your wonderful achievements at university, which Phyllis told us about so proudly when she came back from your graduation! Bravo!

My name is Sister Mary Agnes and I am in charge of the institution to which your mother came twenty years ago, just after you were born. We've never met you, but one advantage of trying to live in eternity, is that you don't have to meet people in the flesh to know and love them. The community here prays for the babies that we have had the privilege to nurture, and for all our mothers and all their babies, so we remember you each day, as Phyllis's daughter.

I'm writing on behalf of Phyllis, whom we all love very much. She is as formidable and blessed a spirit as ever God made, which is one reason we asked her to stay and work with us. She is gifted in many ways and generous to a fault, gentle in her manner and yet tough as nails in her determination.

In all, she has been a wonderful example to the young women who come here. Nor is this anything we have taught her; she was ever so.

On Monday last, your Grandma Vads died. As you know, she had been seriously ill for a while. Caring for her was taxing for Phyllis, who has always been her primary caregiver, the biggest difficulty being that in the course of her illness, Miss Evadne not only became mean, ill tempered and given to rages, but she directed her hostility at Phyllis. We know from nursing our old sisters that this can happen with some illnesses, rheumatoid arthritis being one.

The service for Mrs. Patterson was held this morning at Riverside Methodist Church, but Phyllis agreed to have the wake here since, among other things, many of those going to the funeral would be coming from the convent. Given what she had been through, it is perhaps not surprising that your mother collapsed at the wake. Luckily, Sister Mary Immaculate, our resident doctor, was here. Sister confirmed that Phyllis had had a stroke and she was taken immediately to hospital. Regrettably, the stroke has left her paralyzed on her right side. Her speech, thought processes, and memory are also impaired — exactly how severely, we are not quite sure.

Once out of hospital, Phyllis will need to go to a facility able to provide the necessary care, support, and expertise to help her regain as much of her normal functioning as possible. There is no predicting rate or extent of recovery from a stroke, but complete or almost complete recuperation is possible. Our sisters run a wonderful place called

Mary's Haven in Cohasset. It provides services
such as these. We have consulted your Grandma
Daphne, and she agreed that Phyllis should go there.

Please join us in praying for her full recovery.
We continue to ask God to be gracious to you, and
guide you in your decisions. Feel free to call me at
the number above. The sisters join me in sending
our love, and our condolences on the passing of
your great-grandmother.

Yours in the Heart of Jesus,
Sister Mary Agnes, R.S.H.J.

Mercifully she is in her room when she reads all this, so she
alone hears herself muttering and mewling. Not a doubt that it
is her fault that Phyllis is now in the grip of a crippling stroke,
for never mind Granny Vads bad treatment, Phyllis was fine at
the Scotts. So clever, Papa God! So creative! Your Almighty
Big Brain would know messing with Phyllis is the best way
to punish me. As if the whole graduation ruckus wasn't still
rankling, wrecking the excitement of a new place to live and
study, and new people to get to know. Why had she never asked
Gramps to hook her up with his Zeke-It's-Okay-to-Grow-a-Likl-
Ganja-God before he died? That God existed. He and Gramps
were good friends.

"Good tings come from bad, Gracie. Have a likl faith and
look for the good tings." Not Gramps this time but Pa, wiggling
the stumps of his fingers. She admits to missing Ma, Pa, her
siblings. She longs to talk to Gramps, ask his advice. After all,
he helped make the trouble! He could help remedy it! Most
incongruous of all is that she should feel so concerned about
this woman whom she doesn't know especially well, only two
weeks after the horrid exchange in Warsaw. But it's her fault!
She must feel concerned!

Steph used to say people invoking Oscar Wilde's witticism, "All women become like their mothers" forget the last part: "That is their tragedy." This time, it's the other way around, with her mother becoming like her. And the case *is* tragic, if she, Grace, is the daughter Phyllis is turning into! Papa God is clearly amusing himself with this ludicrous reversal of situations: now she'll be writing Phyllis letters that Phyllis won't read! Farcical as well that in Mary's Haven in Cohasset, Phyllis could as well be a baby, if she is to believe the nun's letter. Still, she is plenty better off than Phyllis had been, painfully inscribing teenage thoughts on blue air letter forms and sending them off to a child who would not read them until she was beyond the age when they might have sweetened her nature.

At least Granny Vads, mean-tempered, ill, and in pain is, hopefully, in a better place, though she might have chosen another day to die. Truly, jackass is right when he says "the world not level"! She considers, decides that she'll think of it in a positive way: both she and Granny Vads embarked on a new adventure on Monday!

So what ought she to do about Phyllis *this* time? Repent? She's done that already. Visit Phyllis? She's just reached Ann Arbor and she has neither the money nor the time, given her obligations. Write? She's already decided she will do that. And she will phone of course, Sister Mary Agnes, and the place in Cohasset, if it doesn't cost too much, although she doubts that she will be able to talk to her mother.

All the same, she's sick of being nailed to the Ten Times Ten Commandments. Ann Arbor is a whole new experience waiting. She'd decided that maybe this time she can enjoy it, instead of quaking in terror and hiding in books. Hard work isn't toddling off anywhere soon, but she's not afraid of that. And the whole thing with Phyllis isn't going away either. But maybe the reason she is mean, sour, and desperate is that all she does besides work is flagellate herself.

"Wise man say no point in studying God. Man to study himself" was Gramps's sage counsel. Till the showdown with Phyllis, and Steph's averring that she is a tough cookie, she'd figured on being a pretty decent person. But whoever she is, that person is going to have to do. She will tread light, make sure to watch her mouth, not say or do or plan to do any crazy things, especially since there is no Steph, or Scott family, or Maisie here to rescue her.

A diary. She will keep a diary. She writes down a to-do list every day so as to keep track of work. Fill out the lists a bit, and that can easily be a diary. Pick out the bits and pieces Phyllis will like, and that will make up her weekly letter. Matter of fact, she can use the diary to write a newsletter, and send it to everybody, not just Phyllis, but Ma and Pa, the boys, Steph, Maisie, Daphne, even Pansy and Mortimer. She knows it's a good idea when she hears Gramps chuckling. "If they all get the same letter, everybody would vex. If it name 'newsletter,' that is a whole different matter!"

Church is the next thing. She has to find a church. She knows things would not have turned out so badly if she hadn't given up on Beloved in Toronto. She will ask someone, maybe the St. Chris young woman in the office at Rackham. She has no family nearby, not even distant kin, and she feels as if a load of rockstone has just buried her. All she can think of is the St. Chris remedy — taking it to the Lord, which means church.

The big stained glass window in the Museum of Archaeology stops her like a splash of ice water in the face on the first Saturday. No glass window she has seen anywhere looks like it. At first she sees only a shedding of soft tones, a gentle splashing of well-behaved hues playing into the room. When she steps forward to focus, she sees a royal purple frill outlining a huge arch and running all the way down the two sides and across the bottom of a large, long window. Inside the frill is another border that resembles accordion pleats of thin brown louvres, or dark popsicle sticks ranged side by side. A vine bearing bright, round emerald leaves, or maybe fruit, each in a curled lilac nest, winds its way close to these edges. Some old, overripe balls of Seville oranges, greenish, dirty yellow, brown-and-gold, looking as though they are spoiling or spoiled, roll around in a bold blue circle at the top, and run down in two lines that lead from the blue circle above to the bottom. Everything lands in a leafy design below. Scrutinized, it's not so pretty, but altogether the colours and the design bloom soft rays on everything.

She can't stop gazing the day she finds it. For no reason, it brings back Wentley and rests it on her heart. Gramps sleeping in dark dirt with a passion fruit vine growing on his grave; Pa reading the Bible in his rocking-chair; Ma watering her purple and orange cosmos with dirty dishwater; Conrad, on his way to school, collecting showers of morning dust as he shepherds Princess in her mauve basic school uniform, matching clips in her hair, hugging her lilac lunch pan; and Sam in his olive short-pants khaki suit, lugging his giant brown school bag. Never mind that they are teenagers now, this is how she thinks of them. When she finds out that it is the Student Christian Association that built Newberry Hall, the place where this window is, and that they used to hold prayer meetings there once long ago, she considers her discovery anointed. She's certain of it when Gramps teases, "You don't find church, Gracie! Church find you!"

So this is her church. She stops by almost every day, stares, considers, rails a little at Papa God. In time, she assembles a small group of four or five Caribbean folks who meet here once a week to meditate.

———

Grace volunteers on weekends at Myrta's Home, a women's shelter. She registers women and children, cooks and serves meals, makes beds, does laundry, cares for babies, teaches literacy classes. It is at Myrta's that she loses her diffidence, thrust past it by the unabating stream of battered women and their children.

Felicity arrives at Myrta's one Sunday at midday, holding her left eye into the socket. Somebody has broken her nose and busted her mouth, which is bleeding like Jesus's side. It's Grace's second day there. When she looks up from the desk, she gasps. "Oh, my God!" She runs to the woman and urges, "Talk to me! Who did this to you? We have to call the cops!"

People appear straight off, scoop up Felicity, and take her inside. Babs Fiorito, who's in charge, sends Grace to help with the babies.

Hours later, when Grace is about to leave, Babs calls her into the office.

"Grace, I owe you an apology. We've thrown you into things with almost no training, and that's not fair to you."

"It's my fault, Babs. I shouldn't have reacted like that."

"Your reaction was natural enough. Felicity was beat up bad. But when women arrive, they need to feel that they're okay now, safe. That's why reception is more like a living room than a lobby. That's why whoever meets them must communicate calm, give them a sense that we can make it better, whatever it is."

"And I didn't."

"No, you didn't. But you'll do fine next time."

"Thanks for looking at it that way, Babs."

"I've a grandma who used to say, 'Everything tell a story. You talk soft? That's a story. Talk loud? Another story. Your children smile? A story. Always cross? Another story. The man hold hands with his wife. One story. Never touch her. Another story.' "

"So we have to get their story right, and ours, from the beginning?"

"Quite."

Grace writes Edgar, "Babs says it's her grandmother's philosophy — and effectively, her psychology and media theory as well. You're communicating all the time. Not just mouth, face, hands, but your whole body, and not just one body, bodies together, and their contexts. The design of a building, the order of a meeting, the layout of a city, the smell of a bathroom, they all talk. The world is one big text that we're always reading, consciously or unconsciously, and writing too, to send one message or another. Amazing, yes?"

Beside a big smiley face Edgar writes back, "You learning about tings, sis!"

In fall of 1982, near the end of her second year at the shelter, Grace starts meeting women who complain of dry coughs, night sweats, recurring fevers, tiredness that won't go away, and persistent diarrhea — a disease, but nobody knows what the deuce it is. Handling folks with an undiagnosed plague would frighten anyone, but not Babs. At U of M, Grace has ready access to computers, so she gets the job of pinning down the disease.

So it's at Myrta's that Grace meets someone other than Gramps, Pa, and Ma with a profound respect for homegrown points of view, and it is also at Myrta's that she starts acquiring the skills to track epidemiological data and spot the symptoms of HIV/AIDS, though the plague is still nameless. As she'd tell Charlie on their first all-nighter, borrowing the tagline from Anancy stories, "Is Myrta's make it."

———

Phyllis is still not answering letters, although Daphne says she is making steady progress. Grace is about to make a big move, so she writes a longish letter.

> *111 Edgelake Ave*
> *Ann Arbor*
> *Michigan 48103*
> *12 August 1982*

Dear Phyllis,
Tomorrow I'm going back to St. Chris for the first time since they sent for me before Gramps died. I'll be forever grateful for that visit, though it was

difficult in many ways. That was when Gramps gave me your letters, and the surprise of my life! I'm going home with some trepidation. I'm looking forward to examining the impact of Non-Government Organizations with health-related missions in the region to see how they make a difference to the communities they serve. I've developed a way of taking account of the occurrence of diseases like malaria and dengue fever so that health and related services can respond promptly, as needed. I wrote it up in a paper that was published and got quite a bit of notice, so I suspect the people at UA in St. Chris are treating me better than the average grad student. It all began with work in a women's shelter here when folks started turning up with symptoms of AIDS, which you may know as GRID or the 4-H disease. I figured that if we could identify the communities in which AIDS was likely to occur, we could make interventions that would be preventative and responsive in a timely fashion. I'm hoping to do some teaching as well. However, several people have warned me it's not like here, hence my misgivings.

I've called Our Lady of Good Hope and spoken to Sister Mary Agnes many times, for I promised to stay in touch with her. You will know that I am also good friends with Sister Mary Clement, the phone lady at Mary's Haven! I'd love to hear from you too, if and when. For sure, I will keep sending the newsletter. Meantime, work hard to get better!

Much love,
Grace

Maybe it is the ebullience of the Quad at U of M, the joie de vivre of the students, or Babs Fiorito's undiminishing hope; perhaps it is the green splash of the city, the glory of the Little Church of the Tiffany Window, the helpfulness of the people who teach her, or maybe she simply sees, as she wanders all over, to protests and poetry readings, festivals and flea markets, chorales and slams and jam sessions and jails that she has no corner on "hard life." It boxes everyone about. Perhaps she is simply tired of the hair shirt. Whatever the reason for the sea change, in Ann Arbor she becomes someone else: Charlie's Grace.

31

Charlie

Grace meets Charlie in January 1984, or, more accurately, Charlie meets her, at the St. Chris airport, because Edgar can't make it. Edgar was going to the Canadian High Commission to collect his visa, which he had to get that morning, because Lindsay, whom he was visiting in Ottawa for a few days, had found a cheap flight leaving that afternoon. He's managed to get the visa just in time.

Charlie is rum red, tall, and powerful. His straight, dark brown hair has reddish tints. His blue-green eyes are the colour of the sea at Richfield. Edgar says on the phone that she is sure to know Charlie, and "Anyway, he'll know you."

She walks out of customs, looks round, and somehow recognizes him as he says he recognized her. "How?" she asks him.

"Your aura. It's turquoise. Means you are efficient, a leader, excellent organizer, multi-tasker, resilient, really good at working with people. "

"You're joking."

"All the time, but not about your aura." He laughs, and informs her that he has a yellow aura, "meaning I'm very spiritual, like Buddha and Jesus."

"You *are* joking!"

Grace has been in Antigua for two weeks collecting data. She had to change her flight, and since the new one gets in late to the smaller international airport and she's brought a few things with her that she wants Edgar to take to Wentley, she plans to spend the night at his digs in Queenstown, leave the things there, and go to her flat at UA the following day.

Charlie takes her to her brother's tiny apartment, one of three in a converted bungalow. Another, slightly larger flat, is Charlie's. His base, he calls it. She doesn't stay at Edgar's though. She spends the night with Charlie, talking, listening to a steel band as they practise in a yard down the road, drinking fruit-and-vegetable juice in strange colours that her host concocts in a blender, eating johnnycakes she cooks when they get hungry.

Charlie is thirty-four, American born. His mother, from Louisiana, is half-black and half-Native American; his father, from Maine, is half-French and half-Irish.

"Lord! What a mixture!" She catches herself. "Sorry. I don't mean it in a bad way."

"Didn't take it in a bad way. You look stirred and shaken yourself, you."

"Please don't go there, Charlie."

"There be dragons?"

"Demons more likely."

"Never mind, sweet lady. Give me a chance, and I'll banish them."

They laugh. From the start, Charlie makes her laugh. Because his parents are missionaries, he's been to school on several Caribbean islands.

"That must have been interesting."

"Bloody hard on a child. I'd fly in, say hi to the kids down the road, play one game of cricket, and they'd yank me out!"

He was a late bloomer. Unmotivated at school, he hadn't done well until, persuaded by his parents who had retired to

Lafayette, Indiana, he enrolled at Purdue and got acquainted with his first computer. Then he was off at mongoose speed: a degree in computer science there, then an MA at Stanford and doctorate at Carnegie Mellon, all on scholarships. On and off, during the summers, he spent time in Silicon Valley, attached to software outfits with big names.

"So what are you doing here, holy man?"

"Well, some of the time I'm at UA, setting up IT systems and teaching courses in computer science. The rest of the time I'm in Haiti. Which is why this lovely flat is *one* of my bases."

She's learned a lot about computers and software, helping out at Myrta's. She's done courses in measurement and stats in preparation for her research, although the Real Time (RT), Real Circumstance (RC), Tailor-Made Interventions (TMI) model comes to her while thinking of how they deal with basic matters in Wentley, like what to do about mosquitoes, cow dung, and the outhouse when the rains come, the water table rises, there are breeding pools everywhere, and the *aedes aegypti* mosquito inspector is not due for another six months. Of course, she's been obliged to devise stats to support her model, and has done a good job, but what Charlie tells her about that night is at another level, a skill set that she recognizes as likely to add flexibility and versatility to approaches in her current research, as well as projects she's thought about pursuing post doc.

"So what are you doing in Haiti?"

"You know there's this idea that AIDS started there? We're trying to track how it got there, where it went after, and how."

Grace glances at his wall clock, an enormous Mickey Mouse affair, and says, "We'd better go to bed. It's after four."

After that she makes the one-hour trip to Queenstown to see Edgar, and do some shopping about once a month, saving her trips to Wentley, a four-hour journey, for occasions like birthdays or anniversaries. At Edgar's, she makes lunch for her brothers, for quite often Stewie is passing through to buy school materials as well. If he is home, Charlie joins them, after which they all go to a movie or for a stroll down by the harbour.

Pretty soon her visits are solely to work with Charlie. Edgar doesn't mind; he knows she is in a hurry to get her research done. As she gets further into analyzing the data, the visits become overnights and then weekend stays. If she comes in on Friday afternoon and works at Charlie's till Monday morning, she gets far more done than she does in the rest of the week, when she also has to teach. Eventually she is doing this every weekend that she isn't in the field collecting data, whether Charlie is there or in Haiti.

It isn't all work when she is with Charlie. They make lunch or dinner together, walking through the vegetable garden in back to cut kale or lettuce, pick tomatoes, pull up onions, gather thyme or parsley.

"So how come you're such a big gardener?"

"You forgetting Edgar is my flatmate, you?"

"How you talk so funny?"

"You're talking about talking funny?"

Sometimes on a clear night he teaches her about the stars, telling her stories his Cherokee grandmother told him.

"Gramps showed me," Grace recalls. "the Little Dipper, Big Dipper, Southern Cross. And the Milky Way!" She identifies the powdery trail of stars.

"Bet you don't know who made the Milky Way?"

"Who?"

"Grandmother Spider. It's a web she spun and threw across the sky so she could steal the sun from the other side of the world and take it back to her side, where there was only darkness."

"Ha-ha!"

"Honestly."

She spends countless nights with Charlie before they make love. One October night with the wind lashing trees, the sky overcome by a lightning show accompanied by 3-D sound effects, she burrows her whole body, migraine head and all, under the spread on his divan. When Charlie rolls her up in it and takes her into his bedroom, her body is ripe in a second, like a flower, pistil sticky with juice.

Kissing her belly-bottom, he announces, "You smell like flowers."

"Flowers? What kind of flowers?"

"Jasmine."

"You making fun, Charles?"

"Always, but not about this inflorescence."

He closes the dark blue curtains against the lightning, but like an inquisitive adolescent, it peeks in, flashing around them through cracks and crevices. Water beats on the roof in one solid, undifferentiated sound they hardly hear, but there is no mistaking it racing through gutters, crashing over paths, streaking for the trenches into which it dives, oblivious.

"Didja have fun, you?" he asks her afterwards.

"Is that what you call it?" She sits on his belly and thumps him.

"Why are you beating me up?"

"How come you kept this from me all this time?"

"We can do it again," he says.

She drops asleep with Charlie croaking foolish love songs at her. The next morning she walks around content, Charlie having kissed her goodbye and left early for a restive Haiti. After that, they are almost always together. He helps her with the statistics related to her research, and reads drafts of each chapter before she sends it off. They talk about whether she'll be confident defending some of the statistical measures Charlie has suggested, and he runs her through their comparative advantages, insisting that the choice of approaches be hers, and one she can argue for.

Charlie is counselor in other matters too, especially when time comes for a dust-up with the powers-that-be in the matter of Vie MacMillan, a PhD candidate whom she's mentored in a small way. Vie has been assigned a thesis examiner against whom she's previously filed a sexual harassment complaint. He gives her an excellent report, but threatens to destroy it unless she withdraws the charge.

"Don't let them disturb your serenity, sweet lady," Charlie advises. "If you plan to pursue a career in the region, think about what you do carefully. Black backra massa have long memory, just like the white one. Whatever you do, if you decide to resign, write on paper, and make clear why you're doing it."

She resigns but, against Charlie's advice, gives no reason why. Is it going to be something that she'll regret in time? She doesn't see how. She's kept her own counsel, and it is a matter of principle. Nor is it selfish. Rather it concerns a vulnerable person for whom she feels some responsibility. If humankind has sunk into lawlessness, murder, and war, it's because people don't keep faith in small things. It's the plantation all over: the mighty doing things because they can. Frantz Fanon would weep, for in this case, though the powerful and powerless are all descendants of slaves, the mash-down is just as callous.

She leaves in time to be back in Ann Arbor for Christmas. Charlie takes her to the airport, saying he will call her from Lafayette, where he'll be with his parents for New Year.

———

She hasn't been able to afford weekly calls to Mary's Haven from St. Chris during the two and a half years she's been there, although she continues to write Phyllis. Daphne has been her source of up-to-date news. She reverses the calls to her grandmother, but often, when she calls, Daphne is out. When she does get her, the reports of Phyllis's health are not especially encouraging. She is still progressing, but very slowly.

Once she is back in Michigan, pinning down Daphne is easier, and she is glad to hear that Phyllis's news is good. She is still in Cohasset, but almost fully recovered. Since the community at Mary's Haven is on retreat over Christmas, Grace is to call her in the New Year. Which she tries to do, on New Year's Day and a few times after that, but with no luck.

"Probably gone for a walk," Sister Mary Clement's wobbly voice says every time. "She likes that, whatever the weather. I'll tell her you called." It doesn't matter if she doesn't talk to Phyllis. If she is well, that is forgiveness.

Not everything is well, though. Andrew Shelton, econometrician on her committee, takes issue with some of her stats, and there are harsh exchanges between him and her supervisor. Grace is puzzled by Andrew's ill will, which is in sharp contrast to his original helpfulness. Then she remembers that early on he asked her to his apartment to "discuss her statistics" — ha-ha — more than once. On further reflection, it occurs to her that she has also talked about Charlie's helpfulness in perhaps over-enthusiastic terms. Still, it is hard to imagine that he is being mean because he is jealous. It is weird and very troublesome.

In the middle of the wrangling, during the course of which Andrew becomes more and more unpleasant, Grace has a dream. She is back in Wentley. It is Christmastime, and she is baking at the Williams's next door. (Because there is no oven in their lean-to kitchen — only a small kerosene stove — when they bake, they borrow the Williams's stove.) It is a blue December day, cool breeze blowing up the frilly curtains in the small, blue kitchen. Grace is making a cake, about to break three eggs into the batter. She puts down her wooden spoon, and takes up the first egg. As she breaks the shell, it turns into a miniature Fillmore Buxton, his foul face filling up the round rim of the bowl, his body shrinking down into the batter. With a sneer, she flicks her wrist and mashes him in, and then takes up the second egg, which becomes an equally ugly Andrew Shelton. She cracks him too, blending blood, bones, and bits of body parts into the mix. Reaching for the third egg, she forces herself into wakefulness and sits shivering, never mind the day is already warm, and dry retching into the nightgown she is clutching in front of her mouth.

"It's only a dream, sweet lady," she imagines Charlie soothing. "You're annoyed with those men. It's good you can resolve it in a dream."

She doesn't agree. It is as alive and urgent as the current nasty heaving of her stomach. Worse, she is far too satisfied cracking the two egg-men, watching their innards fall into the bowl, grinding them into the gross mixture. It is more than just outrage. Maybe she should get dressed and head for Emergency Psych at the University Hospital right away, where she will say — what? "I just had a nightmare, on the basis of which I've concluded I'm crazy?"

She decides to take one of the tranquilizers she always has on hand because she hates to fly, and hope it will put her to sleep. She'll figure it out tomorrow.

In the end, with the other committee members bullying Andrew a bit, they all agree on changes, and she revises and hands in the dissertation. By then, the dispute has taken so long to sort out, and been so traumatic that a letter comes from Cohasset before she manages to reach Phyllis.

> *Mary's Haven*
> *Easter Day*
> *30 March 1986*
>
> *Dear Grace,*
> *How are you? I hope enjoying a rest after all the hard work. Well, here I am, back pon spot! I'm so grateful to you for all those letters, and sorry not to have answered. Happily, I can now explain my prolonged retirement from the world. I've had a psychotherapist these past four years. When I began to have some world-class nightmares and was screaming in my sleep fit to wake the dead, not to mention the folks here, the sisters arranged for me to see her. She's been immeasurably helpful! It was her suggestion that I cut off contact with*

pretty much everyone till we agreed I was ready for the world again. So in addition to working on my body, they've been helping me fix my miserable soul.

Much of what I've grappled with is the result of situations in my childhood and adolescence. It's not just having a baby when I wasn't quite thirteen. There were plenty other things and it was well time that I sorted them out. One thing I know now is that it's not enough to cope, make a go of it, indeed to even succeed brilliantly. You need to believe that you are a good, worthwhile person. I pass that on for what it's worth.

When I was finally more or less functional, I asked the nuns here if I could help in any way and they let me slowly get back into the rhythm of work. It's admin, like what I did in New York. The difference is this big, old residence by the sea is a beautiful, restful place, far from hassle and botheration. Whether winter or summer, good or bad weather, it's utterly peaceful. I'll get back to New York in time, but not just now.

Daphne tells me you are set to get through your final PhD exam with flying colors. If you tell me the big day, we'll send up a noisy prayer from here.

Time for Mass! I hope you make good choices about the paths to pursue now you have the papers you need. The Holy Spirit will guide you. God bless. Much love. Big hug.

Phyllis

P.S. Bet you thought I'd forgot! I hope you had a wonderful birthday! We prayed for you especially at mass and I played the flute for the first time in a long time!

She defends her dissertation on 21 May. Charlie, back in St. Chris since the end of April, comes armed with champagne and the offer of a job in the Haiti project.

"Exactly who am I working for, Charlie?"

At first he'd understood that the Centers for Disease Control were running one arm of the project, with sideways money from the National Institutes of Health. Now he was saying, "I believe that the CIA are on board as well."

"Don't kid me, Charles."

"Sweet one, even I, chuckling Charlie, wouldn't do that. I'm not certain, but I have to tell you what I suspect, don't I? Duvalier is gone, but the new National Council is rickety. Their assembly is only just tackling the constitution, and our friend Father Aristide and the youth of Ti Legliz, his little church movement, are making the establishment nervous. At the best of times there's not much in the world those CIA goons don't stick their fingers into."

It isn't unlikely. Haiti is always more or less uneasy.

Charlie assures her that, as long as they are cautious, level headed, and sensible, they will be safe. She joins the project in January 1987.

On 19 April, Easter Monday, Charlie leaves for the office early. He is opening the locks on their door when she wakes, aware of a queasy belly and a funny taste in her mouth, migraine symptoms she hasn't had in a long while. The taste is different this time, though, like ashes. She slips into a robe and makes it outside in time to call goodbye as he enters the long grass that swallows the track going downhill to project headquarters. The blades shush as they bend and rise, mimicking his answering wave. Then, like a sea anemone's tentacles, they sweep him in. No one ever sees him again.

Grace spends the worst six weeks of her life alone in their small house, waiting for news of Charlie, forcing herself to work, downing pills so she can sleep at nights. When no news of him interrupts her tremulous vigil, she starts to look for him herself, until she is expressly forbidden, the order pronounced with menace by the blue-eyed, crew cut ex-marine who is in charge of security at headquarters. Josée, their translator, must have told him. Grace's Kwéyol isn't good like Charlie's, and so she asked Josée to come with her to help her search.

Then, for the second time in her life, she has an attack of migraine in which pain comes packaged in total blindness. After she has lost vision for three days, she panics. It makes no sense to stay in Haiti and risk complete physical and psychological breakdown. She'll be of use to no one then, least of all herself. Charlie alone has understood her, and loved her for who she is. And Charlie is gone, victim she is sure of some calculated or accidental act of lethal violence — it hardly matters which.

She decides she will make a place inside, a special space for Charlie, and put him away there. She will ration her thoughts about him because not to do so will be to risk total disintegration. She packs a few clothes, gives away most things, heads back to Daphne in Edison. Charlie's death is Papa God's coup de grâce. He shouldn't expect to hear from her anytime soon.

MARK

32

Coming to Order

This afternoon, even the subdued banter that council members normally bring into the meeting is absent. Not that they're a drab and sober lot, but close to year-end they're tired from travel, the pressures of island politics, the burdens of teaching and administration. Still, that is life in these parts, and these fellows get good money for dealing with it and plenty of perks.

He puts down his papers and looks around for Celia. She's on the other side of the room, in animated conversation with another admin officer. She will come over to him shortly, passing along any new information, conveying last-minute apologies for anyone delayed or unable to attend.

But she isn't the person approaching him. It's the principal, Gordon Crawford, skin bloodless, grey pupils skittering like marbles across the whites of his eyes.

"Jesus H. Christ, Mark! They've killed him!"

"Killed who? Who's killed who?"

"Langdon. They've shot him!"

"Langdon? Who's Langdon, Gordon?"

"Shit. Fucking place's turned into Jamaica. Jesus Christ! I need a drink."

"Gordon, get a hold of yourself. Who's this who's been shot?"

"Edwin Langdon. The Minister of Education."

Gordon says that, because the minister has been shot dead, the vice chancellor, who is talking to the Office of the Prime Minister, will be late. Based on this communication, council will decide whether graduation on Saturday should proceed. Edwin Langdon is not a friend, but he is, or was, in the first batch of students that Mark taught and was someone he had worked with often. If there's such a thing as an honest politician, the deceased is that.

"Who shot him? Anybody have any idea?"

"Just happened on his way here! Jesus, I'm cold. Mark, you don't carry a flask, do you?" Mark shakes his head, surprised at the younger man.

"All the same, you're a rum man," Crawford babbles on. "Can't think how you drink that rot-gut." Mark doesn't appreciate the remark, not because it says his taste in liquor is suspect, but because St. Chris rum is superb.

"So the police have no idea ..."

"Of who? Naaah, don't be stupid," Crawford cuts him off. "How could they? Of course, that slut in the admin office is saying it's Langdon's wife."

"You mean she's been killed, not him?"

"Good God, no, man. Use your head. It's him that's dead all right. Flap-mouth was saying his wife knocked him off or arranged for it."

Mark decides that, even in the circumstances, he can't excuse the principal this degree of, to put it kindly, informality. "Gordon ..." His voice portends.

"What?"

"Restrain yourself." He's never known anyone who died by anything more violent than a road accident. He doesn't fear death but he does fear dying, if that makes sense, and a bullet doesn't strike him as a bad way to go.

"Why don't you take five in the chancellor's suite and have a nip of brandy? Here's Celia." He beckons her. "She'll see you in."

"Celia," he speaks before she does. "The principal is feeling unwell. Would you take him to Garvey, please? Organize a cup of tea?" He hopes Gordon notices that the nip has shape-shifted.

Celia hands him several files.

"For me? Thanks. I take it phones are in good working order?" He points to a red phone and a black one on a table immediately behind his chair.

"Yes, sir. They were checked earlier."

"Very well. I'm going to start things off. I think it would be wise to have a car with a driver downstairs, just in case. Can we do that?"

"I'll ask admin to arrange it." She reaches for the black phone.

Council must still meet, if only to decide if graduation should go ahead. Several hundred people will shortly arrive in Queenstown. Indeed, they are arriving already. Preposterously, it's Grace he thinks of, in Haiti for meetings, wondering again why she never answered his letters. Mona can't come! The magic of the words envelops him, like the heat of liniment on aching muscles. "Mona can't come." Not in these circumstances!

Of course he's not just worried about Grace's safety, and Mona's, but about the safety of the families and friends coming for the ceremony. Most aren't wealthy people. It's a moment of triumph for them, dividend of many sweat-invested years. To be cheated of that is hard. Might there be some connection with the university, some mad student with a grudge? Nowadays, that's what angry people do, grab a gun and shoot. At any rate, today the politicians, senior civil servants, academics, and other pukka sahibs can sweat a little to earn their bread.

"Good afternoon, everyone. Thanks for being on time. It's as well, since our normally difficult circumstances have turned catastrophic. I'm distressed to have to inform you that Minister Langdon has been shot dead on his way here."

There are gasps, exclamations of horror. He allows a pause, seconds during which some gape, faces stung, others turn to jabber at their neighbours, so the noise increases. When some start to rise, he returns them to their chairs.

"We will, of course, continue with council. Before calling the meeting to order, however, I would ask that we stand and observe a moment of silence out of respect for the Hon. Minister of Education. May his soul rest in peace."

In the silence, he peeps from under lowered lids, curious about whether any of these men has screwed Grace.

Shifting feet and papers tell him the minute is up.

"Sorry. Got distracted there. Please be seated." He sits, pours himself some passion fruit punch and sips. The meeting will trundle on until late, no doubt reconvening tomorrow. He sets the glass down. Ice tinkles as the sun makes crisscross explosions in the crimson liquid.

GRAMPS

33

Ralston

"Beg you take it from me and rest it on the table yonder, Zeke."

Evadne stands in the doorway with a wooden tray on which there is a jug of lemonade and two glasses.

"Take your time, Vads," Ezekiel Carpenter counsels, taking the tray from her and settling it on the wrought iron table that occupies most of the length of the small verandah, commanding the space like an altar. He returns to give her a hand as she steps down from the polished wood of the parlour onto the shiny red-stained concrete.

"I thank you for the help, Zeke. I am really very well indeed, except for this arthritis. It useful for predicting the weather, but when it ready, it transform me into a cripple. And God Almighty knows I already have troubles enough to cripple me!"

She settles herself on a high straight-backed bench, at the same time waving him into an old-fashioned dark green verandah chair, its seat sloping down to meet a long angled back.

"Maybe you best come to the troubles straight off, Vads," Gramps begins. "Nothing to be gained by beating around the bush. We know each other too long. If Elsie was here, she would say, 'No way to kill the chicken other than put the pan over the head and bring the knife down.'"

"Is a hard thing for me to speak about, Zeke." Evadne beats her fist on her small bosom. "I don't mind money troubles, for I am accustomed to being poor, and in sickness, I pray for endurance." She holds up her hands, the joints swollen, the fingers curling over. "When storm and hurricane come, I recall the Book of Job and know God is master and I bow to his will and the might of his sceptre. But when evil come as close to me as my family, when I see a viper in my bosom and don't know when nor how it come to be there, I deem it hard indeed."

Ezekiel knows her trial. He stepped off the bus in Hector's Castle and was making his way across to Hector's Hardware and Grocery, intending to buy a couple bottles of beer to take up the hill, for Vads enjoys a Red Stripe, when he came across her grandson, Ralston, and two other young men leaning against the wall of the shop, each with a bottle of warm Red Stripe — "hot hops" — and a cigarette in hand, though it was only ten in the morning.

Ralston was idling at full throttle. "Elvin, him that see it, know it. And him that feel it, know it better." He sputtered on the swill of beer he'd just taken, finding his own joke funny. "I go show you living proof that if cousin boil good soup, sister boil better!"

Gramps wondered at first if under the bravado he detected something tremulous, a degree of unease. One good look at Ralston said it was wishful thinking.

"Morning, Ralston," Gramps greeted the young man. Ralston raised his chin somewhat, but made no further response.

Gramps entered and threw his voice into the cool darkness of the store. "A howdy to you, Mr. Hector. I hope your day goes well and I would thank you to reach a couple Red Stripes for me."

"You rather them cold, or you prefer them just so?"

"Just so is fine. Time I walk up the road, they going be hot anyhow."

276   **Pamela Mordecai**

Mr. Hector emerged from the shelves and came to the counter to see Gramps searching in his pocket for the wherewithal to make his purchase. "I beg your pardon, Mr. Carpenter. I never see it was you. Welcome to Hector's. Last time I see you was in fifty-eight, right? Good to see you after this long little while." He looked uncertain as he settled the beers into a paper bag and handed them over. Then he ventured, carefully, "I take it you come to see Miss Evadne?"

"You know that's why I come, Mr. Hector, excepting of course for my regular November visit to Elsie's grave."

"Miss Evadne will be glad to see you, for sure, sir." The grocer inclined his head, gesturing with an eyebrow in Ralston's direction. "I am slow to pronounce it, but it's as well I be the one to tell you. Ralston boasting out there these past days that he make a baby on his sister."

"Is there truth in that, Mr. Hector?"

"I put nothing past that one, Mr. Carpenter."

Now Gramps is looking at Evadne as she pours the lemonade for them both, She's put the Red Stripes in the ice-box, for though many people maintain that warm beer is good for lungs, teeth, and general well-being, they prefer their beer cold. Given the twisted fingers, he considers taking the jug from her, but she is managing, and he knows the importance of a person feeling that they have control, even over small things, when they have lost much bigger control. He notes his own hands on his knees and realizes he is clutching them. Never mind age and experience, if what Mr. Hector says is true, he is in alien waters. Still he's never been a man to shirk a hard thing. He goes across to Evadne, takes the glass she offers, and says, "Thanks, Vads. I need something to cool me down."

Seating himself again, he takes courage. "First things first, Vads. How is Phyllis? Is she here?"

"How you mean, Zeke?"

"I mean the plain words I'm saying, Evadne."

"You mean to say that you know?"

"I know what Ralston is broadcasting in the shop piazza."

"In that case, you see why I had to send her off. How could I have her here exposed to the cruelty of that boy and the bad-mindedness of people? You know all this time, she washing and ironing his clothes along with hers and mine? For is not much I can do with these now." She displays the fingers again.

"I'm sorry Vads — "

She cuts Gramps off. "Not only that, she cook food if I can't manage, clean this house from top to bottom, and all the while," Evadne reaches down between breasts rising in swift tremors for a handkerchief, "the child is trying to keep up with her schoolwork."

"And you're sure he did it?"

"That girl never yet tell me a lie."

"And is she now in good hands? Is she safe?"

"I think so, Zeke. I s-s-send her to Alton Mount." Evadne sniffles into the kerchief. "It's a place the church recommend."

"Which church, Vads?"

"Which church you think? The Church of England, which I was brought up in." She adds, with some ire, "The self-same church you and Elsie attend when you live here, for there was no Methodist Church then. You don't recall?"

Evadne's annoyance at his question helps her to compose herself, which is his intention.

"I don't mean to suggest that it was a foolish thing to do, Vads. I'm just concerned that Phyllis is in a place where people can offer her comfort as well as care for her and the baby, when it comes. She not the first to make a baby at her age, but having her half-brother's baby is another matter."

Evadne's hands flutter up to hide her face.

"Think about Phyllis and you will manage it better, Vads." He pauses. "So. You still don't tell me where she is."

"They start a home for girls pregnant like she in Alton Mount. The home is Archdeacon's idea and his wife is running it. Reverend Myers say he would talk to Archdeacon. It's not many girls, but they are all high up in their teens, so Reverend Myers was worried about Phyllis."

"It's the child's age that is worrying me, as well. Twelve years is very young. Pikni making pikni."

"Well, Reverend Myers say we will tell a kindly lie and say Phyllis is nearly fourteen. And till the baby come, because of the circumstances, Archdeacon Miller say he and Mrs. Miller will have her in their own home. I praise God for that. You know Mrs. Miller's work is to counsel young people."

Gramps wonders what there is to say to a twelve-year-old having a baby because her half-brother raped her.

"Not that I don't try to comfort her, Zeke. I tell her is not her fault, and I work quick to move her once I know what happen, for people too unkind. Everybody know her mother was working on papers for she and me, so I put it out that they come through. That time not a soul but me and Phyllis and Daphne know about the baby. Then Ralston start running his mouth down at the shop!"

"Sound like you did the best you could, Vads. How far along is she?"

"Two months. That boy is wicked to advantage her. The day he force himself on her, I wasn't here. When I come back about four, she vanish clean-clean. I search and I search, walk and walk, examine everywhere, saying over and over, 'The Lord is my shepherd ...' "

Evadne is distraught, her tale a tremulous outpouring, but Gramps doesn't stop her, conscious that the grief and powerlessness and guilt of it all are trying her sorely, and the words are a way to get it out. Gradually her speech fades, and her head falls to one side.

He looks across the road to a white scar of track running up a steep ridge on the other side. There is an old quarry up there. He must ask Vads when she wakes if it is still in use.

———

Evadne starts at the sound of metal banging against metal, as someone slams the gate. It is at the side of the property, the house placed on the land so it is parallel to the road. Done before Evadne and Malachi's time, it meets the need for privacy ingeniously. An arbour running down the side of the house prevents people from seeing through the bedroom windows, with the hanging orchids a further obstruction to prying eyes. They were Malachi's comfort as he dwindled into dementia, and mercifully, death.

The front verandah faces beds of gerberas and roses, a wide lawn of zoysia, bounded on the near side by a new fence, then guinea grass for the goats, and for the larger livestock grazing grass that continues to the steep mountains known as Long Backs. There is also a view across to the lower hills on the other side of the road.

"So why you let me sleep, Ezekiel?"

"You were such a pretty picture, Vads. How could I disturb you?"

"That's why I warn Elsie Dixon about you! That day she come back from Queenstown carrying on about how she meet somebody on the bus that was reading poems. 'Imagine, a man *reading*! And poems, Vads, poems!' "

"You warn her about me because I was reading poems?"

"I warn her when she say you tell her, 'This parting is sweetest sorrow.' "

"Nothing wrong with making a good line better."

Ezekiel is glad of their banter, for Evadne needs the diversion. He fears her reaction when they get to serious talking again.

"That's what I warned her about. Cocksure of yourself from the start."

Clang. Clunk. Clunk. Whoever is coming round to the front of the house is announcing his entry by hitting the containers that hold the orchids.

"Is so your acquaintances have licence to assault your property?"

Evadne's top lip pushes out, her chin muscle pleating her bottom lip so she resembles an angry fish. "That is my grandson, who do what he like, more so since he is now owner and controller of the piece of land yonder," she flaps a wrist at the new fence, "as of his sixteenth birthday, just past, his no-good father having prevailed upon Malachi to sign a paper to that effect."

"Come again, Vads? All this not your house and land?"

"No, siree." Ralston swings the corner, a stout stick in hand. He is using it to swipe at the rose plants, *slap-slap-slap* the rails of the stairs, and thwack at the empty chair before he slouches down into it, exuding fumes of beer. "She own right up to that fence." He gestures tipsily. "Me, Ralston Patterson, is rightful proprietor of what lie beyond."

Having asserted his right of ownership, Ralston sets his stick to one side, pulls a pack of Lucky Strike from his back pocket, offers one to Gramps, to his great surprise, and when Gramps declines, lights up and blows a mighty puff of smoke in Miss Evadne's direction.

"How much time I am to tell you that I don't like that cigarette smoke, Ralston?" Miss Evadne rises. "I know with dinner in the offing, *you* not getting up to go nowhere, so I will just excuse myself. Ezekiel, I hope you plan to stop with us. I'm going to finish frying plantain. Once I done, dinner will be served."

The two men sit in silence for a while, Ralston taking long drags on the cigarette and blowing smoke rings, Gramps staring out across the garden and up to the hills. Thank God, Phyllis and the baby are safe for the moment. His concern is now Evadne. Obviously it takes every effort of will for her to be in Ralston's presence, and he wonders why the fellow is still in her house. Perhaps Ralston has threatened her. Gramps doesn't know what kind of company he keeps. Though the young men with him are rough sorts, they don't look like thugs, but who can tell? As he sees it, ensuring that Evadne has a plan of action for Phyllis and herself is half of what is necessary. The other half is what to do about Ralston. They can go to the police, rape and incest being against the law, but the case will have to be made on Phyllis's word, and he is loath to put her through that ordeal.

Before she dozed off, Evadne had related more of her wretched tale. "That evening, I pray, Ezekiel. I ask the neighbours to help, and we search outside and up and down the road with lantern till late-late, and then I lie awake in what was left of the night begging God to show me where she is. When morning come, he lead me to the bruck-down shed by the river, where Malachi tend his plants. Is there I find her, sitting on a piece of old crocus bag, shivering with cold, wet from the dampness, and coughing like she have TB, her eyes red, for she couldn't stop crying. She wouldn't tell me what happen, why she run off and hide herself. When I see the blood on her, I remind her that we talked about that. I say, 'That mean you're becoming a woman, Phyllis. You remember, don't it?' Same time she start a cow-bawling, and roll herself from side to side, and wouldn't stop."

Gramps beholds the cause of all this trouble enjoying his smoke. He doubts that Ralston has any feelings for the half-sister whom he raped, any interest in what is happening to her, and the child he boasts he has put in her belly. There are a lot of things it behooves him to discover, but somehow the idea of a composed discussion on Evadne's verandah seems atrocious. He has to persuade Ralston to go somewhere else with him.

He decides it is as well to begin with some embellishments to the vagabond's status. "Ralston, I wouldn't mind if you and me could have a talk, seeing as you are now a person of property and in a position to help your grandmother, who will shortly need care and assistance, for you know she is not well."

Ralston is taken aback at the request, but after a lengthy pause, he replies. "Don't see any reason why not."

"What about we take a walk?" Gramps says as he gets up. "Then whatever we say will be between you and me."

Ralston looks askance at him, and Gramps realizes the fellow would remember how close Elsie and himself had been to Malachi and Evadne. He had been a big boy when the Carpenters left Hector's Castle, old enough to recall their many interactions.

Gramps can envision him sitting in the moonlight on these same shiny concrete steps with Malachi and Evadne, his mother, Daphne, cradling Phyllis, who was still sucking her finger, Miss Elsie, and himself, listening as the five grownups told duppy stories. Pretending that there are things between him and Ralston that he'll keep from Evadne makes no sense. He rectifies his mistake. "Not to say is anything secret we going to be talking, but I would like to spare your grandmother's feelings. She been a self-sufficient woman all her life, and her sickness will in time make her weak, in need of support. It's a hard adjustment to make."

Gramps is twisting the truth, but just then all he wants to do is get Ralston's backside up out of the chair and out into the road. After that he has no inkling what he will do or say, where they will go, what kind of arrangement he will try to make so Evadne can live in some kind of peace.

Ralston achieves his feet, checks to see that his parts are secure in his trousers, and with his free hand pats his shirt pocket to make sure he has the pack of cigarettes.

"A-right," he says to Gramps. "So where we going?"

Gramps leaps down the stairs like a man half his age and is barrelling down the path by the side of the house, headed for the gate.

"What happen, Zeke? Where you going? You not leaving?" Evadne calls to him through the kitchen window.

"Me and Ralston just going for a walk, Evadne. Coming right back."

"Hold up, Mr. Carpenter. Is bus you running to catch?" Ralston pauses so Gramps can grasp that he doesn't jump to anyone else's rhythms. "Only one thing I put on so much haste for!" He guffaws so loud that he chokes on his cigarette, whereupon he regards it with annoyance, observes that it is down to the butt, and hurls it into the bush.

Ezekiel makes an enormous effort to restrain himself from thumping Ralston. Knowing that won't help the cause, he grunts in a manner he hopes Ralston will interpret as appreciative of his wit.

"Listen, Ralston, if you own land, you have to behave like a landowner. You don't know that flinging a cigarette butt into the bush can start a fire? You could burn down your whole property from one careless act like that!"

Ralston absorbs this. "That make sense. I will heed it in future."

He is tempted to think that perhaps Ralston isn't an entirely depraved creature whose most decent act is the consumption of hot hops in company with hooligans. Then, letting Ralston walk ahead of him, he notices the young man has a stout knife in a case attached to a leather belt that also sports a metal ring with a length of sash cord looped through it. The implements are in plain view, for the landed proprietor has on a tight white shirt that stops at his waist, and a pair of expertly laundered jeans. Gramps decides it is probably better not know what the knife and rope are for.

They are on the road now. Gramps halts for a bit and surveys the track running up the ridge on the other side that once led to the quarry. "You ever go up that road yet, Ralston?"

"After nothing not up there, no food, no diversion, no female company." Hope flickers again at the relative delicacy of the remark until Ralston chuckles, groping his parts. "Me only go where the freeness is."

"They used to have a quarry up there. That's where the stone that built your grandparents' house comes from."

Ralston does not regard this as worthy of notice. Instead he offers, "One time few years ago, me and the fellows take slingshot and shoot bird up that way. The pickings wasn't bad, but is a long time now we don't go back up there."

"I tell you one thing, Ralston. If you want a good idea of the size of your property, up there is the place to look from."

Ralston debates Gramps proposal for a while Then he says, "Me don't have nothing better to do, so yeah, we could walk up there."

Gramps doesn't know what he has in mind when he makes the suggestion. He certainly isn't worried that this strong, well-armed teenager may choose to hurt him. Malachi and Evadne Patterson were fine people who painstakingly raised their one child, Daphne, Ralston's and Phyllis's mother. But what he knows of Desmond, Ralston's father, is not encouraging. Clever, moody, own-way, Desmond gave up school to join a gang that trafficked in weed. An amiable fellow when he chose, he could be generous and funny, but his ganja smoking worsened his moods so that during the bad ones, even his comrades avoided him. Daphne lost her innocence to his charm at a church picnic when she was sixteen. She'd given birth to Ralston, who spent his growing-up years missing his father, for Desmond was by then as often in as out of the penitentiary. By age ten, never mind his grandparents' efforts, Ralston was as truculent as Desmond.

If the father has bad blood, what evils might lurk in the son? But they have no quarrel, Ralston and he. Besides, as Gramps often said when provoked, "I go to war and come back. Plenty never return." He can handle Ralston, if need be.

They climb for five or six minutes, taking the steep slope without difficulty. When they reach a ways up, Gramps addresses Ralston's back. "If you stop now and look, you will see the whole place, starting from the river over yonder and coming all the way forward to the fence on the road right under us, and also going up, Long Backs way." He gestures as he speaks, towards the slim line of wetness glinting through the trees, then down to the barbed wire threading the posts on the road below them, then north, towards the mountains shrouded in low black clouds.

Malachi and Evadne's holding is a fairly large one, as far as the property of slaves' descendants goes. With each succeeding generation, it has been broken up, and yet fifteen acres or so still stretch away from them through clumps of mahoe and cedar trees, with groves of breadfruit and a huddle of otaheite apple trees near what they call "the river." It is just a large stream, but it never runs dry, not even in the worst drought. There is a pool there, where Gramps failed hilariously in repeated attempts to teach Elsie and Evadne to swim. Ralston's portion, marked off by the new fence, more or less splits the place.

"So it reach to the river all the way across?" Ralston is trying to sound detached, although Gramps can see he is impressed by the size of his acquisition.

"The bottom boundary of your grandmother's place is past the house, down in the gully by the primary school." Gramps waves towards an untidy kraal of small buildings in a depression further down the road. Ralston uses both hands to shade his eyes against the afternoon sun, a yellow glare in the sky. "Your land, which starts at the fence, goes up so." Gramps arm sweeps the other way, towards the mountains.

"So where it stop on that side?"

"I don't rightly know. I don't think even your grandpa rightly knew. It get into some thick bush as it start to climb and the gradient steep like a rock-face, so nobody know where private land stop and government land start."

"So how I would know the bounds of my land?"

"You could ask a surveyor to come and measure."

Ralston takes a step forward. He folds one arm across his chest and strokes his chin with the other, as he swivels his head from side to side pondering the extent of his acreage. Gramps stands behind him, looking down at Evadne's small property. Seconds later Ralston is in a heap at the bottom of the cliff.

34

Open Secrets

"Zeke, you never ... ?" Evadne contemplates Ralston in his coffin.

"How could you ask me that?"

The irony doesn't fail to strike Ezekiel. It was Evadne's question when he asked if Phyllis should perhaps have an abortion.

He isn't sure himself what transpired on the hillside, so he concentrates on his conviction that it is for the best. His report to the district constable states that the young man leaned over too far and fell. There are lots of people to witness to the fact that Ralston was drinking that day and enough who will think "good riddance," for Ralston has not endeared himself to the small world of Hector's Castle.

After the funeral, Gramps promises to pass by Archdeacon and Mrs. Miller to tell Phyllis the news. There is no point in not telling her. Information in small places is, like the wispy flowers of the silk cotton tree, lifted by air and dispersed on its numerous currents. Never mind no mouths admitted to telling tales, accounts find their way across yards, then miles. It is magic.

This does not mean secrets cannot be kept. If people are determined enough, they can band together to fervently guard history. Gramps met an American negro in the war who swore he was descended from Thomas Jefferson. He carried Jefferson's face, his body shape, and his name.

When Gramps asked if people knew, he replied, laughing, "Plenty enough. But still, we be good at hiding what we choose."

35

Two Letters from New York City

114 Riverside Drive, Apt 2G
New York, NY 10024, USA
12 June 1960

Dear Zeke,
We don't long since get here, just a week now. I
am so sorry for leaving with no goodbye. This is so
you don't hear on the street that I am gone. I could
not forgive myself for that. Part of the reason why
we leave so quick is that the papers come through
sudden. God is good, for I was at my wits end
worrying about Phyllis in the home at Alton Mount.
As it turn out, I went to collect her just days after
Gwen and Moses came for the baby.

After what happened, keeping on in Hector's
Castle was impossible, never mind it has been my
home for all my life. It reached the stage where I
could not even think of the good times, the precious
moments with yourself and Elsie, me and Malachi,
the child I bore and raised there. I beg God to help

me so I don't curse and condemn that grandson of mine, but rather find it in my heart to forgive and pray for him, so his soul don't fry in Hell. I am not sure I am able but I try, for that is Jesus's instruction and he has given me no leave to ignore it. I think if men could understand how with one sex act they can destroy a whole world, make people want to forget their whole life and every good thing that ever happened to them, they would take pity and satisfy their lust without benefit of partner. God forgive me, but if a man spill his own seed to spare the kind of evil that we are going through, I don't see how God will hold it against him.

Daphne's apartment is in Manhattan. The first woman she was companion to when she came up gave her a room to stop in and when the woman moved to Florida two years ago, she let the place to Daphne at a reasonable rent for she didn't want to trouble with new tenants. And we have a church. Daphne goes only a few times a year, but a more devout church sister introduced me to the pastor, a Rev. Morris who looks like he could be coloured. It is a mixed congregation, half us and half them. The services are what I am accustomed to although I find the singing half-hearted.

When we came Daphne took time off work to show us around so we know our way and understand how to take the bus downtown. I tell her I am not going into any subway. Underground is for worms and moles, not human beings except they are dead. The one time she took me down there will serve for the rest of my life.

Phyllis is settling in very slowly. She is still grieving for that baby. I find it nothing short of a miracle that *she could love it any at all, though it was a pretty child with good colour and soft hair. Daphne has got her into a school for young mothers, run by nuns. She is one of just two girls who do not have their baby with them, which must cause her more pain.*

I will write more soon, but I never wanted time to pass before I let you know how we were doing. I pray God's blessings on you for all your help, and Gwen and Moses who have opened their heart and home to a child that is no relation. I hope she has settled in well. My good wishes to the family.

Your friend always,
Evadne

12 June 1960

Dear Mr. Carpenter, sir,
I reech to this big city safe, so I writing to let you know. With how Granny Evadne feel about Hector Castle and everyting with me it dont make no sense for we to stay in that house. Everyting happen so fast I reelly dont get no time to say a good thank you so all I can do Mr. Carpenter is to say a big THANK YOU now I mean it with all my heart I hope is not a bad ting but I miss that likl baby for true an I will pray far it every day as God send life and also for you sir for kindnes to me. Granny Vads say that she long to have a lettre from you and I am hopin you give my likl dawter the lettre I rite on July 18. Remember pleas sir you promise to see she get her birtday letter that I will rite evri year.

Yours fatefuly,
Phyllis Patterson

MARK

36

Mirando y Dejando

He calls Mona every night when he's away, but he isn't looking forward to tonight's call. He's exhausted. They all are, though council wound up early, at about five, so they could make it to their hotels before the six o'clock curfew. The meeting had not been able to address any of the agenda items, some of which were urgent. He's especially worried that they hadn't got to the report from the Standing Committee on Information Systems Management. It addressed Y2K-related plans, and there was no postponing that to a subsequent council meeting, not with 1999 less than two months away. Tomorrow they'd have to get past the security and other issues relating to graduation and consider those items. But sufficient unto the day. He strips, throwing clothes on the bed, and stepping cautiously into the shower. He's fallen at home more than once, and his doctor suggested some of the slips might have been episodes of cataplexy.

He worries about Mona. Not that she can't manage by herself, being an independent and capable woman. She'd come to the United States to go to Georgetown University when she was only seventeen, and although she'd intended to, had never returned to Trinidad to live. After her first degree, she'd done an MA, then a PhD.

He'd met her at the university in St. Chris when she was doing research for her dissertation, although, unlike Grace, she hadn't joined the faculty. She'd been sitting on the side of the senior common room pool, thick black hair a waterfall over her shoulders, toes playing in the water. She had unusually well shaped legs for a coolie woman and a nicely filled-out bottom. He liked East Indian women, but for their skinny legs and skimpy backsides. The tar brush must have slipped in somehow to round this one out.

"How're things, Manny?"

"Observing and going my way, sir." The bartender in the senior common room made his usual rejoinder as Mark slid onto his accustomed barstool, massaging his forehead as he issued the order for his daily ration.

"What's this 'observing and going my way' you always on about?"

"Funny, you know, sir. You the first person ask me. Make me think that maybe if I say a obscene word to these good folks when them ask me how me doing, them wouldn't even hear it."

"Don't do that, my friend. They'll hear anything that could be considered even vaguely offensive."

"Don't do it up to now, sir, but many times tempted."

"But you still don't tell me what it mean!"

"Something my great-granny used to say, sir. She come from Cuba. Name me herself, Manuel. And she would say, if you ask her how things going, 'Mirando y dejando.' It mean you watching how things going and proceeding on your ways, minding your own business."

From ten in the morning when it opened, until seven at night when he signed off, Manny was at his post behind the bar, ready with towel and good nature.

"Right, then. Cheers!" Mark hoisted his Red Stripe.

He liked Manny. He liked the bar. That day, the beer was a reward for teaching steadily since nine o'clock. He'd been pinch-hitting for a colleague.

Refreshed and pleased at learning about observing and moving along from Manny, he was en route to his office when Mona asked him the time as he walked by. She was still poolside. He'd obliged, then pointed to her watch.

"Oh!" She'd laughed, embarrassed. "It doesn't work."

He'd nodded, still smiling, and said goodbye, pretending to leave but circling back to the bar to ask Manny who she was.

"Seem you omit important info from the update, Manny." Mark rolled his eyes in Mona's direction.

"Is you omit to ask me, Prof. She name Mona Mansingh. Writing doctor thesis, something about patois. I not too clear. She live over by Stokely."

"Bright as well as beautiful, then?"

"Guess so, Prof, if doctor thesis mean you bright."

"Point well taken, Manny."

"I could tell you one thing though, Prof. You got to be careful with these coolie ladies. I a coolie man myself, on two side, mother full and father half, so I could tell you. They very high strung, sensitive, like them thoroughbred breed of horse. Need careful handling."

"Thanks for the advice, Manny, but for now I am just observing and going along, as you say." Landing Manny a good-natured punch, he set off again.

His relationship with Mona had seemed fated. In uncanny ways, it had unfolded in tandem with his prospects at the Caribbean-Inter-American Development Bank. The next time he'd seen her (it was at the pool again), he'd asked her to have a drink with him.

"I really shouldn't," she'd replied.

"Why not? Is there someone who would object?"

"My mother mightn't like the idea."

"You never do things that your mother disapproves of?"

"That's a pretty personal question from someone I don't know!" She was on her feet by then, pool bag in hand.

"You're leaving because I asked you to have a drink?"

"I'm going to change."

"I'll be here when you come back."

He'd stayed, she'd come back, and the drink became lunch, during which he'd enjoyed being the centre of attention for he was with by far the best-looking female there. When he'd returned to his office, there'd been a letter saying he was short-listed for the bank job. The day after their first real date, he received a phone call inviting him to DC for an interview: he was one of the final three candidates. He'd wooed her as he waited for the verdict, and once certain of the job, pressed his suit home.

"So, who do I ask for your hand?"

"Whom, not who," she instructed. They'd been walking from his office towards the sub-warden's flat where she stayed.

"Sorry. Whom do I ask for your hand?"

"It's mine so I'm not sure why you'd ask anyone else."

"Well, I know your Dad is dead, but there's your Mum in Trinidad, and that bro, the one with the vile temper somewhere in Canada, not to mention sister Nora in Maryland, all of whom I'd prefer not to get on the wrong side of."

"And there's you ending a sentence with a preposition and, far more important, not being very romantic about asking me to tie my future to yours."

He's deeply fond of her and glows with pride when he considers that she's his. He thought he'd never be bored for her mind was quick and her interests broad. Superbly qualified as wife and mother, it grieves him how it went awry.

"Bad luck worse than Obeah," he speaks into the mists of the shower. He'd call after the ten o'clock news and pilot their conversation carefully. She probably hasn't yet heard about Edwin Langdon's murder.

GRACE AND JIMMY

37

Grace Arrives in Mabuli

"Are you alright, Dr. Carpenter?"

"I'm fine, thanks."

"For sure, a bit weary?"

"A bit weary, yes."

The priest is silent again, studying the way ahead. A waning moon offers glimpses of a humpty-bumpty worm of road showing its dusty back in the headlights now and then as it wriggles its way through scrubby blackness.

The only flight from Geneva to the airport near Benke is on Thursdays and she wants to be in Mabuli early in the week. She leaves Geneva on Monday, but by the time she emerges from the airport in Ouagadougou, it is past one o'clock on Tuesday morning. Usually they meet her on the tarmac and escort her through officialdom, not that she regards it as de rigeur, but after twelve hours flying during which she's been serenaded by snores and suffocated by exhalations of foul air, any intervention that spares her extra minutes on her feet is welcome.

Once on the ground, she looks for the priest, but with no luck. Her laissez-passer takes her through immigration and customs, and when one of a tangle of lean, eager young men offers to put her bags onto a cart, she lets him heft the heavy cases. He oughtn't to be helping her at all, given a sign that warns that only porteurs are authorized to handle baggage, but there are none that she can see. Like countless touts inside the continent's airports, he is operating under the radar. As she sets off with the laden cart, she palms him his tip with a conspiratorial smile. When he looks at the money, his smile widens and he bows to signal the extent of his gratitude. It is a bigger-than-usual tip, in the spirit of Christmas just past. She hopes it will help launch him into prosperity in 1994. The new year is barely four days old.

Strong-arming the cart, each wheel with its own mind, she emerges onto the pavement to inhale a dusty mouthful of cool air. She manages to arrest the trolley, and is looking about for the priest when a tiny old woman heaves into view, also fighting a cart. It towers with boxes and bags and is crowned by an oversize suitcase. As the cart, overloaded and tipsy, wobbles across the pitted pavement in front of Grace, it hits a rut and the case on top flies backwards towards its driver. Grace lunges at the large missile and catches it, yanking her body around as it carries her to the ground with its weight. She straightens up, a sharp pain shooting across the bottom of her belly. The woman, though startled, has managed to halt her cart and is limping toward Grace.

"I am so sorry, vraiment désolée. You are okay, mademoiselle? Merci. Merci beaucoup. The barrow, it is stubborn."

"I'm fine, thank you." Grace lies. In truth, the pain in her lower abdomen, though not quite as severe, still lingers. The suitcase might have seriously injured the diminutive person in front of her, however, and she is glad she caught it. "Are you all right? I think we need …"

As she looks around for help, a man steps up, lifts the suitcase onto the woman's cart, and turns to scan the lines of youth squatting in front of the exit, warming themselves at small lanterns. The outside hustler crew, they hawk local transportation, food, "necesites" like toothpaste, soap, combs, deodorant, and also "hebergument aculliant" translated with equivalent aplomb and equally poor spelling as "horspitable accomodashun." Four young men leap forward. The man chooses one, dismisses the others with a few words at which they laugh, and speaks to the fellow he's chosen. A bill passes hands, and the old woman's errant cart moves off as she smiles, bobbing her head up and down to show her thanks.

"Dr. Carpenter?"

"Father Atule?"

They shake hands. The priest is somewhere in his forties, tall and very dark. He takes charge of her trolley, guides her towards an old Land Rover, holds the door open so she can get in, loads the bags, and relinquishes the cart to eager palms.

"I apologize," he says as he settles into the driver's seat and starts the Rover. "I'd hoped to meet you planeside, but I had a breakdown on the way in."

"It's fine. It's not something one can anticipate." She looks across at high cheekbones, an aristocratic up-tilting chin.

In a short time the environs of the airport have slipped into deep shadow, but for the odd street lamp and prickles of light in the distance.

"I am so sorry. I forgot. It's because I am reminding myself to concentrate on these roads." Which is just as well, for though it is very late, lorries and buses overtake and chase past them, their fleeting lights illuminating a bald landscape interrupted occasionally by grey factory-like buildings that loom against the blackness. "It's Harmattan, so it's cool at nights. I brought you a wrap, for it won't warm up till the middle of next month."

"Thank you, but I brought ... " She glances into the back. "Oh no! I must have mislaid my jacket in the airport."

"I'm sorry about that. Please use the wrap. It's very warm. Sœur Monique made it. She's always glad when it can be of service. She says it has good juju."

"Well, I could do with both wrap and juju. Thanks very much."

"We'll see what we can do about your jacket tomorrow."

She hugs the wrap round her, a tight weave in dark cotton, warm but not ticklish, and sinks back on her seat, biting her lip against a next twinge in her belly. Dozing off, she muses, "I'm thirty-four on my next birthday. Getting too old for this."

A couple of big bumps jerk her eyes open. The Land Rover is now squirming through dimly moonlit darkness, its headlights flitting here and there, picking out bushes and fence posts like follow spots on a shifting stage. She listens to the irregular rhythm of wheels on the rutted road, now and then a shuddering of wings in branches, and when the vehicle slows, a faraway pounding like rain. She doesn't see how it can be and is thinking of asking the priest, when she drifts off again.

"We're almost there, Dr. Carpenter," his voice cuts into a dream, of water perhaps, though once she opens her eyes she isn't sure. "The going gets a bit rough from here on, so I thought to warn you. You should perhaps hold on."

She hangs onto the dashboard against a mile or so of formidable pitching and tossing, until she sees in the gloom ahead a lighter place, as if someone has erased the spot. Shortly, the priest drives through rough-hewn gateposts, stopping on a small rise. The point of expunged dimness is a lantern held aloft in the hand of a saint of twisted wire, a holiday garland round his neck. A child sits in his other hand. The sculpture is fixed to the front of a building that stretches back into blackness.

Her host looks towards the house as if expecting someone, then shrugs, opens his door, and jumps out, vanishing momentarily, reappearing to open her door. The light from inside the car shows cheeks freckled in a pattern of scars, a mouth pinned at one corner by an odd smile.

"You must be sleepy as a sulcata, Dr. Carpenter. She's our Sahara tortoise. We'll get you something to eat and then install you in your room. Is there a bag with your essentials or will you need all these cases now?"

Grace figures that the person he had looked for was meant to help with the suitcases. She nods, her attention distracted by a flash of lightning so bright and near she swears she hears it fizzle. She is feeling odd and very cold, despite the wrap, the pain in her belly nagging. Maybe she should have forced herself to eat more of the dreadful airplane food.

"I'm a bit tired," she begins, collecting her briefcase and carryall.

"Why don't I take those?"

Easing herself from the high seat, she hands him the two pieces of luggage and reaches out her hand to grasp his.

"Thank you," she says and faints.

———

She relishes the cover of the soft African night, large enough to wrap her up many times over, alive with sounds so she doesn't feel alone. She nuzzles up to it like a human body, comforted by its snores and hoots and sighs, sleeping the sleep of childhood, wedged between Ma and Pansy, surrounded and safe. Strange that on waking, she feels deflated as popped Mary's tears, tiny, red bell-shaped flowers they'd stop and burst on the way home from school. She is in a white metal hospital bed, knees raised on a pillow, shoulders bare, looking up at a tall black man whose long, slim hands hold a stethoscope.

"You're awake, I see. How are you feeling?"

"It's afternoon, isn't it? It feels like afternoon."

"Early afternoon," he says. "I asked how you felt?"

"Like a squished tomato. How did I get here?"

"You fainted coming out of the Rover. We brought you in and put you to bed."

There is a lump of something between her legs. A sanitary pad! Good God. She never uses those things. It's warm and damp down there. Perhaps she hurt herself falling — but hardly there. She tries to sit up, feels faint, and drops back onto the bed.

"No, don't. You should be quiet. Are you hungry? You must be. We'll get you something to eat."

Past where he is standing by the window in the small, grey room, bright sunlight splatters on dark vegetation. In the near distance some trees, mango maybe, are tall enough to block the light, but enough comes through, dappling in a breeze. Right next to the rails of what must be a verandah there are paw-paw trees laden with fruit. Further away, sun shines on domes of red-brown bricks, just visible through the trees.

The priest has on glasses, round, with pale frames, hitched halfway down his wide nose. She is seeing him properly for the first time. He resembles a schoolteacher, but he is handsome behind the spectacles.

"Father Atule," Grace considers what she wants to say and decides that since she doesn't know, she will simply speak and find out herself. "This is all highly peculiar. We have a lot of work to do, a lot of ground to cover."

"It's Jimmy."

"Jimmy. Thank you. It's Grace. I'm sorry about last night, the trouble and embarrassment."

"Grace," he leans towards her and asks quietly, "Don't you know?"

"Know what?"

"You're pregnant. And you may be losing the baby."

"How can you possibly know that?"

"I'm clairvoyant," he says, or she thinks he says. His smile fades as she slides back into dreaming.

————

A mountain blots out everything. It is alive, sputtering, the earth vibrating with each explosion. Then it breaks open, emitting lava that gropes down slopes, breaking into streams that fan out and cook everything they come upon, frying, boiling, roasting. Chickens burn up, sizzling in their own fat. She hears the feathers catch fire, smells their scorched smell, the flesh aflame in seconds, the bones, first brittle, then ash. Pigs burst, oil spitting from their crackling. Melons and cucumbers stew in their own juice.

Something moves in a green grove towards which a finger of molten rock is winding, a small thing on the ground, thrashing in a frenzy of waving brambles as it wrestles to be free. She wakes, anxious about the furious little creature. The tastes and smells from the dream are sharply present.

It is night and cold. She is in a hospital gown, under a blanket. The gown is raised up, the bedclothes rolled down to her hips. A man is touching her belly.

"Takes twelve years to make your average Jesuit, if there's such a thing."

"Do I detect sarcasm, Don Jaime?"

Jesus! What is she saying! The man must think she is crazy!

"I think the child will be okay," he readjusts gown and bedclothes so she is fully covered.

"It's hardly a child, is it?"

"Whatever it is, it's put you on your back and it's keeping you there."

"Shouldn't we talk about whether there's any point to my staying? We've not even had a conversation about what's brought me here, plus I'm interfering with the centre's routine." She is deciphering what she is saying as it comes out of her mouth.

"Man proposes, God disposes. In your country they say, 'Man pour pint. God take quart.' "

"You've been to St. Chris?"

"I told you about those Jesuits, didn't I?" She must have been asleep for that too. Off-her-head and narcoleptic!

"Why would they have sent you to St. Chris? Isn't there a big enough need in Africa?" His bio said nothing about him being a doctor, or being in St. Chris.

"I did my regency there, at St. Aloysius College. It seems a long time ago now. Jesuits go anywhere there's a need. We are men of the world in that sense. Africa isn't the world, after all. I've studied at Oxford; I've lived in St. Chris. Among other places."

"Oxford? So I was right to call you 'don' then?"

"I preferred to think you were celebrating me as a ganja baron. Suits a big black man better than the other kind, doesn't it?"

He is teasing, but it irritates her, maybe because she still feels outside the fold of black people, though it's silly to call anyone black or African here.

"What makes you think I didn't mean them both?"

He only smiles. "Tomorrow we'll see how you're doing and we'll talk some more. Now we'll send Amitié with food."

He is almost through the door, when he pauses "One more thing."

"Yes?"

"It's not my business, but what of the baby's father? Oughtn't he to know?"

———

Next morning she gets up to go to the bathroom. Through the window, a sky with an old woman's face glowers at her. It is the flinty face she has seen on mothers taking care of wasted daughters spotted with lesions, skin scabbed, or turned to powdery grey; the worn face of grandmothers looking after orphaned grandchildren for whom food is scarce, clothes and shoes are luxuries, and doctors and medicine are fictive things. Wentley folks are poor, sick, and often sad, but she can't recall ever seeing a face or a morning sky like this.

On her way back, she yields to the temptation of peeking through the door. Footsteps sound on the floorboards outside as she is stepping in that direction, and she scampers under the sheets in time to pipe, "Come in!" when there is a knock.

"I heard footsteps. How are we today, then?"

"I'm fine. We're fine, thank you."

"Good. I see you are assessing our weather."

"Please." She is reluctant to say his name. Now that yesterday's delirium has given way to sanity, calling him Jimmy seems too familiar, never mind that he told her to call him that, but Father Atule or Father sounds too formal. Irresolute, she skips it. "I'll die of boredom, if I stay inside. Not to mention curiosity. I need to see what's going on. It's why I came." She is glad to sound businesslike. "Otherwise, what do I tell my employers?"

"Last point first." He sounds serious but there is something playful in his eyes. "I wouldn't worry about them. I've been in touch. They're apprised."

She sits up, *zoom*.

"You told my employers I'm pregnant?"

"Please. You must be quiet." He pats her back onto the bed. "For sure, you can't think much of me. I'd hardly have done that without your permission. Your office called to check on whether you'd got here safely. We told them you were somewhat indisposed but recovering comfortably."

Stupid. All the same, it alerts her to the fact that she isn't sanguine about letting her bosses know she is having a baby. Not that there aren't any single mothers among her colleagues, but it is inevitably a long-time-ago matter, occurring early enough that the children are grown by the time their mothers are senior people.

"And you have been in bed not even for three days. There are women who have to lie in bed for an entire pregnancy if they want to keep a baby."

"Don't lecture me." Remembering Ma and manners, she adds, "Please. I'm surely not one of those women."

"Perhaps not so surely."

"How can you know? Are you an obstetrician?" She is being boorish again.

"There's no escaping some obstetrics if one works with HIV/ AIDS. Women and babies are a big part of what we endeavour to do here, as you know."

She finds the word "endeavour" quaint and humble. He can easily speak of achievement, for as far as the World Health Organization is concerned, the MATE Centres are considered outstanding. He is weird — modest, bossy, and hip at once.

"Isn't there an ob/gynae clinic nearby?"

"I'm afraid I'll have to do. The nearest hospital is in Benke, hours away."

"There must be someone who can get me on my feet … "

"I'm sorry. I have to go," he responds, not really answering her. "There are some other folks I have to see. We'll check on you when I get back."

"Father Atule, we can't keep delaying … "

But he's gone.

———

She puts down Jimmy Atule's manuscript: "Jesus and HIV/ AIDS." He brought it in at lunch time, suggesting she have a look at it since it told the history and work of the centre at Tindi, but how can she read while she staggers among emotions, reeling between fear and confusion? She folds her arms. Exhales in exasperation. First she flirts with the priest. Now she sounds like something out of a bad novel. What is wrong with her?

She has not thought of aborting the baby. She is Gramps's grandchild, Gwen and Moses Carpenter's child, from the barracks' yard in Wentley Park, sister to Pansy, Stewie, Edgar, Conrad, Sammy, and Princess, a family who made a place for her. As she reasoned when Maisie's daughter got pregnant, dashing away pikni isn't part of their tradition. And she is Phyllis's daughter, lost to her mother and cherished anyway. But the priest is right. Should she tell Mark? Less than two months ago, she left him at Logan, feeling not madly in love, but warm, content. She hasn't heard a word since. That surprises her. They worked well together. She hasn't thought of their Cambridge interlude as the beginning of anything earthshaking — she has known earthshaking with Charlie — but it was surely important enough to warrant his being in touch, just to say he treasured it and wouldn't forget. He can find her; people do it all the time. If he wanted to, he could have called. Still, she dallied two weeks in New York to see Phyllis and do a bit of work, spent another three weeks in London, and stayed for a week and a half over Christmas in Geneva before flying to Mabuli. But if he'd phoned or written, she'd have known. That being the case, she isn't sure she wants to give him this news.

The pregnancy is a surprise to her. It had been a while between her last two periods, but the last one happened right before the workshop in Cambridge. Her periods have always been erratic, measured by the once-a-month criterion. Sometimes she has only half a dozen in a year. So she hadn't really been worried about getting pregnant, never mind her teasing question as she left Mark at Logan airport.

"Cock mouth kill cock!" An old Gramps adage.

How do you tell a man you haven't seen for ages then make love to one morning that there is now a bond between you that nothing can erase? Besides, when they parted, she released him from obligations to any baby that might come as a consequence of their lovemaking.

If she hears from him, it might make a difference. She'll wait and see.

————

On the verandah late the next afternoon, Thursday, Grace is enjoying a small triumph. Some good-natured gutter fighting in the morning secured her leave to be outside for a bit. There is to be no walking up and down, but she can sit and read. It is warm, the sky tinsel bright. Dry grasses and shrubs are a dusty olive that holds its own against the jades of pawpaw and date palm. Set against a backdrop of red domes scrabbling through dark green mango leaves, with behind it all, the glittering, overarching blue, the panorama reminds her of Christmas in Wentley, tipping as it always does into January drought.

She has been enjoying the priest's account of how the design for the centre at Tindi came about. At the start, he and the two nuns saw everyone in a large, round, thatch-roofed hut. Those waiting fell into groups: men talked together; women stood or squatted, some with babies, many with toddlers; pregnant mothers sat on benches, often with a baby slung behind or balancing another in front; older women leaned on canes and crutches, no strangers to HIV for having left childbearing behind; restless folks clutched birth, land, and medical papers, for HIV/AIDS affected many things.

When the staff grew (two nurses part-time, another midwife twice a week), they'd used woven screens to divide and extend the hut.

The building rose on the plan traced by people's feet. From a central, all-purpose space, walkways lead to satellite structures housing wards for men, women, mothers with newborn babies, a kitchen-cum-refectory, and an administration section.

Alternating male and female voices interrupt her concentration, singing in a language she can't understand. Laughter breaks in, and then the singing resumes in French, and then English. A lusty tenor asks, "Will you, will you, will you be my mate?" to which a saucy soprano replies, "No sir! No sir! You already have a mate!"

Little rooms are the boast of the facility at Tindi, according to what she reads: bathrooms, a library, a playroom, a prayer room. The priest relates the story of his trying them out on the first day, and, in so doing, treating the superior to a display of his elevated bottom, clad in the rose pink of the chasuble worn on Gaudete Sunday, as he prostrates in the prayer room.

"Allah-o-Akbar, Jimmy. Contemplating conversion?"

"Yes, Father, of kneelers to prayer rugs and kneeling to the Sajda. Our imams and marabouts endorse the Sajda for prayer and the constitution. I agree."

"As long as you ensure the air in this room stays sweet," Father Kitendi retorted.

"Cruel!" I lamented my fate: persecuted for the whims of my bowels. I tried out the playroom too, slamming my ankle into the ground, twisting it badly as I came scooting down into the sandpit from a slide meant for the children. Sister Monique rescued me, eyes full of fun, asking, "Father Jimmy, have you lost your age paper again?"

Atule's account is the story of a brave community, laughing and singing, praying and chanting, sustained by the call and response of purposeful work and instructional songs, the ululation of mourning, the priest's and muezzin's summonses to prayer. It argues stubbornly that the principle of double effect allows the use of condoms if one of two partners is infected, since in that case it is intended not to obstruct life, but to prevent death. Grace is thinking that he's brave to take on Rome as well as powerful, ignorant politicians, when he rides up, parks his bike, and comes upstairs to the verandah, banana in one hand, loose condom in the other.

"Isn't that waving a red flag at a bull?" she jokes.

"If the bull is oceans away, it's not dangerous." He chuckles briefly, reminding her of a younger Gramps. "I wanted to give you an example of what we do. It is simple, deals with the basics, and is easy for community workers to replicate." He becomes subdued as he reports this, sombre even. "Also, it's time for you to be back inside."

She's stayed outside all afternoon. Now she knows what the buildings are, she can distinguish a big dome swelling in the pink sunset, and some of the small domes peering through the mango trees, the eyes of their double-baked bricks winking in the fading light. She closes the manuscript. "I'm on my way." He waits on the verandah, no doubt meaning to watch her go in, but she isn't ready yet. "Father ... Jimmy, I'm way behind. Would it hurt if I sit at my table a few minutes at a time to make notes?"

He takes his time about replying. "I daresay it wouldn't. But be sensible and don't overdo it. For sure?"

"For sure, Jimmy." Luck is with her, so she bets again. "Do you think you'd have some time this weekend for a chat?"

"I couldn't say just yet."

"I'll be up and about next week, won't I? I was hoping to go with you on your rounds soon." She adds, thinking it politic, "I'll do as you say, of course."

"The chat is perhaps possible. For the up and about, we must wait and see." He dithers a bit, then hazards, "You must please do some writing for me, then."

"Absolving you from blame if anything happens to me? Of course."

"Not that, no. I told my editor that you were going to be here. He said that I should ask you to write a foreword to the book."

She thought he was going to ask her to sign some kind of indemnity. It would be a very sensible rule. "Well, I'd ..."

"Don't answer now. I'm truly embarrassed to bother you. I said no, but you know these people, they've don't know what the word 'importunate' means."

"It's no problem. I haven't finished but I've enjoyed the story so far. If I don't think I'm a good person to write the foreword, believe me, Jimmy, I'll let you know."

"Thank you, Grace."

"So, what about the chat?" pressing her suit home.

"I say Mass in three places on Sunday, but perhaps at the end of the day."

"Thanks very much. So may I go with you to the centre one day next week?"

"Why don't we leave it all for Sunday?"

38

Troubling Trouble

He needs no more women in his life. His sisters, Alleme, now gone, Aisha, Ansile, and Angélique have always been a fistful, not to mention his Ma. He loves them with all his heart, which is easy, for they are generous, funny women, but they are still a big responsibility. Alleme, wife, mother, poet, and storyteller like Mapome, joined her grandma in the family plot in Benke at the start of the previous wet season. Aisha and her daughter are living with HIV/AIDS and so are on his radar, always, as is Alleme's younger daughter. Ansile struggles with depression. Angélique, his baby sister is fine, thank God, but she has just started sociology at the university and is finding it a challenge. She plans to work at MATE.

Many women at the centre are also in his mind and heart's keeping: Sœurs Monique and Tekawitha; Amitié; the twins originally from the novitiate, Elise and Lili; the part-timers at the clinic — not to mention staff at the other centres. And there is Nila, near as his next breath. And of course, the women who come to MATE (there are men too, but mostly it is women) who have for six years made up his life!

He gets into his clothes, scours his teeth, trims and scrubs his nails; he will shower later, after Mass. Stepping outside, he gazes north towards the gentle curl of the Bandiagara Escarpment visible in the distance, despite the haze — country of the Dogon, his mother's people. Mabuli's northwest border curves with the escarpment, then stretches southwest towards the River Bani, finally working its way south through savannahs, wriggling down to the border with Côte d'Ivoire.

In the far north, a region of dry scrubland dwindles into the great desert out of which come traders, mostly Tuareg, a people restive, aggressive and, when, as now, they judge it fit, rebellious. His father claims ancestry with Kel Tamasheq, through Mapome's forebears — Mapome, whom he still mourns, who told a tale about her great-great-grandfather entertaining a short white king in his tent near the shores of the Red Sea, Sea of Qulzum, the Great Water. Not everyone believed his forebear met Napoleon, but they were rapt each time Mapome detailed the appointments in Atunkle's tent, so opulent they overwhelmed the emperor of ashen skin.

It is true one Professor Egbert Johnson, an Englishman who was a member of Napoleon's team of scholars, returned to Mabuli with Atunkle, but less certain that he was responsible for disseminating the English language long before the French came. Jimmy prefers another tale, about the Tellem people who lived on the Bandiagara before the Dogon, and who, it was believed, could fly. When some Tellem youth were stolen and sold to slave traders, a group of holy men flew to the coast and snatched an equal number of white men, depositing them in the desert north of Mabuli. They turned out to be English. Those who survived made their way south to barter and then intermarry with Mabuli clans, bringing the gifts of blood and language at once.

As so often happens, the truth very likely lay somewhere between legend and history, but he treasures the myth of the avenging holy men who inadvertently made a present to the country of the English language. Like him, many young Mabulians are happy to be proficient in it. Often people will code switch, speaking French one minute, English the next. As a Jesuit in training, Jimmy had been glad of his fluency.

Thickets of kinkeliba and bakin gumbi spotting the steppes remind him of the dwindling benefits of the last wet season. Mabulians farm the green belt that runs south of the scrubland, continuing farther south over low hills, and then across flat country, ending in forested ranges near Côte d'Ivoire. On the Oti's counsel, farmers keep faith with Mabuli's sandy soils, inter-cropping annuals and perennials, employing neem, gum arabic, and balanzan trees to improve crop yields. For bees especially, the balanzans are vital. His father, Andri, was once a farmer growing sorghum on land in Oubisi, a town towards the south. As a boy, Jimmy worked in those fields. He also minded the family goats, for farmers were often pen-keepers as well, raising some sheep but mostly goats. Like many others, the Atules kept them for milk, cheese, and meat, but Pa Atule had grander plans and went into keeping pens for gain.

The Atules' migration to Benke, the capital in the north, was not desperate. Having learned many lessons from the droughts, his father wanted to form co-operatives for both pen-keepers and farmers. Benke was the obvious place to set them up, for in Benke everything and everyone are to be found. The co-operatives never got off the ground, and his father turned, disappointed, to buying and selling. The Atules grew rich from trading.

Now Jimmy stretches his ears past the clinic, trying to discover the bleating of MATE's own herd of goats. From Oubisi days, he's been a fan of goats, "because" his mother always claims, "you and they have so much in common! Stubborn and stink!" He checks his watch. He has a minute to reach the chapel. He'll steal some seconds to pause on his way past the visitor's room. Tiptoeing near the window, he slows down to listen. "Boy child," he can again hear his Mama Makda say, as she pinches his ears, "rank as a goat, with antennae keen as a bat's!"

Grace Carpenter's exhalations are steady, regular, so he presses on to the chapel, his emotions contrary. It bothers him that he doesn't have more cordial feelings towards Dr. Carpenter, partly, he admits, because of what he may have to tell her in due course. In the small sanctuary he robes for Mass, giving thanks for all the women who stitch amice and alb, chasuble and stole, who see them prepared every day. His mother is one. He remembers the tiny needle prick on the day of his first Mass. They had that custom in St. Chris too: if you mend a garment on a person, you give them a little jab.

He counts hosts into the ciborium, for the six communicants: Monique, Tekawitha, Ousmain, Amitié, Elise, Lili. Then he sits in the chapel to consider again the events that brought him to this place, and his life since. If Dr. Carpenter has a reason for not telling her baby's father, it is none of his business, although no one is more aware than he why the father ought to know she is pregnant. He thinks of all his orphan babies. Dr. Carpenter may be a bright woman and a senior bureaucrat, but he has no doubt about who is in control as things stand. They will do what is necessary to secure her wellbeing and that of the baby. If that means she has to stay close to her room till it is safe to travel to Geneva, so be it. He isn't his father's son for nothing.

It is his tea break, ten stolen minutes before going to give classes to community workers at the centre. He blows on the hot liquid, reflecting. Their visitor hadn't known she was pregnant. He's yet to come across a woman at MATE who didn't know she was making a baby. Amitié, who runs the main house, arrived at Tindi self-diagnosed. A fusillade of thumps on his door early one morning brought him out of bed, sure the house was on fire. She wasn't twenty, her face and body a mosaic of cuts, scabs, and bruises.

"Vous êtes le prêtre, Atule?"

"C'est moi."

"Je suis enceinte, et j'ai aussi le SIDA. C'est mon mari. He gave the baby and The Skinny to me."

"Come," he led her inside, through the corridor, down to the room they sometimes used as a surgery. Whatever else might be wrong, she was severely beaten. Ousmain slept on the floor on his mat at the T-junction of the corridors. He nudged the young man awake.

"Find Sœur Monique, vite!"

They spent two hours cleaning her wounds, stitching, bandaging, plastering, patching up her body.

"Did you report this?" Monique asked her.

"How can I? It is my husband's doing."

"You can report it to the Oti," the nun insisted. "Your clan chief must take it to them, if you inform him."

"Ce n'est rien. Heal my baby. Give me the chance to bring him up."

"But why did he do this?" pressed Monique, a terrier, bone in her teeth.

"He was away. He went with whores. I tell him no sex. You are sick."

"What did he say?"

"'The day I bought you, you swallowed the word "no." I will show you that you cannot vomit "no" upon me.'"

Neither Jimmy nor Monique saw how she could be so sure she had AIDS.

After a week at the centre she came to Monique. "Je vais bien, oui?"

"Yes, your cuts and bruises are healing well, Amitié."

"Je partirai demain. I cannot go to my home, but my place is needed for those more sick." It was true. A dozen new people came to Tindi each day.

"Where will you go? What about your children?"

"Ma mère. She is strong. That man will not cross her. The twin healing women say a grandmother in town is dying. Her body is full of sores, and no one wants to look after her. I will care for her in return for lodging and food. The priest says maybe I can have the test in Benke. I pray it may be so."

She tested HIV-positive. Her baby came on the date she'd named. In between, she stuck to her plan, guarding her health, tending the old woman until she died. After that Monique suggested they try her out at the centre.

Jimmy asked Amitié how it was she knew that she had the disease.

"This body is my home. I know if there's a guest or if the building needs repair." Perhaps he should ask Amitié to consult in the case of Dr. Carpenter.

39

La Sage-femme or The Midwife

"You look tired, Jimmy."

"I am, for sure. But I'm good for the discussion, as promised."

"Do you always say Sunday Mass in more than one place?"

"Almost always."

"So you're never back here before nightfall on a Sunday?"

"Not often. But I made you a promise."

"You spend most time in the Tindi centre?"

"I visit one other centre two days each week. I'm in Tindi otherwise, except of course on Sundays."

"Are all the centres like this one? The domed brick structures are beautiful, but they're not typical, are they?"

"Certainly for Mabuli, these days, typical enough. But it's so in other places too. Perhaps a decade ago we realized we couldn't afford to build with adobe and timber anymore. We had too few trees. The Mabenke gives mud; we can fire clay as well as anyone. We must use what we have wisely. That includes time. What can I tell you?"

"I've big and little questions. Maybe we could tackle both?"

"This is entirely business, then?"

"Yes. If I can't be up and about, at least we can talk. I've learned a lot from your book."

"Not a book yet, but God willing, soon. Shall we start?"

"When you consider how to deal with HIV/AIDS in Sahelian Africa, what first comes to mind?"

"Political will."

"You mean strong government policy?"

"I mean it much more broadly. Every citizen. You. Me. Our parents, our siblings, our families."

"Has your family played a part in this work, Jimmy?"

"I'd certainly not have got involved, were it not for my family."

"How come?"

"I won't tell you the whole story but it began with our discovering, after one of my brothers-in-law died, that my sister was also HIV-positive. She died too."

"I'm sorry to hear that."

"Thank you. It was just after my ordination. It led me to this work."

"You've been very successful in implementing community-based education and treatment here, through the MATE Centres. You know they are our primary interest at WHO."

"I do. But ours is a small effort and Mabuli a small country, so I wonder why you ask me big questions. I'd do better with little ones, like how much easier delivering babies would be if we had running water through Harmattan!"

"Let's compromise. I'll accept your quirky definition of political and look forward to hearing how Mabuli's citizens made a difference, if you'll admit that the folks we usually call political did come on board. They must have."

"Okay. I admit it. They did."

"What made them so discerning? Many African countries haven't addressed the disease with enough seriousness. Did Mabuli policymakers know a lot about HIV/AIDS? Did they know of the studies using Tanzanian data, for instance?"

"I knew of them, and a few other people, but that's not what made the difference. I'd say God's grace is what did it."

"Well, I'm all for God's grace, but please tell me how it showed itself."

"The chiefs of our largest clans lost their eldest sons, one this week, one the next, one the week after."

"Good grief, Jimmy! How awful! That's hardly grace! Sounds like Old Testament vengeance, with first-born sons slaughtered and similar horrors."

"Clan leadership passes through eldest sons. The deaths of those three had a profound, immediate effect. It was a bad thing out of which came a good one. That can be grace too. And number three is very significant in our culture."

"But did they know it was HIV/AIDS?"

"There's knowing and knowing. The three princes' deaths forced people, the Oti included, to admit the fact of the disease and to recognize it as HIV/AIDS."

"Aaah! The Oti! Mabuli's umbrella council of religious leaders."

"Forgive me! I've not asked how you are feeling. Are you okay?"

"I'm fine. Excellent."

"For sure, Grace?"

"For sure, Jimmy."

"Good. We can go on, then. Back to political, in your sense: I suppose, ironically, we could say the Oti fit the political bill."

"You mention the Oti often in the book."

"The Oti need a book to themselves. They include imams, shamans, priests, and marabouts from many belief systems. The organization is quite unique."

"That's a pretty motley crew."

"It is. Nature bound them together, long ago, or God, if you wish."

"Bound them together how?"

"It's a long story, myth some would say, involving our Kenbara Stone Circle, perhaps best saved for another time."

"Tell me more about the Oti."

"The Oti account for much of our success. Their wisdom extends to all aspects of life in Mabuli: the relative advantages of growing millet over sorghum; habits that make for good hygiene; water conservation; sound agricultural practice."

"That's most unusual."

"The Oti also have strong influence on our ruling classes — chiefs, elders, elected officials — politicians, as you say." The priest smiles, lifting his chin, raising his eyebrows, blinking, St. Chris style.

"Your father is a clan chief, isn't he?"

"Yes. It's a small clan. He was frantic after Alleme's husband died. When AIDS took Munti, Pa and I insisted my sisters and their families be tested. Some tested positive. His frenzy galvanized him. All of us."

"I'm very sorry about your family, Jimmy."

"Thank you. As I've said, Alleme died. The others are doing well."

"So your focus on person-centred therapy arises from your family's encounter with the disease?"

"I've not thought of it that way, but for sure it's influenced my approach."

"What about prevalence? How do you keep track?"

"Our systems are basic. Many come to the centre, but many others ignore their symptoms for as long as they can, so we like to use Amitié and her daughter as examples of the advantage of early diagnosis, especially for pregnant mothers. Even health workers, ashamed or in denial, fail to come forward. My father had to ride roughshod over our family."

"I'd like to meet your father."

"Don't be so sure!" He pats his knees, rocking his upper body from side to side. "Aisha's a nurse, and she was hardest of all to persuade. She told me that she was a medical professional and would know if she were ill."

"Taciturn health workers? That's a severe setback."

"I'd say. Plus, where prevalence is concerned, things look different bottom up, from top down."

"Meaning?"

"We don't have resources for testing at the centres. There's now an excellent facility in Benke, but it's overworked, and in some ways, in the worst possible location. We diagnose from symptoms, and then we try to have persons encourage their sexual partners to come to MATE too. Like my father with his sons-in-law, though we use a lighter hand."

"A light hand with HIV/AIDS, huh?"

"The disease is heavy-handed enough. While we're talking to people about who they've had sex with, agencies consider prevalence. It's not that data isn't crucial, but it's individuals who have the disease. We teach people to be alert to symptoms, aware of their health, and the health of those around them."

"So your method is incremental, beginning with the individual, building out from there?"

"Yes."

"And is your emphasis on treatment? Or education?"

"The treatment par excellence is education, whether to prevent or to live with the disease. You need to come to one of our sessions, see the twins do their 'Pat-a-Cake, Take Your Pills' handclapping song!"

"What about money, Jimmy? Where would it be most useful?"

"Well, God forgive me, but maybe some well-greased palms here and there, to make gatekeepers do the right thing!"

"You mean, bribe governments to come on board?"

"No. Bribe executives in corporate boardrooms so they vote to make drugs available and affordable."

Something alters just then, she isn't sure what. It has nothing to do with what the priest is saying. Almost everyone agrees about the need for affordable drugs. It's as if she is suddenly aware of the vulnerability of every person, a weight so heavy the struggle to keep going seems pointless.

"Jimmy, this is to switch direction for a moment. What actual medical training do you have?"

"Some."

"In what?"

"CPR."

"Anything else?"

"Bit of bush medicine." He is teasing her.

"Is that it?"

"I'm a certified midwife."

"You're joking."

"I can show you my diplomas. On top of which I've delivered scores of babies. I'm especially trained to deliver babies at risk for HIV/AIDS, and to teach other midwives. You must have read the background documents?"

"We probably mislaid some pages."

"It's hard to believe that you put your well-being and that of your child into my hands without being satisfied that I knew what I was doing."

"You said you'd have to do when I asked for a specialist, remember? What choice did I have? No offence, but we're somewhere behind God's back. I arrive, fall flat on my face, and the next day you inform me that I'm pregnant and that I could lose the baby. The evidence supports this, so I assume you know what you're doing."

"You might have asked me to show you my bona fides."

"I was half-awake a lot of the time. Plus, you might have laughed in my face."

"May I take your hand?"

"Of course. You needn't ask. You're my ... doctor."

"You're in my care but you're also clearly in excellent health. You probably don't realize how rare it is to see a pregnant woman thriving. That guarantees nothing, where AIDS is concerned, but still. It's not for me to ask if you're at risk for the disease, although I'd be lying if I said I've not thought of it. But just seeing you hearty reminds us of what we work for each day."

"Well ... that's good, Jimmy. I'm glad to be here, then, and pregnant, if only for that reason."

"One more thing. Have you decided about telling the baby's father? I'm interfering, I know, but I think you should."

40

More Wordplay

Gatekeepers. Their visitor misunderstood about the gatekeepers and the palm greasing. G words — gatekeepers, grease. Is it narrow, western, stupid? Why is the greed always in African governments, never in the European lust for gold, oil, diamonds? Why is it never in the foreign letch for immoral local partners in depredation? Perish the thought! That's good business, not greed.

God. The G word of g words. Word of words. G force. Gravitation. Gravity. The Gravitas of God.

He is playing Mapome's dictionary game again.

She wasn't the gushing type, but they galloped along from the get-go.

"When you were about three months old, James, your ears used to wiggle when you heard singing."

"But ears don't wiggle, Mapome."

Her wiggling ears opened up a new world for him.

"Don't assume, James. Don't swallow anything because someone says so. Never behave as though the world is a small place. It isn't. Never be scared if someone is different or something is new. That's the whole point of creation. It would be very boring if all grass were green."

"But all grass is green, Mapome."

"Go outside now into the garden and bring me back grass in six colours."

Go. Garden. Grass. Green.

Some philosopher says that if you call a man a communist, killing him becomes easy. What names are people calling Africans so that they die in droves without anyone lifting a hand … well … a glove, for the sake of the game? (He is playing well. It is the first time he's deliberately chosen a g word.) Gorillas? Gibbons? Goons?

God grant to Simeon, his graceful, God-fearing brother in Christ whose life of generous service was gutted, God grant him rest, and in good time, glorification. Simeon Lubonli would not have harmed a gecko. He shudders to think of AIDS drawing down Simeon's body, already starving so there was not a spare ounce on it, rendering it ghastly, ghostly. He was a skeleton when they found him, barely alive, in his tiny, isolated, God-forsaken parish in the Gambisi — another G! He'd thrown himself into work, but some monster, no good Muslim for sure, put it about that he was a giaour, infidel, threat to the community. Abandoned by his small flock and bereft of their modest support, Simeon sweated it out in his lonely Gethsemane, he who never did ill to anyone. Even Jesus had the three to keep him company in his grim garden. There are gibbets and gibbets: Simeon's cross was a grass mat on the tamped-down ground that constituted the floor of his tiny rectory.

G for Gethsemane, grim, gibbet, ground. G for Gospel, the good news, the spreading of which constitutes the reason for his life and Simeon's.

Enough! Mapome's game sometimes makes him dizzy. Dizzy! He is running out of Diazepam. He must get some on their next trip to Benke. Anyway, time to leave the game and address the dilemma of what to do about his special patient.

It is as well they talk easily. Not that he is intimidated, never mind she is an important bureaucrat who might prove enormously valuable to their work at MATE. Sometimes in their conversation, he is reminded of his first interview with J.J. Perhaps it is a matter of cultural difference.

He grew up in a household where New World black folks were regarded with cynicism. His father had no patience with so-called Afro-Americans who claimed pride in Africa, but were unapologetic about their ignorance of the continent's history, geography, languages, weather, cultures, and customs. One October, talking to a businessman from Atlanta, his father remarked that Harmattan was just round the corner. He was stunned when the man asked if there were good roads to get there.

Is the xenophobia about which Mapome warned him dictating his reaction to their visitor? Or are his feelings not at all what they seem? Why had she suddenly ended the conversation, saying she was tired when she'd assured him she was fine? He prayed for her, prayed for all those under their care. MATE stood for Mabuli AIDS Treatment and Education. Angélique thought of the name, a perfect fit, since much of the success of any HIV/AIDS intervention depended on mates, whether they were partners, friends, brothers or sisters, grandmothers or grandfathers. He hopes Grace Carpenter has a mate.

G. For Grace.

41

Offspring

There was nothing untoward in his manner, nothing suggestive in how he held her hand, so Grace is alarmed that she finds Jimmy Atule's touch erotic. She puts it down to the fact that her hormones are doing strange things. He is cool, solicitous, and delicious eye candy, to be sure, but she meets many sensitive, attractive men in her work. She is here on business, he is a person dedicated to God, she's caused trouble enough, arriving pregnant and unwell, making a call on his time and creating extra work for the staff.

Suddenly aware of the pointlessness of it all, she changed tack, then ended the chat, after his interfering advice to inform the baby's father. He was so sweetly apologetic.

"Can we finish this some other time, Jimmy? I'm suddenly weary."

"You're sure it's tiredness, not anything else?"

"Just tired."

They got up. He reached over and made the sign of the cross on her forehead, saying as he did it, "You don't mind?" She shook her head, no.

"Good night, Grace."

"Good night, Jimmy." She stood watching him as he went, one hand sliding across her stomach. She's still heard nothing from Mark. Fine baby-father, never mind he's no idea she is pregnant. She is increasingly coming to the conclusion that she isn't going to tell him, whether he gets in touch or no. Charlie said when they first made love, "If you get pregnant, Grace Carpenter, I'll be over the moon." She'd been daftly oblivious about contraception that time too.

In her room, she undresses, lies down, turns out the light, and settles into the sheets, preparing again to consider this lunatic attraction to — she rehearses the litany — her professional colleague, her host, her doctor for all intents and purposes, a man vowed to celibacy and a life dedicated to God. Jesus! Then the enormity of what he said hits her. She doesn't know a thing about Mark, has no clue about his personal life, let alone his lovemaking habits, so she and her baby can well be as risk-prone as any Mabuli woman having sex with a mate who frequents prostitutes.

"Oh my God!" she says aloud. "Oh my sweet Lord Jesus. What is this foolishness I've done?" She opens her mouth to scream, then she realizes where she is, who she is. Screaming would be selfish and silly, but she needs at least to talk to someone. Maybe she can wake the priest, or that nice Sœur Monique. She jumps up, starts to dress, almost falling over her feet as they search on the floor for her shoes.

"Turn on the light, stupid!" Having turned it on, she lies back on the bed again, her mind going back to conversations in Geneva. They all take it for granted that since any new sexual partner might be HIV-positive, everybody insists on a condom. She knows it is neither the case that new sexual partners are mostly HIV-positive nor that everyone makes that assumption and so uses a condom. Otherwise AIDS wouldn't be epidemic. Still, she has no excuse, she, of all people!

Up on her feet again, no shoes on, she walks end to end of the small room. She sneezes and, too agitated to search her bag for tissues, uses the sleeve of her nightgown to wipe her nose.

Maybe it is better in this kind of situation to be dirt poor and have no prospects. Then it is less of a big deal.

She is immediately ashamed. The thought is selfish, supremacist. Sinful.

There must be some sensible thing to do. She remembers an Outward-Bound-type program Steph coaxed her to join one Canada Day weekend in the second year she was at U of Toronto. She tried at length to explain to her roommate why she didn't want to participate, reasons having to do with bears and the icy water in rivers and lakes, but Steph, indomitable, prevailed. She learned some useful things, one being what to do in states of panic. She tries to remember. Take long deep breaths. She does. Check vital signs. She is all there, maybe losing a baby but still, all there. Sum up the danger. Right. If she has AIDS, there is nothing to do about it, not immediately, anyway. If she doesn't, there is nothing to worry about. Either way, panic will achieve nothing.

It doesn't work. She is going to the priest. She doesn't care if he is terminally exhausted. She doesn't care about anything except the fact that she has to talk. She gathers the blanket round her shoulders because she is freezing and is turning the doorknob when she hears Gramps, clear as a bell. "You're a big girl now, Grace." A big girl who's done something superbly stupid! Just then Jimmy Atule's celibacy strikes her as a mighty shrewd choice. She decides she will talk to him in the morning.

Next day she sleeps until eight. She doesn't know exactly when the priest gets up, but she knows that he says Mass quite early in the chapel. Since she's been better, he's given up passing by her room in the morning and now leaves by nine most days, the time at which she's been waking up. She has to speak to him before he leaves for the day.

"Father Jimmy!" she shouts from the verandah when he's riding by on his bicycle, heading for the centre.

"Morning, Dr. Grace!" he shouts back, "Comment ça va?" When he sees her running for the steps, he directs the bike towards the building and brings it to a stop near where she is standing.

"Look, you can still lose that child. Rushing to and fro isn't a good idea."

"I'm sorry," she doesn't quite hang her head. "I must talk to you. Please."

"You're not hemorrhaging again?" He is off the bike, up the stairs, ushering her back into her room. She sits on the bed while he pulls up a stool. "Something wrong?"

"I'm fine."

"Absolutely for sure?"

"Absolutely." Get on with it, idiot. "This isn't professional, Jimmy. It's personal. It will take fifteen minutes. I know you're busy."

"Why don't you just tell me?"

"Suppose I have AIDS? Suppose I give it to the baby? I couldn't bear that. The child doesn't deserve that. I don't know what I'd do." She is looking at him, hands over her belly, hugging herself, starting to cry.

"Chances are that you and the baby are fine."

"How can you say that? You can't know. I can't know till I'm tested. And that's not possible here. Right?" She wipes her face with the back of her hand.

"Yes. Benke is too far for you to travel to, in your condition. Abortion is an option, but I can't advise it, of course, nor could you do it here. And you'd still be at risk."

"But you just said I'm probably fine."

"That's true. And the baby too."

"But you can say anything. You're not pregnant. You're not at risk for HIV/AIDS."

"I'm not pregnant, that's true." He hands her a big blue kerchief. "But nobody who works with HIV/AIDS patients avoids being at some risk."

"Makes you very brave, doesn't it?" She is being horrid, but she doesn't care.

"Grace, life is hard, even if you're rich as the King of the Ashanti and healthy as a hippo. When you come down the hill to the centre, you'll see women, children, and men who embarrass us all by their courage."

"I'm sorry. I'd no right."

"It's okay. As you said, I'm not pregnant."

"I just feel stupid and powerless and responsible."

"What do you know about the baby's father?"

"You mean do I know if he sleeps around?"

"Is he someone you just met? Or someone you have a relationship with?"

"I knew him a long time ago. We worked together at the university in St. Chris. He was dean of my faculty. I hadn't seen him for ages."

He sighs. "Is there anything to be done to help you to feel better?"

"Well, maybe I could call him. You know, ask him the questions I ought to have asked before I slept with him."

"So this is a new relationship?"

"New, yes, but I wouldn't call it a relationship."

"Well, what with recent sandstorms, we don't have the best phone connections in the world, but we can usually put a call through. You'll have to come to the centre, though. And we'll have to know the destination of the call to figure out when to make it, given time constraints."

"It's Washington, and they're six hours behind us, so if we called at about three, I should be able to get him."

"I'll ask Sœur Tekawitha, then. Do you have a number? And we'll need his name of course."

"His name is Mark Blackman. He's Executive Director of the Caribbean Inter-American Development Bank. I'll find his number and bring it with me."

"Good. We'll organize it, then. Have you had breakfast?"

She shakes her head.

"I'll ask Amitié to hurry it up."

42

One Night with You

Grace is taking her evening stroll down the verandah at about nine o'clock. It runs the length of the building, meeting the chapel at one end and the dining room and kitchen at the other. If she walks back and forth a few times, it amounts to exercise. She is encouraged to do that, taking it slow. She passes Jimmy's room going and coming. There is no light in his room when she first goes by. She presumes he is still working at Tindi or out at one of the other MATE Centres, so when she walks past his door again, she is surprised to hear something crash and shatter, followed by a regular, violent thumping. She waits a few moments, knocks, hears no answer, and opens the door. In the dimness she sees the priest lying on the ground in his pajama bottoms. His body is vibrating like an old wind-up car engine refusing to start. It hammers the hard wood boards. His eyes show only the whites, brilliant in the half-dark.

She reaches for the light switch, flicks it on.

"Jimmy? Jimmy?" No response. Around him on the floor are shiny blue shards of a broken pottery lamp.

God! What is it that you do for seizures again? A heavy, carved walking stick standing against the wall catches her eye, and she grabs it, resting it on the ground so it won't fall and hit him. He is biting his tongue, but she knows she shouldn't do anything about that. As she is pushing the broken pieces of the vase away from his body, she sees pills on the floor and an open vial with a few tablets inside — Diazepam, according to the label. Container in hand, she surveys the room for something to put under his head as a pillow. She puts down the pills and is bunching up the bedspread when she notices that though he is still sweating, the spasms have slowed, so she waits. When the jangling abates and his eyes are back in place, she asks, "Can you hear me?" He nods. She offers her hand, but he hangs on to one of the bedposts and with effort pulls himself to his feet.

"For sure, this is awful. Upsetting for you. I'm fine. Please go back to your room. Thank you so much for your help."

"How's your tongue?" She watches as one hand starts to go to his mouth, at the same time as the other begins slipping from the bedpost, as if in slow motion. Then the first one falls to join the second as his face and limbs begin to go slack and crumple.

"Do you need the Diazepam?"

He nods, clutches at the bedpost again, fighting to stay upright, groping his way onto the bed. She takes a pill from the box.

"Water?"

He gestures towards a small glass beside a statue of the Virgin on his bedside table. She wonders if it is holy water, but gives it to him anyway, along with the pill. He swallows it, but too late. His body stiffens as he slides into semi-consciousness again. At least he is on the bed. She doesn't know what to do. If she leaves him to get help, something worse might happen with no one there. She has CPR training and she's seen fits before, so she decides to stay.

The colour has leaked out of his skin so that it is the dirty grey-brown of St. Chris river water after heavy rain. This time he lies entirely still. It occurs to her that rousing him might help.

"What can I do, Jimmy? Can I get you anything?"

His pupils swivel and he looks at her goat-eyed, so she wonders if he does indeed see her. Then he is patting the bed for her to sit. She hesitates, but the gesture is insistent, so she eases herself onto the opposite corner near the bed head, all the time looking at him. He pushes himself up, resting against the plain metal headboard and faces her.

"I killed her." It is barely a whisper, so she has to bend to hear.

"Killed who?"

"I killed Nila."

"Who's Nila? Besides, that's absurd. You couldn't harm a flea."

"You want to split hairs? I can do that. I'm a Jesuit. Remember."

"That isn't funny."

"Indeed, it's not."

"Like I said, Jimmy, you couldn't … "

"Very well. I caused her death. Her name was Nila. She was my wife."

Another time she may have been surprised, but not now. "I don't believe that either."

"You mean that I was married? Lying isn't one of my sins."

"I've no reason to doubt that you were married. I meant that you caused her death. Didn't you love her?"

"Very much."

"Well, it doesn't make sense. If you loved her, why cause her death?"

"A sin of omission. Not what I did; what I didn't do."

"What didn't you do?" Persistent *cokee* noises all around in the dark remind her of the tiny tree frogs that used to comfort her in Wentley when she woke from a bad dream.

"You know Descartes, Grace?"

She nods. What has he to do with anything?

"He's supposed to have made this body/mind dichotomy, echoing the ancients' flesh and spirit division. These days the fashion is, 'Forget this mind nonsense. There is only the body, the tangible material thing.' I've always wondered if they never heard of Huxley, hallucinogens, LSD, even good weed."

She reminds herself that he has just been through something harrowing at the same time as she marvels at this Catholic priest who sounds so accepting of mood-enhancing drugs, psychedelics, marijuana.

"The idea that space-time is a continuum and black holes can double back time on itself is sound science, as any Trekkie can tell you." He is talking quickly, flecks of spit banking up at his mouth corners. "But any other predicting is suspect. If you're a scientist forward-seeing from your vantage point on a wormhole and you foresee what I foresee, your foresight is valid but mine isn't."

He's overwrought. Suppose he lapses again? She is unsure about what to do, decides she can't leave him. "Can't I get you something?" she interrupts, distracting him.

"It's all propaganda," he goes on, ignoring her. "Trouble is, while some people are peddling religion, science, philosophy, and so on, our African Everywoman is having sex with a man whose AIDS-infected penis is going about its traditional, historical, as-by-divine-right man business." He is gesticulating, his voice rising. She must get him back to talking about his wife.

"We were talking about Nila."

"We are talking about Nila, about how she died. We're discussing the fine phenomenon you just witnessed."

"What exactly is it, Jimmy?"

"I fall into some kind of trance —"

"Seizures aren't so unusual."

"It's not just seizures. Everyone else falls down. Me, I fall down and prophesy."

She allows a respectful time for that to settle, and then offers, "In our part of the world, seeing the future isn't so strange,

Red Jacket   339

though Ma and Pa didn't like us fooling with horoscopes, tea leaf reading, and the like."

"I'm not talking about astral charts and palmistry, Grace. I wish I were. I've read all about clairvoyance, sweated on my knees, fasted for days. It's real. It can run in families. God knows, I do foresee things! I wish I didn't, but I do."

"So what has that to do with Nila's death?"

"The night we were married I went into a trance, before we had sex, before the union was consummated. I could have called it quits and packed her off back to her parents. I didn't. Even after we'd sealed the deal, in the terms of Holy Church, I could have stopped her when she insisted we go to the Alps. I could have said, 'Not there. Bad things will happen if we go there.' "

"You saw that Nila was going to die, but you didn't stop it?"

"It would have been easy. This is Africa. I'm her husband. I could have said no, absolutely not, and that would have been that."

"You may have done that and she might have died anyway, somewhere else, in another way."

"I've told myself that. I've told myself many things: that the clairvoyance had happened only once before; that prescience isn't real, I was imagining things. But I knew I wasn't. We made love, went to Switzerland on our honeymoon, and she died."

"What happened?"

He shuts his eyes, presses his fingers against his temples, utters each phrase like an old-fashioned Teletype machine, slowly clacking out data. "We were in Montreux, standing on a hillside, looking down at Lake Geneva. A small avalanche erupted, jumped her from behind, like a giant, leaning down, flicking snow right at her, with his finger. It rolled her down the slope. They rescued her in no time. But she was dead."

"And you had foreseen that?"

"Clearly."

"I still don't think you can blame yourself."

"I'm long past blame."

"Oh? What then?"

"I've grieved for her every day since she died. I've forgiven myself to no avail. I haven't worked out why I didn't prevent it. When I contemplate it all, my thoughts end up in bad places."

"In that case, don't think about it."

"I have to. For one thing, never mind Diazepam, the seizures haven't stopped, as you can see."

"You just now saw stuff that's going to happen?"

"I just now saw stuff." He is mimicking her, but he is shaken.

"So what do you do when it happens?"

"When I was a novice, I had an awful premonition during the Ignatian retreat. I reported it to John Kelly, my retreat master, and the novice master, Erasmus Azikiwe. They eventually organized me, sent me to Rome. I saw neurologists, psychologists, psychiatrists. In the end, they arrived at a protocol."

"What protocol?" Protocols she understands. Maybe she can help.

"I take the pills if I can get to them fast enough. I meditate if I discern up ahead that it's coming on. I'm supposed to consult my spiritual advisor and my superior, if it happens. And my shrink."

"Does the protocol work?"

"Well, the pills and meditation haven't done badly with short-circuiting the clairvoyance. They've worked up to now."

"Can I ask what you saw just now?"

"You can, but I wouldn't do that to you."

"Is it always about death?"

"Yes."

"And the dying is always bad? Death doesn't have to be, after all."

"It's awful every time, in itself, and because I feel trapped, out of control. I can do nothing about what's going to happen. This one was monstrous."

"Why?"

"Not just one, but thousands of people, slaughtered, mutilated."

"I'm sorry."

"Me too."

They sit in silence for a while.

"Here's the thing. I'm the only son in my family. My father is not without resources. I'm educated, travelled, well read, ostensibly cultured, some would say handsome. I've no excuse for being anything other than a well-adjusted fellow with no reason to harm anybody. I didn't want Nila to die. I loved her. But when it came to choosing, I didn't choose for her good or even mine."

"Maybe the Devil made you do it." It is superficial, trite. She is angry at having said it, for she believes him, wants him to know she isn't taking his story lightly.

"You're right," he says, wryly, sadly. "They say he's in the details."

"I've seen him there often enough."

"Me too. At any rate, I've figured things out this far. It's about courage, which we have in different doses, and faith, which we also have in varying amounts. But mostly it's about 'man and man,' as you Christophians say, a concern for others embedded in us, a sense of community, if you want, which is why I'm glad the protocol involves others."

"That's good progress, don't you think?"

"Maybe, but that's not the details, that's the very general picture. And we both agree on where the Devil is."

She knows where the Devil is all right. She hears Charlie's flip-flops slapping along the dry, impacted earth as he walks away for the last time. Who took his life? Then Charlie is there, saying, "Tell him! Tell him you know about death taking someone you love!" But she shoves him back into his Charliebox, telling herself it is the priest's troubles that need attention.

"Can I do anything now?"

"What I want most from you, Grace, you're in no position to give me. Which is just as well." She takes a while to grasp what he means and doesn't entirely till he reaches across and pats her stomach. "If there wasn't a baby in your belly, I'd make love to you with every ounce of strength in my body, long and hard."

She is mortally ashamed afterwards and begs Charlie, beloved of men, and the child inside her, to forgive her, but she wishes the baby out of her womb right that very minute. She is sure that Jimmy's arms around her, his mouth on hers, their tongues rolled up into one sweetie ball, his penis stroking her insides, will banish all evil, renew every shrivelled thing, heal the sick, raise the dead, and create enough heat and energy to light his MATE Centre for years. Then she recalls that not six weeks before she was twined around another man, sucking his mouth, behaving like the nasty girls who wait behind Wentley Park Elementary School until games are over, so they can hitch up with sweaty, force-ripe boys, and do it in the cane fields, quick and careless.

43

An Occasion of Sin?

Grace leaves for Geneva two weeks after she arrives. Monique and Ousmain drive her to the airport, where she collects the jacket they've been holding for her at the ticket counter. She and Jimmy decide that it is best. She can go to Benke for tests, and the care at MATE is excellent, but she won't be able to do what she's come for, and she'll be an extra responsibility.

Jimmy said that if she wasn't pregnant, he would make love to her, and he meant it, at that time and moment, although having said it, he knew he wouldn't do it. But he doesn't have to take it back, doesn't want to, because it was true, right then. He isn't in love with her and he hasn't known her long enough to love her, except as he loves all of humankind. He is confident the impulse that prompted his wish to be inside her has nothing to do with wanton desire, about which J.J. and he spoke. He wanted to empty everything inside of him into her body in a kind of purgation. What is desperate to come out is a force, a rage, a ferocious resentment at being his own prisoner.

Mapome warned him. "James, they can take everything else from you, but you will always have words to tell your stories." Except he isn't looking for words. He wants to get past them, past thought, to where he can fix the thing that possesses him the way a lepidopterist pins an insect, so he can see it for what it is. But he can't get far enough away to trap it. It traps him, so he has to expel it. He doesn't fail to notice that the place where he wants to dump his wretchedness is a woman's body.

He sees Nila, wild, nappy-headed Nila whom the snow ate with his baby in her. He imagines the three of them searching for njamra in the stream by the farmhouse in Oubisi. On their wedding night, Nila didn't stop nagging until he told her what happened. She'd told him how his body stiffened and battered the bed, how his eyes rolled over, how he bit first his tongue and then her finger till both bled. She'd been afraid he might never return from his mummified condition, bound in sheets like Lazarus.

And now here is Grace. He knows about her work, but not much about her as a person. In some ways she appears distant, dispassionate. But for sure she is worried about the baby, and she's been open, vulnerable about it, and when she saw him at his worst, she didn't run. If she'd gone for someone, it would have opened a huge can of worms. He asked her.

"Why did you stay? You could've left me, fetched Ousmain or Monique."

"I wondered if I should do that. But I'd seen seizures before. I decided, all things considered, I ought to stay."

He said he'd always be grateful. She said she was glad she stayed and then asked if she could do anything for him. And he told her. Why did he, happy in his calling, find himself wanting her then? "Wanting blooms, like a yawn," J.J. said, He'd wanted her as naturally as that.

For sure it can be argued that he should shun Grace as a

likely occasion of sin. For sure he'll have to keep working with her if the project in the Sahel gets off the ground. For sure he'll pray about it. But he won't ask to be sent off anywhere. He lost a woman with a baby in her belly, and now he has one back. And he knows this child is his as surely as if he put it there.

MARK

44

Waiting

Vodka and passion fruit juice is Mark's end-of-day drink. He lies back on the bed having watched the first few minutes of the seven o'clock news, from which he has learned nothing new. No progress in finding Edwin Langdon's murderer. Disturbances continue in several coastal towns, and there is now unrest in Halcyon and Stanton, the two largest tourist centres. Extra detachments of police have been dispatched to both places. Speculation is rife about a state of emergency being declared in the next twenty-four hours.

Towards the end, a reporter addresses a question about HIV/AIDS in the Caribbean to a Grace Carpenter departing the day before, at which point Mark switches to a program about the migratory habits of whales. The sight of her, skin aglow and hair aflame, burns. *Cetacea* are easier on the soul.

What had transpired between them had happened five years before. He'd written and then waited and waited to hear from her. He'd left his home number with his personal assistant, to be given to her if she called — something he'd never done before, for, ironically, Mona and he had agreed to keep a distance between work and life.

It upset him when he had no response to the postcard, the one that told her thanks for the advice concerning prowling about. He'd sent it to her at WHO and put it into the postbox himself; he knew the day and time. And then he'd written the first letter, and then the next, both of which he was confident Mona had mailed. At that point, he discovered where she was. Newspapers in D.C. had been running features about impending baseline studies that were to be part of an initiative to retard the spread of HIV/AIDS in Sahelian Africa. One of the articles profiled a controversial Jesuit priest from Mabuli named James Atule. He knows about Mabuli, although he's never visited. It's a small, landlocked country, Mali to the west, Burkina Faso to the east, sharing a short border with Côte d'Ivoire in the south.

Once he'd read the *Post* profile and seen that WHO was setting up something in West Africa, he'd guessed. Thereupon he'd experienced some inner turmoil. He applauds himself for admitting that his reaction was sourness at being rejected and pique at things not going his way. Apart from whatever could be included under the large heading, "Grace," he is not sure what he wants. At the beginning he'd been glad that, since she had her own life, no untidy repercussions were likely after their couplings in Cambridge. At the airport that ground had shifted, how radically he hadn't known till he'd written the first letter. By the time he'd written the second one, he'd passed through suspecting, then admitting that he wanted her to be, like some nineteenth-century New Orleans placée woman, not just his, but lodged in close proximity for anything that might strike his fancy, never mind his lawful wife.

The day he saw the article in the *Post*, he'd ordered a big bouquet of roses for Mona and arrived home carrying them, as well as wine and supper from the Table d'Hôte, a gourmet catering service with a select clientele of Washington subscribers. Mona opened the front door for him.

"What happen?" he asked, kissing her. "You send home the butler?"

"Wow! Thanks for these," she'd said, ignoring the comment and taking the flowers. "They're lovely. All the same, you can hang up the jacket yourself, and if that's dinner, just rest it in the kitchen. I'll be there in a minute."

"Body servants supposed to do everything for their masters you know. Where my slippers?"

She sucked her teeth. He hung up his jacket, found his slippers, and followed her to the kitchen.

"Want to open this?" She gave him the wine, a Merlot they both liked.

He set to work. "So how come you don't ask me what's the occasion?"

"I know what the occasion is."

He kept on at the cork. "In that case, you better than me. I just thought," he emphasized the next word, "whimsically, that it was a good way to start the weekend, so I got Elaine to ring the florist and the caterers, and they did the rest. Besides," he pointed outside, "it looks like spring might be consenting to arrive ahead of schedule. You love that tree. Let's say we celebrating the blooming of your tree!"

In the courtyard of their townhouse a small pink magnolia was covered with very early buds. Mona hung on for it to flower every year. While he showered and changed, she had put dinner on the table — coq au vin, salad, warm-from-the-oven baguettes.

"So what you did all day?" En route to his chair, he bent to smell her hair. She kept it long because he liked it so.

"Mostly read. Took a couple of calls for you."

"Would you pass the butter, please?" Aware of the number he'd left with Elaine, his hopes rose.

"So who called?" He loaded his bread with butter.

"Some person passing through named Frank Nuñez who said he'd been at UA with you. The number's on your desk." Her elbow was on the table, thumb propping up her chin, fingers curled over her mouth.

"Who else?" He was hoping dangerously.

"A woman. Wouldn't say who. Said she'd try again."

"American? Caribbean?"

"She sounded Latin. Maybe Cuban."

Not Grace.

They'd tidied up afterwards and gone upstairs where he made love to her tenderly and at length. It had gone so well he'd thought to raise the idea of another baby, but he gave it up quick enough. She'd know something was up.

He thinks now that, never mind his circumspection, Mona guessed that day, if not who he was dallying with, certainly that he was dallying. There was nothing lacking in her response to the flowers, dinner, or his lovemaking. It was something in her expression, her eyes. He can't say she looked resigned for resignation is now written all over her, inscribed by Adam's death. This look was something else.

He's not always been faithful. After Adam died, she hadn't wanted to make love for ages, almost three years. No full-blooded Caribbean man went that long without sex, and not even the craziest woman would expect abstinence for such a period. As far as he's concerned, they'd reached an unspoken truce. They never spoke of infidelity, and she never noticed anything amiss. He wasn't careless, but small things had to show.

Still, she's not a woman to come to terms. What he believes now is that she's been biding her time — the inscrutable East in her, no doubt. He can't blame her. Nor is there any sense in imagining their positions reversed. That situation is inconceivable. So it isn't something to be tackled, just something to be waited out. He has a pass yet again at telling himself she couldn't have known. The letters she'd mailed to Grace were like hundreds she's always posting for him: his extensive personal correspondence includes people all over the world. She always dispatches it faithfully, a couple times a week, sticking on stamps, popping the envelopes into the mailbox.

Nothing identified the letters he'd sent Grace as in any way different — unless the intensity of his feelings had somehow imparted vibrations to the paper.

As for Grace, it hasn't occurred to him that he might forgo his greedy need for her. He wants to consume her and still have her there, ready for eating again. It's not that he doesn't love Mona. He loves her, and making love to her, and taking care of her. How he feels about Mona has nothing to do with how he feels about Grace. With Grace, it's like being caught in a powerful current: there's no point in struggling. All you do is exhaust yourself, so you go with the flow and hope to be washed ashore safely at some point.

The whales, getting smaller and smaller in the ocean blue, and then disappearing under credits for the program, remind him there are things to do before tomorrow. Gordon, who'd promised an update on developments and a run-through of the revised agenda, has been silent. He looks at his empty glass. "Bird can't fly on one wing," he thinks and fixes himself another drink.

GRACE AND JIMMY

45

Landings

"You see how your womb stay? You just going to have to take time! If you hold on, that baby will hold on. Mark my word, you get off light, for one time it would be full bed rest. I telling you straight: take it nice and easy."

Dr. Joyce Zaidie-Klein wears her lavish head of hair in thick locks. Each day she puts on her white medical coat over some new creation: a patchwork frock of Bob Marley T-shirts, a dramatic dress of mud cloth, a long skirt of batik, or bandana cloth. The outfits blaze against her skin, for she is pale as any Irish colleen, her veins a network of indigo streams and rivers under skin pervious as mist, the tight twists in her hair defying its pale blonde and the startling blue of her eyes.

Grace stared when they first met and felt obliged to apologize.

"Yup. Them baby blues just stopped me short of being a dundus — you know, albino? My mama was a very white lady, and my papa black as the ace of spades. You grew up in St. Chris, don't that's right?"

Grace nods, too happy to meet her, and in Geneva of all places. When the doctor smirks, posing to show off the day's outfit, tie-dyed in green, gold, and red, Grace remembers Miss Carmen in her dashikis and matching trousers. Heritage, Miss Carmen used to say, was a legacy that you could draw down on whenever you were ready. These two mixed-blood women, her relative obviously a woman of colour, her doctor almost imperceptibly so, are happily drawing down on that inheritance. Unsure what she has inherited, Grace envies them.

"Brighten my day and wake up my patients. For colours, I praise Jah."

Grace does as her doctor instructs: keeps herself shipshape and guides the tiller at work with the lightest touch, pretty much handing things over to Jimmy and project managers in Senegal, Mali, and Burkina Faso. Jimmy leads sessions with the managers every two months. Each country has its turn as host, and he reports to Geneva afterwards.

It is hard to let go. She loves her job, gives it all she'd got, for that is what Gramps had charged her to do, what he, Ma, and Pa taught her by example. And her siblings inspire her: Edgar looks over her shoulder when she writes, Stewie when she draws a plan. Pansy's willfulness she emulates when she advances an argument. Sam and Princess, whom she still thinks of as children, happy and healthy, embody the reason for her work. And she does her job every day in tribute to a man she doesn't dare remember, not the way she remembers, say, Gramps. Gramps she resurrects whenever she wishes, seeing him in the circumstances in which he had been most himself, like when he was making his ganja infusions or tending his provision ground. But Charlie, the man who gave her many of the skills she now uses, is enshrined in a place she never goes to. With him she breathed and smelled, walked and drank, ate and slept, made love and felt hurt with a scope and intensity she'd not felt before. Once he'd gone, she'd worked and functioned and responded at a remove, as if she was dead too, watching herself from below, through thick layers of earth under which she remained buried until she met Jimmy.

She couldn't have him, but he at least makes her want to push her way up from underground.

As for Mark, she can't account for Mark. But for the baby, he can as well not have happened. Maybe the now-and-then lunacy that prompted her attempt to seduce Lindsay and led to her rudeness to Phyllis had overcome her again. Perhaps one day she'll figure it out.

———

When she is about six months on, she gets up one morning, studies her belly, and thinks about her mothers. Ma is a perfect mother, but for myriad reasons Ma can't come to Geneva. She understands then why so many parents from the Caribbean send their children home to their islands for grandmothers to raise; she remembers that Phyllis had said in one of her letters how happy she was that Grace had grown up in St. Chris. But she is never going to part with this baby. She phones New York.

"Hi, Phyllis?"

"Grace? Are you all right? How's the baby?"

"Baby fine, as far as we can tell, and me too."

"Good. I pray for that every day. So how things?"

"Pretty good. I've just a couple months to go, so I'm taking it easy. No problems, knock wood. Except I look like a chopstick with a dumpling stuck on the front."

"Graphic."

"Mum, it make no sense for me to beat about the bush. I have a big-big favour to ask you."

"Okay, Grace."

"Is really big, you know." Her tone kneads caution, hesitation, pleading.

"Grace, I understand English. Just make your request."

Her mother is well named — Phyllis, Green Bough of Great Calm.

"I need you to come and help me mind this baby."

Long pause. "So is now you decide to ask me that?"

"Is long time I been debating about it, Mum, but is only now I make up my mind to just bite my lip and ask you."

"How much time I have to think about it?"

"Whatever time you need."

"I could take till next year then." Phyllis's humour lurks in the pool of conversation like a turtle, elevating its head unpredictably.

"Mum, you know this baby is coming long before next year."

"So you want me to come before the baby born then?"

"Lord, take time with me, nuh?"

"You just phone halfway round the world to say, 'Phyllis, how you would like to give up your work, your life, your home, and come to a strange place where you don't speak the language, don't know nobody, and nobody know you, so you can look after my baby?' And I must take time with you?"

"My baby is your grandchild — very likely, the only one you'll ever have."

"That is perfectly true, as is the fact that you are the mother of that child. Baby-minding responsibility thus falls to you. At least, that is how I know it."

"Mum, you know full well I can't do this job and mind the baby at the same time. If we're going to eat, I have to work. You want me to put your grandchild in a nursery for a set of white people to mind?"

"So since when white people can't mind pikni? Look, Grace. I best tell you right now. If I was to decide to come over there, I not going to be no surrogate mother, so make us be clear on that."

"Your mother left you. They forced you to give me up. You think I'm going do anything like that with this baby?"

"Don't judge about things concerning which you know nothing!" Phyllis snaps, something Grace can hardly ever remember her doing. More turtle behaviour! "There's no comparison between your present circumstances and mine when you were born, or yours and Daphne's when she left to work in foreign and send back money to support me and Ralston. You think if I'd stayed in St. Chris and brought you up, you'd be where you are now?"

Grace knows better than to answer. "Mum, we'll discuss it down to the smallest details, work out how it's going to go day to day, hour to hour, if you want. But you and I both know that I didn't have to keep this child. Having decided to, I'm not likely to behave as though it belongs to somebody else."

"If I come, Grace, I am holding you to that."

"Agreed, Mum."

"One more thing. You haven't seen fit to speak about the baby-father. I've asked no questions, but if I come to mind that baby, I must know who his pa is."

Transatlantic burbles. "I really don't want to talk about that."

"Listen, Miss. I am not ecstatic about giving up a perfectly good life here, which is what you've asked me to do. I'm not going to do it, only to have some man knock on the door one day, come to collect his child."

"This is 1994, Phyllis. Those things don't happen anymore."

"They most certainly do, Grace. Not to say you'd let the baby go just so, but don't fool yourself. Parents do snatch children. If there's a chance of my finding myself in the middle of such an abduction, I must know."

"Suppose I tell you every last thing about him: age, profession, height, weight, shape of nose, skin, and eye colour, education, earning power, political persuasion — all except name and address. That will suffice?"

"What about marital status?"

"He's married, Phyllis."

"Fine barrel of brine water you land yourself into!"

"That's very helpful."

"Have to think about this, Grace. Take it to the Lord in prayer."

"That's more than fair, Mum. I know you'll need time."

"I'll speak to Reverend Mother tomorrow. You're lucky. Is only forty-seven I am on my next birthday, but I been working here thirty years now, so I have my pension, plus I have some leave saved up."

"Right. I will call you in another couple days. Take care, Mum. And thanks for even thinking about it."

Being pregnant has been no cakewalk, seven months of whether the baby would miscarry, morning sickness, World Cup football in her belly, and the belly in the end so heavy that there is no good position to sleep in. Ironically, all that has been to the good, immediate discomfort overriding neurotic doubts about whether the baby has AIDS, never mind all the tests she's done say she is fine.

She's enjoyed preparing for the baby, though the most important preparation is the one she's that day hopefully put in place. Someone has to mind the child because she has to work. She'd considered, and then had the brainwave, and then the misgivings, so she'd talked to Jimmy.

"Do you think it would be fair to Phyllis?"

"Ask and you shall receive. Can't hurt to ask."

There was a bit of a tug-o-war between herself and her Rasta doctor about where the baby should be born. She started asking around for a good doula, for she wanted a home delivery, so that the child could be born into the smells, sights, and sounds that would surround him or her in the first years of life. These are to introduce the baby not just to home but to Wentley Park and his or her extended family as well. To that end, the nursery is painted the blue of the sky in St. Chris. There is a wall with a mural depicting a small shop, like Pansy and Mortimer's Ital Cookshop; she paid one of the children from the high school nearby to paint it from a postcard of St. Chris. The shop is on a roadside prettified with oleander and allamanda bushes and blooming poinciana and acacia trees, with the road running past a swathe of cane fields backed by a stand of tall coconut palms, the whole set against the glow of a perfect St. Chris sunset. It is tourist stuff, to be sure, but if she gathers two or three places in Wentley and puts them together in her imagination, the picture is not too far off.

There is another wall devoted to the Carpenter and Patterson branches of her baby's family tree, which she has drawn and then painted herself, and to which she has affixed photographs of Gramps, Ma, Pa, all her siblings, Daphne, Granny Vads, grandpa Malachi, and of course Phyllis and herself. Even Pansy and Mortimer's children are there, for they are first cousins, after all.

Joyce Zaidie-Klein discourages the doula and the home birth. She reminds Grace that she is older than the average woman giving birth for the first time, and she needs to bear in mind that there may be complications with the delivery.

"Hospital is the best place for old lady who just starting to make babies!" her doctor declares, ready to pick a pretend fight with Grace. Grace doesn't given her the satisfaction: she capitulates straight off.

"But of course – you're absolutely right!"

So Jeremiah arrives in the hospital, though, thank God, there are no complications. She does not debate about naming the child. She has little to give Jimmy, or that he allows her to give him, but she knows how much he mourns John Kelly, and she's told him if the baby is a boy, she is going to name him Jeremiah.

Phyllis was to have come a week before the baby was due, to be part of the warm and welcoming Christophian cocoon in which Grace is determined the child will find himself when she brings him home. But he was in a hurry, which is why at this moment, three months after her phone call to her mother, she is all alone, shushing a two-day-old small person who can't even lend a hand with shelling peas!

As she pats his back, she checks the wall clock. Phyllis's plane should be touching down any minute.

46

The Lady in the Park

Grace can't imagine what possesses Phyllis.

"Grace, I bring a visitor." Phyllis empties Jeremiah out of a light jacket, shrugs off her own, and hangs them both in the coat closet, as the person she is speaking of stands in the vestibule, plainly uncomfortable, timid about coming in.

"You can bring whoever you like as long as you bring back my son. Come here, Jeremiah. Come tell your Mama what you and Grandma did in the park."

"Got a lady in the park, Mama."

Jeremiah points at a woman standing in the doorway, tall, black hair, dark sloe eyes.

"Hello, Dr. Carpenter."

She knows right off. It is the woman who answered her call from Mabuli, who said she was Mark's wife. She is sure of the voice, the Trini accent. It reshaped her life in ten seconds, told her things she didn't know before, including the fact that in Mark she had hopes and expectations. She dropped the phone and would have fallen down herself, had Sister Tekawitha not grabbed her. The words, like warts, returned again and again to mock her, "This is his wife."

Get a grip! she tells herself. Wife, ex-wife, lover, it doesn't matter.

"Hello. Have we met before? Do, please come in." What is this woman doing in her home? Jeremiah says they got her in the park, so Phyllis must have invited her, and so must know who she is. Maybe the woman on the phone lied and wasn't a real wife. Maybe she was Mark's live-in paramour, a euphemistic wife. Whichever applies, she has to hand it to him. He can pick a damn good-looking woman.

Outside, blue skies say Phyllis's invitation has nothing to do with the weather, and the woman doesn't look ill, so it isn't Phyllis's Good Samaritan instincts. The stranger's eyes are all over Jeremiah as he backs off his sneakers and runs to his toy box. Is Phyllis up to something? Has she had found out Mark is Jeremiah's father? And even if she has, that is a quantum leap away from bringing his wife into their home. She can't conceive what may have prompted that. Never mind. In due course, her mother will have the length of her tongue.

The stranger, relieved by Phyllis of her classy coat and scarf, is walking down the wide corridor towards Grace.

"Would you like something to drink?" Grace produces her diplomatic self. "Some lunch, perhaps?"

Jeremiah's favorite toy, a capuchin monkey, is stuck in his toy box. As he tugs at the monkey, the tail starts to rip away from the body. Upset by the noise and frustrated at not getting the plaything, he starts to cry. His distress persuades Grace that it may be better for them both to escape. She looks at her watch.

"Oh my! Is it so late? Come, Jeremiah. Put your sneakers back on. Remember? Mama has to take you to the doctor." Big lie, but Phyllis won't dare let on.

"I leave you in Mum's capable hands," she bares her teeth at the woman as she walks over to the coat closet. "Do excuse us. We must rush." She puts on her jacket, picks up her purse, scoops up Jeremiah, and collects his coat and shoes. "We'll put these on in the car. Mother ... " Phyllis will know she is furious, for she never calls her that, "we'll be back as quickly as we can. Perhaps you'll still be here?" This she says to the woman whose eyes are still stuck like tar on Jeremiah.

"Jeremiah, say goodbye, sweetheart."

"Bye, sweet-art!"

———

When Grace brings Jeremiah back in the late afternoon, he is asleep. A refined snore flutes from the dining room. Grace looks in to see Phyllis napping, her head on the table. She puts Jeremiah into his playpen, opening one of the French windows to let in some air. There is no cloud cover, as there often is, and no afternoon rain. That is part of what angers her. They could have had lunch on the deck, maybe gone for a drive after that. Instead, her mother and Mark's woman manage to spoil a beautiful day. She lies on the carpet, fuming, and dozes off too, waking when Phyllis comes in.

"How exactly did that woman come to be here, Phyllis?"

"I honestly don't know if I can give you a good answer, Grace. Jeremiah and I are sitting on our bench in the park and I'm reading his Anancy book to him. Of a sudden, I hear somebody say, 'Oh my God!' So I turn round and I see this woman. She start crying, so I tell her to sit down. I give her one of Jeremiah's bottles of water and a mint. When she compose herself, she say she don't mean to make any trouble, then she address me by my name and say how Jeremiah look like his father!"

"I don't need a blow by blow. I just want to know what you were thinking when you asked her to come here."

"I guess I wasn't thinking too straight. Look, all this time you making a big secret of who Jeremiah's father is, then a stranger appear, call me by my name and show me a photo of a man who look like he spit your child out of his mouth!"

"Okay. I admit you must have been taken aback … "

"Taken a back? Plus a side, a front, a top, and a bottom! She say she know you, and she look like she was going to start crying all over again."

"Spare me the gory details. You asked her here, and you shouldn't have."

"Grace, she showed me the man's photograph! Jeremiah don't only look like him, he slim same way, smile same way, tilt his head one side same way."

"Fine. You've met, she's been here, scrutinized Jeremiah. I need your undertaking never to do anything like that again. She could have created a very unpleasant scene, and most important, upset Jeremiah. Do I make myself clear?"

"Perfectly. Do I pack my bags, get on a plane, go back to my yard, and pick up my life where I put it down?"

"Don't be melodramatic."

"Hardly. If we're going to be on tension about this, day in, day out, that won't do Jeremiah any good. No use hemming and hawing. Best get down to the nitty-gritty."

"The nitty-gritty is we're perfectly happy here, and we couldn't manage without you. Let's put it behind us. Okay?"

"Kidoki." Jeremiah murmurs in his sleep.

"Lord! We need to talk soft! I totally forgot he was right there."

"I am talking soft, Mum. Anyway, just so we get this straight: you don't know who Jeremiah's father is, nor does the woman, and it will stay that way."

"She hasn't told her husband, you know, and she says she won't till she's talked to you."

"I have no intention of having a discussion with her. It's not her affair."

"Best not to introduce that word, don't you think? If you listen to yourself you'll see what you're saying is nonsense. Even somebody as tough-headed as you must admit it concerns her. It's generous of her not to tell Mr. Blackman till you two talk."

"Didn't you hear me, Phyllis? I don't intend to speak to her, about Jeremiah or anything else. What she elects to say to her husband, if he is her husband, is her business. She can speculate at will about my son being his child."

Phyllis kisses her teeth. "Grace, this is 1996. They can prove paternity. I know that. It's been in my line of work for many years now."

"I'm done discussing it."

"Suppose something happens to you?"

Grace is examining the monkey's torn tail.

"I'll mend it," Phyllis says. "I did it once before."

"I can easily buy him another."

Phyllis doesn't pursue it. "I promised Mrs. Blackman to keep in touch with her and I'm going to. I don't break my promises."

"I would rather you didn't, but I can't stop you. Perhaps, being the prayerful person that you are, you should ask God for guidance in the matter."

"You know, Grace, I pray my whole life against it, but there are times when you behave exactly like your father."

"My father? If I were to judge from the times you've mentioned him, I'd have to conclude he was either non-existent or the Devil incarnate."

"Well, insofar as you are here, he existed all right."

"And the Devil part of it?"

"Best to let it go, Grace. Best to let it go."

47

Another Visit and a Summons

"God bless you, Jeremiah!"

"Sleep tight, Jeremiah. Remember, Mama loves you."

"Night, Tules! Night, Mama!"

"Good night, son. I'm putting out the light now. Okay?"

"Kidoki, Mama."

As Grace reaches for the light switch, Jimmy gently restrains her so he can look around the child's room. It's decorated with Jeremiah's drawings, mostly firm strokes of blue crayon at all angles, with roundish scrawls of orange nearby. Grace sees him looking from one to the other, all sea and sun, and explains, "Phyllis has been telling him stories about pirates." She is pleased when he points, smiling, to Jeremiah's self-portrait on a large piece of paper where one side of the family tree now ends. His smile shrinks at the sight of a photograph of himself, affixed near to hers, though it's not connected to the tree. As he steps out so Grace can close the door, she wonders if it bothers him. "Forgive my son, please. When he's a bit older, I'll work on his form of address."

"I kind of like 'Tules.'"

"So, shall I call you that?"

"Jimmy's fine. If you flirt with me, I'll insist on Father Atule."

"Very well. I promise to behave."

"Good. Don't you say prayers with him, Grace?"

"Phyllis does. Not me. She's out visiting friends."

"Pity. Good night prayers are comforting."

"I know. Ma and Pa would be mortified." She shrugs. Jimmy knows she has pretty much parted company with God. "I should have asked you to do the honours."

"Next time."

"Anyway, I'm glad you could come. He so looked forward to his second birthday party with you. Of course, if we keep this up, he's going to expect a string of parties till his next birthday."

"Why not? He's wiser than we are. Every day a celebration!"

"Only if someone else is party organizer! I didn't think five children could create such havoc!" Grace gestures for Jimmy to sit as she collapses onto a chaise longue and lets her sandals fall to the floor.

"I'd volunteer, if I were here. I do a good party."

"It's great for him to have you around, Jimmy. He doesn't see many black folks, and almost no black men."

"I can't be his stand-in daddy, Grace. You know how I feel about that. But I'm always glad to be the second black man in the house when I visit."

"From you, I take whatever I can get. And as ever, I'm elated to see you."

It's true. She's long since decided that she must have Jimmy in her life, whatever the terms. But she knows and accepts other people's claims on him. He feels responsible for his family, especially his mother and sisters. He cares about the staff at all the MATE centres and knows in detail the stories of their lives. His patients' histories have become part of the lore of his life. Even Nila he still speaks of now and then.

"The drug baron, Don Jaime, is happy to see you too."

"Man, you don't let a person forget, eh?"

"C'mon, Grace! It's too good a joke!"

"Why don't I get you a drink?"

"Just a glass of water, thanks."

She gets up, goes over to the small bar and pours him a glass of Perrier, which he comes across and takes from her, with a smile. He'd once told her why he liked to drink water and preferred it without ice, some wisdom acquired as a young man from a Chinese business associate. Like all Caribbean people, she considers water better with ice in it.

"I'm having a taste of St. Chris Ten Year Old. I've worked hard this last week. Massa's overseers chewed over every last cent in every line item in the budget."

"Sorry to hear that. I hope it won't seriously hamper the work."

She gestures dismissively as she lifts her glass, and he lifts his in a silent toast. "We can only ever get what we pay for. One day, they will all learn that. But on to more important matters: I'm worried about you, Padre. You look perkier now, but when you passed by the office this morning, you looked beat."

"I'm a bit weary, for sure, but a couple nights' sleep will set me right, and I can count on that when I'm here. Good Swiss bed and board!"

"You can always stay here. You know that."

"We both know why that can't work, Grace."

"Okay. Okay. Is it the project that's taking it out of you?"

"Not really. It's true there've been a couple setbacks at MATE Tindi, but nothing we can't cope with."

"As you'd say, why don't you just tell me?"

"One or two things have been nagging at me. It's not to do with MATE specifically. It's occurred to me that while the country projects are up and running we should look further down the road."

"At what specifically? Are you thinking of money? Expansion?"

"I'm thinking of emergency plans. Suppose we had a real catastrophe, Grace? Suppose we found ourselves in a state of civil war, for instance?"

"Are you saying there's trouble in Mabuli?"

"If there were, I'd have told you. I'm saying, 'What if?' Doing a hypothetical."

"Okay. Political upheaval. Any other what-ifs?"

"I'd say volatile weather. It's true weather in the Sahel has been variable for decades, but we need to consider it nonetheless. And what about the possibility of our losing staff, massively, overnight?"

"But we have understudies, don't we?"

"We have understudies for some key people in each project, but not all. Mali's project manager has no understudy, nor have I. Monique can handle Tindi, but not all the MATE Centres."

"Jimmy Atule, if you're leaving the Jesuit order to run off with anyone but me, I'll hunt you down, club you on the head, and drag you back to my cave!"

"I've not forgotten the mating rites in St. Chris. For sure, you've no competition there. But since you raise it, suppose my superior got it into his head to send me to Fiji?"

"Is someone sending you off somewhere?"

"I said 'suppose,' Grace."

"Okay, you've made a good point. So, any ideas about what we do?"

"We could talk about it at the next bimonthly."

"We can do that. I'll set it up. Is that everything, Father?"

"There is one other thing. Peter-Hans has summoned me."

Grace sees the slightest ripple of change over the pattern of his facial scars, and she thinks, Aha! We've come to the trouble.

"Peter who has summoned you?"

"Peter-Hans Kolvenbach, the Jesuit Superior General."

"The Jesuit Superior General? But why?"

"I had a run-in with our new regional superior. He must have reported me."

"I remember you said you'd miss Father Kitendi."

"For sure, the new superior is no Kitendi!"

"But if they've called you to Rome, that's serious."

"Yes."

"What can they do to you?"

"Pretty much anything they like."

"They wouldn't move you, would they, Jimmy?"

"They might."

There is a mild thump in Grace's abdomen. She hesitates to call it foreboding. She cannot conceive of the West Africa project without Jimmy. More truly, she cannot conceive of her life, their life, hers and Jeremiah's, if they saw him less frequently than they do now.

"Is that why you brought up contingency plans?"

"It was what brought them to mind."

"I don't understand, Jimmy. Why all of a sudden?"

"Father Agbidi probably spoke the words 'rebellious' and 'disobedient.'"

"Are you scared?"

"Peter-Hans is our capo di tutti capi, so yes, I guess I am."

"You'll see him?"

"He's a busy man, and I'm small beer. Someone else will bring me to heel."

"But they know you're doing crucial work. Why would they want to stop you?"

"The Jesuit Order is a human institution, Grace. There are superiors like Agbidi and like Kitendi, just as there are popes like John the Twenty-third and popes very different from him. I don't know what the thinking at headquarters is. We obey the Holy Father. He's an even bigger capo than Peter-Hans, and, to pick an issue at random, he's not a fan of condoms."

"So we can't count on reason prevailing then?"

"You make me laugh. No, I don't think we can count on reason. Wisdom we can hope for. I'm praying hard that wisdom will prevail. Help me pray."

"You're teasing. What if I promise to think of you?"

"As you'd say, I'll take what I can get, with thanks."

She can tell he doesn't wish to pursue the matter further, because he moves quickly to asking about each of them, herself, Jeremiah, Phyllis, and listens with the complete attention that he once told her he'd learned from J.J. She reassures him that they are all fine, but she is happy, in her mother's absence, to report with indignation the incident of her bringing Mona Blackman home.

"Why did Mrs. Blackman come?"

"My question, precisely. I've never met this woman. In fact, I've deliberately avoided knowing about her. I do know, to my cost, that she lives in Washington, which is not to say she can't come to Geneva, but I don't expect to see her here unless I invite her."

"So Phyllis must have invited her. Surely she had a good reason?"

"You don't expect me to be sanguine about that woman being in my home, do you?"

"Not sanguine, but it's hardly the end of the world. And you haven't answered my question about Phyllis."

"She's not my friend! Not even my acquaintance!"

"You slept with her husband and had his child."

She isn't surprised at Jimmy's bald characterization of her encounter with Mark. His smile challenges her to contradict him. Which is his way. In St. Chris, they say if you do it right, you can tell somebody to go to Hell and send them off with a smile on their face. Jimmy has that talent.

"We're not talking about that. We're talking about whether or not she has any right in my home, uninvited."

"I thought you said Phyllis had asked her."

"The point is, Phyllis shouldn't have."

"Did Phyllis explain why she brought her home?"

"She said she wasn't thinking straight, and started a long story. I told her I didn't want to hear the length and breadth of it."

"Maybe it was a good, but complicated reason?"

"No good reason is possible!"

"Well, if you put it that way. How did the visit go?"

"You don't think I stayed to have a chat with her? I scooped up my son and concocted a reason to leave. She was devouring Jeremiah with her big coolie eyes, gobbling him up like she was one of Asia's starving millions, and him the last morsel."

"You're shocking me, for sure."

"Oh, please! You're no white-as-the-driven-snow saint with pure-as-pasteurized language."

"For sure I'm no saint, and even if by any stretch of the imagination I could be white, I would prefer it not to be like the driven snow, which, as you know, has bad associations for me."

"I'm sorry, Jimmy. I forgot." Lord! How could she say that? She knows he still feels responsible for Nila's death. She remembers a proverb Gramps liked to invoke, clapping his hands by her ears to get her attention: "The tongue does not love the throat." She has no excuse. She knows better, especially after years of having to speak with circumspection in her job. "I'm sorry, Jimmy. Me and my big mouth are very sorry."

"It's okay. I think you're angry because you can't get your way in a matter you've decided concerns only you."

"It concerns me and my son."

"In other words, not you alone."

"I decide for Jeremiah till he's old enough."

"His father has an equal right to do that."

"I won't discuss it."

"Any talk about Jeremiah is a discussion about that."

"This isn't a discussion about Jeremiah."

"His step-mother merely looking at him just prompted you to use some rather colourful language."

"His what?"

"The wife of his father. That makes Mona Blackman his step-mother."

"Why are you being so cruel?"

"You're the one who always advocates being sensible. Is it sensible to object to Phyllis's actions without giving her a chance to explain them?"

"I gave her a chance. I just said not to give me a song and dance about it."

"Oh, come on, Grace."

"What reason could she have requiring more than two sentences?"

"I don't know. You don't either. You can't till she tells you. Don't you find that there's also something, shall we say, perverse, about sleeping with someone else's husband and regarding yourself as the aggrieved party?"

"He said he didn't have a relationship with his wife. How was I supposed to know? And my aggrieved-ness relates to her intrusion into my home."

"What about your intrusion into her life?"

————

Shortly after Jimmy's visit, Grace decides that a strategy is called for to deal with any claim to rights over Jeremiah that Mark and Mona Blackman might advance. She consults Joyce Zaidie-Klein's husband, a lawyer specializing in custody disputes, and by reputation, a tough litigator.

"I'd like to discuss a hypothetical situation, Mr. Klein."

"I don't do hypotheticals, Dr. Carpenter."

"Why is that?"

"People make things up, or leave things out, and my time is expensive. I want them to get their money's worth."

"Understood. The facts. I have a son. His father has no idea that he exists."

"You are not married to his father?"

"No."

"Never were?"

"My son is an accident of misfortune, you might say, though, being perfect, he undoes his origins. As I say, his father is unaware he exists, and the longer I keep it so, the better, partly because I assume the law will be on my side if I can prove, should the occasion arise, that his father has had nothing at all to do with him."

"I wouldn't assume anything on the part of the law."

"The assumption seems reasonable enough to me."

"The law isn't reasonable. And since I'm the lawyer, why don't you let me form the opinions?"

David Klein advises her that, since Jeremiah's father will probably find out about the child eventually, she should tell him directly. When she refuses, he tells her that if he wishes, Mark Blackman can easily get access; indeed, sue for shared custody.

"Wouldn't he have to prove the child is his?"

"Of course. But that's easy to do."

"What if I don't let him near the child?"

"For Jeremiah's sake, you'll want to avoid the trouble that would bring."

48

Secrets

Grace knows everybody hides things, good things sometimes, like she mostly hides Charlie. She knows Phyllis has secrets, maybe not of her own making, but still secrets. She is sure the biggest one is her father, Ralston, whose name Phyllis spewed at her at the end of their quarrel the day her mother brought Mona Blackman home.

Gramps warned Grace when he gave her Phyllis's letters that her father was a bad man and made it plain he did not wish to speak of him. Phyllis's attitude has always been much the same. Out of deference to Gramps and consideration for Phyllis, she'd asked no further about him. Once Phyllis says his name, though, she reckons he is up for discussion. She is curious about him, wicked though he may be, and besides, her child is his grandchild. That justifies her interest. What if Jeremiah has inherited some congenital disease from his grandfather? She asks about him repeatedly, insisting she has a right to know whose blood is in her body, whose genes have gone into her child.

"All in good time, Grace," Phyllis responds. "All in good time."

The "good time" arrives one Sunday afternoon, about a week later. Phyllis invites her to sit at the kitchen table and sits facing her, just as Gramps had done.

"It's hard, Grace, what I'm going to tell you."

"It's better for me to know, Mum, even if it is hard."

"That's true. Can't quarrel with that. But he ... Your father ... Ralston Patterson was not a good person."

"We're making headway. I now know his name."

"Don't his name is on your birth paper?"

"The space where my father's name should be is empty."

"I've never seen that paper, so I never knew that."

"Gramps gave it to me with your letters. Anyway, now you know." So Phyllis's surname and Ralston's are the same — but surely they weren't married?

"Somebody was being considerate, so they never put it down," Phyllis says.

"Meaning what?"

"I'm going to tell you how he and me share a name. I'm going tell you everything."

"Good."

"Far from it."

Through the long windows, Grace sees a crude wind force its way through trees and bushes at the same time that some ghostly off-switch suddenly outs the light in the sky. She shivers. Phyllis too. Asleep in his playpen in the living room, Jeremiah moans.

"I am sitting on my bed, reading, when I hear Ralston coming, banging on the metal gate, flowerpots, front door, and then he come in and slam the door to his room. I wonder if I should ask him if something is wrong, but I decide to let sleeping dogs lie, so I go back to concentrating, for that time I can't read so good.

"All of a sudden I smell somebody beside me stink of beer, cigarettes, and sweat. I feel the bed slope as he put his weight on it. I never even have time to ask him what he is doing in my room, and he never even say 'dog' to me, just shove me onto the rug on the floor beside the bed. To this day I don't know why he never just do it on the bed. I make that rug myself when I was eight. I walk all up and down Hector's Castle begging people for cloth, and the rug remind me of so many people: Ma Phelps up Loomy Road that give me a piece of tartan, say her sister send it from Scotland for her eightieth birthday; Mrs. Budhai that give me a scrap of green silk, a bit of the sari her grandmother wear when she step off the boat from India; Sister Mingo that give me a strip of heavy navy blue cloth her mother use to cover the windows in wartime, still strong and sound as a drum.

"Is there he pin me, wiggling his underpants down his legs. Is only when I see his prick stand up, big and sticky, with the front part peel off that I realize he come into the room without no trousers. I see plenty man bathing in river and at standpipe, but I never see a penis in that state before.

"He drop down on me, haul up my skirt, lock his knees round my thighs, and wrestle down my panty. Poor me, fool, just staring, surprise mix up with fright, when I should be doing something to save myself. Not that I could move that easy, for he holding me down, and never mind he slim, he strong like the wiss vine we use to play Tarzan in the guango tree."

Upstairs, a window bangs. Thunder rumbles far off. Raindrops, small frightened birds, peck at the windows.

"When I could speak, I talk so soft is only me hear. The worst part is the words follow the motion of his hips, like the penis was poking them out. A pain like a knife cut my belly, then blood. I pass out as his seed was coming in me."

"Mum ..." Grace starts to get up. They need something. Rum, maybe, or brandy.

"I am not finished yet. Please sit and hear me out. Ralston was my mother's child by another man. He was my half-brother. Daphne give us both her family name."

It is a long time before Grace speaks. "And that is the person you say I am exactly like?"

49

Graduation

They celebrated first in the morning with a sung Mass in the dining room. Mass isn't strange to Grace. She had gone to Catholic ones with Steph and to Anglican ones at St. Chad's. Jimmy explains that a sung Mass is just that: a Mass that is sung. She's heard the "Missa Luba," but never in a church, and she's never heard Jimmy do more than hum a few notes.

His face is many smiles, the clan markings describing new patterns all the time.

All twenty graduates attend Mass. Families come too, which is why they use the dining room. The musicians are a surprise: Ousmain on the kyondo, Monique and Tekawitha on kikumvi, Elise and Lili controlling the boyeki, called "scrapers" in St. Chris. As she listens to Jimmy leading the call and response of the Kyrie, she is tempted to forgive his wicked God a little. Then she recalls the news Phyllis gave her about Ralston, and the tiny well of forgiveness dries up.

That evening twenty Mabulian community workers trained at the centre sing a song of their own composition and dance to its music across a makeshift stage lit by banks of torches on either side. They set up the stage in front of the main communal hall, between the arms of covered walkways that lead from the central structure to the women's and children's wards. Sitting out front, the families of the graduates, friends from the surrounding villages and nearby towns, most of the community of persons living with HIV/AIDS at the centre, the centre staff, and their distinguished visitor all clap and stamp out the rhythms played by the five musicians. Thunder rolls in the distance, background to the drums and xalams that accompany the performers.

The graduates studied for the first four months of the year: how to type, use a computer, keep a journal, input data on a spreadsheet. They learned more about HIV/AIDS. Many live with the disease, so they already know a great deal. Amitié is an expert. "I will teach you. I am a diagram. I am a history." Whereupon she recites the stages of the disease, its earliest symptoms, how it spreads, finally producing her daughter, Azzara as evidence that, with AZT, it need not be passed to babies. "Mabuli, c'est un bon pays. Vous pouvez être testés. You can be tested. Vous pouvez avoir des médicaments. You can have medicine. The Oti told our government to spend money on health workers and education, to support community efforts, to work with international agencies. We know the power of the Oti. Nous connaissons bien la force d'Oti!"

They perform the "Pat-a-Cake, Take Your Pills" handclapping song invented by Elise and Lili, the dazzling display of their quick arms and bouncing hips prompting the audience to prolonged cheering. Then, in sometimes deeply moving, and often wildly funny presentations, graduates saunter, leap, or sashay onto the stage and announce, coyly or mock-tragically, ranting or quietly, "I am a person with the Skinny. I live with HIV/AIDS. Je vis avec le VIH/SIDA." Then they dance or sing or act out their individual stories.

If the core staff at Tindi are proud, the graduates preen like ibises as they sing at the end of the ceremony the song with which they started:

> We who come from the land of walking stones
> whose forbears overthrew a tyrant
> when they met and chanted hymns
> and histories and holy songs
> will overcome also this cruelty
> with bonds of solidarity;
> will overcome also this cruelty
> with mighty bonds of solidarity.

50

A Hypothetical

Jimmy doesn't go to sleep right away that night, upset because Grace is clearly ill. She is thin, her skin dull, her eyes sunken. He asks her what is wrong.

"It's nothing, nothing a good night's sleep won't cure, as you would say." She is a bad liar. She goes to bed after the ceremony, pleading the avowed tiredness. So does he. Unable to sleep, he gets up, pokes his head out, smells rain, and reckons it will come before morning. Further down the verandah, he notices the light on in Grace's room. He dresses, walks down to her door, and knocks.

"Who is it?"

"It's me, Grace. Jimmy."

"Is there something wrong, Jimmy?"

"That's what I came to find out."

"I'm fine, thank you. You can't come in. I'm in my nightclothes."

"I've seen you naked, Grace. Besides, you have robes, dressing gowns, wraps. Put something on."

"You need sleep, Jimmy. I need sleep. Go back to bed. I'm turning out my light."

"If you don't open this door, you will regret it, Grace Carpenter."

"Is that a threat, Jimmy Atule?"

"Not a threat. A promise."

She is hugging a robe around her when she lets him in. Invited to sit, he chooses a chair by the door. Birds honk, squawk, whirr like rusty machinery. Fat bugs bounce against the window screen.

"I don't remember it being so loud."

"Nature continuing the celebrations." He is proud and not hiding it.

"Your graduates are going to do great things."

"I hope so. But they're not why I'm here."

"Why are you here, Jimmy?"

"We need to do a hypothetical, Grace." It is Grace who introduced hypotheticals to him. He often runs them with Monique and the folks in admin now, as well as at project meetings.

"If you insist."

"Over to you, Dr. Carpenter. What are we looking at, hypothetically?"

"Let's say someone just discovered incest in her family." She doesn't answer right away, but once she starts, she soldiers on, quick march. "She's beside herself. She's a person of colour, abroad, in a strange place. She's not European, so the experts available aren't the best fit. What can she do?"

"Can you say all that again, please?" He has taken it all in, but retelling will mitigate some of her revulsion.

"The subject is a woman of colour, from my part of the world, living in Europe, who has just found out about incest in her family. Okay?"

"Okay." Skating over life on a surface of irony.

"What do you recommend?"

"How old is this woman?"

"I don't know. My age."

She is talking about herself. Once he is aware of that, he decides he has to take her through it, step by step, all the way, regardless of where they end up. Rites are reassuring. That is their nature. Careful rehearsal, a path cut gradually, firmly through. At the centre they prepare the dying and their families in this way.

"And is she involved in the incest, in other words, has she discovered that someone with whom she is having a sexual relationship is a family member?"

"Jesus, Jimmy. That's sick."

"Come on, Grace. You know it happens all the time."

"I know, but … "

"But it's not supposed to happen to you or me?" He isn't being hard. She has to see people in incestuous relationships as "we," as "us."

"I'll avoid the 'It's fine for you to talk' bit and just stick to the matter at hand. It's her parents. They were half-siblings, different fathers, same mother."

"Mmm. That would be difficult too."

"I'm not sure she'd be better off in her home country, which is very conservative, but I don't know how she can find help in the place where she is."

"How well do you know this person, Grace?"

"Well enough, I guess."

"And has she just learned about this situation?"

"Yes."

"I think I understand the 'if this' part of the hypothetical."

"Isn't the 'then what?' part obvious? Then what can she do?"

"She's a well-adjusted person?"

"I suppose so."

"I'd say she should be cautious about seeing any old professional. Does she belong to a church? Have any ties of that kind?"

"She's not so good with God."

"Right. Is she living with anyone?"

"She has offspring, but no spouse."

"Does she live with the incestuous parents?"

Her "no" is ferocious.

"Does she have a relationship with her parents?"

"In touch with her mother. Doesn't know her father."

"Did the parents have a relationship?"

"I just said it was incestuous!"

"That doesn't answer the question."

"The father raped the mother."

"Okay. The incest was a matter of just that one time, was it?"

"Christ, Jimmy! They had a child. This is about her."

"I can't answer you off the top of my head. I need to think about it."

"She may jump off a bridge."

"Okay. I won't be responsible for any deaths. I think you should suggest to this person that she find the best, nearest available help from a professional from her part of the world, or whatever culture, society is most similar. If that's impossible, then find the best, nearest shrink."

"A professional from her region; failing that, the best therapist. Is that it?"

"It is if I have to make a call so she won't kill herself. If she isn't allergic to religious places, I can suggest a couple institutes. There's a fine one in Rome, run by a Jesuit: staff highly trained and diverse. One in Syria too. Damascus."

"Well, since you recommend them. Can you give me contact info?"

"Absolutely."

"Thanks. I think you'd better go now."

"Will you be okay?"

"Yes."

"I'll see you in the morning."

"Good night, Jimmy."

"Good night, Grace." He wants to hold her in his arms, hug her, comfort her, but he doesn't.

———

En route to Ouaga Airport, Grace and Jimmy make a detour, stopping at the novitiate.

"What's a Catholic seminary doing in Mabuli?" Grace is sulking.

"There are places they should and shouldn't be?"

"Oh! I forgot. Fair numbers in Mabuli are Catholic. Your church, sticky paws all over, has numerous hostages from among whom to entrap the unsuspecting."

"It's not a very large number of Catholics, and you needn't be mean to my church. I wouldn't be mean to yours if you had one." They are on stairs that sweep down to a courtyard in a stand of date palms. "The novices just made a new stone garden. There." Jimmy kicks a stone all the way down the stairs. "At the bottom, with benches."

"A what?"

"A stone garden, my beloved. You're meant to rake the stones and be soothed."

"Oh. A meditative raking of stones! My life, absent the meditative part."

"Mine too. Lots of us have lives of raking stones, or lives raked by stones."

"You sit too," she instructs when they get to the bottom of the stairs. "You haven't told me about Rome, Jimmy, though I've inquired more than once. For all I know, they called you up to discover what some woman was doing in your room in the middle of the night."

"They don't summon us for that kind of stuff. They'd have too many Jesuits to deal with."

"Seriously, Jimmy. What happened?"

"It wasn't so bad. I told them the woman who'd been in my room was generous with her favours."

"I said, don't joke."

"They were kind, Grace. They read me Father Agbidi's letter. I assured them that I wasn't flouting church teaching, but I said my conscience insisted that I tell mates of both genders whose partners had the disease that condoms were an option. If I failed to, I was effectively condemning people to death, women especially, and with that my conscience had serious problems. I said I was preaching only the best behaviours — fidelity and chastity."

"They bought that?"

"I wasn't selling them anything. It's true."

"Did they send you to your shrink?"

"I saw him."

"Did it help?"

"A little."

She leans her head back, closes her eyes.

"Don't you want to talk about last night, Grace?"

"What's more talking going to do?" She remarks on the three baobabs patrolling the fence line. He explains about the Father, Son, and Holy Ghost, and the chapel inside the third tree.

"The Father looks ragged, like he's on his last legs."

"It's a tough job." He chuckles, by himself, then confesses. "I know it's you, Grace."

"I know you know."

"You still don't want to talk about it?"

She shakes her head. She is crying. Eventually she stops, wipes her eyes and blows her nose on a tissue.

"Can we go to the chapel now?"

"No chapel, Jimmy."

"What I want to show you is in the chapel. We must go before sunset."

"Okay. The chapel, then Ouaga. I want to go home to my son."

They go to see Manokouma's windows. He makes her cover her eyes, open them in front of the Angelus window with the ruddy, freckled Mary.

Back in the stone garden looking at the bloody sky, he takes a stab at it. "There's more to it than this, though, isn't there?"

She nods.

"You might as well tell me."

So she off-loads her cargo of grief, the burden of a self that she now judges to be ruined at the root: Grace, the dump pikni; the red jacket in a black family; the child too terrified to open her mouth; the sibling with a sister who disclaimed her; the misfit at St. Chad's. She rails about the evils that fate has engineered, things for which she can have no responsibility: Fillmore Buxton, family member and would-be rapist; Colin who died by hunger in rich Toronto; Ralston, incestuous despoiler of her teenage mother. She berates his God for not breathing a word of warning so she could avoid the humiliating débacle with Lindsay, for not restraining the mean tongue that engineered the argument that led to Phyllis's stroke. They are actions for which she is responsible, but his God might have extended a hand of gentle caution.

And then on tiptoe, for the first time at last, she lets Charlie out of his box.

They spend the night as guests of the novice master, leaving for Ouaga early next morning. Jimmy drives like a madman, and she makes the plane.

MARK

51

To Come or Not to Come

It's late now, nearly eleven, almost time to call Mona, and certainly time to stop thinking about a woman he screwed once, or more accurately, on one occasion, and hasn't seen for four years. Besides, tomorrow isn't going to be just another day. It doesn't appear from Gordon's call that either police or army have made any progress in discovering who has killed the minister, so any number can play.

Mona and Grace are still tumbling about in his head with occasional others from the past: Mireille, a stunning Haitian woman and the only student he'd ever been involved with, and Irene, a professor of his when he'd just started graduate work, brilliant, moody, way out of his league. Stop! he tells himself. He's a one-woman man. Grace is his woman now, his wife.

At this point he knows he is in serious trouble.

There's always been a heated argument in St. Chris about fidelity and the pervasiveness of men's "wild-willy" habits, with the good churchmen (often the most wayward) maintaining that men are perfectly capable of keeping their particles in their pants, except for church-sanctioned use; social historians averring it was the white colonial oppressors who had encouraged wanton rutting to create new human chattel; and randy fornicators insisting, "If God make man, don't wild willies must be part of His plan?"

He admires fidelity, probably because infidelity stridently broke up his parents' marriage, the offending party being his father. When the union was collapsing, punctuated by quarrels at dusk and daybreak so loud they blasted through concrete walls, his mother would tell his father, "I love you to distraction, not destruction. We can't go on like this!"

Mark had just turned twelve when she left, straight for the airport. His father married his pregnant girlfriend as soon as the divorce was final. Although the agreement had been that Mark and Ben, his brother a year younger, would stay in St. Chris with their father until their mother sent for them, his father's bride was not happy about old offspring being imported into her new marriage. They'd gone to his mother's cousin in Barbados as a stopgap measure. It turned out to be a big gap: it took six years to stop it.

In many ways, he's grateful for that. Barbados, also known as Bim, was a much better place than St. Chris to get a taste of what the world was like. A small white élite, wealthy and powerful, had a heavy hand on the economic and political life of the island. Not that you'd get that admission from too many black Bajans, whose version was that whites were in the island on their sufferance. Black Bajans were mostly content not to buck the status quo. Bim sported a rock-steady dollar, a high level of literacy, a wild Atlantic coast in the east and sweet warm Caribbean waters in the west. For many tourists, it was the paradise of the Caribbean.

Barbados had been salvation for Ben. Mark had suspected that his younger brother was homosexual even before Ben was a teenager. By the time they finally talked about it, Ben had figured things out, no doubt with help from friends also struggling with being who they were. St. Chris has a barbaric attitude to people attracted to the same sex, men especially. Ben's rite of passage had been easier in Bim than it would have been in St. Chris. So Mark is grateful to Barbados. It gave himself and Ben an education, beach cricket, and sun-warm sea, and it gave Ben the chance to be safe and sane. Sex is such a vexed and vexing business. Or should he say gender? He supposes he means both. Now, with this HIV/AIDS business, it is impossible, in the way that his mother used to say to him and Ben, "You children are impossible!"

How on earth do young people manage? Not that old people manage much better, but chances are if you stick with a faithful wife and with one or two women whose habits you know ... The absurdity of what he's thinking doesn't escape him, just as he knows there's no comfort to be taken in the idea that sex with a condom is safe — if it doesn't slip, leak, burst, all of which have happened to him. Maybe they should characterize condoms the way they do polls, "accurate to within three point five degrees nineteen times out of twenty." Sometimes he considers whether one day, in a store or bank or classroom, he'll encounter a young person behind a desk, a counter, a lectern, maybe a pulpit, whose face will tell him unequivocally about one of those leaky prophylactics. He doesn't dwell on it; all men must wonder. A few years before, the island's funny bone had been tickled by raucous jokes about shipments of condoms from China, the downfall of greedy local investors who'd neglected important baseline statistics. By no means a laughing matter!

HIV/AIDS is not funny either. They all know that, he and the other Caribbean males who "run tings," women being among the "tings." Still, most have no intention of forgoing bareback riding to go undercover in rubber contraptions.

He'd proposed to Gordon Crawford that they arrange for Grace to meet with the seven UA deans and the principals of teachers' colleges, most of whom would be at graduation. He knows she's been pushing regional governments to consider an

HIV/AIDS education program for secondary schools, but she seems less concerned about universities and he wonders why. Perhaps she assumes they will all come on board in time, or perhaps it's personal and has something to do with him.

Which is of course ridiculous!

He is suddenly furious with himself that even now, after her clear dismissal, after her stalwartly maintaining her distance, even now he would be glad to be assured that he means something to her.

He checks his watch. Eleven. Time to call Mona.

"Hi Mona, honey. How are you?"

"Much improved."

"I'm glad. Listen. I better tell you right off. Bad news ... "

"Oh, no, Mark! You sick? I can change my flight and come sooner!"

"I'm fine. It's you I'm concerned about. I don't think you should come."

"But I just told you I'm okay."

"It's not you creating the problem, sweetheart. It's the damn place that's boiling! Nobody know how much hotter it's going to get." He doesn't know why it comes out that way.

"Queenstown hot in November? Not that all those academics and politicians don't deserve to sweat. But that's no reason for me not to come. Is Trini I grow up in!"

"I'm sorry, hon. I'm dead tired and my brain and mouth are not connecting so well. It's got nothing to do with temperature. You've not heard any newscasts?"

"Nuh-uh. One of the perks of your not being here! No newscasts."

"You remember a fellow named Edwin Langdon? Came here as a mature student? Graduated the year we got married?"

"Cute chap? Short? Dark? Used to capture the podium at speaker's corner and preach the virtues of self-reliance?"

"Him same one. He's minister of education since the last cabinet shuffle. Was. They shot him this afternoon."

"Shot him? You mean shot him dead?"

"Dead."

"Good God Almighty! Who? Why?"

"No one's sure, so I won't give you what's mere conjecture. There's been unrest in some of the tourist towns, including Halcyon and Stanton. People in the party have been attacked as well."

"But are you all going to be okay? What about graduation?"

"That's why council's going on into tomorrow. We stopped early today so people could be in by six. The city is under curfew till the fellows figure out what's going on, if maybe the bullet was meant for someone else. Makes most sense and would be the best scenario."

"A sorry business when a confusion in murder victims is the best scenario!"

"We've talked with the PM's office, the police commissioner, and the army folks. They feel it's a bigger risk not to proceed, so we'll probably go ahead with graduation, and at that point UA will use all media to confirm that the ceremony is still on."

"But what a tragedy, Mark!"

"It's going to be under tight lock and key, and any jollifications that were planned for afterwards have to be cancelled, what with the curfew."

"That's really sad for the graduates and their families and all."

"We'll do our best to keep everything as normal as possible, but there'll be soldiers, police, etc. So you see why I'm saying you shouldn't come."

Short pause. "If you're there, the graduates, their families, I don't see why I can't be. In fact, I should be."

"They're different, Mona."

"I don't see how. What sort of signal does it send to people, if you let students, their families, and friends run risks, but not your wife?"

"If you come, you're taxing an already over-taxed security system."

"No more than anyone else, Mark." It is the tone she uses when she's made up her mind. "My flight leaves early, so I'll be at The Xooana in good time."

"Fine." It is the tone he uses when he's yielded against his better judgement. "Council shouldn't go past midday, so I'll be here. Celia will meet you."

"I'll look for her. Don't collide with any bullets."

"I won't. Fly safely." He falters. "I love you."

"Love you too. Night-night."

Her mother says her navel string is "cut on stubborn," an obstinacy now compounded with foolhardiness. It's just a fact that if she doesn't come there will be one less person to worry about. He replaces the receiver and sits back with such force in the antique armchair that it nearly tips over. Truth is, the whole business with Grace promised to be a lot easier if Mona wasn't coming.

GRACE AND JIMMY

52

A Pain in the ...

17 November 1998

Dear Gracie,

We plan to come to see you at the SCR Hotel tonight but like how they shoot the Minister nobody must be in the street past six. We come in early yesterday for we get a drive in the morning with Mr. Sampson and we get in just a little past two. We are safe here and the church folks taking very good care of us. Not all of us come up from Wentley I will explain when we see you like how you leave to go Haiti this morning and also seeing as they never consider to invite us to anything only the ceremony never mind we is your family. We sorry we don't have no way to see you before the graduation on Saturday. Edgar say he meeting you at airport when you come this evening but if we all come with him to collect you he not going have time to bring us back down here and then go all the way to his place so we will all just have to wait till the very occasion. There is plenty talking about the horrible shooting and Pastor is holding special midday service to pray for the country and against the violence and of course for the peaceful rest of Mr. Langdon soul. We will go to the service and if they keep a vigil here in pastors residence tonight we will stay up for that too. I know that God still in charge and life taking is serious matters. Lord help the person who take the Minister life for his soul in grave danger. As usual your Ma cannot stop talking. Is just glad we glad to have you nearby.

Everybody here and leave back send love.

God bless.
Ma

Grace folds up Ma's letter, puts it in her handbag on the floor beside the bed where she always keeps it, and turns off the bedside lamp. It's early, not even seven, but already dark outside. There is no noise on campus, which is odd, until she remembers the city is under curfew, the prime minister having read the riot act the previous afternoon because of the shooting of the minister of education. Luckily, the plane from Haiti had landed at four on the dot with almost no one on board, so she'd been at The Xooana by twenty to six. She had expected Edgar to meet her, but he hadn't turned up. Someone from UA had come, a Ms. Achong, and they'd reached The Xooana quick sticks, for the roads were empty.

She'd tried to call Ma and Pa at the number for the church house where they were staying, but it just rang and rang. She wonders how the letter from Ma came to be at the desk and worries about where Edgar could be. She hopes he is okay. She feels odd, disconnected, as if things are slipping away, awareness, alertness, energy: it's not so much fatigue, more an ebbing, as if someone is modulating her life the way you turn down the volume on a radio or TV.

Mark Blackman. She gives herself special permission to think, "Jeremiah's father," for she has taught herself not to regard him in that way. She hadn't seen him at the seminar, but then chancellors don't wander around universities, never mind she still thinks doing walkabout is a good idea. She'd told him so once. Right now she doesn't care where he walks or if he can walk at all. But he is Jeremiah's father and, as Phyllis often points out, the odds are he'll in time find out, and if he does, he might assert his rights to his child. She's certain Mona hasn't told him about Jeremiah, or she'd have heard from him long ago. But what if Mona decides to? She's thinking about Mark and his wife only on Jeremiah's account. For that reason, quickly in and out of UA suits her fine. Mona is bound to come, she of the greedy coolie eyes, so the less time around them, the better. Mona nags at her though, an irritant like the blister that's developed over a small cut on her little finger since yesterday afternoon. It first itched and now it aches.

Why doesn't Mona make her own baby and stop sniffing round Jeremiah?

The two men she'd gladly have made a baby for are unavailable, one dead and the other as good as dead, for making babies, anyway. So Jeremiah is it, all that there is to her life, the resolution of all her dilemmas of unbelonging. He's certainly black enough to be a Carpenter, and he's the person who binds her to her impossible birth mother, twelve years her senior, day in, day out; the person who erases by his bright, rumbunctious self every dread aspect of his and her heritage; the person whom she can wallow in caring for and being kin to. If his grandfather is his grandmother's half-brother, and his father, who doesn't even know he exists, is another woman's husband, so what? If he isn't the fruit of a great passion but merely of the passing encounter of two bodies in the night — well, morning, more

Red Jacket   **403**

accurately — he is still her joy, her purpose, her completion. He's hers. Not Mark's and not Mona's!

As she rummages in her bag for pain tablets, she wonders if anyone has done a study on how many men in the Caribbean have children about whom they know nothing. She swallows two pills with a long drink of ice water and turns off the light, but her arm won't let her be. She can't figure out what's wrong with it, nor resist gazing at it in the dimness, turning on the light to peer at it, imagining there are tiny dots forming on the skin. Nor can she find a place to put it when she instructs herself to go to sleep once and for all.

———

"Jeremiah, you've had two stories. Time for bed now."

"Phone, Mama. Phone. I'll get it!"

"It's okay, son. I have it."

She turns and reaches for the phone with her left hand, for the pain in her other arm is fierce.

"Hi, Grace. It's me, Maisie."

"Hi, Maisie. How you doing?"

"You sound sleepy. I hope I never wake you up?"

"I need to get up anyway. What time is it?"

"It's nearly eight."

"What! What am I doing sleeping at this hour? Plus dreaming I'm at home with my son. I always get up at five!"

"I know. That's why I didn't feel any way about calling now. But you don't say yet how you doing."

"Not so great. I have this blister thing on my hand and it is madding me. Getting bigger and bigger and burning me like scotch bonnet pepper. I'm looking for tablets as we speak."

"Real sorry to hear."

"Maybe a bit of fever too. Must be my heavy heart. Too much horrors in the world and now it come and find we right here in St. Chris."

"You mean the minister? He is your friend?"

"He wasn't my good friend, but is somebody I know. They should have left him in the ministry of youth. It would have been safer."

"You think somebody kill him for purpose?"

"I don't know, Maisie. We not Jamaica yet, but we getting close. Remember what you told me years ago, about why your family left?

"I couldn't forget that, but I thought things was improved."

"Mr. Langdon and I were to talk about HIV/AIDS education early next year."

"I'm truly sorry for the loss of your colleague, Grace. Anyhow, you busy, so I best state my case. I call for two reasons, though one sound real foolish."

"Girl, you know you can tell me anything."

"Mama big toe swell up last night, and she say every time that happen, bad things always follow."

"I think the bad things happen already, Maisie!"

"Maybe so, but I still worrying about you. You should go doctor if you don't feel good. UA hospital is right there. Better safe than sorry!"

"It's really not so bad. If it get any worse, I promise to check the hospital."

"I also call to tell you that is not only Sylvia I bring with me; Carlos come too. Sylvia wanted to come so bad I couldn't tell her no, and then she decide that we have to bring 'your baby,' Carlos. Two of them insist they coming to celebrate with you, so if you hear cheering from all the way up here, is them making noise."

"Why don't you bring them, Maisie? I'm sure I can get another couple of tickets to the ceremony."

"They would love that, but I know everything is now a big confusion, so if is any worry, don't bother yourself. All the same, Grace, I would really love you to see Carlos now he grow up!

One good-looking boy! Kind of on the short side but handsome can't done. Grace? Gracie? You hearing me?"

"Sorry, Maisie." The blister is insistent. It is larger now, reaching onto her hand. The flesh nearby is red and warm. It strikes her that a small balloon of risen skin should not be the source of such wicked pain.

"So what about your boyfriend? I know is plenty money to come so far, but I figure the gorgeous beau would be here to cheer you in your triumphal hour."

"I don't have any idea who you could be talking about. You see me have time for any beau?"

"I mean the big black dreamboat that God grab for himself before you could even stake a claim."

"You mean Jimmy? No, man, Jimmy have serious work to do. I wouldn't ask him to leave it for this frivolousness."

"I don't think you should make them hear you talking bout their big UA award as frivolousness!"

"Maisie, no award could be more important than Jimmy's work."

"Yes'm. Whatever you say. I going say goodbye all the same. You have enough to do."

"I'm glad you called. Say hi to everybody for me. Ring the UA switchboard a little later and ask for the Events Office. They will tell you where to pick up the tickets."

"Okay. Check a doc if you keep feeling bad. Promise?"

"Promise."

"Thanks, Grace. Bye, now."

Water. She must have water. Her lips are so dry that the skin is flaking. On a table nearby she sees the plastic ice bucket she put there after she took pills before falling asleep last night. It's full because the ice cubes from last night have melted. She drains it to the bottom.

53

Two Widowers in Barcelona

Amphitheatre full of dark bodies, cheering. Grace in the purple kiloli they gave her when she came to graduation at Tindi, her afro glowing around her head like the halo of the angel in Manokouma's window. The weaving women who came to the centre had made the cloth on an old-fashioned loom under Sister Tekawitha's guidance, not for Grace, just against the day when cloth for a special occasion would be needed. Sœur Monique padded the hem and embroidered on it, in Kufic script, a pattern made from the words "good woman." Grace sobbed and hugged Monique when she explained the meaning.

She accepts her award from the chancellor, a shell carved in luminous pink stone, a lantern glowing in the last light of a prize Christophian sunset, when her right arm swells, the skin leaving the flesh and becoming a huge, shiny bladder. It explodes, scattering bits of bloody tissue, leaving only a skeletal appendage of white bone, bent at the elbow in its gesture of acceptance. The shell falls, but it does not break.

He shoots up in bed. It is a dream, prescient, for sure, but not as clearly present as usual, and he hasn't had a fit, nor become ill — at least not yet. All of which he takes to be a good sign. But he has to go to her, for sure.

He is in Barcelona, old port city, with its fabulous Sagrada Familia, forever-building cathedral, its ordinary old streets, its simply ornate buildings, its pensións tucked into impossible corners, its scallywags come from all over to relieve other poor of their pennies. Billeted on this hill, Gaudi's Parc Güell up the road, the Monastery of Saint Joseph next door to the residence where he is, he knows for sure that Iberia is African, not Moorish; the entire country's ancient provenance. He'd trod its hard-packed earth all over the northern part of the continent.

The wall clock in his room says four-thirty. He will call Rome at six to talk to his psychiatrist, Fra Mucelli, and Benke, perhaps to get Leviticus Kitendi out of bed. Levi, Benke's new bishop, has just replaced one of his handlers. The third man, Padre Alonso, is here in the monastery. He has to get to St. Chris fast, but before he leaves he will try to observe the protocol. If he doesn't find Mucelli and Kitendi, he is going anyway. Alonso can tell them.

Mass is at five. He'll see Alonso there. He should hurry.

———

He is glad he'd been there when they found Jeremiah in her belly; grateful she'd been with him the night he'd foreseen the slaughter in Rwanda, foul corpses mucking up his sandals, rancid flesh clinging between his toes. He'd trudged through fields of headless, limbless torsos, scattered body parts, gourds of skulls mouldy with putrid brain matter, the whole a banquet for swarms of flies who clothed their dinner with a shimmering coat, glinting green and murmurous.

The pills she'd given him then had prevented a second trance. He'd be forever grateful that she'd come in time to stop him from going back to that horrific place, though sometimes he wondered whether, if he'd returned and seen some sign, noticed some clue to where it was, whether he might have helped prevent the massacre.

"Padre, teléfono." The boy waylays him on his way back to his room.

"Gracias, Tomás. Ya vengo."

In the office, he takes up the phone. "Hello? It's Father Atule. I'm calling about that flight, Barcelona to Heathrow? Have you managed that? Thanks so much. And to St. Chris? Yes? Perfect. Many thanks."

He goes back to the church and, having brought Alonso up to speed, slips into Joseph's chapel. Two widowers, Jesus's father and he, chaps who'd married wives and had dreams that plunged their lives into chaos. The bearded builder looks at him across a vase of dead flowers, as tired as the saint must so often have been. Over time, Joseph told Jimmy his story. The foster-father carpenter, who could have come from any Mabuli village, had been near fifty with three male children by his first wife, all grown and gone. His two girls, nine and ten, needed a mother's care, though. The woman, Mary, cleaned, cooked, and ran a house on swift, assiduous feet, minding his Ruth and Rachel with a sweet cunning, as if they were all girls together. And once he folded her in his arms, his blood danced. But Jehovah himself had wanted Mary for breeding and how could he face that competition?

He isn't fighting anyone for Grace. Mark Blackman is Jeremiah's parent by blood, but he, Jimmy, still loves the child and loves his mother too, perhaps in a way he didn't understand, but so what? They are colleagues, friends, but he also finds her physically attractive, not in the way that Nila or Rita Rose had been, but in ways that drew them together, tethered them tight. They've navigated afflictions of body and spirit, a bond embracing and transcending the erotic.

He smiles. Never mind what he's told himself since then, he might well have made love to her that night, save for Jeremiah in situ.

There is a way, Joseph keeps saying, always a way. A month after John's death, a plane ticket had come. In Rome he'd begun seeing a grizzled Italian friar, Pedro Ponti, a psychiatrist. For years Ponti, in his eighties, had ministered to mystics and stigmatics, including the saintly Padre Pio. Who'd have thought there were enough of those to make a life's work? The friar treated him for six months, designing a way to negotiate the visions through meditation, writing him the first scripts for Diazepam. When Ponti retired, Friar Mucelli succeeded him. So far, so good with the pills: he's been grateful for a way to muddle through. Once his handlers knew of the nightmare he had when Grace visited Mabuli for the first time, it became their affair to manage. They elected to hold a watching brief, and Rwanda began five months later.

He'll be airborne in an hour. He is still hoping to speak to Mucelli and Kitendi, but he has to go. The dream about Grace gives him hope this trance at least might help keep someone alive.

It is Mucelli who suggested that his closeness to people is what enabled him to sense their impending deaths.

"Once upon a time, Giacomo, there was a cat called Ascension that lived in a home for old priests in Assisi. Anytime it climbed into the bed of one of the old men, he died within days. People swore it had a demon, but the priests loved the cat, welcomed her putting them on notice, so they could have the last rites, summon their families, say goodbye." Mucelli suggested Jimmy might be like the cat who knew and loved the old men so well that she breathed in tandem with their lives. For sure Mapome and he had been thick as thieves. As for Nila, whom he'd loved more than life, if what killed her on that snowy hillside was some infirmity he'd intuited, he'd have some peace. And this time, Grace.

"Padre, el taxi!" Tomás, his dark head bobbing as he dances across from the residence, arrives at the chapel door with his backpack.

"Adiós, amigo." He takes the bag, hugs the child and goes out.

54

An Unexpected Trip

"Grandma Phyllis, gottagoagain."

"Are you going to come with me into the Ladies?"

"No, Grandma. Is not for men."

"And you're a man?"

"Yes. I need a papa so I can pee."

"I'm not a papa, Jeremiah. I'm a grandma, and I can't go into the men's bathroom, so I think we have a problem."

"We have a problem."

Jimmy hears the conversation before he catches sight of the speakers. He sees Jeremiah stop unexpectedly, so Phyllis nearly trips over him. They are in the midst of Heathrow's morning turbulence, with a stream of bodies, people, and occasional dogs eddying about them, but the child's eyes find him in the confusion with the swiftness of a homing device.

Jeremiah runs to Jimmy, throws his arms around the priest's legs, and shrieks "Tuuuules! Jeremiah going with Tules!"

"Hello, Jeremiah Carpenter."

"Gottagoagain, Tules!"

"Jeremiah! What kind of greeting is that? Jimmy, what are you doing here? Not that I'm not glad to see you. And I'm sorry for this young man's forwardness."

"Tules! Gottagoagain!"

"He's been wanting to go every ten minutes and fussing about using the women's. I've been having a time of it."

"Give us one twitch of a monkey's tail. We'll be right back."

Jimmy returns minutes later, the child asleep in his arms, his little-boy frizz of hair damp on his head.

"Thanks, Jimmy. What did you do?" Phyllis unfolds the child's stroller.

"Breathed Mabuli desert air on him."

"When does your plane leave?"

"I'm actually on the flight to St. Chris." He settles into the seat beside her. "I decided," he looks at his shoes, "to join Grace for the big day."

"Well, seems like she decided at the last minute that she wanted everybody at the party."

"It is a very big day."

Half an hour later, Chrisair calls the flight. Jimmy lifts the child from the pushchair, Phyllis gathers their paraphernalia and they head for the gate. The priest settles into the seat by the window in the bulkhead with Jeremiah beside him, and Phyllis sits in the aisle seat. The plane is full, the passengers mostly tourists.

"Are we going to have to be really quiet so we don't wake the prince here?" Jimmy asks. "Or is he a pretty sound sleeper these days?"

"We woke before five to get the plane here, so he should sleep," Phyllis hesitates, "which is good, for I'd like to talk to you. Serious matters."

"For sure." They've gained altitude, but still haven't cleared the clouds.

"I been on a greasy pole with Grace for months now: up, *swish*, down, only to begin climbing again. She told you we had a fuss?" She makes a querulous face, looking at him for confirmation.

He smiles, doesn't answer. "Why don't you tell me the trouble, Phyllis?"

"She's angry about a barrel full of things, but most of all because I say she's exactly like her father. The minute it come out my mouth, I know I should never say so. I don't think about her father. I never have the two of them in my mind at one time. But true is true, and when she's ready, Grace behave own-way exactly like Ralston."

"You're worried about her?"

"Worry not the right word. That girl have so much education and still so foolish. Sensible people take lessons from experience, and look to consequences, but crazy people do neither. Sometimes I think that even though she do her work so well, is like she just going from one thing to the next without it really involving her. Like she there and not there at one and the same time. You don't have to agree with me, Jimmy, but you understand what I mean?"

"Yes, I think so." He remembers Grace's unburdening at the novitiate the day he showed her the Manakouma windows in the chapel. He'd tried to tell her about letting past things go so she could wallow joyfully in the present. She'd smiled, shaken her head, said, "Too esoteric for me."

"At the convent Sister Mary Agnes was always saying experience is not the same for everybody," Phyllis continues. "Some people have twenty years' experience, others have one year's experience twenty times. Well, Grace clearly learn from her work, but I not sure she learn from her life."

"Why do you say that?"

"Two times now Grace just throw any semblance of sanity to the winds. The first time is obvious, with the result sleeping beside you. But now she won't tell the child's father about him. Does that make sense?"

"I've told her that myself."

"I don't see how she can enjoy that child while she is hiding him from his father. Better she let everybody know, share him with all concerned, especially since it going to happen eventually anyway."

"There's a lot of wisdom in that."

"You know what start the fuss?" It isn't a question — just a prelude to the story Phyllis wants to tell, which he already knows. "I meet the child's father's wife one morning in the park near our house in Geneva. Jeremiah is running up and down after ducks, and this woman just arrive and announce Jeremiah is her husband's child! I nearly faint, but my state was nothing compared to hers. She was slobbering and bawling so bad, I invite her home with us. That is over two years gone, and Grace won't get over it. She think I was out to cause trouble, and if anything, it was the exact opposite."

"I would have been upset too, if I were Grace."

"I don't say no, Jimmy. But till now she won't let me explain. And me, all the time minding this child, seeing him watch other children's fathers, sure he is wondering where his father is. You yourself hear him just now say he need a papa to pee. Which is not to say I was thinking about all that when I asked the woman home. It just seem like the decent thing to do. What was I to do? Say, 'Oh well, is your husband's child, but you better get over it?' "

He nods, non-committal. He's glad he can't look at her directly on account of a brilliant shaft of sunlight coming through the window opposite.

"Anyway," Phyllis is an indignant storyteller, "that is how it went. I suppose I was thinking the child could do with a father, and if his papa were willing to be involved in his life, it would be a good thing. Furthermore, if after she foolishly go and have a baby for a married man, his wife turn out to be decent and reasonable instead of jealous and vindictive, that is more than a blessing."

"I'd say that was lucky, and pretty unusual, yes."

"Grace was royally upset when she find out who the woman was, and I'm not saying she didn't have a right. We had a discussion about it the same day ... "

"Discussion?" The light has moved and he is smiling at her.

"Okay. Quarrel. She won't listen, just keep insisting that it's her child, and she can do what she like. It get heated, and I liken her to her father."

"He's dead, isn't he?"

"Long time aback."

"And Grace never knew him or anything about him?"

"She was eighteen when Mr. Carpenter, her adopted grandfather, told her about me. At that time he made her to know that her father was a wicked man."

"Lots of people say that about lots of fathers."

"If Mr. Carpenter say he was a bad man and St. Peter say he was a angel, she would believe her grandfather."

"So it's natural that she was hurt when you compared her to this man her Grandpa said was so bad?"

"I tell her I was sorry if I upset her or cause Jeremiah any distress. I even offer to go back to New York. She move right past it, don't want to talk about it, tell me is her business who the child's father is, she not admitting it's Mr. Blackman and we must just pick up where we leave off, go on as usual."

"Do you think that's what she's done, as far as her relationship with Jeremiah's father is concerned?"

"Seem to me that's how she deal with all her personal problems: never identify whys and wherefores. Just pass through, swallow like medicine and press on."

"Medicine should make you better."

"Maybe not medicine, then, maybe spit. The thing is, when she talk about her first boyfriend, Charlie — not that she say much, mark you — or when she speak of her visits to you in Mabuli, she turn into somebody different, or maybe she turn into her real self, I don't know, but she is another person those times."

Jimmy scribbles this down mentally as something to think more about. "She's not told me a lot about Charlie either. Losing him the way she did must have been hard and she and he seem to have worked very well together. As for Mabuli, she knows we think of her as family, and she sees the difference she makes in the lives of many people. That may have something to do with it."

"Well, I suppose that could be why. I just hope she figure it out soon. I must say I have a lot of sympathy for Mrs. Blackman. She want to stay in touch and keep seeing Jeremiah, and I didn't see how I could say no. Jeremiah is her step-son. If the man ever decide to take the case to court, dog nyam Grace supper. So Mona and I write and talk on the phone. Not behind Grace back neither. I tell her I was doing it."

"That's as it should be."

"I tell her that my keeping in touch with Mrs. Blackman would cause no problems, which I knew it wouldn't. After that, Mona stop by the park and visit us when she come to Geneva. It wasn't so often — maybe four times since the first time. Jeremiah know her good. He never talk to his mother about her, though I don't tell him not to. I suppose children just know not to do some things."

The priest yawns, then hastily apologizes.

"I can see you are tired Jimmy, and I soon finish, but I need help deciding what to do. I don't ever talk to Mona about the ins and outs. It's not my business. But it's not right where Jeremiah and his father are concerned. His step-mother too."

"You keep encouraging Grace to tell his father?"

"But after this child is not going grow up, graduate from university, and get married without his father finding out that he exist!"

"It would be unlikely."

"Then this year, the university write to say … "

" … they were giving her the DIS Award."

"I can't understand why she never tell them no. Can't you say no to these things?"

"You can, but that would create awkwardness, especially given Grace's line of work."

"Well, she tell them yes, she accept, and that is what lead to the most recent disturbance."

The plane bounces as if on cue. It is a drop of maybe twenty feet. The seat belt sign goes on, and the captain announces there will be turbulence for several minutes. Jeremiah stirs, flaps a hand as though to brush away some creature bothering him, then settles down.

"Don't repeat that last word," Jimmy shakes his head, pretends to warn, wagging his finger.

"If she was going to get this award, that mean St. Chris papers, regional papers, maybe even the overseas papers would be researching her life, doing articles about her, and so on. I decide I better tell her, for if it was to take her by surprise, I wouldn't forgive myself."

"Tell her what, Phyllis?"

"That her father was my half-brother, which I expect she told you. But there is more she doesn't yet know."

The plane is surfing another series of big air waves.

"How did she respond to what you told her about her father?"

"She don't talk to me so much these days, which is okay, in a way, for it's Jeremiah I'm most concerned about. These are grown-ups, responsible for a child's life!"

"Is Grace certain Jeremiah's father doesn't know about him?"

"I'm sure he doesn't. That's why I don't understand this alteration of plans. When she said she wasn't taking Jeremiah to St. Chris, I assumed she didn't want his father to find out about him."

"You were right. She didn't change the plan. It was I who arranged for you both to come. But go on. You said there was something you hadn't yet told Grace."

"After it come out that I was making a baby, old Mr. Carpenter visit my grandma to see if he could help, and he and Ralston take a walk up a hillside near where we live."

"What happened?"

"Some say Ralston lose his life in a accident; some say Gramps push him, and good riddance!"

———

It is a brilliant one o'clock. Clouds like the meringues Mapome used to whip up in her blue earthenware mixing-bowl are just mounting the northern sky, a basin paler than he remembers from his last time in St. Chris. He gets them quickly through immigration, takes Jeremiah to the bathroom again, and then installs the still half-sleeping child in his stroller. While Phyllis changes his clothes and coaxes him to drink something, Jimmy finds the bags, loads up a cart, and leads the three of them out of the airport.

"We're going to The Xooana Inn, please," he says to the cabbie, then turns to Phyllis. "I made bookings there. Grace's office pulled rank. They'll move her into a suite big enough for you and Jeremiah. Graduation is at four-thirty. We'll make it just in time."

At half-past one their taxi is rattling down the slope of the promontory on which the airport stands. Jimmy sees the bridge across Boatman's River, rusty girders like strings of a huge old harp, and the highway that goes up into the hills to the UA campus.

Jeremiah is awake, staring out through the window at a huge bird, flying escort. "Look, Grandma. A big duck!"

"That's a good guess, Jeremiah, but it's actually a blue-crested gull. It's the national bird of St. Chris."

"Whazaanashnalbird, Grandma?"

"It's a bird that all the people love and want to represent their island."

"Whazanisland Grandma?"

"It's a small country that has water all around it. Look out through the window. See the water?"

"Yes, Grandma."

"Keep looking. See where it goes."

Jeremiah resumes gazing out of the window and shortly is asleep again.

"Jimmy, you said you arranged for us to come because you knew something was wrong with Grace. How did you know?"

"You won't believe me if I tell you."

"Try me."

"I had a dream about Grace receiving her award at the ceremony. She was reaching out and — " The image of Grace's exploding arm makes him pause. Also, he isn't accustomed to the fact of a mere dream telling him what is to come. He usually has an epileptic seizure, followed by something like a vision. The fact that it's a plain old dream is less harassing but it leaves him in doubt. Ironically, the violence of the fits or of some accompanying illness stands as a perverse guarantee, underwriting the reliability of what he foresees. That isn't the case this time. Still, his instincts say the dream is the real thing.

"And what?" Phyllis urges.

"Something was wrong with her arm, so she dropped the award. I could see she was seriously ill."

"What was wrong with her?"

"I'm not sure, but I know it's bad."

"Why didn't you tell me right away? Why wait? I've a right to know."

"It was a dream, Phyllis. This has a long history that I can't go into now. It explains why I'm less confident in the present case than I might otherwise be. I didn't say anything primarily because … " He thinks again of the seizures, the absent warranty. "I worried about upsetting you, only to get here and find Grace perfectly fine."

"But you seem so certain."

"I am sure — and I'm not!"

"What are we going to do?"

"We can pray."

They join hands and close their eyes. The child's breaths, a gentle tide, go in and out. Phyllis opens her eyes and speaks first. "How did you arrange for us to come? Can you give instructions for Grace?"

"I have her power of attorney. I've had it since Jeremiah was born."

"Isn't that untoward, you being a priest and all?"

"It's unusual, yes, but not untoward. I have it *because* I am a priest."

"You're speaking in parables now, Jimmy. She gave you power of attorney because you are a priest?"

"Want to listen to some more hard-to-believe stuff?"

"You know my life. Want anything harder to believe?"

"Okay. When I was a novice, I made a thirty-day retreat with a priest named J.J. — for John Jeremiah — Kelly."

"Is that where the child's name comes from?"

"Yes. J.J. was murdered before the retreat ended."

"Where? In Mabuli?"

"Yes, but in all likelihood, not by any Mabulian. He and I got very close, just talking twice a day over two weeks."

"Mmmm. It can happen. I know."

"Well, this tale takes a lot of knowing. I'd been married as a young man, very happily. I lost my wife in an accident not long before I entered the priesthood. She was pregnant. I was so broken up, that, awful as it sounds, I was glad to be giving my life this time around to someone who couldn't die."

"Never thought of it that way."

"Nor had I, till then. I was very concerned on that retreat about being able to live a life of celibacy, having been married and all that."

"Hard, eh?"

"Maybe. Maybe not. Anyway, J.J. gave me an assignment. There's a big stained glass window depicting the Annunciation in the chapel, with St. Joseph in the background. We call it the Angelus window. I spent most of my meditation time there. John said to ask Joseph if he wanted Mary the way a man wants a woman."

"That's never occurred to me either. And what did Joseph say when you asked him?"

"He gave me a puzzle. I couldn't figure it out for a long time. When I met Grace, the pieces began to fall into place."

"How?"

"Joseph said I'd lost a woman with a baby, but God would give me another, also with a baby, to take care of."

"And Grace and Jeremiah are who he promised?"

"For sure."

"The sea's done," Jeremiah turns from the window, wide awake, and announces precisely. "And I have a secret."

"What's the secret, Jeremiah?" they ask together.

"Is not a secret if I tell you. Is a secret for Mama."

"Is it a story?" Jimmy knows his secrets are often stories.

"No, Tules, is not a story."

"Make sure you keep it in a safe place. All right?"

"Kidoki."

MARK,
JIMMY, GRACE

55

Showtime

Mona suggests it.

"Why don't we ask Grace to join us for a glass of sherry before we go downstairs to lunch?"

What is the woman thinking? If she and Grace meet in public, neither will risk unpleasantness. St. Chris is too small. In private is another matter! Mark hopes they will be cordial, but if they aren't, his insurance is the presence of others. Time will pass, it will eventually be over, lunch, graduation, the award ceremony. The curfew will mercifully have them indoors early, and that will be that.

He is immediately ashamed of himself for thinking in these terms about these two women for whom he cares. Neither of them is a shrew, though Grace has a viper's tongue on her when she is ready, and Mona, in her element, can hold strong men at bay. But who knows women? Who can predict what they will do, when?

"Mark? Are you dozing?"

"Not just dozing, dear. I'm soundly asleep."

"Listen, outside this door you is chancellor, but you is no chancellor in this bed. Didn't you hear what I said?"

He rolls over, lies on his back, and opens his eyes. The sun is conducting an inspection through clerestory windows along the top of the east-facing wall, focusing families of motes and a pair of tiny twin spiders suspended on invisible threads. In a move he strongly encouraged, the refurbishment committee had asked the architects to preserve aspects of the original building — cedar floors, coolers on the windows, fretwork along the eaves. The light troops at an angle down the wall and masses on the floor, warming the old wood. The last bit of night shrouds the corner of the room where the bed is, for the windows on the adjacent walls are shut tight. Mona didn't want any lizards wriggling in. One has come anyway: a yellow-brown curry lizard is standing guard at the foot of a pot containing a prosperous croton, its leaves a fiery green, the tracery of veins outlined in orange.

The trick would be to have some kind of collapse and stay holed up here for the day. He pulls his feet back under the sheet. Maybe he will. "I don't really think it's necessary, Mona. We'll see her at twelve for lunch, and she probably has any number of things to do between now and then."

"She'll be ready long before twelve, Mark, and twiddling her thumbs till it's time to go down. She's right here in The Xooana. Why don't we just ask her?"

"Fine. Are you going to ask her?"

"I don't know her. You can just run down to her room."

"I should think the phone would be fine."

"Don't you think a friendly rap on her door would be nice?"

What is she doing? Does she know? And if so, is she encouraging a tryst minutes before lunch? Planning to barge into the room seconds after he enters and catch him with Grace in his arms?

"If chancellor's wives don't do that, for sure chancellors don't."

"I thought you were a different kind of chancellor."

"Dear, we wouldn't want to catch the lady en déshabillé, and the only way to avoid that is to call and ask if she'd receive us, in which case you might as well issue the invitation on the phone."

———

He hears Mona answer a rap on the door.

"Dr. Carpenter. Do come in. You look lovely."

"Thank you. So do you. That sari is exquisite."

"Originally my mother's. She'd thank you for the compliment. Do sit. Mark will be out in a minute. What can I get you to drink? Sherry, perhaps?"

"Sherry is fine, thanks. It's six o'clock somewhere."

"Mark always says that. I tell him it's six o'clock in two places, actually."

Grace is sitting directly in his line of vision as he enters the room. She has on an embroidered and beaded white m'bubu against which her skin flares. Her reddish hair, with more gray strands than he remembers, is twisted into a chessboard of small bumps with cowrie beads threaded through them. He studies her face, the slope of the gown on her shoulders, the peaks of her breasts.

"Hi, Mark. I'm pouring Dr. Carpenter a glass of sherry. Will you join us?"

What to do now? Kiss Grace? Shake hands? Do nothing?

"Allow me," he says. He takes the glass of sherry from Mona, picks up a small side table, and walks it over to Grace, who is biting her lip, worrying what looks like a large blister on her hand. Pleased at resolving the problem, he sets the glass on the table. Neither kiss nor handshake needed!

"Grace, how nice to see you after so long, and in such magnificent circumstances." He is being a bit over the top, but never mind; the idea is to keep going. He doesn't look at Grace long, though he hopes he has done so warmly, then he is swiftly back at the bar, taking the glass of sherry Mona offers — she already has hers — and raising it.

"I think a toast is in order. Congratulations! You honour us by being the first person from St. Chris to receive the university's Distinguished International Service Award. May your work prosper so that the health of our region and the world may prosper!" More overkill, but he is going to roll along like an army tank.

They lift their glasses. Sip. Mona speaks. "How's Jeremiah, Dr. Carpenter?"

"Please call me Grace. He's very well, thank you."

"Is he here?" Mona goes on. "Has he come with his grandma?"

"No, not this time. We thought it would be hard for him to make two long journeys in so short a time."

"Who's Jeremiah, if I may ask?" Mark inquires, pleased that things are going well between the two women.

"Jeremiah is my son," Grace says, eyes meeting his.

"Oh, really! I didn't know you were married."

"I'm not."

"Foolish of me. Of course you needn't be. But I certainly didn't know that you had a son. Wonderful. Congratulations on that too. How old is he?" It flies straight into his head. Their bodies had rolled over each other for three hours one morning, with no prior or subsequent contact. But any number of other men might have done exactly that, days before or after. The child needn't be his.

"He was four on the twenty-ninth of July." With math and the calendar he is quick, has to be for the sake of his work. With the cycles that women's bodies ride, he is familiar. It is a way of being doubly cautious. It was almost exactly nine months. Jesus, Grace, what fine fellow followed me? Then again, you were probably already pregnant. Maybe you don't even know whose child it is!

He finds himself gazing at her tummy, a delightful African tummy, a motherly prominence, like the dome of a miniscule hut or a tiny mosque. In a second he is back in Cambridge, regarding tummy, breasts, legs, all of her stark naked, stretched out under him. He loses his grip and spills the sherry. Mona catches the glass in time, but her sari collects the escaping drops, which mark the red silk.

Grace stands, comes quickly towards Mona. "Oh, no! Do you have salt? Seltzer water?"

"It'll be fine. I'll be out of it and into another in two seconds. Do keep Mark company. I'll be right back." She vanishes down the corridor leading from the sitting room to the bedroom.

Grace goes back to her chair, collects her glass, comes over to the bar, and sets it down. "Thanks very much for the drink and good wishes. I should go. I'll see you both in the dining room at twelve."

She turns towards the door. He is about to say goodbye, when to his horror, he hears himself asking, "Is he mine?"

"I beg your pardon?" She spins around to face him.

"I said, is he mine?"

"I'm not sure what you're talking about." Her voice is controlled, but her fury fans the redness in her skin, makes her nostrils flare, forces her shoulders back, her head up and her chest forward. He's sure he sees her nipples harden under the white cotton. As he becomes aroused, he's aware of the damn cataplexy kicking in again. He curses how it works: any strong feeling makes his knees buckle and his muscles go weak. He holds on to the bar for support.

"Gracie, don't —"

"Don't under any circumstances call me 'Gracie.' "

She has every right, but it still hurts. "But ... "

"As Prince Hal said, 'But me no buts.' "

"I'm sorry. I'd no idea that I was offending you." He doesn't tell her that it isn't Hal. "This is important."

"*You* are telling me what's important?"

"I want you to answer me."

"You've no right to an answer."

"I may have no right, but the child has a right." His quick wits surprise him; the child has snuck in on his own.

"That child is as fine and happy as a child can be."

"That's now. Now is changing into tomorrow as we speak." He is struggling. "I wrote again and again. You never answered, not even a postcard."

"I don't know about any letters. I do know you lied."

"I didn't lie."

"You said your marriage had broken down, that you hadn't slept with your wife in years."

"I said I hadn't slept with her, and that was true."

"Don't bring your sophistry to me. Have you any idea of the grief you caused me, caused us?"

"And what about the grief you caused me? You simply expunged any possibility of communication between us."

"I called your office from Mabuli when I found out I was pregnant. I was worried sick I might have AIDS."

"You thought I might have a sexually transmitted disease?"

"Arthur Ashe died from AIDS. Better men than you have had it. What did I know about your sleeping habits?"

"Watch yourself, Grace."

"Don't you bring any of your testosterone into this, Chancellor. It's already caused enough trouble."

"And which of your hormones do I indict?"

"Indict any of them, all of them. I don't care. I call halfway across the world and get your secretary who says, 'He's at home. This is the number.' "

"Which I left precisely in case you called."

"Precisely? Could I have supposed you'd have done that with a wife commanding centre stage? And guess who answered? Some woman saying she was your wife — unless, of course, the person changing her sari in the room next door isn't your wife? Maybe she's a figment of both our imaginations?"

The figment joins them. This sari is blue-green, trimmed with gold braid, and she's altered her jewelry and eye shadow, shoes, and purse.

He feels the skin of sweat on his face, sees the sheen on Grace's.

Mona observes them, a cat studying mice. "It's ten to. I think we should all go down. Thanks so much for spending this time with us, Grace." Mona waves Grace before them as they go towards the door and smiles up at him. The bindi on her forehead is a bright third eye peering at him from the face of some enigmatic creature out of the *Ramayana*.

In the foyer downstairs Mona goes over to greet the principal and his wife. As he and Grace stand together, he asks again, "Is he mine?"

She looks up at him and mouths a prolonged and exaggerated "No."

56

Groaning Towards the Spirit

After lunch the women return to The Xooana to change for the graduation ceremony, while the men go to be further briefed on arrangements for security.

Upstairs, Grace is unsteady on her feet because of the pain. As she shoves her door hard to open it, she notices that the blister now covers almost all her upraised hand. It has acquired black spots, and the itching has turned into soreness. The blister and spots make her think of jiggers, though, what with the size of the bubble of skin, they'd have to be gigantic! Once when she was maybe eight or so, Ma used her slimmest needle to pick a female jigger, swollen with eggs, from under her second toe. She explained to Grace that you had to remove the whole creature in one piece, for if the eggs escaped, each one would plant itself, lay its own eggs, and eventually the heap of jigger fleas chomping away would devour your foot, leaving only bone. Sort of like the AIDS virus injecting its DNA into healthy cells, spreading as they multiply.

"It's the way with nature, Grace." Ma held the miniscule creature up against the light. "Everything fix on growing and making itself again, groaning like Romans say towards the life of the Spirit. Everything, jiggers included." Even then, Grace thought that peculiar. How could her mother see flesh-eating fleas as nature "groaning towards the life of the Spirit?" Might HIV/AIDS be a manifestation of that groaning towards the Spirit too?

As she steps into her room, she trips on the carpet and falls flat. When she tries to get up, she can't move. At that point she admits what she's known all along. These are no jiggers. These are symptoms that all WHO personnel are familiar with, manifestations of a macabre disease, the stuff of science fiction. Jiggers, even giant ones, she'd be grateful for. She can't face this. She closes her eyes, falls asleep instantly and dreams that Jimmy is showing Jeremiah how to fly a kite which gently lifts them both aloft into a dark sky out of which grow ground orchids in purple, pink, and orange. Jeremiah is about to put one in his mouth. Her impulse to stop him wakes her up long enough to drag herself to the bed, where she collapses again. Pain is ravaging her hand. Trust Papa God! Her shining moment, and she's going to die right in the middle of it! Punishment no doubt for saying she has more brains in her little finger than God has in his head. It's all on account of a finger; one tiny digit has given mortal offense. She thinks of Pa, envies his placid stump.

She's dreaming again, making her way through snow falling in plump, heavy flakes that are warm to the touch. She is crying, tears and nose-nought mixing up with snowflakes on her face to make a kind of elemental mush. Now and then, she takes the sleeve of her down jacket and swipes the sticky mess. Not so smart, for the jacket's material, whatever it is, can't absorb any of the stuff, so her face is wet, and pale green slime streaks the sleeves.

Standing on the sidewalk waiting to cross Baldwin and walk the short distance to Beloved, she slips and nearly drops in front of a car making its way around the corner. A big, tall, white skinhead man puts out his hand and catches her, and she looks up into mismatched eyes, one grey and one green.

"You all right?" he asks.

She can't smile, can't talk, so she nods her head, swift bobs up and down. The man looks around, not sure what to do, maybe trying to find somewhere to take her, or someone to help him, and she realizes he's still holding her up. He's starting to speak when Maisie, all in white — mink coat, Gucci purse, and boots — emerges out of curtains of snow, a glittering goddess, commanding the space on the sidewalk, grabbing Grace, smiling, and saying, "Many thanks. I'll take care of her."

Maisie is a strong woman — just as well, for she is able to sling one arm around Grace, and use it to steady her and keep her on her feet. The warm, close human body is a comfort, and the familiar smell of Maisie's perfume, French, expensive, over-proof, Belle Mademoiselle, or Jolie Madame, or something, marches into her nostrils with such firm strides that it wakes her up.

The bubble now covers the hand beside her on the bed and is making its way up her arm. Underneath feels like soup. It's not itching any more, only hurting worse than labour pains, worse than toothache, worse than any hurt she has ever felt in her life. Her body is full of awareness, every cell responding to an alarm bell, a siren, a wailing korchi. She can feel the spaces between nerve endings in her brain, and she knows the moment of knowing, the vibration of the old word, "korchi," as it leaps across her synapses. She must get up and force herself down the hall to their door. Mona is there changing for the ceremony. The woman is no fool, she who called and invited Grace to join them for sherry, who asked about Jeremiah, who retired to change the wine-sprinkled sari. Grace recalls how she'd looked at the two of them when she came back outside.

She's about to knock when the door opens to reveal Mona, regal in purple, dark hair falling around her like a silk wrap.

"Grace! What's wrong? You look awful."

"I'm in dreadful pain, and my arm is doing something peculiar. Look. I think I'm really ill, so you, you should probably stay far from me." She knows that probably won't do any good — except perhaps persuade Mona Blackman she's a thoughtful person. "Could you call an ambulance, please? I'll wait in my room till it comes." The last thing she hears is Mona shouting, "Mark!" as she crumples in the doorway.

57

Your Cheating Heart . . .

Having come back from the graduation ceremony by six o'clock, Mark and Mona are sitting, quiet, in their room at The Xooana, which is dark and cool. She asks for an update on the murdered minister, but there is no word on him. The curfew is still on, and the security situation is much the same.

Mark thinks he'd better get on with it. "So, aren't you going to say anything?"

"Anything like what, Mark?"

"Anything like anything, Mona."

"Okay. Anything."

"You sound like a child playing a game."

"And who has been behaving like a child playing a game, Chancellor?"

"Me, I suppose?"

"Throw a stone into a pig pen, the one that go *quee-quee*, is him it lick."

"If I'm a pig, then that child is my piglet. If he isn't, I have a pig double somewhere in the universe."

"Mark, that's such an endearing admission of adultery."

"Mona, we been married a long time. You're as familiar as my own bad breath."

"Thank you. You're Prince Charming this evening."

"That's how I'm certain you been on to this thing from the start. All along I had a feeling, though, honestly, I've no idea how you could have found out."

"You listening to yourself? I need to be sure I'm hearing what you're saying."

"I know very well what I'm saying. I'm saying you knew about Grace and me. Not that there's very much to know."

"If you gave her a baby, there's enough to know."

"That's all there was to it. I suspect you knew about the child too."

"Don't you think you've got hold of the wrong end of the stick?"

"I'm not dealing with any stick."

"You quit that then? Good. Glad to hear it."

"Grace, this is not a laughing matter."

"I'm not Grace, Mark. I'm Mona."

He fumbles. She doesn't pause. "That makes it even less of a laughing matter. I thought I knew men from these islands pretty well. I thought I knew you very well, but you manage to astound me. You've just found out you have a child, just admitted you've been unfaithful, and just seen your baby-mother go off to hospital looking like she's at death's door, and all you can say is the child looks so much like you he must be yours, and you've no idea how I could've found out about your infidelity?"

"They're the first two things that came to mind, so I said them. What's wrong with that?"

"Nothing at all wrong with saying what's on your mind. But I'd have hoped those thoughts might have taken second place to expressions of concern for even one of the three people I've mentioned. Jeremiah is four years old. He doesn't know he has a papa, and, never mind that Grace has been raising him without letting you know that he exists, you may jolly well end up being his only parent. I won't bother to go on about the gravity of her present circumstances, and I'll resist making any comment about where I stand in all this."

"You stand where you've always stood."

"No, Mark. That's where you're wrong. You're only just learning about it, but I've known that you were Jeremiah's father for over two years now. Jan Leighton called me and told me she'd met Jeremiah and his grandmother in Geneva at a luncheon put on by some Caribbean social group, and he was your dead stamp."

"Trust your mouth-a-massy friend."

"She doesn't like you either. So I went to see for myself and found out that my husband had not only been unfaithful, but he'd fathered another woman's child, conceived like spite after our baby dies, swatted like a fly in his sleep. Ergo, I am married to a Royal Rat — and I'm not talking about Reepicheep either."

"Who the hell is that?"

"A mouse of noble lineage in the *Chronicles of Narnia*."

"Oh, for the love of God! Not in the middle of this! Mona, let's cut the crap! We both know this isn't the first time I've been unfaithful."

"Is that so?"

"You expected me to be celibate when you were looking at me like I was something that smelled bad every time I touched you?"

"Being celibate is not impossible, my village ram. Some men are celibate for their entire lives."

"That's unnatural."

"You sound like some born-again fundamentalist. Celibacy is old as man's belief in God: holy men of every tradition — monks, priests, shamans — are celibate."

"They have a religious motivation. Marriage is about two people becoming one flesh. It's carnal. Your body abdicated a responsibility to mine."

"Our baby had just died! It can't have been easy for you, and I'm sorry. But I was ill. I couldn't help myself. We've been through that."

"Well, I couldn't help myself either."

"If you say so. We're straying from the point."

"Which of the many?"

"I'd have been reassured if your first thought had been for the child, or for the child's sick-unto-dying mother, or for me — somebody other than yourself."

She goes to the bar. The lights are still off. "You want a drink?"

"No thanks, Mona. I want a clear head for this."

"You'll permit me?" She pours herself a glass of rum.

"You don't plan to chase that?"

"Sipping it slow, like I've stepped slow finding my way through every day since Adam died. And it's just as well you're not drinking, what with calling me 'Grace' when you're dead sober."

"We're different in the way we use language. You use words precisely, and speak with lots of pauses, because you're organizing what you're going to say. I blurt things out. I submit that my excitement about the child — "

"His name is Jeremiah."

"... about Jeremiah looking so much like me is very much related to the fact that I'm concerned about him, that I will indeed be responsible for him, and take care of him, whether his mother dies or not. My anxiety to know how you found out — I repeat, not that there's much to find out — is related to the fact that I knew it wasn't something you'd be happy about, and like every good husband, wished to spare you distress."

"Mark, you know, in a crude way, both those things make sense? I should probably be packing my bags and threatening to leave you, as I well might, in time. But you didn't see that woman's face at the door, or the balloon on her forearm; you didn't see her slither down that doorjamb. And you haven't been watching that little boy grow up over two years. He's funny and smart — "

"I'm sure he's a fine child, and I'm very happy that you're so fond of him, but right now, I'm just keen to establish that, however it may have seemed to you, I wasn't just thinking about myself and why my attempts at sparing your feelings failed so miserably. I still can't figure out —"

"Don't push your luck, Chancellor. You're already way ahead of the game. He's a great youngster. His grandma takes care of him, and she and I like each other. If his mother dies, he can walk right into our lives. If his mother lives, it's a whole different kettle of fish. Which is not to say that I want her to die. But she's worked hard to keep you out of his life. If she refuses to name you as his father, are you going to press the matter? All this, assuming, of course, that the two of you don't choose to rush into each other's arms once you find out that it was I who purloined the letters that were intended to fan the the flames."

"Thanks for telling me."

"You're welcome. I brought them, if you want them."

"Really?"

"Why not? I'm not going to fight to keep you, Mark. You need to make up your mind. And I may as well tell you. She called you at home from that African place, the one with the weeping stone that's been in the news these past couple years."

"I think there's someone at the door, Mona."

"I'll get it. Maybe it's news about Grace."

He turns on a light as she moves to the door.

"Father Atule? How nice to meet you. Phyllis has told me all about you. Just a minute, please. Let me take off this chain. Do come in."

"Hello, Dr. Blackman."

"It's Mona. Please. I'm Trinidadian, God's most laid-back people."

"I'm Jimmy. I think you know Jeremiah?"

"We do know each other. Hi, Jeremiah. You did very well at graduation, going to collect Mama's award."

"With Tules. From him." He points to Mark, standing by his chair, intent on the child holding the priest's hand.

"Yes, that's the person who gave it to you. He's my husband. His name is Mark. How are you doing?"

"Kidoki. Mama's sick. Grandma is at hospital 'cause Mama's sick!"

"I'm sorry. But your mama must be happy to have Grandma with her."

The priest had walked up with the child to receive the award, a shell carved from pink marble, mounted on a base of granite, the mote in its lip a black pearl. The child was grave, courtly, saying, "Thank you, sir," as he took the shell.

"Mona, would you to take Jeremiah for a walk downstairs, maybe around the pond in the atrium?"

The request strikes Mark as presumptuous, but he says nothing.

"I was about to say 'the duck pond,'" the priest continues, "but he insists there are swans."

"There are, actually, statues of two swans," Mona says, "I'd be happy to take him. It's lovely now. They turn the mood lighting on at six when happy hour starts and everyone deserts the atrium for the bar. We'll have it to ourselves."

"Jeremiah, how'd you like to go and have a look at the swans?"

"Kidoki."

"We'll see you in a while. Say, half an hour?"

"Half an hour would be good. Thanks very much."

Mona takes the child's hand. He looks up at her and smiles as they go through the door.

58

Throwing Words

"Can I get you a drink, Father Atule?"

"Yes, thank you."

"Something hard? Soft?"

"Water would be good, for the moment."

"Seltzer water? Perrier?"

"Anything at all. Out of the tap is fine."

"How is Dr. Carpenter?"

"They've given her something stiff for the pain, so she's knocked out. Ms. Patterson will let us know if there's a change, for better or worse."

"You wouldn't be doing what we call 'throwing words' with that 'for better or worse,' would you, Father? This is Perrier. Will it do?"

"It'll do fine, thank you. And James is fine, or Jimmy. I assure you I don't throw words. That's a St. Chris thing, and subtle. I'm not from St. Chris."

"And not subtle?"

"The present situation isn't one for subtlety."

"Do we have something to speak frankly about, then, James?"

"Jeremiah isn't exaggerating. His mother is ill, perhaps terminally." Jimmy pauses. He has not told anyone what Grace's illness is. The words "flesh-eating disease" are liable to send people into a panic, not least because hospital personnel are often at a loss as to treatment. UA has an excellent Centre for Medical Research, however, and doctors on call to deal with situations like Grace's, for the Caribbean has its share of ugly outbreaks of disease. She is very lucky.

He sips his water and studies Mark's face. It is inscrutable, guarded, even impassive. Is that the kind of face that senior bureaucrats cultivate as part of the job? He decides that since Mark is Jeremiah's father, it gives him a right to know how ill Grace is. Besides, the discussion he intends to have concerns their son. For sure the news of Grace's bizarre disease must undo the man's deadpan countenance!

"The survival rate for necrotizing fasciitis is thirty to forty percent." Jimmy speaks the doctors' verdict slowly, emphasizing the scary figures.

"I'm truly sorry to hear that."

"We all are, for sure." Jimmy doesn't spare the irony in his voice. Mark's countenance is unaltered. If that is his entire response, Jimmy can only wonder what persuaded Grace to go to bed with the man. "I'm also confident you know what we need to be talking about."

"We're dispensing with subtlety, right? So why don't you just tell me?"

"You should tell me, Dr. Blackman. The responsibilities are yours, not mine."

"I'm sure I don't know what you're referring to."

"I'm referring to what's to be done if Grace dies."

"I think that's for her family to decide, don't you?"

"Her family will decide whether Grace should be buried here in St. Chris, and when, and so on. As far as I know, her affairs are in order, and there's a will."

"I'm glad you're sure about so many things. I won't ask how since it's not my business. I'll just say it all sounds as well arranged as one could hope. It will be very trying for those concerned, but we'll have to cope. That's life, isn't it?"

"I'm glad to note that 'we,' Dr. Blackman."

"For God's sake, man. Do I have to ask you to call me 'Mark'?"

"I wouldn't think of doing so otherwise. Still, the only important name that needs calling now is Jeremiah's."

"I feel deeply for the boy. It will be difficult for him, initially, but children are resilient. He'll get over it. And he's clearly attached to you and to Grace's mother, who I understand is his primary care-giver in Geneva."

Jimmy is still on his feet. Mark hasn't offered him a seat, and he thinks of taking the initiative — "Why don't we sit?" — but decides not to. Somehow the situation needs them both erect.

"I won't say this is awkward for me, Dr. Blackman. It isn't. In my line of work, there's not much that's awkward anymore — horrible, heartrending, desperate, but not awkward. My dilemma centres on whether or not to betray a confidence in order to do the right thing."

"And what confidence is that?"

"Ah! Grace still hasn't told you. Is that it?"

"Told me what?"

"Who Jeremiah's father is?"

"She's not told me who his father is, but she's said he's not my child."

"And you believe her?"

"Shouldn't I?"

"If Grace dies and the child's father is alive, he's Jeremiah's nearest kin and must assume responsibility unless there's some serious reason he can't."

"You don't need to instruct me, or to sound like a law book. What you say is obvious enough. I'd like to know, however, how any of this is your business."

"For sure I don't need to instruct you. As for the law book, your reference to it may not be ill advised, but I hope it won't come to that. And it's my business because Grace made it my business. I promised her I'd look after him."

"He's a fortunate young man."

"Your wife knows Jeremiah and is obviously fond of him. She also knows Ms. Patterson quite well. If I have to, I'll break Grace's confidence and count on her to forgive me, since I've always thought you ought to know the truth."

"About what?"

"You know very well what."

"Aren't you effectively breaking that confidence now?"

"I've not said anything to do so, nor am I responsible for the understandings that you take from this exchange."

"Man, the Jesuits do an amazing job with you fellows. And you're in the best company: Thomas More. Bill Clinton. And priest or no, only one thing explains all this. You love her, don't you?"

"I love them both very much, yes."

"Right. For all I know, you've screwed her."

"That would be none of your business. Jeremiah certainly isn't my child. We met when Grace was two months pregnant and in danger of losing him."

"Christ, man. Sit down. I'm sitting down."

"Thank you, but I'm fine standing."

"If I don't sit, I'm likely to fall down. Could you get that phone?"

"For sure." Good God! On top of callous, the man is weak, self-absorbed. "It's for you, the principal."

"Hello, Gordon. What? Right. Thanks a lot. We'll be right there."

59

A Dream

So Maisie folds Gracie in her arms like a baby and takes her down the road to Beloved. When she reaches the storefront church, she reverses into the heavy wooden doors, forcing them open with her broad backside, and the two of them go through to see Reverend Douglas, who is waiting. Several ladies make up the congregation, and there is even a small choir, a bright blaze of birds the colour of parrots and macaws. Reverend Douglas walks up to receive Maisie and her whimpering charge, arms wide open, big as a baobab tree, and she folds the sobbing Gracie into the great tent of her white robes and takes her up to the altar where Jeremiah is waiting, dressed in red and white, the youngest of seven altar boys who swing gold censers as they wait for Jimmy to begin saying Mass.

Gracie sees clear-clear the miniscule red crosses alternating with green banana trees that decorate the stole gently riding on Reverend Douglas's ample bosoms. She sees the large golden flamboyant tree emblazoning the front of Jimmy's chasuble, a cross set against a background of myriad tiny red crown-of-thorn flowers. They are Ma's work, Ma who is sitting in the rocking chair on the ramshackle porch at Wentley, painstakingly embroidering crosses and crowns, bananas and flamboyant trees, as she hums, "Have thine own way, Lord."

And there at the altar is Gramps, straight and strong, instructing Jeremiah on how to tend the forest of medicine plants that he has set out in rows and rows of pots at the back of the barracks hut in Wentley.

"Tell her, Gramps," Ma says, fresh as morning drizzle.

"You've got to get up, Gracie. It's time to go."

Ma walks over quickly, for though she is stout, she moves light as wisps of silk cotton seed. She leans down to give Gracie a hand, but Gracie can't move, sake of pain. Her entire lower arm is blown up, a fat reddish balloon. The pain inside is hot like boiling water. If anybody offered to cut her arm off, she would let the knife do its terrible work without a moment's thought.

She understands. It is Carnival, and the inflated arm is part of her costume, and they are all dressed-up to play mas, a whole band of players in green and white. They wear masks, and their heads are covered with caps like the old-fashioned bathing caps that grandmothers wear at the beach. The party room is tiled green like the birthing room in Geneva where Jeremiah was born. She hates green. She hates this room with green tiles for walls.

There is one very black face that she recognizes, even though he has on a mask. The half moons of his tribal markings won't let him hide. It is Jimmy, and she can see that he is smiling because his eyes are sideways slits. How she loves his long curling eyelashes! How his touch floods her body with light and movement! His face is red-brown and his eyes are blue-green like the sea at Richfield. He calls to her, "Your aura is brilliant turquoise, my sweet lady." She reaches for him, but he fades away with the slip-slop sound of his slippers. She calls, "Charlie, Charlie!" but he doesn't hear.

He wants her to pay attention. He points and she follows his hand, which is covered in tight-fitting sterile rubber gloves and is directing her gaze to a huge circular glass window above them, with people sitting around, looking down, as if they are in a theatre. They are a most attentive audience, leaning forward, rapt. Some look through goggles or long lenses like periscopes. Perhaps they are filming the party. She will try to be pleasant though her arm hurts so much. She must ignore the cameras, so she looks away, but Jimmy beckons and points again.

Her gaze follows his outstretched finger. A small hand is holding ground orchids in yellow and purple, pink and orange! The trailing flowers riot against the dark skin of this little person. As he waves them, the flowers turn into birds.

"It's a secret, Mama. I can make the flowers fly."

"That's amazing Jeremiah, but where the hell is your grandmother?"

"Don't curse, Grace. You know better than that."

It is Gramps, and he has called her Grace. Gramps doesn't know how hard it is. They don't know, any of them. Only Colin, the red boy who died from kwashiorkor knows, and Sylvia, the yellow-turd girl, and Carlos, her fit-to-be-dashed-away baby. They are the strangely coloured people who belong nowhere, who exist as diversions for God and everybody else. Well, she's had a baby that she could have dumped. What else is required of her? She has studied hard, worked hard, tried to make the world a better place. Charlie knows. Charlie showed her so many things. She giggles. "More, Charlie," she says. "I want more."

There are more costumes, many more revellers. They wear medieval hats, dark gowns with braid and hoods of gold and black, mauve and green. First they march. Some sit above, but most are herded together on benches below. From time to time the herded ones stand up, throw their hats in the air, then sit, and open bottles of effervescing drink, which they spray at one another, laughing. Wave after wave, they stand, sit, and pop open fizzy bottles of white smoke.

There is music, tambu music: penny whistles, drums, fifes, and rhumba boxes accompany a grand procession. There are so many faces passing that she knows. She must try not to be sour and sick. She must join the procession, attend the party, but she is hot all over, full of fire. The man with the rubber gloves speaks. "Grace! It's me."

"I figured it out, Jimmy. God is Anancy, a trickster spider. His time's run out. That's all. That's the explanation for the way the world is."

"There's a children's storybook called *Waiting for the Thursday Boat* in which God is a little black girl. I daresay he could manage to be a trickster spider as well."

"Don't get all clever on me, my Jesuit friend. I am sick unto death. I deserve the truth."

"Pilate asked about the truth, but he walked off before he got the answer. It would have been better if he had waited. He'd have discovered that nobody deserves truth; we all wait for it, humbly."

"I deserve it, Jimmy. I worked and worked. Isn't that enough?"

"There's no enough, Grace. There's not even the best you can do, only what you manage at any given time. Sometimes that's brilliant; sometimes it's barely sufficient. It's necessary to accept that, to recognize limitations, yours, mine, everybody's; to know that when we get things done together, it's a bloody miracle; to understand how many miracles have happened every day, go on happening every day, just so we can continue to be here."

"Sounds like platitudinous bullshit, to me."

"First Corinthians, chapter 1, verse 19. It is bullshit."

It is dark now. The sun has gone down, or the lights have gone out. She hears sounds, women singing softly, a lullaby perhaps. There is a procession: Granny Vads and Grandma Elsie; Ma and Phyllis and Daphne; Pansy and Princess and Pansy's girls; Miss Constance and Mrs. Sampson; Miss Carmen, Miss Glosmie, Miss Isolene, and Mrs. Buxton; Reverend Douglas; Mrs. Scott and Stephanie and Susie; Felicity and Babs; Maisie and Sylvia; Sister Monique and Sister Tekawitha, Elise and Lili; Amitié and Azzara; Joyce Zaidie-Klein; Mona Blackman; even Mrs. Sommersby.

The woman who leads them wears a red sari spotted with drops of something, wine or oil or blood. Each person in the line holds onto the sari, which stretches longer and longer as more women join, walking up a path covered with petals of red, purple, yellow, and orange. The leader is someone she knows, but the wind blows sheets of sand across the line of singers so she can't see who it is.

At the edge of the desert in Mabuli, dunes flare and subside, one minute lit by a ferocious sun, the next dragged down into the swell of dark night sands. A small boy is in a boat, oars in his hands, silver pinpricks of sweat on his face. They get larger as he ploughs through the brown drifts. Two men push the boat from behind, white haired, white bearded. One is black, and one is white. They melt into each other, and change, and change again. A tall black man lifts the child from the boat and hoists him over his shoulder. He has been weeping. Tears leak from under his long lashes into the tiny indentations that pattern his cheeks before they spill again, myriad eyes. The child wraps his arms round the man's neck. The door of her room opens and, as they come in, she sees them both, clearly.

"Jimmy? Jeremiah? Don't cry!" She opens her arms. "Come to your Mama!"

The boy, a bird, a kite, lands on her bed in half a second, trailing his limbs about her.

"Kidoki!"

She folds her arms around her son, but he isn't there. She looks up, but the weeping man with the scarred cheeks is gone. Never mind, she thinks as she closes her eyes, she will see them soon. When she does, maybe she'll get back into the ring with Papa God. It was Gramps way, after all, hassling with the Almighty Father. Perhaps it might work for her too.

Acknowledgements

First of all, I am grateful to the taxpayers of Ontario, who, through the Ontario Arts Council and the Toronto Arts Council, allowed me to eat and have a home while I wrote this book. My considerable thanks too, to Margaret Hart for her commitment to placing this novel, long after I had moved on to other projects.

It is not possible to say what I owe to my husband, Martin Mordecai, who readily and without complaint reviewed the book in its many versions; to our son, Daniel Mordecai who offered helpful comments, and to our daughter Rachel Mordecai who more than once lent it her keen critical eye. The book is much improved by your interventions, and I count myself very blessed in you.

My thanks must also go to our once-upon-a-time online writing group, especially Nalo Hopkinson, who instigated it, and including Hiromi Goto, Larissa Lai, Martin Mordecai, Jennifer Stevenson, and David Findlay. The group provided an impetus to get the writing out, and it introduced us to fine writers and fine people. In that regard, my thanks go especially to Jennifer Stevenson without whose generous support, comments, readings and re-readings, the book would not have come to completion. That it exists is very much her doing. Special thanks also to James Fitzgerald Ford, who allowed me to credit my heroine with an academic paper that put forward principles cribbed from an article of his, and who gave me the benefit of his experience in more than one of the locations in the book. For saving me from embarrassment, I thank Barbara Shepherd, who set me right on the Thirty Day Spiritual Exercises of St. Ignatius, and Dr. Michael Hawkes who gave me the benefit of his experience as a physician and as one who knows the region.

For their various contributions, by reading part or all of the book, by supplying, in some cases, encouragement, and in others, practical help, I am indebted to Edward Baugh, Ian Bolton, Marlene Bourdon-King, Kamau Brathwaite, Andrea Conroy-Cresser, Carol Duncan, Molly Tobin Espey, Esther Figueroa, Shivaun Hearne, Keith Lowe, Stephanie McKenzie, Stephanie Martin, Rethabile Masilo, Marie-José Nzengou-Tayo, Timothy Reiss, Elaine Savory, Derek Walcott, M. G. Vasanji, Betty Wilson, and Priscilla Zamora. I crave the indulgence of anyone I may have forgotten, for many people helped with this book over a long time.

Finally, to Diane Young at TAP Books, who saw the virtues of the book, took it on board, and shepherded it to completion, and to the ever-helpful staff at Dundurn Press, my sincerest thanks!

Glossary

Ar = *Arabic*;   DT = *Dread Talk*;
ECE = *Eastern Caribbean English*;   G = *Ga*;
It = *Italian*;   JC = *Jamaican Creole*;
JE = *Jamaican English*;   MT = *Mabuli Talk* ;
TC = *Trinidad Creole*;   Tk = *Turkish*

abeng (JC)   = bull's horn used by Maroons as
                          a signaling device or as a musical
                          instrument

backra massa (JC)   = originally used of a white person,
                          especially one who owned or exercised
                          authority on a plantation; now a
                          person, white or not, in a position of
                          authority; metonymically, those who
                          wield power; oppressive authority

bakin gumbi	= *Acacia macrostachya*, shrub common in the southern Sahel used for live hedges, fence posts, fuel. Its seeds can be boiled and eaten and its young leaves can be boiled to treat gastrointestinal disorders and also as an antidote to snake-bite.
bangarang (JC)	= echoic word meaning (and representing the sound of dragging) assorted paraphernalia
bissap	= *Hibiscus sabdariffa*, annual or perennial species of hibiscus used for a variety of purposes in cooking as well as for making a variety of drinks. Other uses include a number of medicinal ones: as a diuretic, a gentle laxative, and a treatment for cardiac disease, nerve diseases, and cancer
bissape	= red drink made from calyxes of the sorrel/bissap plant
bourgou grass	= grass native to Africa
boyeki	= African percussion instrument; güiro in Latin America; reco-reco in Brazil; scrapers in the Caribbean
braps (JC)	= echoic word that represents the sound of a sudden fall, collapse, or development
brought-upcy (JE)	= quality of having been well raised
bruck (JC)	= break
m'bubu	= flowing wide-sleeved robe; kaftan
capo (It)	= chief of a branch of the mafia

capo di tutti capi (It)	= chief of all chiefs (literally); the term designates the head of the most powerful Mafia family
Cetacea	= scientific order that includes whales, dolphins, and porpoises
cho (JC)	= exclamation of annoyance, impatience, irritation, disgust
cocoa tea (JE)	= chocolate (drink)
coolie	= an East Indian person, according to the *Dictionary of Caribbean English*, used derogatively. However, like "nigger," it is also extensively used, especially self-referentially, without pejorative connotations.
cotta (JC)	= coil of cloth used to cushion a basket resting on the head
crosses (cross) (JE)	= difficulty, hardship, burden
djembe	= African percussion drum
don (JC)	= a crime boss, originally and still especially in the Mafia; crime boss engaged in the ganja trade
dungle (JC)	= garbage dump, dung hill, rubbish heap
duppy (JC)	= ghost
escoveitched (JC)	= from the Spanish "escabeche" meaning pickled, a method of cooking (mostly fish) with vinegar, peppercorns, onions and scotch bonnet or chili peppers; perhaps also related to ceviche, a Peruvian seafood dish
facety (facey) (JC)	= brazen, forward, impudent
favour (JC)	= resemble, look like

gallery forest	= forests that form along the corridors of rivers or wetlands and extend into other otherwise sparsely treed areas
giaour (Tk)	= modern Turkish word for infidel, unbeliever; an offensive ethnic slur used by Muslims in Turkey, the Balkans to describe all (especially nearby Christians) who are not Muslim
gizzada (JC)	= Jamaican or Portuguese pastry made of grated coconut baked in a pastry shell. It is also called "pinch-me-round" in English from the rippled edge of the pastry and guizada in Portuguese.
Gourounsi	= ethnic groups inhabiting north Ghana and southern Burkina Faso
grater cake (JC)	= a Jamaican sweetmeat made of grated coconut cooked in a paste of dark or white sugar
homo ludens	= Latin for games-playing man
imam	= Islamic scholar, community leader, worship leader
Ital (JC)	= derived from English vital, with the v removed so the initial I can affirm oneness with the essential i-force of nature; (Rastafarian) food, which is salt free and largely vegetarian
jacket (JC)	= outside child, born of intercourse between a married parent and some person other than his/her spouse, but accepted as part of the household
Jah (JC)	= Rastafarian name for God

Jonkonnu (JC)	= Christmas festival of African and European origin, in which masqueraders in traditional costumes (e.g., the Devil, Wild Indian, Belly Woman, Actor Boy, Pitchy-Patchy) parade in the streets dancing to fife and drum music, collecting money for their prowess in dance and mime
jook (JC)	= to stick, poke, pierce
juju (Fr)	= originally used for traditional religions in West Africa; now used for the supposed magical power of those religions or for objects used in witchcraft
karst	= landscape formed from dissolution of limestone, characterized by conical hills, sinkholes, underground rivers, and cave systems
kas-kas (JC)	= echoic word meaning quarrel, contention
Kel Tamasheq	= (recent self-designation of the Tuareg) speakers of Tamasheq, the Turareg language
kikumvi	= tom-tom; used in the musical accompaniment to the Missa Luba
kiloli (MT)	= garment, worn by men and women
kinkeliba	= Combretum micranthum, shrub species native to Western Africa. Known as kinkelib in Senegal and Gambia, it is used to brew a

traditional bush tea (nicknamed "Lipton Tea" due to its popularity) used for weight loss, as a diuretic, an antibiotic, to improve digestion, and to relieve minor pain.

kiss-teeth (JC) = contemptuous or dismissive sound made by sucking air through closed teeth

korchi = loud factory whistle used to indicate start and end of the workday

kotch (JC) = take a temporary seat, mostly in a place not intended for sitting

kouri = dry water course

kwashiorkor (G) = acute form of childhood malnutrition

kyondo = a type of slit (log) drum common in the Congo, especially the southern part; used in the Missa Luba

lectio divina = divine reading

lick (JC) = knock, hit

macca (JC) = prickles, thorns

marabout (Ar) = Muslim religious scholar, scholar of the Koran, teacher, and leader in West Africa

Maroons = slaves who freed themselves by running away or guerilla-style warfare and established self-sustaining communities in isolated places in the mountains or forests

mas (EC) = see play mas

mbuni (MT) = species of rodent

millet	= small seeded, ancient grass yielding grain of many variations, for human and animal consumption
mouth-a-massy (JC)	= talkative, given to gossip
néré trees	= *Parkia biglobosa*, perennial deciduous tree with a height ranging from seven to twenty metres and impressive red spherical blossoms
njamra (MT)	= large dark-shelled river prawns
nose nought (JC)	= mucus out of the nose, possibly a corruption of "nose snott"
nyam (JC)	= eat
Obeah (JC)	= African derived belief system and practice, similar to Voodoo and Santería, that uses supernatural forces to achieve or defend against evil intentions; any evil spell cast by a practitioner of the art
Old Higue	= creature in Guyanese folklore, an old witch by day, a blood-sucking vampire at night. Able to shed her skin, she travels in a ball of fire and feasts on the blood of infants.
Oti (MT)	= umbrella association of religious leaders of all belief systems, imams, shamans, priests, and marabouts
own-way (JC)	= self-willed, stubborn
palampam (JC)	= echoic word meaning noise and confusion
pasero (JC)	= friend, possibly from Spanish pasajero (fellow passenger)

pawpaw (JC)	= papaya
picong (ECE)	= from Spanish picón, which means mocking; originally, a verbal contest between two Calypsonians in which wit determines the winner; teasing or sarcastic repartee; friendly teasing and heckling
pikni (JC)	= child
pimento dram (JE)	= pimento liqueur; herbal liqueur with a rum base that tastes of allspice
placée woman	= woman of colour (African, Native American, or mixed-race) in eighteenth-century Louisiana, who became a sort of common-law wife in a recognized extralegal system in which white French and Spanish and, in time, Creole men entered into the equivalent of common-law marriages. Placée women were not legally recognized as wives, but were supported by their partners and had families for them.
play mas (ECE)	= take part in the masquerade, the procession of dance, music, and costumed bands that celebrates Carnival in some cities (e.g., Rio de Janeiro, New Orleans, Port of Spain) on the days prior to Ash Wednesday when Lent begins
praedial larceny	= theft of growing crops
pyah-pyah (JC)	= insignificant, worthless

rass cloth (JC)	= (employed only as an obscene expletive) a used sanitary napkin
Rasta (DT)	= short form of Rastafari or Rastafarian
redibo (JC)	= (red Ibo) person of colour with red skin, red hair, grey eyes, and often freckles
saga boy (TC)	= a man who likes to dress well and chase women, a fop, a playboy
sajda	= Muslim prostration, the bent-over, head-to-the-earth posture for prayer
sand puppy	= burrowing rodent, similar to the East African naked mole rat *Heterocephalus glaber*, which is also known as the sand puppy or desert mole rat
sappi (MT)	= beer made from bissap
scotch bonnet	= *Capiscum chinense* also known *inter alia* as Scotty Bons and Bonney pepper. Named for its resemblance to a Tam O'Shanter hat, it is a variety of chili pepper found mainly in the Caribbean islands, as well as in Guyana.
shaman	= spiritual leader; medium between physical and spiritual worlds
sistren (DT)	= sisters (in Dread Talk, the language of Rastafari)
The Skinny (MT)	= slang for AIDS
sorghum	= genus of several species of grass, one of which is a grain
steups (JC)	= see kiss-teeth
suck-teeth (JC)	= see kiss-teeth

sulcata	= *Geochelone sulcata*, the African spurred tortoise, which inhabits the southern edge of the Sahara desert
susu (JC)	= gossip, rumour
susuing (JC)	= whispering gossip, spreading rumour quietly
Tuareg	= a Berber people, with a traditionally nomadic pastoral lifestyle
xalam	= name for a stringed musical instrument from West Africa
yabba (JC)	= earthenware bowl, glazed on the inside, used for cooking and baking preparation

CPSIA information can be obtained at www.ICGtesting.com
Printed in the USA
LVOW06s0902130415

434314LV00004BA/243/P